THE EASTER HOUSE

ALSO BY
DAVID RHODES

Driftless

The Last Fair Deal Going Down

Rock Island Line

THE EASTER HOUSE

DAVID RHODES

milkweed
editions

The characters and events in this book are fictitious. Any similarity to real persons, living or dead, is coincidental and not intended by the author.

Published 2009 by Milkweed Editions
First published by Harper & Row in 1974
Printed in Canada
Cover design by Betsy Donovan
Author photo by Lewis Koch
Interior design by Steve Foley
The text of this book is set in Griffo Classico.
09 10 11 12 13   5 4 3 2 1
First Paperback Edition

Please turn to the back of this book for a list of the sustaining funders of Milkweed Editions.

ISBN: 978-1-57131-077-4

The Library of Congress has catalogued the cloth edition as follows:

Rhodes, David.
    The Easter House.

    I. Title.
PZ4.R4755Eas   [PS3568.H55]   813'.5'4   73-14322
ISBN 0-06-013544

This book is printed on acid-free paper.

For Luther Rhodes

THE EASTER HOUSE

THE EASTER HOUSE

The beginning, with Cell's story, and the story of C, Sam, and, one year later, Glove, is more than enough.

THE BEGINNING

Seventeen candles would be enough, thought Fisher (Fish) Wood. He silently stuffed them inside a folded army blanket and checked the bundle on both ends before picking it up. The attic was mostly dark except for a cold, dimly lit area around the window. Fisher stood at the edge of this light with his hidden candles and watched large, ragged snowflakes hurry across the square of outside afternoon; some of them climbed up the window, and once a pinwheel of snow came together in the upper right-hand corner. He was old enough to think that snow acted oddly when seen from the attic window because of wind getting trapped under the eaves of the roof. He carefully set down the blanket and tried for a final time to open the window, being quiet. No, seventeen candles would be enough, he thought. They would have to be . . . everything else of value was too large to be taken directly out of the house, and the noise of hammering, which was what it would take to open the window, would draw attention and his stupid sister might come upstairs. He pulled the cardboard box farther into the light and punched more holes in it with a nail, for air. Though birds were not necessarily afraid of the dark, Fisher reasoned, they could very well be afraid of the inside of cardboard boxes. Speed was essential. He would be back.

Fisher put on his rubbers, a tremendous winter coat, a Russian-like protective hat, leather gloves, and a scratchy scarf from Marshall Field's in Chicago. He picked up the folded blanket and began a silent descent down the thickly carpeted staircase, letting his right hand slide easily down the brass banister rail, noticing in horror that the door at the bottom was ajar. He heard the toilet flush and stopped, keeping well back away from the partially opened attic door. Stupid, he thought, leaving a door open, and tightly concentrated on his breathing. Eight Wood left the bathroom in a businesslike manner, shutting the attic door with a casual kick from the side of her foot, and went down the red-and-gold hall and into her room. Fisher heard the stately click of the chrome-plated door handle.

It was not as though the attic door had been shut in his face (he was a good three feet from it); it was that a member of his family could be so much like his sister Eight, could walk by a partially opened attic door and not notice it . . . no! notice it and shut it! That she could care so little about the real things, the mysteries and murders. Fisher felt he had been humiliated. With a bird in the attic and someone stealing candles, she had shut the door. He waited until his anger went back up into the attic, for fear his mother would see it and have reason to waylay him from going outside— asking him questions about his face, which, when angry, resembled his father's normally haggard expression—then he opened the door, moseyed on by Eight's room and down the stairs.

His mother was in the kitchen and he had to go through it. He had expected this and was prepared. In a single glance she could tell if he was sufficiently clothed; all he needed to do was get close enough to the door so that she had time to see the clothes, but not enough time to ask about the blanket or the remnants of his anger. Arness, the maid, was in the kitchen too, and he used her body as a foil in order to cross half the length of the kitchen before coming into complete view of his mother. Another four feet and Mrs. Rabbit Wood saw him. Fisher's face fixed itself into a look of belligerent concentration, an attitude of disguise that always made his parents think, "Children are always having secrets, secrets that amount to nothing . . . better to leave alone."

"Where are you going, Fisher?" she asked, just as he arrived at the door.

"Outside," mumbled Fisher, and was gone into the snow.

"He's got a blanket!" said Arness, looking out the window above the sink. "What do you think—"

"Another trade," said Ester Wood. "He's got something he wants from Easter's Yard, and there's something wrapped up in the blanket to trade for it. He wears that scarf to be invisible."

Fisher ignored one of his father's neighbors who called from the open window of his automobile, "Hey, Fisher, where you going with that blanket?" pretending that the snowstorm made hearing not necessary. He walked six blocks, his tracks leveling off behind him.

There was only one house in Ontarion, Iowa, larger than Rabbit Wood's. Not only was it the largest house, it was the only house with an entire square block to itself. It was built in the middle of four acres of metal rubbish, old cars, washing machines, railroad ties, furnaces, radios, bathtubs, sinks, muskrat traps, threshing machines, elevators, wheels, stoves, doorknobs, refrigerators, typewriters, and, as far as Fisher knew, everything. The house had not probably come after the junk, but if the townspeople—other than that handful living inside the gray, pillared house—could have wished away either the Yard or the house, they would have moved the house very far away. They were afraid of it.

There were other differences between the two houses; one was a fine, immaculate house with aluminum windows, a house precise in all ways. The other was not, and Fisher had to step over a sign that had fallen from the porch roof: EASTER'S YARD. He knocked on the door. Someone from inside called for him to come on. He removed his rubbers, went in, and hoped, like all of Ontarion, that he might catch a look at The Baron, an odd child believed to be three years older than himself, who never came out of his room upstairs on the third floor, and who was crazy and probably chained up and tortured by his mother, mad as well, and frightening.

"Fish," said C Easter, shoving his head out backward through the doorway of the Associate office, as though he were leaning back in a swivel chair. "What can we do you out of?"

Fisher was forced to smile, but held his ground and asked to see Glove; he had a better chance with Glove; the rule was that if you wanted something from the Yard, you could get it for free if one of the Easters didn't know the exact location of the object, and C Easter always knew. Fisher would have a better chance with his son Glove.

"GLOVE," hollered C Easter, and Glove headed for downstairs. Fisher listened to sounds moving across the ceiling, thinking, So odd, a house where people moved so quickly, without finishing paragraphs or waiting for commercials, to answer a call.

"Fish!" he said, midway down the open staircase.

Fisher did not move, and waited until the young man had cleared the distance between them.

"I want that aviary," said Fisher, looking down to the floor.

"Birdcage. You must mean the birdcage, Fish. The one between the bathtub and the stack of angle iron. Do you know of another one?"

"No . . . that's the one."

"What did you bring to trade?" asked Glove, carefully noticing the blanket bundle. "A blanket?"

Fisher put down the blanket on the wooden floor and opened it up.

"Candles," said Glove.

"Seventeen," said Fisher.

"Come on, Fish, you know the rules . . ."

"I know, same size, same weight. But I couldn't get nothing else, this is all I could get."

"You plan to trade the blanket?"

Fisher hesitated. "No, I can't trade the blanket."

"I see." Glove would not trade.

Fisher was despondent. "But what if I let you see what I got?"

"What is it?"

"I can't tell anyone now; but someday I'll show it to you and you'll be the only one to know."

"How big is something like that? A secret?"

"I don't know," said Fisher. "Bigger than an old aviary."

"Birdcage."

"Birdcage."

"O.K. It's a deal." Glove procured a hat from an off room, put it on, wedged a brown sack into the slight blue jacket he had already been wearing, and waited on the porch for Fisher to stretch the rubbers over his $45 wingtips.

"Good pair of rubbers, Fish."

"They're O.K."

They walked out into the yard, Fisher walking behind the older boy, but to the side, refusing to walk in Glove's track. The snow had not covered the cage, and the top of it reached out into view. Glove lifted it up and shook the snow out of it. But Fisher took it away from him and didn't care about the snow, wrapping it up in the blanket so that he could carry it from the swivel on top while letting the blanket fall down from its sides, disguising it.

"Why do you want a birdcage, Fish?"

"I dunno."

"Oh."

Fisher looked up to the third floor of the house, hoping to see The Baron staring out of a window, wrenching against his chains. Then he said goodbye to Glove and began walking home. Had Fisher been older, he might have wondered why several years ago half of Ontarion seemed to live at Easter's Yard, spending days and nights inside the giant house and out into the Yard—why in the summer full-grown men, without drinking or playing cards, would gather at Easter's Yard and watch the colored time move through the afternoons. He might have wondered why today no one went there—why even though the Easters and the other three men there were "good people," as his father called them, no one would go there . . . except at night. He might have wondered what The Associate was—what it had been and what it was now. But if Fisher had been older, he would have known these things. He might then have wondered about the killing and the money.

WITH CELL'S STORY

Glove took careful notice around him, and watched Fisher merge into the snow, as though walking into the rounded folds of a curtain. He removed his hat and struck a farmer's match inside it by popping it with the tip with his thumbnail. Then he lit a cigarette. He thought of the gray smoke coating his nerve endings, deadening them, seeping into his head and smothering those uneasy, sad feelings that even now he could pick up from the house. Even through the storm the sadness that they would not put in their faces or use in their words, that got into the corners and empty rooms because it must go somewhere, got to him. Even through the snow.

Last winter was when he had known for sure that his house was suffering. He had thought then that it was a disease, something that happened when stale air attacked wood. He had thought it was the winter. Shrinking wood and ice and wind and furnace heat. He waited for spring, when the clear morning air could rip through the rooms; flies and mosquitoes and birds—not squawk birds, but songbirds with colors (he would let them in)—could swarm into the corners and eat the disease; when the night sounds could watch over the Yard while he slept. Winter was so damned quiet, he thought; if only you could open up and let everything in, let everything out, get everything out in the open: then your house would be all right. He had been right about a lot of that. But when spring came, the colored birds were kept out with screens, and in the summer the metal roof was like a grill and even those astringent trickles of breeze that crawled through the mesh and into the house seemed like a slow-burning flamethrower. It was

6

better to keep the windows closed during the day.

But this winter was worse . . . perhaps because he had watched it come, from his window at the level of the third floor, his headphones on, listening to his powerful radio and the voices.

He flung the last three quarters of an inch of cigarette into the stack of angle iron and did not hear it strike the snow. Looking carefully along the street and through the immediate neighborhood, he walked deeper into the rubbish yard until he finally arrived at a stand of weed trees growing around an assortment of automobile wheels and engines. A grain elevator. For a final time he checked the windows of the house to be sure no one was watching, then walked in toward a 1946 school bus that he had towed into the cover of the trees in order to hide it completely. He had insulated the underneath with tightly packed straw. Inside a back compartment he had put an 80,000 BTU heater that blew into the bus, drawing air back (circulation) through an apparatus that seemed to all superficial inspection like a grain elevator that had fallen on the roof of the bus. He looked in the window and two black eyes stared back at him. Baron rolled down the window and Glove handed in the sack of food. Baron opened his mouth as if to speak, but Glove put his finger quickly to his lips. "Shhhhh," he whispered, "shhhh." The window was rolled up and Glove went quietly out of the cover of the trees back toward the house.

Genius, he thought. Sometimes the characteristics of genius pass not from father to son, as one might suppose, but take a leap in time and land in a grandchild; and stay there, and end there. Three hundred years of family go into the making of these two, and two hundred years of aftermath. Every family has them, though not always do both of them rise to the surface; usually only one—the first. Sometimes after one hundred years a small cluster of an old family will gather to talk over their heritage and anything else they have in common (which is usually very little), drinking lemonade and eating potato salad from picnic tables. Someone will bring a family album and they will see a picture of an ancient relative and his eyes will be wild and they'll fit together all the information they can gather about him (which in most cases will be scarce); and finally later, much later, a young member of the family will be talking to his girlfriend about his family (as though selling them), and say, "That's John T., we believe he was a genius." And the girl will look down into his eyes, and from then on everyone will believe it. The other one, the second, will stay in the ground.

Glove knocked the loose snow from his shoes and went inside. He hung his coat in the off room and went upstairs, hearing his mother come to stand behind the door to her room. The voices from the men downstairs grew louder. He heard his father laugh, but there was shouting too. He tried to make it by. She opened the door.

"Glove."

"Yes," he said and stopped walking.

"Where you been?"

"Oh, the Wood kid came over for a birdcage. I went out to get it for him. And we talked."

"I just wondered." She smiled.

Glove felt the grip of the house on him. He began to walk away.

"Glove," she said, "you got to keep the windows in your room closed . . . it ain't healthy for that cold air to be in your room. I shut it for you."

"O.K., Mom." He stood there.

"Isn't it a comfort . . . I mean how good Baron must be getting on . . . happy, I mean?" She was still standing behind the door, holding on to it with her left hand.

"A comfort."

"You ain't seen him, have you, Glove?"

"No, Mom. I haven't, but I'm sure he's fine." Downstairs the shouting grew louder. "Those are real doctors up there."

"Yes," she said, smiling. "He must be so happy. He deserved to be happy . . . such a comfort."

"Yes, Mom."

"Why . . . why don't you ever"—she laughed and tossed a thread of hair away from her face—"call me Mother?"

"Mother! What do I call you?"

"Mom. Plain old Mom."

"What's the matter with that?"

"Nothing. Nothing." She laughed. "I just wondered, that's all."

More shouting from downstairs.

"I wonder why they're . . ." Glove began.

"It'll get worse," Cell Easter said. "It's for the good, though," she added, and then smiled.

"What do you know about it?"

"I know. Before, I didn't. But now I know . . . and it'll get worse, but then it will be better."

"How can you say that?"

"Because I know."

The angry, harsh voices exploded again downstairs, and the walls extracted the meaning of the words, leaving only the hard consonants to come up to the landing. To Glove it seemed as though the floor sagged under him.

"This house was poorly designed," he said. "Your grandfather built it, Ansel Easter."

Glove leaned against the hallway. How could it have been overlooked to tell him that? Why had he had to find out by himself, and put it together? Why did information never move through his family? Why, when in other families even the children knew the names of their parents' parents' friends, did his family seem to have come up out of the ground like a mushroom?

Suicide, he thought. It was the only explanation. A family suicide.

"Suicide," said Glove.

"No," his mother answered.

"Crazy. He was crazy, wasn't he?" He was talking fast. "He was crazy. Of course. That's why you think that—"

"He wasn't crazy . . . not like Baron. He was misunderstood . . . by your father mostly . . . but he wasn't crazy."

"What happened? Something happened." No, he thought then, I don't want you to tell me.

Cell Easter and her son Glove went up another flight of stairs and into his room, because it was cooler there and the shouting downstairs could not reach them. She nudged him along with her hands. Glove's gigantic radio, with its five aerials, switchboard, headphones, speakers, and interchangeable tuners, occupied a good one quarter of the room, spreading itself onto the table and connecting to three of the four chairs in the room, with the earphones draped over one post of the bed. With this radio he could hear men sending messages to each other in Alaska—lonely, isolated men who laughed to each other over their radio sets about trivial but grand things. Cell sat down in the only unconnected chair and told a story that she had ferreted out of her husband's carefully protected history. One single green point of fierce light betrayed that Glove had it on; the glowing tubes of the transmitter were hidden.

"To begin with, the people here killed him. In the dark of the moon, at night, they came in this house to murder. They went through the house. They cut open his throat and kept him from screaming so that down on the second floor C and his brother Sam heard nothing; and it wasn't until the next morning, when the blood came drip by drip onto the hallway from the boards above, that Sam went up and found him lying there, his head nearly off. Another slice had cloven his face. The blood stained the floor, but is covered now by a rug nailed down on top of it. I don't tell this to make you sick, but to show what it must have been like for your father and Sam."

"What people?" he asked. "Why would they do that? Things have reasons."

"Because of hate . . . because of fear. Because evil will destroy goodness, will seek it out and destroy it, and Ansel Easter was a minister."

"There were other preachers. There must have been——"

"No, not like the ministers we have now; they administer to
the people. Your grandfather was a minister of God.

"In the beginning he was just a coal miner. He never went to
a church school or learned how to compose sermons. But people
would ask him to come up out of the mines and talk for them,
organize their feelings and bring them out in the open. What I
mean is that he never had any polish, the way the ministers are
slick now and talk like funeral directors. Ansel Easter's voice
was cracked and, in the pulpit, throwing back his head to begin
a hymn, would sound like yelling down a shaft for more light.
Opening his heart. Even later, when C was almost a full man,
Ansel's old, hard arms still seemed to quiver, as though they were
ready again to go back grubbing in the ground for pieces of coal,
as though he had just taken a short rest and the screeching whistle
was about to begin. His face was hard.

"God looked through his eyes. The good things that Ansel
saw in the world He saw in the world. Those things that were
not good, the ugly and evil parts, made Ansel despair. Once—if
you can imagine such a man—he went to a traveling carnival and
saw written on the side of one of the wagons: COME SEE THE MOST
HIDEOUS CREATURE IN CAPTIVITY, HALF HUMAN, HALF BEAST. BEWARE.
Pictures in color of the thing; awful pictures. Children stood in
front of the sideshow screaming and crying and holding on to
their mothers just from these representations. Ansel stood along
with several other men, paid money, and went inside. The canvas
enclosure smelled of human feces and rotting meat. There, inside
a cage, fastened to an iron ring set in concrete by a log chain
welded on the other end to a steel collar around the neck, was a
thing so horrible that many of the men fled back outside for fear
their wives or children would venture in, hurrying them on down
the dirt midway. Two of the younger men made fun of the thing,
but could not laugh.

"I have a picture of it." And she pinched open one of the

gold trinkets hanging from her bracelet. She pulled out a small, tightly folded photograph and unraveled it to its full $1^{1}/_{2}$-inch size. The likeness had yellowed, which, compounded with numerous cracks, made the original impression nearly impossible to decipher by merely looking at it. But there was just enough so that by studying it several times, turned in varying degrees to the overhead light, up close and at a distance, at first making presumptions about what it might be—primeval creatures, water reptiles, larvae, and large insects—then thinking what it must be, Glove saw beyond a shadow of a doubt a photographic representation of something ghastly . . . something the height of an old woman, with pale olive skin, completely hairless, stretched taut like a drumhead over its bones and sinews, the entire body seemingly without cartilage, both feet perfectly symmetrical, all toes even. And its face . . . hardly larger than a shrunken head, but the eyeballs of natural size, pupils the same color olive as the skin, surrounded by a yellowish white, its nose long, narrow, a covered knife bone so sharp down the front that the skin seemed about to break apart there, leading to an irregular hole of a mouth with pointed teeth inside (possibly filed down by the manager of the carnival, for the effect). Its tongue thick but long, able to reach out of its mouth and into its nose. Its five-fingered hands slight, as though made from number-ten wire. An olive sexual organ, shaped like a piece of corn smut.

"My God," said Glove. "What are you doing with this? Why do you carry it around? Get rid of it."

Cell took it back and replaced it devoutly in its hiding place, snapping the gold plastic heart shut on it. "It's to remind me," she said, "that there are such things in the world."

"I should think you could just remember."

"Maybe I could, but, anyway, your grandfather stood there with these other two men looking at Ernie."

"Ernie!"

"Ansel named him Ernie."

"Named that thing a human name! Ernie!"

"Stop interrupting. If you don't want to hear the rest, just say so."
Glove was quiet.

"Anyway, again, those other two men stood there until a fly lighted on Ernie's shoulder, and despite the stretch of the skin, the whole covering of his shoulder flinched over his bones, the way a horse's does. The fly fluttered away, but settled back again. And again the olive skin flinched. The two men shoved their hands in their pockets and stood with both legs close together, staring. The fly was buzzing back over the spot, and Ernie turned his head slightly towards it and his tongue snapped out of his mouth, his feet jerking a little, and stopped it in mid-air, carrying it back towards his mouth. Then he rubbed his feet together. One of these younger men made a heaving motion, but gagged successfully instead, and both went back outside and hurried off away into the sultry heat.

"'Why do you let them do that to you?' Ansel asked the thing. The canvas walls were hot and the sunlight came through in streaks of dust. Ernie's eyes snapped from their gaze at the floor to meet your grandfather's eyes.

"'Nothing should live like you do,' Ansel said.

"Into the dirt-filled showroom came the barker, wiping his forehead on his sleeve. From his stashing place behind a fold of canvas he pulled a gallon water jug wrapped in a dripping, badly worn towel, a precaution he had taken against the heat. He unwound the metal cap on top and, not bothering to use it as a cup, drank directly from the round mouth of the jug, and water ran down both sides of his chin. His thick-brimmed hat fell off. There was not much water left.

"'That thing can't talk, Mister,' he said. 'He's stupid.' He took another swallow and replaced the cap, holding the water for a minute in his mouth.

"'He's not,' said Ansel. 'How can you keep him here like this?'

"'He's not that stupid,' the barker said and picked up his hat, not bothering to dust it off, 'like a rabbit, that'll chew its foot off to escape. He'll eat when you throw food in and will even use a blanket to keep warm on cold nights. I even see him picking at the locks as though he were trying to open them . . . he's smart, for an animal.'

"'He understands talking,' said Ansel. 'It's a man.'

"'That's crazy,' said the barker as he looked outside at the dust and the blinding light and the three or four people still standing far away, watching. Things were not well with him. He had not made good money since Kansas City, where some people came back to pay three and five times for another look. He didn't like the Midwest. He didn't like anything about it. Everywhere there were flies. It was useless to return outside; he would sell no more admissions today.

"'Look at his eyes,' said Ansel. 'He understands.'

"The barker came over to the cage and looked in absent-mindedly. He pointed his finger. 'You call that understanding?'"

"'Yes,' said Ansel. 'I do.'

"'Down South, where I got him, people were hunting him with dogs. But he was a good climber and could lose them in the creek willows and live oaks. I got a glimpse of him one night eating out of a garbage pail and decided to trap him. Because of the way he looked, most people thought he was like a human.' The barker sat down on a box. 'But I just thought to myself—Now, where would something like that be safe in the daytime? So then I knew he'd have to live up high—not wanting to be bothered by the large ground animals, or the dogs. He'd also have to be up high to see from a long distance when the wolves were out, because they could run him down on a flat, even ground. At first I figured he'd be in trees. The people down there thought like you, that he might be human-like, because he could move along on his two legs, and had eyes that didn't fill up the entire eye socket. Naturally, because of thinking like that, they also thought he was some kind of a super-natural thing, with powers and abilities beyond the comprehension of normal people. Further, they thought these powers and abilities were not good and attributed murders and pillages, most unexplained, to them. That, and they couldn't catch him.

"'But I reasoned again he would have to live up high in the daytime, but not always in trees. Cross-over trees—trees that he could use to escape—weren't tall enough to give him cover. So I knew he'd have to be up high, with a clear view, but not always in trees.'

"Your grandfather hadn't taken his eyes off the cage, but was listening closely to the barker, knowing that they liked to talk by the nature of their work.

"'But I noticed one thing that no one else'd taken into consideration. While he was leaning over the garbage pail, taking out and sifting through the heap, I noticed his hide, and, as you can see, there was no fur. He was shivering in the morning air, his breath misting down from his nose. This thing needs heat, I told myself.' Inside the cage Ernie hadn't taken his eyes away from Ansel. Ansel's hands twitched unconsciously.

"'So where could he be safe and warm? I wondered. It was winter and I began looking. I knew the thing would be too stupid to burn wood itself, and would have to use the heat of people. So I knew it would be in an attic somewhere, half sleeping in the daytime, watching through a window for dogs and danger.' Ansel sat down and waited for the end of this. The barker continued talking with no regard for time.

"'I couldn't find him. I knew he was in an attic somewhere, but I supposed that he had several to choose from, and people weren't overly friendly about letting me into their houses. So what I was finally forced to do was rent an old place near the woods, jack the heat up, and wait in a darkened corner of the attic. Nothing, for a long time. Then I heard him early one evening scrambling up the side of the house like a spider. I saw his head looking in through the window. Then he was gone again. I knew he'd be back and sat quietly, wrapped in a wool blanket, eating dried fruit. I'd been there for so long by then that the rats and mice roamed freely across the attic floor. Later that night he came back again for another look and I saw his head outside the window because it was dark against the sky. Then he scrambled back down the side.

"'The next time, opening the window by sliding his fingers in through the crack and flipping the latch open, he came onto the floor without making the slightest noise. The rats fled into the walls. He left the window open and began walking cautiously in a circle along the walls, covering the room. I think by the time he was almost to where I was he knew something was wrong, but by then it was too late and I had the net over him. Nearly as strong as two men, he was.' The barker stopped talking.

"'You got to let him go.'

"'I might be persuaded to sell him,' said the barker. 'But I'll never just let him go . . . though this would be fine country for him.'

"'He can understand words,' said Ansel. 'He can think. He's a man.'

"'No, he isn't. That's crazy. Have you ever seen anyone else like him? Look at his feet. Look at his organ, man.'

"'He may have been distorted, by birth, or by chance . . . but to keep him like this is against God.'

"'Even if what you say is true—about the birth—even so, after something's been that twisted it's no longer the same thing as it might have been if everything had turned out normally.'

"'But he understands,' said Ansel. 'Nothing should live like that. Turn him loose. Let him stay with me.'

"The barker thought of the few coins in his pocket. He coughed. 'It'll cost you money,' he said. 'Of course you can get some of it back, though, here and there. People will pay.'

"Ansel did not press to insist that this was immoral. 'How much?'

"'Three hundred.'

"'Too much.'

"'For a human being!' said the barker indignantly. 'Too much for a human being! How can a man be not worth three hundred dollars? *That's not much money for a human life.'*

"This line of reasoning presented your grandfather with some problems. He left, and when he returned, groups of two and three people were slowly coming into a much larger group in the dust outside the sideshow. This gathering at first was timid, brought together by accidental interest. But some of the men who'd gone into the show began talking, and then the group decided that something would be done. Though unsure of what that would mean, they were generally becoming hostile. One woman suggested that a fire be set to the canvas, for fun, and as the momentum of the idea was being drawn into actuality your grandfather stepped out into the dust, the creature stepping so carefully beside him, the chain gone. The barker, watching them from inside, counted three hundred dollars out in ones and fives and silver— collection-plate money. The crowd moved back and was quiet. They made a passageway and your grandfather walked between them with Ernie glowering up at their faces from his some four feet, thick, dark marks on his neck. Some of the people followed them nearly home, watching at a distance. Before the two stepped up onto the front doorstep of the house on Everett Street, where they lived before moving here, he'd been named, and Ansel introduced him to C and Sam and your grandmother as Ernie. And he lived with them.

"Actually, he didn't live with all of them, because your grandmother left shortly after that, never to return. Can you imagine a man with principles like that?"

Glove sat and listened, becoming very interested.

"So then there was this man (this was a little later) Johnie Fotsom, who I think lived—It doesn't matter. He started writing these novels about your grandfather, true stories, and sold some copies, and it came out in a cheaper edition and sold some more. *The Holy Man, Man of Faith, The Broken Lantern.* Critics hated them. All men of learning—any learning—deplored them. Young people hated them. Atheists found them 'cheap sensationalism' and 'hocus-pocus sentimentality.' But still they sold. There was one scene in *Man of Faith* where Ansel was pictured walking toward town during the Depression with seventeen cents in his pocket and a starving family at home when a freshly, cleanly killed rabbit falls out of the sky at his feet. He looked up, expecting a large hawk or eagle, and saw nothing. There are several then about how close to God he was and how God would purify the impure people around him—one account of how Dr. McQueen lost a hand to an exposed window fan that he had forgot about being behind him as he reached for a piece of billiard chalk on the ledge. One where a man's wife hangs herself. And so almost overnight Ansel received a fairly immense sum of money from Johnie Fotsom for the use of his name and his life. Ansel took the money and everyone in his church thought he shouldn't have, because a lot of money . . . for nothing! No honest work. Of course everyone knows writers are a seedy lot, but to accept money from one, especially a not very good one, and be glorified in the public eye . . . Whatever, there was a surge of resentment against your grandfather (spearheaded by Rabbit Wood's father) and some talk of ousting him from the ministry of the First Friends Church. Many in the congregation were afraid of him, because they couldn't understand saintliness, and most felt that Ernie was an affront to the community.

"But before a real confrontation could arise, a half-dozen carpenters imported from Cedar Rapids—strong, hard-eyed men that never talked while they were together—began working on this house; and even before the foundation was set, it was obvious to everyone that it was going to be a building of giant size, much bigger than many of the rural people had *ever* seen, and bigger than any Christian man could ever use. The town people, at noon, stood back and watched as our front porch went up, as the studs for the walls climbed up three stories."

"Wait a minute," said Glove, showing signs that his mother

recognized, signs of becoming very upset, his hands twitching nervously. "So someone begins to build a house, on his own land—his own place! What business is it of anyone else? What can it possibly matter to them? Why can't people just mind their own lives?"

"I don't know," said Cell, sitting up straighter in the chair. "C could tell you. He's been to college, and that's what's the main thing of education—showing you what's *your* business and what's somebody else's."

"Still," said Glove. "It was none of their business." The green light shaded his hand.

"Maybe I didn't explain well enough. There were whole families destroyed, little children had terrible, uncommon accidents, disease would break out among healthy people. And all this they thought might be Ansel's doing. They were afraid. And so, with things like that, everyone was going to be absolutely sure that something was *not* their business before they ignored it for even a little while. Maybe I didn't explain that there was more, that Ansel worked his sons into the ground, making them cut wood with him. There were stories of how much corn he could pick by hand, ungodly amounts."

Glove then remembered the only other thing he knew, at that time, about Ansel Easter . . . he remembered someone saying that his grandfather had taken all the broken, cracked, and rusted parts from his automobile as they'd worn out, the mufflers, clamps, old tires, hoses, brake shoes, carburetor gaskets, etc., and put them in the trunk, like a chain the car must wear for its sins. They said he didn't beat his children for their transgressions but inflicted nightmarish lectures upon them that would live like weights in their memories.

AND THE STORY OF C

And so it may be imagined that C Easter, on the supposedly unmysterious death of his father, after the expenses of the burial and the more than adequate fee charged by attorneys for extricating the actual man Ansel Easter from his partnership with Johnie Fotsom while retaining his name for possible printed material in the future, had little more than enough money to rent a small basement apartment in Iowa City, enroll in the University with the intention of going on to law school, eat moderately, live as though each moment was a new one and might fool him into remembering those things he wanted to forget, and be secure that this way of life might last five and three quarters years until the money ran out. And C intended to do that—run his money out. He was just under twenty, shy, reticent, and fearful of things he couldn't see or identify. He believed the world was hostile—that if in any way it could direct misfortune and calamity toward him, it would. His own mental image of himself was one of victim. Nightmares filled his sleeping. He did the things he had to do by living in a sense of routine: this thing now, that thing at five thirty. If he could go through a whole day without emotion, it was a success. Everything he did had a plan. Going to the University amounted to giving himself time, five and three quarters years, in which to discover a friendly attitude toward living. If at the end of that time there was no change—still the same gnawing hope that it might improve—then he would let the trickling out of his money be the end to everything, and have no more moments that might ever again fool him.

With an enforced serenity and one thin carpetbag, C said

goodbye to Sam and went away to school, not so that he might learn, but to nullify all the rest. Apartment hunting nearly finished him, and though he finally succeeded in finding one, it was a meager success. The rhetorical lectures at the University were a comfort to him. He studied late into the night in his basement, a gaudily furnished, L-shaped, concrete room with pole lamps, a space heater, pictures of musical instruments, and everything that a non-student might imagine a student wanting in his place. The only change he made in this arrangement (after obtaining with difficulty an approval from his upstairs landlady) was to streak black and white brush-width stripes along the walls and across the ceiling, converging on the outside corner of the L at the spot in front of and slightly above the top of his study desk. In this way he changed a kitchen-living-room-bedroom-dining-room space into an area for work, and the means for forgetting. The stripes could not be ignored. There was no place in the entire apartment where he could rest his eyes without their being led to his desk. And at this place the moral questions of the day neither disturbed nor distracted him from studying for long hours until sleep, and he would crawl off into his "Hollywood bed" and wait/ sleep until morning.

The months rolled by. The only break in the routines he set up was the operation of setting up new ones, registering for new classes and fitting into different time slots. So each semester varied his life only that much. For instance, he might be getting up at eight thirty instead of nine o'clock. Everything else was the same. He took summer courses in the summer. The seasonal changes passed almost without notice. His professors' names he forgot after the first two weeks of their classes. The other students he never talked to or looked at, in the halls looking at his feet and sitting at the lectures taking volumes of notes. And when the professor would make a joke and the room would roar with laughter, he would write it down: *Joke made here, about how ancient culture seems like ours today.* Years went by.

His upstairs landlady thought he was not right and probably for that reason fetched him upstairs whenever she could bring herself to impose on his solitude, to eat dinner, lunch, and breakfast with her four children. She'd never had a renter stay so long, and she felt this was a kind of intimacy, at least compared to the few students she'd had before whose lives were so erratic that they'd be here one day and breaking leases another with no regard for any responsibility.

C dreaded her children. He dreaded eating with them. He dreaded eating. After two and one half years he still dreaded living. And then what he dreaded most of all and knew would happen happened on a dreaded afternoon in winter. Mrs. Sorenson, his upstairs landlady, had slipped silently into the apartment. She often did this and would sit—C did not know for how long—watching him work at his desk (he imagined for hours) until he finally turned around or got up for a drink of water. At first this so distressed him that he made a point of turning around every ten minutes in order to catch her (he could not bring himself to lock the door). His studies suffered. His plan suffered; and he finally turned the desk around so that he sat with his back toward the wall. Even with this she managed, despite her lumbering size, to enter without being noticed. This particular afternoon she did not wait to be caught, but spoke out from her seated position on the Hollywood bed.

"How did you get a name like C?" she asked.

"My father," C said and did not look up from his books.

"Your father called you C?"

"Yes." He looked at her now—dreading. "That is, he called me Cecil and my mother didn't like that because it was too long."

"Then your mother named you C," she concluded, with satisfaction, and crossed her heavy legs.

"I suppose so."

"I'm not old enough to be your mother," she confessed and re-crossed her legs the other way.

Dread, thought C, staring into the pages of his book, through the desk, through the cement, and into the ground—hoping she would think he was reading.

"I'm only thirty-six."

"Your children," said C.

"No; we're a very liberal family. I have made it a point for my children to be completely used to their bodies and mine. There's nothing dirty about it."

"I can understand that," said C, "for you."

"You too, C. You study too hard. Come upstairs and let me stick you between my thighs and shake something loose."

He'd expected it might come in that way, nothing but the terrible facts of the desire. There was no other way for her. It was her attitude. Dread, thought C . . . but he believed then, and always, that relationships between people were like nothing else—that somehow it was partly his own responsibility for his landlady feeling the way she did, and because he was partly responsible for agitating this desire, then it would be wrong not to help her satisfy it. Dread, he thought. Involvement, maybe, but like this, now . . .

"Can't you think of anything else to do?" he asked himself, "like shopping, or laundry, or working, or . . . no, I don't suppose you can." And he got up and they went upstairs and upstairs again and into her room, where he stood nervously next to the door.

"First time, ain't it?" she said, pulling her sweater over her head, beginning to let her full self out. "Come over here," she said, stretching her arms out to him. "Don't be shy."

"I'm not," he answered.

"Come over here," she cooed.

"I can manage," he said and quickly removed his clothes, giving himself more time with the socks as he noticed she was having some difficulty in undoing her bra and finally peeled it off downward.

"Must have been rusted," he said.

"Come here," she said, and he saw that outside the window was rain, slush, snow, ice, and wind, and this made him feel smaller somehow. He walked over to her as gracefully as he could and she laid hold of him and sat him down on the bed with one of her hands around behind his buttocks and the other already stroking and pulling at his shrunken penis.

"That's better," she said. "You'll be all right." C had his eyes closed and was concentrating on intellectual theories—names and dates. Mrs. Sorenson wrapped her legs around him, pressed him neatly into her with the backs of her calves and heels, rocking him gently with her hands on his shoulders. The front door opened and closed. Feet clambered up the steps and into the room. C's soul slipped to his feet.

"Mom, where's Benji?" asked the seventh-grader, soon joined by his younger sister.

"I don't know. At the neighbors' . . . maybe Mrs. Myers let him in the house again. Why don't you go look?" C had stopped and was looking at them, apologetically, fearfully, hatefully. Mrs. Sorenson began rocking him again with the tremendous power of her legs. "And tell Dennis to turn down the radio or turn it off."

"Did you have a good day, Mommy?" asked the smaller one.

"It's been all right. Now run along and don't go wandering off before dinner . . . and take off your boots," she called after them. They left.

"You have very liberal children, Mrs. Sorenson."

"Don't think about them now," she said and closed her eyes.

AFTER SOME TIME C WAS ALLOWED TO ROLL OVER ONTO A MORE SPA-cious part of the mattress and Betty trotted off to the dresser drawer. She extracted a large manila envelope and carried it over to the bed. C had sat up and was watching the summing up of the afternoon outside.

"Look at these," said Betty. "These were taken at Lake of the Dells—at night, of course." And she lifted out a clump of photographs and spread them out on the bed . . . pictures of her in the nude standing beside pieces of furniture, trees, lying in the grass, eating candied apples, playing a guitar . . . "My husband took them."

"Where is your husband, Mrs. Sorenson? Is he dead?"

"No. He was in the reserves and in 1949 volunteered for active duty in Korea, and stayed there."

C looked outside again.

"Here's one taken at Okoboji on our first vacation. That's Jack," she said, pointing into a black-and-white picture. C got off the bed and went over to his neat pile of clothes on the floor, and began putting them on.

"I've got a lot more here," she said.

"I don't have time to look at them, Mrs. Sorenson. I've got to be going."

"Back to your studying, I suppose."

C put on his lost shoe and walked downstairs and then walked downstairs again. Margie, the first-grader, opened the basement door for him and stood watching him descend the open staircase. He looked around his apartment and of course saw nothing but the stripes he had painted. He looked at his desk and went to it and put a paperback edition of a contemporary philosophical position in his back pocket. In the other pocket he put his check-book. He put on his jacket and left. After the money was gone, there would be nothing.

He walked down Burlington Avenue and into town. He had never been downtown much before except to buy books—so went into the first tavern he saw, on the corner of Dubuque Street. Many of the men and women in the bar turned around as the door opened, but then resumed their private activities after C had securely fastened it—as though they were only concerned with seeing the cold air come in. The bartender was in shirt sleeves and C went across the street to another bar after he refused to accept a check.

C sat alone in a booth and drank and ate until he was sick, and then rented a room in the Roosevelt Hotel and lay down, thinking before he fell asleep that this would not work, that he had only spent twelve dollars, and at that rate . . . well, it would simply have to go faster. The next morning he bought a used car (he could not bring himself to waste money on a new one; no, that would be wrong; but everyone needed an automobile), and drove it around all day, having the oil checked, putting air in the tires, eating four full meals in restaurants, watching two movies, and going finally back to his hotel room with a strawberry ice-cream fizz.

The following few days were like this, except without the food. Then he took the last step, walked into the final phase, and gave his money away—in the manner that his father might have—donating it to needy institutions under his full name: The Reverend Ansel C. Easter, Ontarion, Iowa. Even some to the University.

He was soon without money in the bank and threw his check-book into a trash barrel outside the telegraph office. And walking down Clinton Avenue, he wondered for the first time how he would die—how the money made any difference at all. He would have to stop eating; and he could've done that anyway. Surely something will happen now, he thought, and felt in his pocket—four bits in nickels and dimes. C went inside a drugstore and bought a small bottle of terpin hydrate, signing his name The Reverend Ansel C. Easter and the date, carried it over to a tree in the Pentacrest, sat down, and began drinking it sip by sip, the taste exploding inside his mouth, very badly. There is nothing quite like terpin hydrate.

The cold air bit into him.

A girl came walking through the slush and drizzle across from the drugstore. The wind tried to carry her thin bones away. Once a horn blew at her and she stumbled back to the curb, waiting for the light. Several more people came, talking and laughing, and went into a bar. She did not look up, and pulled her denim coat more tightly around her neck. A large man stopped beside her, waiting for the light, and she turned to him. C saw the man bodily push his way past her, shaking his head and swearing, as though he might have been asked for something he was unwilling to give. She crossed the street and entered the Pentacrest, dragging her feet along in the snow, her uncovered hair wet and streaking across her face like tears. She sat down next to C and lowered her face between her arms and against her upright knees.

"How's everything?" she asked, out loud, dull, expecting no answer, like someone talking to herself. She sounded young.

"Good," said C. "Everything's good. How about you?"

"Good," she said (but didn't look up). "Everything's good."

"Want some cough syrup?"

"Codeine?"

"Yeah."

"O.K." And she took the bottle, swallowed, and shivered from the taste.

"Go ahead," C said, "kill it." And she took the rest of the corner in one quick gulp.

"That's good."

"You're welcome."

These two sat together and the snow and the ice and the cold went on, though they didn't comment on it, or anything. And it grew darker. Those few cars that trudged down the streets beside the Pentacrest were forced to stop at each intersection by the conspiracy of Iowa City traffic lights, and slid sideways when they began to move, as though they were large gray animals being led home on a long rope.

"You got a place to stay?" she asked.

"Yeah," he said. "Sure, I got a place."

"I just thought, because you were sitting here, I mean—"

"Right." And they were quiet again for a while.

"You a student?" she asked.

"No. Not now."

"You mean you were?"

"Sure. For a while."

"What's the matter—run out of money or flunk out or something?"

C almost laughed.

"No. I guess I just quit. You want a cigarette?" He shoved a half-filled pack toward her after his hand had bumped into them inside his coat pocket.

"Thanks," she said.

"Keep 'em. I think I ought to stop."

"Thanks . . . non-filters. That's good."

"You a student?"

"Me?" She was looking at him in the dark. "No . . . oh, no."

"I don't know, I just thought—"

"You sure you don't want one of these cigarettes?"

"Well, maybe one last one." She held them out to him, then gave him her own to light from.

"You cold?"

"No, I'm fine. How 'bout you?"

"You haven't got any more of that terpin hydrate, do you?" she asked, very slowly, stirring the snow around with her high-top work shoes.

"No. But I can get—" Then he stopped. He couldn't. "Are you sure you're not cold?"

"Yeah, sure."

"I just thought. I mean, because of wanting some more cough syrup."

"No. I didn't want any; I just wondered. I wondered if maybe you were addicted to that stuff."

"Oh. No, I'm not."

"Oh."

"How about you?"

"What?"

"You addicted to that stuff?"

"No. Say, you getting ready to go?" she asked. He could feel her shivering, though he had not thought they were touching.

"Go where?" More shivering. "And you're cold. What's the matter with you anyway? Why don't you get on out of here?"

"Damn it," she said, half crying. "I ain't got any place to go. I'm cold, and hungry . . . and I don't know what the fuck the difference is to you. So why don't you get on out of here yourself, Jackshit? I can stay in the lobby of the girls' dorm anyway."

"In the lobby of the girls' dorm!" he exclaimed. "Why do you do that?"

"Why? Because it's free and it's cold out here. That's why."

"You mean you want to go on . . . living like that?"

"Of course not. What do you think, I like it there and wouldn't want to be in a house or apartment or someplace where the campus police wouldn't chase me out? Things are tough now, Pigass. No work . . . and some of the girls bring me food back from the cafeteria."

"Look," he said, wondering how long he had spent inside, outside of this normal flow of things, away from the streets. "Take . . . well, I haven't any more money. You see that car over there? The blue one? Well, here are the keys. Drive it down to 718 Jefferson and in the basement there's an apartment that's paid for up until next month. If the landlady says anything, tell her that I told you to go there. And then sell the car—and don't let them give you less than three hundred dollars. The title's in the glove compartment."

"Listen. Listen, whatever you think, I ain't no kept woman."

"What?"

"Sure, I know, you don't expect nothing. Except later, when you come bustin' in that apartment of yours and start deciding then and there that you got something coming. And then maybe it's better if I don't, so you can hit."

"You stupid bitch," he said, surprising himself with a language that he had until that time only read about in paperback novels. "I don't give a good god-damn what you do. I've given my money away. My father's dead and he was a shit. I quit school because I wanted to stop studying . . . to stop everything. And my landlady has got over three hundred and fifty pictures of herself in the nude and her children are very liberal, and I've had it. . . . Can you understand that? Can you!"

"Fuck off," she said. "I can't understand any of that. I don't know any of those people."

"In ordinary terms, I'm going to sit here until something happens."

"You'll die—that's what will happen, you jerk."

"That's good," he said. "I just wonder how it'll happen. I mean, if it will be the cold or the hunger, or what."

"You got any food in your apartment?"

"Some. A lot. I never got much of a chance to eat it because of the upstairs landlady inviting me up to eat with her fat-faced, liberal, sneering children."

"Let's go back and eat," she said.

"Didn't you hear what I said?"

"I wasn't listening. I was thinking."

"You mean everything would be good with you if you had a place? That's all? Just those things? What were you thinking about?"

"Food. And of course it would. What else is there? Let's go."

"Aren't you afraid that I'll want something from you?"

"I was thinking maybe you would. And it doesn't worry me much. You seem sort of weak, I guess. And I can't drive anyway, or read street signs. And I don't know your name to tell the landlady."

"C," said C.

"My name's Cell," said Cell.

"First," he said, "you should know I'm not so good with people. It's been—"

"Let's go."

These two, Cell and C, drove to C's apartment and entered by the least noisy of the two doors. Mrs. Sorenson and her children—from the living room—watched them cross over the hall and into the entry to the basement, noticing particularly the tracked mud and water. They went downstairs and Cell thought that the way he had his apartment painted was not in the best taste, and he twice had to point out to her what spoiled food looked like before she tried to cook it or put it in a sandwich.

C had waited for something to happen. He was unsure, watching her eat, sitting in dry clothes too big for her, if this thing had been enough of a happening to qualify, but he was at least willing to ride a ways on the wave of it—which he felt was better than having a vague hope. And she knew this. Nothing was expected from her.

But I must be careful, she thought: I must plan ahead. She would not be fooled again. She had been once before, when their automobile killed her parents and her safe place was sold for mortgage. There had been no insurance. A kind, sad-faced policeman had taken her to an orphanage, where the civil servants beat her regularly for punishment and sport, sometimes making her pull down her drawers the next day so they could see the marks. At sixteen years old she was let out. That had been two years ago and she had not been fooled about anything since. She began to plan ahead and moved the bed to the place where the desk had been before she put it beside the furnace. So now the striped walls made more sense.

"HOW ARE YOU GOING TO PAY THE RENT NEXT MONTH?" SHE asked.

"I can sell the car."

"And when that money runs out?" she pressed.

"I don't know."

"You don't work?"

"No." And they turned out the light and went to bed. Cell's

body was thin, tight, and tough. C imagined in a moment of fren-
zy that he was in bed with some kind of smooth-skinned animal.
It was also exciting to have so much to do for himself.

Afterward, exhausted, he sat on the bed, leaning against the
converging stripes, and Cell brought coffee for them with so much
sugar he couldn't drink it. "Well," she said, "how are we going to
get some money?"

"We aren't," he said. "I'm not going to spend my life making
money. I won't do it."

"But when the rent runs out. We need a place."

"I've got a house. My father's house. We could stay in there."

"Your father."

"Don't worry, he's dead. But if all you want is a house, then
we've got one."

"Where is this house?"

"In Ontarion."

"Well, we'll go there. But not until the rent's gone here. It's not
right to waste. So later we figure out about food."

"O.K.," said C.

"What's your last name?"

"Easter."

"Easter!"

"What's with you?"

"Nothing," she said, and smiled. "I was just thinking how
good things are, and how funny for you that Cell Easter is such a
better name than C Easter, and somebody even named you."

She might be right, you know, thought C, as though to someone else; then went to sleep, hoping that what he feared wasn't
true—that everything was going too fast.

I hope he doesn't expect too much from me, thought Cell, because I can always go back to the dormitory and maybe get a job
in a laundry or something; then went to sleep, a broken, fretful
sleep with a stranger.

C sold some of his books to a used-book store with a little room in back of it. They didn't pay him much for them and he had to sell most of those he owned in order to get enough money for gasoline, oil, a sack of bologna sandwiches with lettuce and mustard, and several gallons of fruit juice. They drove to Ontarion. Cell was asleep in the back seat when they arrived. They knew each other hardly better now than they did before they met. The snow had all the sounds and wouldn't let them out. Very, very quiet.

"You mean that's it?" she said, her sleepy voice nearly cracking, rolling down the coupe's back window.

"That's it," he said, and turned the car off. Buttonweeds had overgrown the lot and stood up through the snow, brown and dead. Rabbit tracks went among them. Mice. The windows were still whole, untouched by small ruffians.

"It's so big," she said, and added, "But it sure is a fine house . . . it sure is a fine house." Her voice trailed off and came back again. "You sure this is your house?"

"Yep," he said and got out of the car.

"Sure is a big house," she said and followed him, carrying the half-filled pillowcase of bologna sandwiches up out of the weeds. "Who was your father anyway?" she asked, when they had reached the porch.

"A nigger."

"A nigger!" she said and set the bag down on the snow on the porch floor.

"I mean he was everything as unpleasant as that word. I meant nothing ethnic by it."

"You mean he wasn't black."

"That's right, he wasn't."

"He musta been a lawyer, or some great man, if this was his house. Unless he had it for a hotel."

"He was a preacher."

"Preacher!" she said with more surprise than she had with the other word. "They don't have houses like this."

"I know," said C and unlocked the front door with some little

trouble. A current of snow swept in and across the wide boards
of the hall.

"Hurry," said Cell, rushing in with her sack. "Shut the door,
and don't let any more of that in here. God, this is a big house.
Where's all the furniture?"

C had noticed that too . . . there were only a few pieces left,
scattered around the house as though they'd been caught in a
whirlwind and thrown to the edges of the rooms, upside down
and in corners. Sam, thought C, must have sold the rest—might
have sold the house (he didn't tell this to Cell, who brought
together two chairs into the hall, set them upright, dusted them
off, sat him down and handed him a bologna sandwich, took one
herself, and sat across from him, her feet not touching the floor).
"This sure is a fine house." And ate into her sandwich.

They found some beds on the third floor and picked out the
biggest one. C groped down into the basement, threw the master
switch, turned the water pump on—surprised that there was still
current—lit the oil furnace, and went upstairs to wait for the ice
in the lines to melt so that he could begin to run the rust out and
open the drains. He listened to the popping of the iron casing of
the furnace as it expanded. Cell was collecting all the furniture
from several of the downstairs rooms into one room at the foot of
the open staircase, in order to have a regular-looking place.

"Forget it," said C. "We're not going to keep that stuff."

"It's all we've got," said Cell.

"We'll get some more."

"How? We haven't got any money. We haven't got—"

"Shut up," said C.

The boards creaked from the warmth, frost formed on the
windows. The walls groaned and stretched in the middle, then
everywhere, as the house woke from the dead.

"YOU DON'T BELIEVE IN GHOSTS, DO YOU?"

"Not his," he answered.

The electric lights tunneled out into the yard. The ice melted in the water pipes in the basement and C turned on all the faucets, letting the rust empty into the sinks. They dismantled the bed and carried it down to the first floor, and were asleep before C had time to think about not going on another day, or Cell had time to decide to go back to the dormitory.

C KNEW THAT HE WOULD BE DISCOVERED, AND THAT BY NOW EVERY-one knew that someone—probably him—was living in the gray house. That morning he got up and walked down to the bank. Cell watched him leave and got out of bed thinking, He better not say shut up to me again—just for a little mistake. This goddamn snow, thought C.

The bank was closed when he arrived. C sat on the bench outside and waited for Merle Wood to come back and talk to him. Merle would be eating lunch at his mother's house. C looked out into the street. Tire tracks in the snow, making no noise. Snow swallows sounds. He knew he'd only been away a little this side of three years, and knew that that wasn't enough time to really change anything, and was enough time to change many things a little . . . *If they could only have forgotten about my father.* A short, squarish figure stepped out of Merle Wood's mother's house and stood for a minute adjusting his gloves and coat collar before ven-turing out onto the street and toward the bank. Even from that far away he could tell it wasn't Merle. Rabbit! thought C. That's Rabbit! And Rabbit, Merle's son, stepped down from the porch and came toward him in the slow, lumbering gait of his father, his squinted eyes darting up and down the street, noticing not only C, but that his coat was worn about the elbows and that his skin was not healthy—had not been exposed enough to the weather . . . taking this all in at a glance and seeing that nothing else had come or gone.

"Hello, Rabbit," said C, leaving his arm on the top of the bench.

"Hello, C," said Rabbit. "Good to see you home again."

They looked at each other.

"Good to be here."

Rabbit took out a shining bunch of keys and opened the bank. Then he stood in the doorway, waiting.

"I heard you were going to school. The University, I heard."

"That's right."

"Almost three years, summers too. Graduate?" His fleshy hands played with the keys.

"Nope." C came into the bank. "I went over to the house last night and noticed that a lot of the furniture was gone. I thought that what probably happened—"

"Sam sold it. We helped out—as we could—but there was just some of that stuff that no one could use."

"About the house, Rabbit. I was thinking that maybe Sam had—"

"He borrowed seventeen thousand dollars on mortgage. That was six months ago. Every month he sends money from Springfield, Illinois."

"O.K."

Rabbit Wood sat down on the top of the desk and lit a smoke.

"Your father, Merle, I guess he—"

"He retired and moved to Quincy with his new wife. I noticed you're not alone. Married?"

"I guess. Yourself ?"

"Not yet," said Rabbit. "Not until June."

"Anyone I know?"

"Ester."

"Oh?" He didn't know her very well, but knew Rabbit had been going up to Dubuque to see an Ester Willams since way before he left. He had brought her down occasionally and once introduced her, but he'd forgotten.

"Yep," said Rabbit, and smiled.

"So you and Ester. When's the wedding?"

"June."

"You're lucky."

Rabbit smiled.

"How are you going to live?" Rabbit asked.

"I don't know yet. I'll think of something, or something will happen. It'll work out . . . now that the house is still ours."

"You better get a job, C. Men shouldn't live without work. It isn't right." He was still playing with the keys, but what he said was serious.

"That's probably true. I got to be getting back now. Nasty weather."

"Say," said Rabbit before he closed the door. "I saw you come in last night. So I called Ralph and got him to turn on the current for you."

"Thanks," said C. "I wondered." Then he shut the door and began walking back home.

CELL WAS EATING A BOLOGNA SANDWICH. "WHAT'S THE MATTER?" she asked.

"Nothing."

"We have to leave, don't we?"

"No. But Rabbit Wood runs the bank, and he's this prudish kid that used to be in my class in high school."

"So you wish you could be like that?"

"No. I don't think so. But maybe I wish I could if I could all the way; I mean be like that. It might be better."

"I don't understand."

"Well, he said everyone should work . . . that it isn't right not to. He even said that it isn't right to live if you don't work."

"He didn't."

"That's what he meant."

"So what?"

"So I guess I feel that way too, only I have no intention of working."

"You want me to leave, don't you?"

"No. Why did you think that?"

"Because of saying things that sound bad that I can't under-stand—like maybe you would be better off without me."

"Well, that's not it."

"Then we can't stay here. That Rabbit said we couldn't."

"He didn't."

"Then there's nothing," she said, with a satisfied finality and sat down on her favorite chair in the living room. C sat down too, and they stayed there for two or three days, wandering about the house, while Cell became increasingly aware that every time the furnace clicked on and the warm air swooned into their room, they had no money to pay for it. She turned the thermostat down, and made C read in the same light that niggardly lit her own book. He won't stay here long, she thought. He'll go out and find work. He'll get tired of sitting around. It isn't healthy. He'll start hating; everyone does. Everyone hates.

"Don't you hate things?" she asked him.

"Yes."

"What most?"

"Bologna sandwiches."

"They're almost gone."

"Good."

"No. *Most*," she insisted.

"Iowa City water."

"None of that here."

"I can remember it."

"I mean not things, but conditions."

"I don't know. How about you?"

"Worrying."

"Is that your real name, Cell?"

"Sure, if yours is real."

"It is. But it was originally Cecil."

"Oh."

"What was yours?"

"A long one."

"What?"

"Cassandra, I think."

"Better that both of those names are gone."

"Yes."

"We got no more sandwiches."

"Good."

"C . . ." Then she turned away and went upstairs.

She is like a dark, ancient animal, he thought.

Upstairs, she was looking out at the car, trying to remember everything she had ever noticed about what it took to drive one. I am being tricked, she thought. These days'll bring something from the worry. Something's not good here. I have been tricked.

"I HATE PEOPLE WHO BUY ANTIQUES BECAUSE THEY COME INTO PLACES where other people live," he blurted out, "real people who use things the way they were meant to be used . . . they come in and give them money for the things that they use, and take them back home and put varnish on them, and refurbish their houses with them."

"There's nothing wrong with that," said Cell.

"Not if you think of things that you can use as dead. If you think that they're alive—when they're being used—then people who buy antiques are killers—killers who pay money to kill."

"I never thought of them that way," said Cell, and added, with her eyes cocked to the side, "and I never wanted to."

That night they made love until they both hurt. Cell was glad when it finally ended and C rolled over, facing the wall. The house seemed frighteningly strange to her, moreso in the dark when she could only sense it, and though she knew C wasn't asleep, she couldn't speak to him. There was a barrier as surely as something she could touch. From where it arose, him or her, was no concern—only its realness. In the basement she heard rats chewing on wood, making noises like tiny hammers. She put her hand on her right breast and quickly took it away, it seemed so small and close to the bone when she was on her back. Any curiosity she ever had of her body always ended in the same kind of rejection. He'll never penetrate into me, she thought. He'll never really know me . . . or want to. The wind outside rattled the eave pipes. There was a fence around the orphanage, she remembered, that sounded a little like that, but not nearly so close. C's leg jerked of its own accord. He seems so old, she thought. We both do. Tomorrow, if something doesn't happen, I'll leave: I knew this wouldn't be any good. And once again she felt as though she wanted to cry—forever wanting to join the simple ways of normal living, forever being shut outside.

"Cell."

"What?"

"Nothing. I just wondered if you were asleep."

. . . But C doesn't want that, she thought. Any common sense that he'd had before had been rooted out and so entirely jumbled by the University that although he appeared to be normal—physically normal—he was virtually nothing more than a mad vegetable.

Cell had once been told by her mother, though she could not remember when and often wondered if maybe she hadn't dreamed it (even down to what her mother looked and sounded like because it was one of the few vivid memories she was able to retain through the years with the juvenile home in between), that if she lay still in bed before going to sleep, and did not think about her troubles, they would rise to the surface and float away and be gone by morning. This memory comforted her and she fell off to sleep, confident that in the morning she would know what to do. Periodically the furnace turned on with a *vooroom* sound and ran an almost imperceptible tremulation up through the spine of the house.

But C woke up first. He slipped quietly out of bed and went

up to the third floor and looked out across the yard. The moonlight was being filtered first through a layer of clouds and then
through a low-hanging fog bank, leaving an eerie, almost blue
light to trickle into the town. Through this C saw the upstairs
light in Rabbit Wood's house turn on. He's getting up now in
the dark to get ready for work, thought C . . . now when it's still
night he's getting ready to go to work, and, God save him, he
enjoys it. It was cold on the third floor and C rubbed his tired
hands together and felt once, automatically, in his empty pajama
pocket for cigarettes. And then as though some magic was working through Cell's sleep into his mind, into his thinking, and into
inspiration, he understood that it was these Rabbit Woods that
not only ruled the world, but should, and that same evil that had
been in his father—that distaste for life and the normal activities
in it—was in him. He shuddered from the cold and leaned with
one hand against the window frame.

I've come here, he thought, to be on the third floor looking out
into the yard as though without moving. . . . I have been a part of
the whole way things are, like a child complaining of beets or his
mother's milk. From now on what I have will be mine and what
I do will be me. My father is dead. No one cares what I do any
more, except her. I'm free. I'll have to watch myself and not make
any mistakes. If I fall, it will be because I have stumbled, not because of loose stones on the ledge.

I KNEW IT, THOUGHT CELL, LYING IN THE EMPTY BED . . . HE'D LEAVE
me here and take the car and go away. I knew it . . . all along I
knew he'd do it and I came anyhow. She stared at the floor over
the edge of the bed, making ringlets in the dust with her finger. I
knew . . . and I knew he'd do it at night—crawl away in the middle of the night after the food was gone, with the car, without me,
like a rat . . . leaving me for the police to come and find and . . .

Then she heard him coming downstairs, and did not wonder if
it was someone else because of his way of walking down sideways,

making always a loud thud followed by a smaller clump in rapid
succession.

"Good morning," he said.

"Good," she said and stretched into a seated position and then
out of the bed, holding her open arms out to him, who walked
into them and carried her back. Like magic they were fitted together and Cell screamed softly, "Love me, C. Love me." And C
thought, I will surprise you.

"I'M GOING TO START A JUNK YARD," HE SAID. "I'VE DECIDED THAT WE'VE
got to have a junk yard that in years will cover this whole yard."

"What kind of a junk yard, C?"

"One with everything in it."

"Like cars?"

"Cars, books, planes, stoves, refrigerators, railroad ties, nails,
chains, sledge hammers, oil cans, lumber, window frames, insulation . . . everything."

"Why?"

"Because that's what I'm going to do."

"What's what you're going to do?"

"Run the junk yard."

"Why, C?"

"Cell, listen . . . don't talk. Listen. We are going to live because
people will trade us things that we need for things we don't need."

"We don't have anything we don't need."

"Quiet. Listen. Just listen. We can trade this car—"

"WE NEED THE CAR!"

"—for a bunch of junk—bring it here and leave it in the
yard—sort of display it."

"C—"

"People will trade food for it too. People will do anything to
get something secondhand."

"But—"

"And my father would turn over in his grave if he could

know about his house being surrounded by junk. Antique buyers will tear their eyes out when they can't buy what they want . . . and those kinds of people never have anything to trade. . . . I'll be back." And he threw on his clothes and ran out of the house.

Cell's eyes filled with water. She pulled the corners of the sheet up over her shoulders and tried to fall asleep. They'll fool him, she thought. How young he must be to not know that the world fools people who think like that—think that something can be made out of nothing—that happiness can come just because you decide it should—yes, and that the meek will inherit; children's thinking. I would never have come with him, she thought, if I'd known he was that stupid; and now I can't leave him, can't tell him because children never believe, and have to stay and watch him crack open and watch his childhood drain out of him. I've been so careful not to be fooled this time from one direction that it has come up behind me. C . . . C . . . C . . . And she fell asleep completely covered, her head jammed in between two pillows.

These pillows protected her later on from hearing noises in the front yard next to the street. And by the time she finally got out of bed, wrapped the sheet around her, and walked to one of the huge windows, she saw C standing in the middle of the dreary afternoon yard, standing beside a man in overalls and a tremendous pile of lumber, metal pipes, two oil drums, a stack of half a hundred pieces of ceramic tile, enough fire bricks for a fireplace, holding three giant brown paper bags wedged in between his two arms . . . standing and talking.

Cell stared out of the window. No, she said to herself, it's not natural. He wouldn't have done it . . . he couldn't have done it— not this quick; not in a town this size.

The man in overalls got into his pickup and drove away into the snow, pulling C's car behind him with a chain fastened not to the bumper, but the frame. C, still holding the food bags, walked around the beginning of his yard, noticing carefully the condition of the fire bricks and ceramic tile, not caring much over the lumber, which he knew a man could get anywhere, even steal off an isolated barn . . . if he wanted it badly enough. It began to snow and settle on the top of these things. He went inside.

"You traded the car," said Cell from inside the sheet, thinking, YOU TRADED THAT CAR!

"Here's some food," said C, and set down the bags of frozen vegetables, meat, potatoes, spices, apples, peaches, flour, butter, eggs, and one half-gallon of milk. "We can keep it outside until someone brings a refrigerator."

"That was the only thing we had that was worth anything. Three hundred dollars! We could've had three hundred dollars for that."

"But we've got some other stuff instead," said C, meaning both that they had been better off in the exchange, and that he didn't want to talk about it any more; and stood in the bay window and watched the snow fall on his new pile of junk.

Cell was quiet. The size of the house . . . the size of the rooms and the windows . . . frightened her a little. A hundred people could hide in here, she thought—maybe more, if they were employed and made money. She carried the bags to their one furnished room and separated out enough for them to eat—raw carrots, radishes, green onions, butter, and bread. The rest she put out on the back porch in a cardboard box, put this in the corner and threw an old single mattress from the basement over it as disguise so that no one would steal it in the night, being careful to step only on the aisle of porch next to the wall where the thin film of snow had not reached. We can eat better, she thought, when someone brings a stove to trade, and then cursed herself: Idiocy, plain idiocy; I will simply wait, and after the food is gone—after we've made a fire in the basement, or cooked the meat in the furnace—after no one comes and he finally begins to see things are not like he thinks they are . . . then we'll do something to get on, something normal.

IN FEBRUARY THEY GOT A STOVE THAT C BROUGHT INSIDE, DESPITE HIS reluctance to take anything out of the growing collection in the Yard except furniture, which now decorated three of the downstairs rooms. People traded, and every once in a while, on top of what was already in the bargain, C would say, "We could kind of use some food," and obtain another bag, which was split between the inside and the back porch. Cell wanted a gun in order to be able to shoot anyone trying to steal food from under the mattress. But she didn't tell him.

She watched all this—this dealing in the snow—out of the windows, each time half not believing it, and half trying to guess, from the dress of the man, what in God's name he wanted from the growing heap of trash. "More than equal size and weight," said C, when asked what he wanted for a piece of this or that, keeping the prerogative to refuse even this exchange if he didn't care for the proposed item. In March they obtained a refrigerator and set it inside. "You skinned me on this one, Easter," called the man after him, as he and Cell wheeled it inside. "But next time it'll be different."

"I'll be here," said C, and the two laughed; then Bill Wooly and his boys lifted a bathtub with feet up onto a flatbed. Two of the older boys hopped up with it and steadied it from shifting as their father eased the truck over the ruts in the road toward home.

"Oh, C," shouted Cell, "we've got a refrigerator! This is becomin' just like a real house. Before long all those downstairs rooms will be full of furniture."

"What's more important," said C, "is that Bill Wooly is from up around Tipton, and there's plenty of traders up there, shrewd traders, with lots to trade."

"Things are good, C," said Cell. "What with this refrigerator, we can live the way people were meant to live . . . good people were meant to live."

"With refrigerators?" asked C, smiling slightly.

"Don't tease," said Cell and set about cleaning out the refrigerator and ordering food inside it from the back porch, being happy despite herself . . . despite her knowing, sensing clear back inside her, that something wasn't right, that people shouldn't live in a happy, easy way without money, with others taking care of them—knowing that something would come along, something was bound to happen—like a blinding arrow of lightning—and break everything apart; and the better they got on, the higher they rose, then that much heavier the fall would be, maybe even enough to kill C; and in order that that should not happen, Cell worried, and watched, and waited, suspicious of everything in order that they would not have so far to fall . . . at least her half. C could tell. "Remember?" he asked. "Remember that a place and food is all? That's what you told me. We've got those." She smiled, but waited.

Their food, which could no longer be hidden by a single mattress, began to rot—the three fourths of it Cell couldn't jam into the refrigerator that said GENUINE FRIGIDAIRE on the inside of the door and woke her up for the first few weeks every time it turned on. Near the end of April, C got another one, but by then most of the food on the porch was too far gone and under no circumstances, he told her, was he going to bring another refrigerator into the house and live with three, despite her worries. She accepted this cheerfully, thinking to herself that because she'd been told not to worry, then she didn't have to and couldn't be blamed when the blow came.

The warm weather drew C out onto the porch in the daytime, where he sat in a rocking chair looking over the Yard. Cell read magazines and books and listened to the radio, and finally (with C's approval) got a part-time job working in a fabric shop in order to keep from going stir crazy and to pay the electricity and oil bills. They had a blood test and were married.

In the beginning of the warm weather only those few young men that had been C's close friends before he'd gone to Iowa City came over in the evenings when the light was still out and sat on the front porch or around the Yard with him, talking and laughing. Midsummer, however, saw the porch and Yard filled with people sitting and talking; just enough shade to keep the sun off, and enough to talk about to last at least another hour.

But it wasn't C who brought them. No one ever said, "Let's go over to visit C." It was always, "Let's go over to C's place." Sometimes the women would come too, but Cell mostly watched by herself out of the windows or beside C on the porch, thinking to herself: "They've come like vultures. People don't come to a junk yard just to be." But they did; and later Cell still thought of them as vultures. Even Rabbit, after he was married, came over and sat heavily on one of the front steps in his shirt sleeves and smoked cigars and looked at everyone out of his tiny, squinched eyes.

"Rabbit," said C. "I haven't seen you."

"In a long time," said Rabbit. "No, I guess you haven't."

"Brought your new wife, I noticed," said C.

"Yes. She's gone inside . . . to talk to *your* new one."

That bastard, thought C.

"I noticed everyone coming over here." Rabbit gestured out toward the two or three groups of people milling around out in the Yard, sitting on pieces of broken machinery and drinking soda pop or beer they had brought with them. "Thought that maybe there was something more here than a growing pile of junk."

"No, that's about it," said C.

"I see," said Rabbit, and tossed a cigar butt away from the house. "You got any insurance?"

"Insurance?"

"In case anything happened to you, or to your house."

"No," said C, standing up and leaning against one of the front pillars, watching a blue sedan drive up and stop. "Did you see those plates?"

"Might've been Missouri," said Rabbit.

Two men got out of the car, one older than the other but possibly related, thought Rabbit, because of the protective way the older man acted toward the younger. It was more in the way they moved than anything else—sort of a carry-over from the two men remembering the childhood of the younger man, but only one of them remembering the childhood of the older. Rabbit's eyes were the only ones good enough to be that sure from that distance.

"A man ought to have insurance," said Rabbit, "in case something happens."

"Nothing's going to happen. . . . Look at them. There's some real traders."

Rabbit looked again at the two as they walked along through the junk, talking quietly to themselves, looking over the lumber and angle iron, touching a piece here and there, the way a husband will accompany his wife in the grocery store . . . over to three men from Ontarion sitting on an old tractor drinking beer from bottles. One of these three nodded over toward the porch and Rabbit noticed that the two did not look then—did not follow the nod, but marked it carefully so that later they could take a long, studied look.

"I wonder what they want," said Rabbit.

"How do you know they want something?"

"Because people act like that when they come into the bank, if they want something."

"Curious," said C. "I didn't think it was at all the same thing. . . . It isn't."

"Just the same, you ought to get some insurance. What does your wife think about it? What's her name?"

"Cell . . . you've seen her in the drygoods store. If I could only know what they wanted before I talked to them. She wouldn't want insurance and has a very idealistic attitude about the world.

Everything's always fine with her. And with me. We don't need any insurance."

"How about health insurance?"

"Don't need it. Damn, Rabbit, if *you* want some, or some more, why don't you get it?"

"It's not right . . . living like this," said Rabbit. "How about when you have children?"

"Children!"

"I suppose you don't . . . well, you know."

"Christ, Rabbit! Besides, she's got one of these things that keeps her from getting pregnant. It's a thing that shoots water up inside her and runs all the sperm out. It's kind of a neat gadget. Do you want to see it?"

"No!!!"

"Well. So we aren't going to have any kids," said C.

"Why don't you go out and see what they want?"

"Give 'em too much advantage—thinking I'm curious. Better if they come up here."

"It's odd," said Rabbit, mostly to himself. "Set ways of doing things—procedures, everything like a real job, like real work, but not any money. Your father would have called that evil . . . something that appears to be like other, natural things, but isn't."

"Maybe you better go in and get a pop; you're looking hot and thirsty."

Rabbit got up and ambled toward the door, turned and looked again at the two men, who had by this time pretty much covered the entire Yard, walking easily, not stopping longer in any one spot than another. Then he told C something that C had suspected was true but couldn't be sure of even after Rabbit said it: that everyone had forgotten about his father because even though it'd happened, it was too bizarre to believe, too fantastic for the memory to hang on to—there was no place to put it. "For instance," said Rabbit, "how long can you remember a nightmare?" Then he went inside to find Ester and have a pop.

C sat on the steps and waited, called Jimmy Cassum over to talk to him, and lit a cigarette. The two out-of-state men finally walked up to the porch as though they had just happened to be passing that way, would have been passing that way if no one was there at all, if there was no Yard, no porch, no house—just walking in the fields.

"Hello," said the older man.

"Hello," said Jimmy.

"Do you own this place?"

"No. But *he* does." He indicated C sitting beside him.

"You have some nice things here," said the younger man.

"Real nice things," added the older man.

"Thanks," said C.

"Kind of young to be owning all this, aren't you?"

"Kind of," answered C.

"Do you sell?"

"Trade."

"Good . . . good."

These guys are great, thought C, asking me all this that they already know . . . as if their car wasn't full of things to trade; as if they didn't know what they wanted before they came here. Maybe all the way from Missouri.

"Do you see anything here that you like?"

"Well, not really."

"Well, if you do," said C, and pinched off the lit end of his smoke and put the rest into his shirt pocket. Nearly everyone in the Yard was at least keeping some kind of notice of them, though several of the original crowd had gone back home, and several more—townspeople rather than farmers—were coming in, chewing tobacco and playing horseshoes in the mud pits beside the road, looking back at the porch every couple of throws. The Yard, with rusted metal and a band of red sunset stretching from the horizon clear to the corn elevator standing at the end of the lot next to the field, seemed to be glowing of its own accord.

"I could use a couple of good oil drums," said the man whiskered in steel wool.

"Good," said C, and they walked over to where the oil drums were. They don't want oil drums, thought C; this is just a preliminary, something to warm up on; he hopes to be able to get what he wants for almost nothing . . . maybe asking me to throw it in on a deal for something else he pretends to want.

The two out-of-state men turned the drums over several times by rolling them with the bottoms of their kangaroo shoes and pulling them up onto their tops by grabbing hold of the hand pumps. "Those are good pumps," said C.

"The pumps don't make no difference to us," said the younger man. "All we want them for is to make a barbecue grill."

That was good thinking, thought C, shrewd; these are real traders. "They'd be good for that," he said.

"Probably be better to make it out of something else. These would be hard to cut."

"True."

"What do you think you might take for them anyway?"

"Probably something that was at least as big and weighed at least as much. Probably nothing that you could have brought with you—or I'd see it sticking out of your car from here."

"That's a rough deal," said the younger man. "Very few things are that big and weigh that little."

"Metal things, at least. Maybe a couple of kitchen tables."

"Measured how?"

"Occupied space."

"Then a table would be too small."

"No, I meant two for one barrel."

"That's a rough deal."

"Maybe a lot of small things, then," said C.

"Is that the way you always trade?" asked the older man.

"Generally," said C. "Sometimes for food. Sometimes for tobacco. Other things that I need."

"Oh. Well, what'll you trade that tool box for?"

They don't want that either, thought C, but they're getting ready. The three walked over to the tool box, an oak rectangular-shaped carry-all with a smooth, round dowel across the top, fastened to bell-shaped ends. Several of the horseshoe players went home and a couple more took their places. These replacements were not such good pitchers and Rabbit from clear inside the house could hear the occasional *sproinginging* of the shoes, on end, striking the stake and springing off.

"I don't know," said C. "Probably I wouldn't take anything for it. They're pretty hard to come by, and if I ever get together some tools, then I'll need it."

"I see," said the old man, pulling out his pocket watch, holding it up to his ear and winding it. "Then there's some of these things here that you won't trade. Like that birdbath top, for instance."

"Do you mean that sundial?"

"That thing over there"—he pointed—"that you put on top of birdbaths in the lawn. . . . Maybe it's a manhole cover."

"That's a sundial," said C, thinking, They don't want that either, but they're getting ready. Probably the next one. If I guess right, I can end up with everything they brought to trade. "It just doesn't have the pointer."

"Oh. Then you probably wouldn't think of trading that either. In case you got a pointer."

"I'd practically give that away; for something that weighed about as much."

"Oh. But you probably wouldn't want to trade the cider press."

That's it, thought C. "I might. I'd have a hard time getting another one, though, around here. They're scarce and people hold on to 'em."

They walked over to it, a devious distance of about twenty-five yards.

"But you might—for, say, three lawnmowers."

"Well, most likely not. It depends, though."

They began walking again, over toward the car, past many more pieces of things that these out-of-state men might have wanted. By the horseshoe pits they stopped and watched the game for a while, neither party speaking. That game was finished and another one begun with two other men. C watched as the challengers—obviously better—roared into a lead of six to zero and then threw a double ringer on top of a single one and won nine to zero . . . a skunk game. "Must be depressing," said C.

"It's only a game," said the old man, and they walked over to their automobile.

"Missouri," said C, indicating the license plates on the back bumper.

"That's where the car's from, at least," said the younger of the two out-of-state men. The other lifted two partially broken lawn-mowers out of the back seat and down onto the grass.

"Do they work?"

"No, they're broken. But they could be fixed."

"Maybe."

"Well, what do you think?"

"No good," said C. "That press is worth more than that. Twice as much. I thought you said you had three."

"That's a rough deal," said the younger out-of-state man.

"True."

"How about some water pipe?"

"Galvanized?"

"Sure."

And the two began pulling pieces of pipe from the back-seat floor, ranging in size from several inches to five feet. After they had drained their car of this, making a pile in the grass as big as a man, on top they put two collapsible lawn chairs. They shut the door and looked at C.

"That's good," said C. "That makes up the difference. Almost." I've got them, he thought; all this for a cider press.

"It should," said the older man, took out his pocket watch, and handed it to him. A nice one with a train on the back.

"Good. I'll even let you have that sundial too—if you want it."

"Sure. I guess we'll take that too."

The three went over to the sundial, past the horseshoe players, and through a large group of town men sitting and talking in what little was left of the sunset, then back again toward the car, the dial between the two out-of-state men, carrying it like a stretcher, followed by three or four of the town men. They set it down and leaned it against the car.

"That's almost as heavy as a manhole cover," said C.

"Seems to be," said the young man, and opened the trunk. Inside was a solid foot and a half of prize junk—old bottles, metal screws, scaffolding nails, doorknobs, pieces of chain, and children's baseball equipment, tools and gears, pulleys and brazing rods. They placed the sundial on top of this and the back of the car sank another half-inch onto the overload springs. The two men looked at this trunkful of prize junk that C didn't get, and looked at C, and then away.

"It should be," said the old man. "It's solid silver." And he scraped away a tiny line of the tarnished metal with a penknife blade, revealing a thread of silver. "I'd heard that you had this; that Turner had got a hold of it and brought it up here to trade for some tractor part, not knowing that it came from the Stafford estate in Knocksville."

The town men looked at the men from out of state, then at C, thinking, You poor sucker, too bad you didn't know . . . that much silver's worth as much as this whole Yard put together. Poor bastard.

Damn it, thought C. They would have traded that whole trunkload too. I didn't know they wanted that.

"You can keep the cider press," said the younger man, climbed inside, and they drove away.

One of the town men picked up a piece of pipe and looked

through it like a gun barrel—pointing it up toward the light; then set it down.

"It's too dark," said Jimmy Cassum, and the horseshoe game broke up and the players went home. In five minutes everyone went home—out of the Yard and into the darkness beyond the streetlight and C's vision. He walked through the Yard to the house and met Rabbit and Ester on the steps.

"Going home?" said C.

"I'm a working man," said Rabbit. "This night air's hard on the kidneys."

"Goodbye, Ester."

"Goodbye," she said, and left. C watched them walk down the Yard and by the pile of water pipe, Rabbit looking at it very carefully. Then C sat down in the rocking chair and brushed the mosquitoes away from his face and arms in regular movements. He watched the light go on in Rabbit's house. Cell came out and sat carefully beside him on the wooden chair, waiting to see if it would collapse, trying to be ready if it did.

"Another chair," she said.

"One more," he said, thinking, Those guys were some real traders.

"What's the matter?"

"Nothing. Nothing important. Just that everyone thinks I'm an idiot or poor fool or something for not knowing that this sundial I had was made out of silver. But it's just a sundial to me and I don't care . . . except that they had more stuff I could have gotten."

"You mean it was silver? Real silver? Could you get it back—if you called them up and told them it didn't really belong to you and that you had no right to sell it?"

"No . . . it's just that look on their faces when they thought they'd outwitted me. And they did. If only I'd known."

"It's hard to tell how people feel by what they say," said Cell, thinking, Silver!

They sat, brushing mosquitoes away from their arms and listening to the buzzing of junebugs as they came careening across the porch and bumping into the screen, trying to penetrate through into the light. Small animals crawled silently through the rubble in the Yard. The forest of moonlight covering Ontarion was diluted by rain clouds moving northeast, finally letting down what seemed to C like thin silver strands of rain, beginning at the top of his streetlight and extending toward the ground. "Mist," he said.

"C," said Cell, "do you think we could maybe get some inshoorance?"

CONFLICT. CELL NEEDED THIS, AND IF THERE WAS NOT ANY PRESENT, then she imagined that some was coming. In this manner she was like a professional fighter who, when he isn't fighting, is preparing. Of course this cost her, and her body remained at a tough eighty-seven pounds and C could almost cover her tight little buttocks with one hand and get a good bit of one of her hard-nippled breasts into his mouth. There was hardly enough loose skin on her stomach for him to squeeze, and her thighs were barely larger than his arms at the place where they joined his shoulders. Cell secretly enjoyed this size because she felt that, unlike other women, her husband knew her better because there was less of her and each place could get more attention. Yet she knew he could not penetrate into her innermost thoughts, or even their periphery, for that matter. So when the time of the month of her periodical bleeding came and went without anything happening, he not only didn't know, but she didn't think anything of it. It wasn't until just after missing her third period in a row, after her weight had teetered the scale over to near ninety pounds and she felt queasy in the morning, that she began to wonder if maybe that rubber-and-plastic gadget she had found in a cardboard box full of kitchen utensils C had traded for might not be foolproof. Even though she had used it every time afterward (as much for the sensation of cool, rushing water as for the clinical benefits). And as soon as the idea came to her, she knew it was true. She tested it with her consciousness. She could feel it. She began thinking the way she was sure pregnant women thought. She noticed that her fingers were getting fatter. She waited for when she might have dreams of crabs or fish. She weighed herself several times a day, every time sure that the scale was not accurate enough to record her changes. Things tired her out more quickly. She was sure the other people at work—even the customers—knew.

This is it, she thought. This is the way it will come. Things has been good up till now; but now it comes. Now we're going to pay for all this. It ain't right, being the way we've been, and now it comes—the splitting open and destruction, the screaming and crying. It was meant that it should happen—that even the water couldn't wash it away. We going to be held to it now, C and me. We going to be thrust back to the real world like we was flung from the sky.

By the fourth miss there was no doubt in her mind. She weighed ninety-eight and a quarter pounds, a lifetime record, and she no longer bothered to weigh herself after that. C'll know before long, she thought. He can't help but notice, he knows me so well; and as soon as she thought this, she became anxious that he should notice. Especially when I'm on top, she thought, he should notice.

But he didn't notice at first. At first he noticed that whenever he lay down, his wife would crawl on top of him, many times just to lie there, as though trying to sink into him, sometimes in the morning when neither of them had any inclination at all, despite his erection, which was a phenomenon that always bewildered him to the point of a prolonged astonishment . . . much more bewildering because, he reasoned, it was himself that was doing it, no outside forces were operating, and to no purpose or end. Sometimes she climbed on top of him when he was lying on his stomach. *This is curious,* thought C, and nothing else.

"WHY ARE YOU THROWING UP?" ASKED C, LOOKING DOWN AT CELL kneeling over the toilet, her face red.

"I'm sick," said Cell.

"Maybe we should get you some Pepto-Bismol."

"I don't think it would help."

"You're sick almost every morning. Have you been worrying about something?"

"Worrying? What's there to worry about? Everything's fine. I'm just a little sick, that's all."

"Oh," said C.

"Are you worrying, C?"

"No," he said, and began to leave.

Cell sat down on the floor and put her arms between her legs.

"C," she said, looking not at him but at the bathroom linoleum, "a wonderful thing has happened. Wonderful. I'm pregnant."

"I thought you were getting a little heavier."

"Did you?"

"That's good," said C. "That's very good. Are you sure?"

"Yes. I'm over four months into it."

"That's good," said C and there was a *grand mal* seizure inside his head that drained all the blood from his face, and like a ghost he stole from the room and, half dressed, stumbled outside to sit in the rocking chair. . . . Pregnant . . . pregnant.

For the next five months C had what seemed like a projector in his head that showed a stream of home movies—something that developed by a series of awful scenes, with the only sound being that of C's own thinking voice—something impossible to turn off but impossible not to notice when it was running. These scenes were in black and white and the characters (usually only two, he and his future child) sometimes just fused into the gray background and disappeared, only to reappear in the same place. C of course was always himself in these, but his hypothetical child began as a normal-ish baby somewhere between one and five, and ended up either a belligerent, brutal, egotistical, raving monster or a cowering, crawling, suffering, pale, pink-skinned animal that whimpered and hid under tables and in corners. For instance: one movie would begin with C in some way setting an example for his child—concluding a successful trade—and would end by his experimental child either hating him for being a cheat and enrolling in a monastery, or following in his footsteps and going on to become the biggest swindler in the country. One of the more dreaded of these movies was one in which C told his son that stealing was wrong. This movie had two endings too: one where his son lies and steals his way into Fort Madison Prison and becomes a punk, the other where he is naked in a barren acreage, cleaned out by all the shrewd traders in the world, who manipulate around him with half-truths. C tried to explain at this time in the film that lies are only bad if they are abundantly self-centered—that half-truths are sometimes helpful. But his son looks back and hates him for being wishy-washy and afraid to take a stand on the vital questions and issues of the day.

Another character was Ansel Easter, who would come shifting into a scene carrying a black belt which he offered to C for use on the child. "Bring welts to them," he would say, "big blue and black ones that will last forever. Make 'em scream. Teach 'em the Bible and everlasting glory. Teach 'em of repentance and damnation. Teach 'em of God and his infinite wisdom. Teach 'em Hell." And in these movies C would not only be standing, shaking in revulsion at his reborn character, but searching desperately for the projector, wondering why inside his own mind such a thing could go on, seemingly out of his control.

No, he thought. All fathers are not mine. All fathers are not mine. It doesn't have to be like that . . . things can be different. Someone can be happier than I was, and than I am. It's possible. It doesn't have to be like that—like a living worm that everyone catches from their father—and wishes from then on for the darkness and the warmth and the . . .

But C wasn't sure of this. He wasn't sure that it wouldn't happen all over again, and even when he talked to Cell about how their lives would be changed, and how much joy would come into their hearts, he was watching home movies of what he was sure it would be like. And as Cell grew to well over a hundred pounds, these movies became more frequent and more vivid, many times intruding into his dreams and making his body sweat even outside the covers.

C WAITED WITH HIS WIFE IN THE INDIGENT WARD AT THE HOSPITAL—A large room with many beds and many pregnant and very pregnant women. Cell had insisted that he be there, not during the birth (which she didn't care about because she figured that if it killed her, well, then it wouldn't matter), but be there when they carried in the baby, in order that he would have to accept some of the blame, in order that *she* wouldn't have to show it to him later, in order that they could be together when the blow fell.

C was glad for the large room, the other women, nurses, orderlies, water canisters, the noise, and the activity. It's better here, he thought, than I imagined. There are witnesses. There are other fathers.

He sat beside her bed and they waited, watching everyone and everything that moved in the room, not ever taking their complete attention away from the two swinging doors through which a nurse would emerge carrying the baby.

"How wonderful it is," said Cell, "that we have a baby—a baby boy."

"A boy," said C. "They told you that? That it would . . . that it is a boy?"

"Yes. Before I came out of the room they told me."

"I thought it might be a boy."

"That's what we wanted. Isn't that what we wanted, C?"

"Yes," he said. "I thought you wouldn't be conscious then— that they put you to sleep . . . because of the pain."

"No. I think it's more natural to be awake . . . and I didn't want to miss anything."

That takes courage, thought C. "And you didn't . . . I mean, it must have been so painful. Did you see it?"

"No. No, I didn't. I swear I didn't. I wanted you to be with me . . . to share."

"Do you feel like going to sleep? Are you tired?"

"No. I feel fine. I'm too excited to sleep." Poor C, she thought, he isn't prepared for what will happen.

"Oh. Well, maybe you should be. Maybe it's not healthy not to be. Should I call a nurse?"

"No. It's the best thing to be excited now—because I'm so happy."

A nurse walked through the doors in the other direction, away from them.

And another nurse, a young nurse, not small, with telephone-black hair, came through the doors into the thirty-bed-capacity room carrying a bundle and looking down into it. She stood casually, resting on one leg, and looked across the ward, from bed to bed. Some of the others looked up from their lying or propped-up positions and then looked away uninterested. Her search carried her easily down one aisle and up the other, rocking her arms so naturally that her limbs seemed to swing in time to her heart, until she found the frail little woman with colorless eyes peering out of her covers like a frightened bird, her husband sitting beside her in a straight-backed chair looking like a passenger in a very fast car that had just taken off. First baby, she thought; people are so odd . . . such a simple thing, having a baby. But these people aren't even holding on to each other. She needs comfort now. He should be more compassionate. They're afraid to be kind. And she carried the bundle over to them.

"Mrs. Easter?" she said, in a voice that came sympathetically, automatically, from way down inside her, clear from nursing school.

The colorless eyes did not leave what she was carrying and there was no answer.

"He'll probably be getting hungry about now," she said. "He's a handsome little devil."

Still the two didn't speak and she carefully laid the baby down on the bed between Cell's spread legs. Then she left, feeling slighted, thinking, Stupid people!

Cell looked at it, and it moved. C looked at it and, as though it might be a butterfly bomb, got up from his chair and stalked around the bed, sliding one hand along the metal frame. Cell wiggled one of her feet, then the other, then both. The baby noticed neither. Later, C sat back down on the chair and lit a cigarette.

"No smoking," snapped the woman in the next bed. C pinched off the lit end and put it in his pocket. Cell reached down toward the baby with an extended finger and touched its right hand.

Nothing happened. As though taking apart an intricate machine, she pulled the wrapping away. One of its legs moved. C came over closer.

"Aren't the eyes open yet?" asked C.

The eyes! thought Cell; they will . . . oh, my God; but soon then the baby opened its eyes and looked—at least it seemed as if it looked. And then C touched it and it moved again. Then Cell touched it. After a while it opened its mouth and yawned. Then it made a noise and then it cried.

It's a baby, thought Cell. It's just a baby . . . look, C, it's just a baby. "It's wonderful," she said, as though listening to the sound she wanted to say.

"It's wonderful," said C, trying this also, thinking, It's alive, it's something . . . something different from me. It's all together.

"It's wonderful," they said together and began to laugh, tears running down the sides of their faces. "It's wonderful." The baby screamed—C coming over to the bed and being close to Cell—

she finally picking up the baby, laughing and crying.

"Keep quiet," snapped the woman in the next bed. "Don't you know this is a hospital?" But the Easters did not hear her.

The nurse returned with a paper and wrote down numbers and words from the chart hanging on the bed. Cell was rocking the baby back and forth with the motion of her body, smiling, and C, absent-mindedly, not wanting to take his eyes away from his family, said,

"Glove."

And she wrote it down.

SAM

Sam played mostly three-ball in the honky-tonks, barrooms, and all-night bus terminals with tables. Two fish in Clancy had brought him enough for three weeks in a Hilton, two new sets of clothes, two daydrunks, the evening company of uncommonly attractive women, and cigarettes. It was not always so good. A sixteen-year-old kid in Gary had taken his car, and an old man whom he'd taken to be half blind took him for his playing cue in a nine-ball game. But mostly he lived from quarter to quarter, winning never more than two or three of them from each stranger that played him, and always wearing a white shirt and a wide green tie that fell down over his cue as he took aim and swung from the loosened knot around his neck, his square-blocked Stetson hanging on the coat rack. In this way he was undoubtedly to the hotel clerks, waitresses, and bartenders a neat, perhaps even proud bum. *Sam,* he would sign in the register.

"Sam what?"

"Just Sam."

There was something about Sam that was silently violent, and because these two attributes conflicted so much, he seemed at the edges of his personality to be neither. He lived for involvement. But this was complicated by his nerves, and confused by his drive for freedom, and compounded by his love of tranquility. In any case, these involvements, which he willingly and willfully chose, invariably would defeat him, and each would be one of those all too good examples of self-destruction except that he was powerless over his own desires and couldn't control them. So time and time again he would be caught up terribly in involvements of his own making.

"A man is what he does," his father, Ansel Easter, had told him. "If he lays brick eight hours a day, then for that time he is a brick-layer. He's nothing but a bricklayer if he does nothing else. He's only a drunk so long as he's been drinking. People that do noth-ing are close to being nothing except survivalists, and next to that are those that do one thing." Actually, when he had told Sam that, C had also been there and had asked if a man could be a thinker, and Ansel had left the room and slammed the door back toward the brothers and against the doorjamb.

But Sam had listened and had even remembered that he'd giv-en an entire sermon from the pulpit in explanation of the mean-ing, documented with such glaring examples of real sinners— those people who spend more time at finding fault in others than evildoers do evildoing, and so were very much against the way of the Lord—that everyone left the church feeling as though he too was one of the "parasites of the world . . . moral degenerates, spiritual demigods . . . ingrates." It had been one of his good but not outstanding sermons; but Sam had remembered it, thinking that he might as well believe it was true, not so much out of rea-son but because he knew he was incapable of inactivity, his nerves continually attempting to unwind inside him, and doomed to do many things in order to keep them wound.

Auctioneer's school had barely been enough for him to keep himself together, and he was relieved to be out and into the more complex world of opportunities, where he picked up work from town to town selling animals and farm machinery. Then back to Ontarion, and back again into Illinois. With the money from his father's house he went to Chicago and by merely following the stock market from day to day and watching for the interrelated-ness of companies he nearly doubled his money—every month sending back payment on the mortgage. Then he went to Quincy and sold in the neighborhoods and hired himself out as a speaker for luncheons and dinners on the ground floors of hotels or in private clubs. He was successful. People liked him.

Sam bought a sale barn and founded a company outside of Springfield. He bought up all the stocks himself, and sold very few regular-paying bonds. Each month he sent money back on the loan. For once in his life he could sleep well; he was actually tired for five to six hours of the day.

The sale barn traded in debt. A man would buy a hundred cattle and would pay the sale barn, which would in turn pay the original owners for their animals, extracting a fee for the sale, a fee that fluctuated according to the price of the sale, six cents on the dollar or thereabouts. And so the sale barn had a violently fluctuating balance of money from which checks could be written and cashed all over Illinois with no questions asked. This balance of money was tremendous because of the lag between the time when the buyers put money into the barn and the sellers were given it to take out. At times as much as $200,000 would be resting in the flux, $180,000 of which would go out the next day, but during which time more would come in; and the payments, if need be, could be delayed even by simply mailing them out in the evening mail so that, though the postmark was the same, it made a day's difference in the cashing of the check, which would be further delayed by the handling of the clearinghouse before it went back to his bank and the money was subtracted from the figure representing his barn's account. So although this balance was not Sam's, it could nevertheless be pretty much continuously kept well above the $150,000 mark, and several days' delaying of payments could mean as much as $350,000 in his hands at one time. This money could then be used for investment collateral in the stock market or placed in private savings accounts to draw interest. All of the money earned could then be poured back into the barn and set free into circulation in the same way.

Sam built a movie theater; and reluctantly, but with hideous pressure from his conscience, took on help that in so doing also set them free from the penitentiary and made him in some way responsible (though he was never sure exactly of the extent of this responsibility). He bought shares in a plastic-forms company. He loaned money to finance business ventures of friends.

Into what little idle time he allowed himself, he crammed hunting and fishing expeditions that sometimes found him traveling through four states in a weekend. His women were all cut from the same mold and were wired as tight as the piano tuner could turn the key—women who could go without sleep for days on end without the slightest notice, so long as the good times remained where they lived, on the surface of their emotions. He had two places he lived, one in town and one so far out in the sticks that no one but he knew exactly where the little cabin was, as it was necessary to walk a half-mile through swamp timber to get to it (but usually he'd go there to work, chop wood and clear underbrush). This kind of perpetual activity made him happy—not consciously happy, for he was too busy for that—but when he'd think back to, say, when he and Gladys were in Minnesota, six cleaned walleyes in the trunk, sipping from a bottle of Kentucky bourbon, driving with the green lights of the dash singing country western, through small towns empty and sleepy at four o'clock in the morning, heading for Quincy, where they would lie in for a couple of hours before beginning again—he'd realize that somewhere in there he was happy.

And his business succeeded until Sam began to realize that his dates and figures and planning had gone too far. There were too many enterprises and the line between enough and too much was broken. He could no longer keep the entire bunch together. This, coupled with an unpredictable market that did not conform to any way of maneuvering around it, difficulty from his feelings of guilt concerning a man whom he liked being sent back to prison, a fire in the plastic works, a wife who could spend money in her sleep, a new house with split-level floors, the forced sale of a tavern, a divorce, and fair-weather friends, drove Sam to a realization that not only shocked him but cut off the monthly payment to Ontarion forever. From the outside it looked merely as though Sam and his barn had done so well and was such a solid business that stocks were now put up for sale, no bonds, just stocks, as though Sam wished to get together some ready money and invest in a house or some real estate. And no one thought anything else when the payments were a little slow. What was odd, of course, was when a month and a half later, after selling the stocks and collecting as many bonds as he could buy up, Sam quit and left the barn and business to the two part-time auctioneers that worked for him.

From the inside, of course, Sam went about moving money from place to place, taking out of one pile to bail out a sinking game in another. In trouble with payments, and with sales low, he sold his stocks (from which he'd been paying himself interest) a few at a time so as to build up the market value of the rest, in order to make up deficits. He turned his new brick house, complete with pool table, over to the bank for the down payment he'd made on it (accomplished because of also borrowing a huge sum of money and paying it back the same day from the sale of the tavern) and extricated himself from the entire complex, letting his movie theater float down the river, an impoverished but respectable citizen with three clean shirts and good credit. By then he was much older.

"SHOOT," SAID THE CIGAR-FACED MAN.

"Sorry," said Sam. "Wasn't watching, I guess."

"One more, then I ought to quit." The man looked at his watch as though he actually had somewhere to go and wasn't hopelessly in the wrong competition. Sam tried for two, made one, left himself rotten for the second, made it anyway, and touched in the last.

"Three," he said.

The other man shot once and made the left-end ball on the first bank.

"You know how far Ontarion is from here?" asked Sam.

"Where?"

"Ontarion."

"Never heard of it," he said and sank the second, but left a lot of green for the third.

"About forty miles from Washington. Maybe not that far."

"Iowa. It's about two hundred miles to Cedar Rapids. You drivin'?"

"No," said Sam.

The stranger missed the long shot and put the cue back in the rack, first making sure it was crooked, as he had suspected. Then put a quarter down beside the other two.

"Hitching?"

"Yes."

"Well, take the blacktop down to Six and follow it all the way across into Iowa."

"Thanks," said Sam and took up the money. "I'll never make it anyway. Just a thought."

The man left, watching the players on the other table for a moment before finally buying a six-pack and walking out. Sam went to the bar and ordered a beer with an empty-glass sound of one of the quarters falling on the wet top. The others he put in his pants pocket. The bartender, named Charlie, with a face as small as a midget's should be and a card in his billfold declaring he was an alcoholic taking Antabuse and should be rushed to the nearest hospital in case he ever took a drink, brought it over and told Sam, leaning over the bar, that gambling was not allowed and keep the money off the tables; not that it made any difference to him (who used to use a cue himself when he was in the marines) but he could be arrested and fined for having gambling in his place.

"O.K., whatever," said Sam and drank the beer slowly, raising his eyebrows when the small-faced man motioned that he would let the state pay for that one. I've been here a lifetime, thought Sam, putting the quarter back in his pocket. The violence began to surface, coiling around his nerves. One good woman, he thought, could do it. He was nearly broke.

RABBIT WOOD DID NOT OWN AN AUTOMOBILE. HIS FATHER HADN'T owned one and he didn't own one. His father had purposely walked three blocks out of his way to and from work in order to avoid passing in front of Mrs. Schrock's house, the sight alone of which was enough, even without the dozen or so gray, fungus-infected dogs that lived half-fed in the back yard and slept inside a tool shed. Rabbit didn't, and cut through Mrs. Schrock's yard in order not to have to go even one half-block out of his way. There were other differences. Of course the dogs were gone, as was Mrs. Schrock, and the house interested Rabbit slightly because of the way it changed—altered mostly by the neighborhood children having secret meetings in it and leaving messages inscribed on the faded sides threatening terrible havoc to anyone trespassing onto club territory. Sometimes, coming home from work, he would see just catches of tops of heads being jerked back down below the window ledge on the second floor . . . this and running through the house and sounds like young owls. Twice a month he personally made a complete and thorough search of the building, looking for broken glass and rotting floorboards—things that a child might be harmed by. In the event that a window was broken, Rabbit would kick out the retaining frame, letting the glass splinter onto the ground, and sweep up the floor. Of course he could have had the house boarded up or razed, as a public nuisance, but it was his contention that without such places and a host of secret rituals and imaginary purposes surrounding them, children might well grow up misfits from their family and their true selves. . . . At the same time, he knew he could buy the property or absorb it into the bank for mortgage, but he didn't want to be legally responsible in case some accident he hadn't been able to anticipate happened.

A shiver of satisfaction always passed through him when at the end of his walk home he stepped onto the corner of his own yard and began walking toward his house. This, however, like many of Rabbit's feelings, was not pristine and he had no idea exactly where it came from, or what type of satisfaction this was—one of pride or contentment, security or freedom, function or form. He told his wife that it was because of her, but at least he knew this wasn't true because he had had it before he was married, before he had thought of marrying; when he was living alone.

His bank never made him feel anything. Not even after it was moved into a bigger building and he had brass and marble furnishings brought in from Des Moines and two men and two women were waiting after five P.M. on Friday to be paid for their time. Not even after the three floor-stand fans were brought, in July, to move the air around and cost as much as a bricklayer makes in five weeks, and a few of the townspeople, the very old ones with canes and heavy triangular lines under their eyes, were lured away from the Yard in the heat of the afternoon to his hickory benches along the wall, in the exhaust of the huge turning blades. No, it was not until after the six blocks home, after his tiny sparrow eyes had seen everything in between, and after counting the pigeons on the wire in front of his neighbor's bar-converted garage, and before Ester could hear the soft, heavy touch of his shoes on the front step, there in his own time, that he felt a shiver of satisfaction pass through him like a silent morning train over the dew on the tracks, and be gone before he reached the house.

"Hi, Rabbit," said Ester Wood, who would not call him anything else, though he was accustomed to so many nicknames—fashioned to him by the people who felt embarrassed to come out and call him Rabbit in public, to his face—that he felt obliged to answer to almost anything. Many of the nicknames were so desperate that they were more attempts to establish a new name than revising and reworking the old, or making something of his shape, names like Jack, Simon, Smokey, Root, Art, The Fat Man, Rub, Beef, and Loren. These names of course were not in use simultaneously, and if one was ardent, he might be able to notice the use of one fade and another one come moving into prominence; still there never seemed to be a time when you couldn't use any one of them and be understood, or a time when you would hear someone use a name for Rabbit that you had not heard. The only explanation was that they too had been handed down from Merle Wood, and he had acquired them slowly, and people had learned them one at a time . . . *"Who? Who did you say? Beef . . . Oh, yes, you mean Root . . . that's him."*

"Hi, Sneaker," said Rabbit and let himself down into a kitchen chair with a glass of tap water just as Ester came into the kitchen. Yes, he was the kind of man who could be as comfortable in his kitchen as in any other room in the house.

"The Easters had their baby, you hear?"

"I heard," he answered.

"C named him Glove."

"I heard." He drank. "Why someone would name a child that, I don't know. Must be the only guy in the whole world that when the nurse came in couldn't think of anything better than Glove— that that would be the first thing in his mind, before Joe or John or Dave, before deciding to tell her to come back later. It must be from living in that junk yard." Rabbit finished the water with a long swallow that began as a toss into his mouth, his fat hand nearly hiding the glass.

"What would be the first thing to come into your mind?" she asked, sitting on the edge of a chair across from him, pulling at a button on her blouse as if it were a sandbur, not looking at him.

"And everyone gets tired—or got tired—of hearing over and

over again from both of them what a wonderful thing it was. Every time you went into Parson's, Cell'd tell you again what a wonderful thing it was, having a baby. And C too, as though it were something that only happened to them and no one else."

"I know," said Ester.

"And he, like nothing was . . ."

"Have you been over there?"

"That Yard? I stopped over the other afternoon."

"You know it upsets you to go over there, Rabbit. You ought to have more sense than to do things that upset you. Now you'll be upset for another week—thinking about C."

Rabbit went back to the sink and refilled his glass. "Maybe. But you've got to admit that Glove is a stupid name for a child."

"What would you name one? The first name that would come into your head?"

"Fisher," said Rabbit.

"That's a good name."

"What would you name one?" he asked, tossing down half of the second glass.

"Oh," she said, pulling with both hands at the buttons on her blouse, finally popping one off and holding it as if it had fallen from the ceiling, "I wouldn't care."

"That's what gets you in trouble, not caring. That's why C's son is named . . ."

"I mean I wouldn't mind—anything you would like would be fine with me."

"Fisher would be a good name."

"I wouldn't mind," said Ester.

Rabbit looked into the refrigerator, finding nothing he wanted. "She must have stopped using that thing," he said, half out loud.

"Who?"

"Cell."

"What thing?" she asked, thinking from his voice that the thing might be worse than the using of it.

"C said that they had something they used to keep from getting pregnant."

"What?" she asked, thinking, in horror, He must think that I use one. He is blaming me for using something, some piece of rubber or something.

"I don't know," said Rabbit.

"Didn't he tell you?"

"Something with water that . . ." and the sentence was drowned with the last water in his glass, as though trying to rinse the liquid through his mouth and into his face, quenching his blushed expression. But, unlike some, Rabbit's embarrassment did not hamper his ability to communicate, and Ester understood immediately both why he couldn't continue and what he was talking about.

"Oh!" she said. "One of those things." Solidly, like talking about an ax handle. "Someone should have told her that they don't work, that she could be pregnant before she even went into the bathroom and—"

"Well, whatever . . . they shouldn't have named him Glove," he said, looking down into the empty glass.

"Maybe not. That wasn't his father's name, was it? A lot of times people will name their sons after their fathers."

"No. The burden of C's father's name, Ansel, on a child, would crush it. Nothing small could survive with that name, not around here where people still remember, or would remember if they were reminded by the name."

"I never heard anyone talk about him."

"No one talks about him, that's why; for fear maybe he'll rise up out of his grave or something."

"No."

"Yes. Edlebrook's father broke up the cement foundation of his barn, loaded it in his pickup, drove down to the grave, and piled the pieces on top and around his flat marker, just so if he did rise out of the ground it would take longer. . . ." Then he added, "Of course he did have to bust up the foundation, but he didn't have to dump it there, all of it, all fifteen loads."

"Stop teasing, Rabbit."

"It's true, go out to the place and look, at the bottom of Millet's pasture and look."

"Come on."

"Go look."

"Maybe there's some cement there, but it's not for that reason."

"Honest to God."

"How do you know?"

"Because I spent time studying him."

"Ron Edlebrook's father?"

"No. Ansel Easter. I used to lie in bed and stare at the ceiling, studying him . . . figuring out how it had to be. Then after he was dead I still lay awake, thinking, and when I heard from someone that there was a person in Wisconsin who knew him before he came here, I borrowed a car and drove up to see and talk to him, or rather her, as it turned out to be; the name hadn't given it away."

"What did she say?"

"Only that he was a coal miner, and I'd already guessed that, from the way he talked, and the dust-gray hair on top of his head, and a way of walking that seemed close to the ground and like he would walk through a door or a wall if he happened to turn his head to watch something else and wasn't aware that it was coming. And of course his voice and forearms."

"Do you think I don't want a baby, Rabbit? Is that why you're talking this way—because you don't want to say it or talk about it?"

Rabbit leaned forward onto the table. "If I thought that, I'd've never been able to keep quiet. Besides, I don't imagine that it makes too much difference what attitude you have. It either happens or it doesn't."

"I just thought that on top of us not having any that you thought I didn't want one."

"No, it's just that you never knew C's father. If you had, you'd be interested in those things that with everyone else are commonplace—like having been a coal miner and a boiler man—anything to help fill in the gaps and explain to yourself how someone could begin living in one way, change to another, and then before your eyes shut himself off from the world altogether . . . making his sons go out for groceries, shut up in that huge house with only his boys and the ragged mute that he had taken out of a circus sideshow and kept with him from then after. Except in church, where from behind the pulpit he would throw back his head and sing as though possessed; but he quit that too."

"I'll talk to Cell about him someday," she said. "She'd know about him, from C."

Although this implied of course that Rabbit did not know and had no business talking about Ansel Easter, it came to nothing. He was only listening to her with his face. He was studying C now, and wondering how it had happened that he had named his boy Glove, especially when he had to be so careful, so very careful with everything he did, even covering his mouth when he yawned, in order not to let his soul escape, in order not to find himself being what his father became, like stone. Then his thinking went into another time-out and he could see his yard, where the deerflies, fishbugs, and gnats went in and out of place after place that would have and then would not have bits and pieces of the retreating sunlight.

"It's like someone pulled a plug in the sky and all the colors drained down into it," said Ester, watching too.

"Yes," answered Rabbit, "very much like that. Very much like that."

IN THE WINTER, WHILE TRUNDLING THROUGH THE SNOW, AN IDEA CAME to him that had nothing to do with C Easter, and nothing to do with the bank. It came in that time it took to walk across the last stretch of partially shoveled sidewalk before stepping into his own deeply drifted yard—in anticipation of the satisfaction he knew would then come. His desire (and he could be said to have very few desires, given that his father, Merle Wood, had desperately wanted him to be more than himself and he, Rabbit, wanted only to be as much) could not be traced back to its source, and he could neither negate it nor deny it. He was inescapably trapped, because desires become ambitions become needs, and how could he explain to Ester that he wanted, yes, needed, a new house, a larger house sitting in the exact spot where their perfectly adequate, perfectly congenial one sat now?

"You pretentious slob." She would not say that. Of course no one would say that, and if they did they would be imbeciles because Rabbit did not even have such thoughts about himself. No, what he feared most was Ester's expression as it attempted to cork the tears that began forming in her eyes, her stammered voice and button-pulling hands, asking, "Why, Rabbit?" and meaning in those two words, "What have I done that you need something else, another home? That your own house, the place you were born and your parents lived in, has become, with me, intolerable to live in?" And more. "You accuse me of something, and what can it be, because you knew me full well before we were married, except in bed and that was your own fault?"

And so Rabbit kept his new-found desire smoldering inside him for months, through the winter, into the spring, past the time when C's baby was walking around with only the support of a strong finger to balance with, past the first summer he had ever seen that smelled like the inside of an old army tent, into autumn, when the grass does not grow so well and people wonder when the ground will freeze, thinking they will know by the feel when it does, until he worried that even his tremendous bulk could not contain it, now when he could visualize every room, every light switch, and every closet.

TODAY I MUST GET SOME OF THESE LEAVES UP, HE THOUGHT, STEPPING through his front yard toward the small house, listening to the sound of the wet leaves bending. It would be a disgrace for snow to fall on them. His fast eyes jumped and focused from one place to another with agility and certitude far beyond normal capabilities. As he had grown older, his face had grown out around these instruments, these seeing things, recessing them farther back, as though they became more fragile with age and more likely to meet up with visions which would do no harm to the gently overhanging forehead and eyebrows or cheeks, but would nevertheless be catastrophic to the sensitive gels of his eyes. Ester had once said to him, while staring intently into his eyes from her side while he smoked in bed, the ash tray resting on his stomach, "Sometimes I look at your eyes, look into them and try to see what they have seen." Rabbit had put out the smoke, set down the ash tray on the floor, and turned over, wondering how that all went, almost deciding that it was just something that Ester had said while she was nearly unconscious and therefore not completely coherent, yet fascinating the way those things are, and almost asked her, curled up behind him, if that wasn't the case, but fell asleep.

Today he could almost imagine into a solid form what his house would be like, and went up the steps and into the kitchen, stamping off the snow from his rubbers before removing them with the aid of a boot jack. Ester was not in the kitchen and he took a can of beer from the refrigerator and accompanied it into the predominantly blue living room, where he found her in a chair, reading a newspaper or at least sitting behind it. He took nothing for granted. "Hi, sweetheart," he said.

"Hello," she answered, but did not lower the paper, and although Rabbit saw this, he did not understand it. "Good day?"

"Pretty good."

"What happened that wasn't good?"

"Nothing really important."

"Oh," she said from behind the paper, her hands around the outside shaking, and Rabbit seeing this but not noticing it, wondering to himself how long he'd have to keep paying his own bank every month for the house that C's brother Sam had quit sending money on over a year and a half ago. ADDRESS UNKNOWN had been stamped on the notice and returned to him; he had paid so far, and was ready to quietly pay the next. I must, he reasoned; C has no money and Cell makes only enough for the electric, if that.

Rabbit had to. He only wondered (his only rebellion against this obligation) how long he would have to keep it up before either Sam re-established himself or he could wake up one morning and feel differently about it.

These were empty thoughts and Rabbit drank the cold liquid from the can, his fingers thawing the frost on the outside, remembering that C and Sam and Jimmy Cassum would have called this "skunk beer," beer that has been cooled and then left to warm and then cooled again (it being the remaining can of a six-pack that he and Ester had taken on a picnic to Strawberry Point). They had called it that when they were young . . . back at the same time when Rabbit stood by himself in the crowded parking lot behind the high school and waited for someone, anyone, to call, Hey, Fats, let's go have a brew, or, Let's go hustle some snakes . . . even, Good night. He took another drink.

"I went to the doctor today," said Ester, calmly and slowly.

Now he put the beer down and sat forward, recognizing finally the urgency of the well-disciplined voice behind the paper. "What is it, Sneaker?"

She crumpled the paper into her lap, and with a red face, and enough decibels to fill three rooms, said, "I'm going to have a baby," ending on such a note of satisfaction that Rabbit was for some time at odds to find anything to say.

"Which doctor?" he asked. "Treblem?"

"No, Snobokin, and he said that there's no doubt about it, that in less than seven months I'll have a baby."

"You better go to Treblem too. Just to make sure."

"I'm sure, Rabbit. We're going to have a baby! But I'll go if you want."

He was quiet and the sound of the paper being uncrumpled was more than the creak/screech of the rocking chair's joints loosening under him. The can of beer almost fell off his knee onto the floor, but he caught it, losing only several drops that bubbled and faded into his pants. He got up and went to a window.

"Fisher," he said, "would be a good name. I don't see anything wrong with that, do you?"

"No, Fisher is a good name."

"But is it a good enough name?"

"It's more than good enough," she said, looking now as if she might cry.

"No name could be more than good enough, Ester," he said, and turned to her, "not for a real baby, with hands and eyes . . ."

"You're right," she answered, ready to laugh.

"Are you sure?"

"I'm sure."

"And we'll need to get a fence put around the house. We need more insurance, of course. What do you think of Dr. Treblem?" But he didn't let her answer. "Never mind, we'll get one of the doctors from University Hospital down here, once or twice a week, just . . ."

"Rabbit, there's nothing—" But she knew that whatever she said would be useless, that for the next seven months—probably the next year and a half—she would be subject to the prodding fingers of only the best obstetricians, physicians, gynecologists, and whatever. The house would go into havoc and maids would rush in while she was sleeping to clean the house and put things away in the wrong places before she could get up and throw them out. Nurses would be in and out of the house like flies, crawling over her, taking her pulse, bringing her food. It had happened once before when she had a week-and-a-half flu.

". . . Mother can come over to cook meals . . . or Mrs. Tate; much better."

And she was glad. Though Rabbit was often, perhaps always, this way, the extent to which he was this time exceeded even that time he was asked to chaperone a half-dozen Cub Scouts on a camping trip to Stone City—where a bear had been sighted years before and at one time there was one you could feed by holding out the food in your hand.

". . . And we'll need a new house, of course."

THEY MOVED INTO A RENTED HOUSE, THOUGH NOT AN ORDINARY RENTED house because his mother was living in it too and she, along with hired servants, nurses, and an emergency man equipped with a car set up like a jet, took care of Ester. As for the old house, although Rabbit wanted some of the wood paneling and built-in cabinets, linoleum, beveled glass, doors and floors, light switches, banisters, railings, lattice work, and baseboards removed without even claw marks from the hammer and stored in a watertight warehouse to await replacement, it was for the most part ruthlessly beaten to the ground and the basement busted up and hauled away to the river, where Rabbit watched the men throw the heavy chunks into the water, each making one heavy splash, then sinking fast. He wondered if, were he in the water, he could hear them hit bottom and fall against each other, and if he could, what it would be like.

This new, bigger house was not completed in time—that time being before the baby, young Fisher, was ready to move into it. The reason for the delay Rabbit vehemently attached to the absent-minded daydreamingness of the builders, under the slovenly supervision of Jimmy Cassum, master carpenter, who, having an undisputed reputation of unparalleled craftsmanship and knowledge of all materials and all ways to put those materials together, also held an uncompromising and equally undisputed reputation for an uncontrollably free will which prevented him

from working under anything but the most ideal conditions—
the mere fluctuation of humidity having been known to either
discontinue or begin one of his frequent work stoppages. (This
last part of his reputation was grounded, and for the most part
resided, within Rabbit's own thinking.) The real reason for the
uncompleted house was in fact Rabbit himself stepping over the
boards and watching out for nails, moving among the workers,
making them put in more studs, heavier supports, larger nails,
different brands of insulation (ripping out the old), safety de-
vices on the furnace and electrical system that so far exceeded
even the most outlandish building code that the parts had to be
shipped in from New York City. Staircases were removed and
replaced with shallower steps. Rabbit fired one worker when he
caught him pounding nails while standing on a ladder without
someone holding the bottom of it steady. And so when Jimmy
Cassum was finally told that he and his men must work twelve
hours each day in order to make up for the time they had wasted,
he answered:

"I quit."

"You can't quit," said Rabbit. "We have a contract."

Cassum put his hammer into the loop of his overalls and
said, "You can take that contract and shove it up your ass." As
he left the building site, he was followed by his eight workers, leaving Rabbit standing in the middle of his half-finished
house, with only three weeks (estimated) before the birth of
his child.

Needless to say, Rabbit did not attempt to use the contract for
any purpose other than that for which contracts are made, and in
a matter of a furiously short time Jimmy Cassum's wife looked out
of her window and in an almost I-told-you-this-would-happen
tone of voice called her husband, who looked too at the surround-
ing policemen, listened to the heavy knock, and held out his hand
to receive notice of two $500,000 lawsuits and a subpoena to ap-
pear in court to face the charges of seventeen illegal and unlawful

breaches of contract and specific, elaborately documented examples of malpractice and building incompetence.

"Sorry, Jim," said the Chief of Police, "but Beef's got a lot more power than you'd think by looking at him. He ain't about to let nothin' happen that he thinks amounts to a cheatin', especially his own. He's already got the judge to post bail so high you'll never get out for even a glass of water until the trial, which can be delayed for as much as six months."

"Can I make a phone call?"

"Sure; go ahead. You want his number?"

"No. I'll look it up."

Still it was not done in time, even at ten hours a day; but by that time Rabbit did not notice. Things had happened too fast. Even the live-in nurse did not know; even the University doctors could not predict that Ester would quietly walk downstairs one week early and tell him that the time had come; and Rabbit, opening the back door of the car he had hired and kept sitting in his mother's driveway with a half-asleep driver at that, bent the hinges so badly that it had to be ignored and they went to the hospital taking up three quarters of the narrow streets, running other cars up onto lawns. It was all too fast. Everyone seemed to be screaming in the hospital. Doors slammed. Someone dropped a bedpan down the hall from him. Ester was whisked off into a white room and the doctor wasn't ready yet. That's what they told him and he said, "*Isn't ready yet . . .*" and more, and the doctor must have heard because he came and asked Rabbit if he wanted to be in the room and Rabbit said, very quietly now, "No." It was all too fast. Even waiting was too fast; and when the nurse came into the waiting room and asked if he had decided on a name, he said, "Fisher," and when she said, "For a girl?" Rabbit stammered twice and with a handful of cigarette butts and sand from the stand-up ash tray answered, "Ester." And it was not until several years later that everyone called her Eight because it was the first word she learned clearly and the only number she knew until almost

three and a half years old, so, when asked her age, would always
say, "Eight."

THE DRIVER OF THE CARRY-ALL VAN WONDERED IF SAM KNEW ANYONE
in Ontarion. Sam said no and asked to be let out at the edge of
town, near the graveyard. "Oh," he said, "but it's a poor spot to be
looking for a place to sleep at this time of night," and pulled the
van up alongside the frontage road to the cemetery. A tall white
marker, near the back by the trees, looked like a shaft of light.
Everett Street.

"Sure enough," said Sam and closed the door, resting the suitcase beside him on the ground and watching after the taillights
going away from him, making the fallen leaves in the street and
ditches turn red. Then he picked up his bag and carried it into
town, in among the houses. The sight of the church, the cemetery,
and his old home was what he feared it would be. There was no
traffic on the highway and he knew he would not be able to get
out until morning—something he had already anticipated earlier,
in East Dubuque, and had carefully weighed against the displeasure of being seen and recognized in the daytime, but that now
only irritated him. He would have to spend the night shivering in
the woods somewhere or walking along the highway to keep the
fall air from penetrating into his nerves. People shouldn't live like
this, he thought, and the displeasure so overrode his awareness
that he nearly forgot the meager purpose behind his decision to
come there at all: to look at the house. He was lost as he thought
about the cold, walking. The sense of the present was not gradual,
but returned to him the very second he progressed around the
curve in the highway; and from even that far away he could see
the mounds of junk surrounding the house, outlined in gray from
the moon's neon light. He put his suitcase down and stood beside
it, squinting off into the moisture-laden air at the spectacle, view-
ing it well from where he was before rushing up at it. (This was
Sam's way.) There could be no mistake. That was the house. A

light was burning downstairs and shone through the side window into the yard.

He picked up his suitcase and walked closer, putting it down and stopping again twenty rods on, not so much not believing, but more taking time to wonder—if it was true, why? How could so much junk get there in so short a time? But it had been five-six years since he had been back. No, he thought, I paid on the loan for over four years, four years and six months, and Rabbit wouldn't have let people put junk there on my property, not while he was taking care of it. Merle might have done that, but not Rabbit—not on property that wasn't his. Such thinking occupied his mind all the way up to and into the yard itself, in among rolls of fence, refrigerators, lawnmowers, and tractors. He put the suitcase down and left it behind him, picking his way along, over and between pipes and bricks and broken coal shovels, as far as the steps to the house, where he turned back to look out through the junk to the road; not believing it now that he could see for sure that it was real. The moon went away, leaving only the bleary light from the streetlamps, too far away to be very good.

"Hello, Sam," said C.

"Hello, C," he answered and turned and looked up the steps, but could see nothing, not even the top fifth step. Then he heard the rocking chair begin and he went up and sat down on the chair next to it, finding it with his hands.

"How long you been here?" he asked.

"I saw you coming up from the road."

"I mean how long have you been living here?"

"Quite a while."

"How long?"

"After Rabbit's old man moved away."

"He did that three weeks after Dad went down."

"I didn't know that."

"How'd all this get here?" he said, and C, unable to see his gesturing hands because of the black night, knew what he meant.

"It's mine," he said. "I started out with one car, and look at what I have now."

"I think you'd've been better to keep the car . . . what kind was it?"

"It was a convertible."

"Really? A convertible?"

"With a heater," he added.

"Maybe you are better off. What do you do with all this?"

"Trade with it. That's the way we live."

Here the brothers were silent, trying to keep from laughing with joy at talking together here in the mock matter-of-fact way they were using, as though everything were normal and it was only yesterday. But the joy began to break through and Sam's voice snorted as he tried to keep his feeling hidden.

"'We,'" he said. "And who's 'we'?"

"Cell and me, and Glove."

"Glove and Cell and me," said Sam. "Is this a dance team or something?"

"No. It's not. It's my family."

"I thought *I* was your family, C," said Sam, beginning to laugh.

"You are, Sam, you are—but then you weren't there, and there wasn't enough of me and it took two to replace you, and I've another one on the way 'cause I didn't know you were coming back."

"Maybe," said Sam. "I'm not saying nothin' now. I'll want to look over the place. In the daylight."

"You'll like her, Sam. She's not at all like anyone."

"Not like Mom?"

"No. Not at all. You remember the scar on Mom's arm, where she had two vaccination shots?"

"Sure I do, and it always made you think it would be like torture to have one yourself and you'd rather take the disease."

"That's the one. Well, Cell doesn't have one there."

"That did it. She can't be family."

"No, Sam. You'll love her. You'll see."

"HE WON'T STAY HERE, WILL HE?" ASKED CELL, STANDING NEXT TO THE window on the second floor, where they had moved their furniture part of the house after slow trickles of junk brought in by Glove and sometimes C had squished it up there.

"Not so loud," said C. "He's right downstairs."

"No, he isn't," said Cell. "He's out walking around in the Yard." In his stupid green tie and gray hat, tramping around like he owned it, but he doesn't; it's just as much C's. Why couldn't you have stayed wherever you were? Get out of here!

"You'll like him," said C, and went downstairs and out into the Yard.

"Did you sleep all right?" asked C.

"Fine. Say, you've got some old stuff here, maybe even antiques. Maybe there is some money in this. I'm sure my suitcase is around here somewhere. I was sure I'd remember where it was because it was beside a bedspring."

"I don't make money, Sam. I trade for things—comparable size and weight, food and tobacco."

"Come on, now, I'm sure I left it right around here. You must make some money."

"Cell works at Parson's when she's not too big, but that's only for the electricity and oil. We don't need money."

"Here it is," said Sam and went over and picked up his suitcase. "What do you do, then, trade old pieces of furniture to Rabbit for money?"

Neither of them looked at the other. C sat down on the running-board of a Buick.

"Sam," he said, "I thought you were paying that—the loan, I mean."

"I was until about over a year ago, when . . . but if you're not—"

"Rabbit?"

"That little rat, it's just like him to behold himself to you and not let on." Sam made an unsympathetic gesture. "Well," he went on. "If that's his way."

They were quiet for a while again. Several cars drove by the front of the Yard and the people peered out at them, recognizing Sam but not calling out because it had been too long a time for that.

"It's not right, Sam. We can't let him do it. We got to pay him."

Sam was sitting down now, feeling the backside of his suitcase, looking at the highway, knowing that if he were on it he could make Omaha by late afternoon. It was an agreement, he thought, a simple agreement: the money for payments, no payments, no house . . . further, that if he did not keep up the payments he would not come back; but he'd already broken both of these and Rabbit had broken the other. I wish I'd never come here, thought Sam; starting over would be easy anywhere else—anywhere but here. He even looked at C and thought, I owe you nothing. Dad died and you went to college and I took money on the house. We're even. But it was a lie. Not an untruth, because all the facts were there and in the right place, but a lie because he was a fool and knew he should never have come back and came anyway. From his place in the Yard he could see C's family staring at him through a window on the second floor. A man only owes so much, he thought, some definite amount, to his brother, mankind, the state, and the country, in that order, but he knew that he was well shy of it. His nerves uncoiled a turn inside him and to twist them back he closed his eyes and pictured a table set up for a game of three-ball.

"We'll think of something," he said.

AT THE DINNER TABLE SAM RAVED ON THROUGH THE COFFEE ABOUT THE meal and through one of C's cigarettes about the coffee. Cell didn't make a sound the entire time unless asked to do so by C.

"How was work today?"

"Fine."

Silence.

"There's frogs in the back, down in the ditch," said Glove, shoveling up mashed potatoes with a spoon.

"What kind of frogs?" asked Sam.

"Green ones and brown ones," answered Glove, watching him carefully.

"No, I mean are they crooks or sheriffs?"

"Crooks or sheriffs!" said Glove, forgetting about the mashed potatoes, the suspicions of Sam that his mother had lent him, everything.

"Sure, there's only two kinds of frogs, crooks or sheriffs."

"How can you tell?"

"It's almost impossible, if you don't see them when they're dealing."

"Dealing!" said Glove, sure that this was some kind of story, but resolved to believe it until the last ounce of reality was drained out of it.

"With others, their dealing with others. Some of 'em are cheats and make off with money and food from other frogs."

"Frogs ain't got money," said Glove.

"Not like you or me, maybe, but they've got it just the same. Where we use paper, they use fly wings."

"Frogs eat flies!"

"Not the wings. Great God, you didn't think they ate flies' wings! You wouldn't eat a fifty-cent piece, would you?"

"No."

"So there you are. And some of the frogs are just plain mean and have been known to kill each other for a couple fly wings. You haven't observed such a thing, have you?"

"No."

"Well, what have you observed?"

Glove was quiet and stirred his potatoes around with his spoon.

"That is, what have you seen them doing?"

"Jumpin' in the water."

"So that's all?"

"Swimmin' sometimes."

"Have you heard anything?" asked Sam, his face as serious as if he had just dealt himself a five-card flush in a game of stud.

"Croakin'."

"Then you was too late—just too late, I'd say."

"Too late for what?"

"To catch a look at the crooks fleeing from the scene of the crime."

"I seen one croakin'."

"No, those are the sheriffs. The robbers never say anything and work mostly under water. It's the sheriff frogs that yell out 'CROOKS, CROOKS' after a robbery."

Glove took a bite of potatoes and studied Sam. Sam finished the last of the round ball of hamburger on his plate, chewing it as though he were satiated, yet hadn't eaten anything except crawdads for weeks. Cell brought more coffee. C excused Glove from the table, who walked slowly downstairs, out of the front door, around the corner, and dashed toward the ditch in the back. Sam and C carried their second cups of coffee into the living room, finished their cigarettes, and each lit into a cigar from a box Mike Bloomfield had traded to C for an automobile seat. They talked about how to make money. Cell washed the dishes and listened. C would not sell any of his junk, that was definite. Sam wanted a business, and C wanted only a little money—enough to pay back Rabbit and to keep paying on the loan. Sam wanted more, something with potential. Cell hated Sam from the kitchen because he had not paid the loan (which amounted to owing C money), because C needed him now, and because he might get C to work— something she had always believed impossible. She hated him for the way he looked at her, as though all she was was a brother's wife with no more womanhood of her own than a burlap rag or a record player.

Much of her resentment was unfounded, especially the part about C working. He even told Sam, "I'm not working. I'll tell you that. Under no circumstances are we going to get jobs." Of course this was no surprise to Sam, who felt a similar distaste for work. So what they finally decided that night turned out to be nothing more than a realization that they had no collateral for leisure money-making, and there were too few of them to constitute an effective potential money-making force like an advertising agency or a group of financial overseers and councilors. But it was in that direction they headed.

In the fall, in the horseshoe pits, they talked of what they might do. Others helped them think. C was uncommonly good at horseshoes. Everyone agreed that making money should be easy, if one had the right attitude. It was that attitude which was difficult to decide on, and everyone had his own ideas about what it was. Those without much money thought of it as being ruthless and morally deficient and caring little for the good things. Those with money thought of their own attitudes as being exactly suited for the project, and worthy of admiration. Those in between thought a little of both. C was making some money selling beer out of his house without a permit. Sam played poker in a downstairs room at night, but usually broke even. Both of them became increasingly aware, every day, that they were beholden to Rabbit.

In time, and during the night, Sam, C, Jimmy Cassum, and Keith Kullisky (a mechanical wizard known to both of them from high school who had a straightforward machine way of thinking, uncluttered by theories of science, able to weld two of the most unlikely, decrepit pieces of metal together and who some people believed could weld to wood, but that wasn't true) painted a sign and hung it up on the front porch of Easter's house: THE ASSOCIATE. Jimmy Cassum and Keith Kullisky didn't move into the house for a long time, but lived in their own homes. In fact, they would never have moved at all except to protect themselves and their families after everything went bad, after the killings.

But at first everyone in Ontarion thought THE ASSOCIATE was nothing more than a sign C had acquired by trade and had hung up because he liked it. When someone would wonder enough to ask, C (or Sam, who also watched the Yard now) would tell them that The Associate was a team of specialists for hire who could do anything.

And after its establishment C went to see the banker and said, "Hello," to him, shutting the bank door on the first snowfall of the year.

"Hello, C," said Rabbit from the middle of the standing room, next to one of the two round counter areas for writing. He was refilling the inkwells and checking the chains on the pens.

C went over to him. "It's been a good thing, paying on that loan . . . and not telling anyone."

"I heard Sam was back."

"Well, I came here to find out how much we owe you, because it's going to be paid."

"Nine hundred eighty-seven dollars and sixty-four cents," said Rabbit, letting himself down heavily onto one of his benches, beside a townsman who was either too old to hear the conversation or too old to take it along with him.

"Well, we have an association."

"I heard about that too," said Rabbit. "You, Sam, Keith, and that hoot owl Jimmy Cassum, who claim to hire out to do anything."

"So we'll have the money soon. Figure me up the interest too."

"Maybe you'll have it. Listen, C, it's foolish—that's no way to live. You can't just throw together a group of men and hire out to do anything. Especially with someone like Jimmy Cassum. It's worse than foolish. It's risking everything you have."

"A yard full of junk. Come on." But he knew what he meant.

"Your family," said Rabbit. "You've got a responsibility."

"Not the kind of responsibility you mean."

"What else?"

"Not a responsibility to live up to, but one to live down, a bad taste the old man left in everyone's mouth—in yours."

"I could care less about—"

"But you can't forget, can you, Rabbit? Admit it. That twisted old bastard still bothers you, doesn't he? Doesn't it bother you that so much harm could come from one man? Isn't that why you paid on that loan?"

"No."

"Can you remember how McQueen's hand looked when he pulled it out of the fan, with his fingers spraying around the room? Maybe you weren't there."

"He had nothing . . ."

"But he was there too when your uncle—"

"Shut up."

"—your uncle's face was nearly blown off when the valve broke on the oxygen tank; only no one was there then but him, that anyone knew *for sure*."

"He had nothing—" Rabbit began to say, again, that Ansel Easter had nothing to do with these things—that they had just happened—that there was no design anywhere in the world for them to happen. Accidents. He wanted to say what everyone had for so long wanted to believe, what lying awake in bed at night he would tell himself over and over again had to be true, had to be true. But then he and some others *had* heard Ansel say, "I don't want to hurt you," to Bill Mead, and the next day Bill hanged himself.

He remembered that thing, Ernie, out behind the church, when he'd tied down a tomcat with strings held in the ground with small wooden stakes and burned its hair with a cigarette lighter. The screaming. How he had gone over with a block of wood in case the thing would jump at him, and had shouted for the thing to stop. And how Ansel Easter had come out of the back of the church from the basement, run over, and, breaking a stick from a nearby tree, had beaten him (Rabbit) and sent him home, telling him never to come back again or meddle in the thing's affairs, as though he wanted it to go on.

"And he was there the day before John's wife hung herself out in the garage and John cut his wrists that night in a hot tub of water and screamed until he was too weak. You heard him, didn't you, Rabbit? Your father went next door and lifted him out and you were afraid to go over and look—look at a man drained of blood, and the bathtub."

"Shut up," said Rabbit, menacingly now, holding one of the heavy metal ash trays in his big hand. "It's nothing to me, anyway. He was *your* father."

The old man looked at them in bewilderment.

C stopped his rapid talking and spoke evenly and without passion. "But it always bothered you, Rabbit. Either way you can see it, it bothers you. If it wasn't him, then your father was wrong and maybe, you think, murdered him for no reason. The other way, he was just evil and the idea of that much evil in one place is so different from the way you want the world to be that it frightens you. And it frightens you that I—that Sam and I—could have grown up with it all the while you were being high and dry, protected by your big-shot father."

Rabbit stood up and came toward C, but he continued: "Do you know what happened to Sam? How he saved himself? How he spent some of that precious money you've taken on yourself to pay back? He paid it to a psychiatrist to probe into his self, so deep that finally, and under hypnosis, with sweat rolling down his face, he screamed, 'I hate my father,' and three months later he said it out loud and listened to himself say it, and the doctor told him to say it over and over until he could yell it. And he did. And the idea that you'd have to get down in the gutter like that to cure yourself makes you want to give up the whole thing."

"It isn't that way," said Rabbit. "Get out."

"You didn't have to take it on yourself," said C, and left.

But I did, thought Rabbit, watching him through the window. I had to.

NATURALLY, WHEN CONFRONTED WITH A GROUP OF MEN WHO WERE IN business for everything, it was impossible to think of anything to have them do, even if you had the money to pay them. It was bizarre. Even the name was bizarre, The Associate, when it could have been just as easily The Team, or Hire Out Service, or Odd Jobs. If the Smalletts' car broke down, they could take it to a garage. If Brenneman's water pump stopped pumping, a plumber or maybe even a well man could fix that. But what someone might have for an association to do—a foursome of general specialists, at that—eluded nearly the entire population that frequented the Yard for trading or just sitting.

But it wasn't something that could be ignored. Everyone knew. Everyone playing horseshoes in front; or drinking cold beer from the ice-filled cooler with a tin can on top that Cell had put there for nickels and dimes to pay for the ice and the beer; or walking around the Yard with C, working out a trade or working on his sympathies and telling him how much you needed this or that and promising food or tobacco in the future; or in Parson's, listening to Cell talking about how wonderful the new baby was going to be and how proud and full of joy she was to have C's brother living with them; or sitting on the porch while Sam gave half-hour descriptions that seemed like one continuous sentence of men he had known who could talk 150 words a minute chewing straw, while bidding a hand of pinochle before picking up all the cards, rolling a cigarette in one hand by licking it and slap-rolling it against the front of their shirts, and cheating . . . Everyone knew that there were four men, C, Sam, Keith, and Jimmy Cassum, who had wives and families, had been born in Ontario, and would soon go hungry without work. Besides, it was part of the Yard, which belonged to everyone and could be said to be the town itself on those long summer nights when the air was so thick with water that the hay was too wet to bale tomorrow and the tractor wouldn't make it down the rows in the mud, when everyone was there except Rabbit, who wouldn't come and didn't let himself feel alone even when his wife and daughter were there sitting on the porch, in the house, or in the Yard. And though that kind of burden—that kind of joy—is dead now and there are hardly even families any more . . . at that time, if a group of people did not take care of its own, no one could sleep and locks had to be put on doors.

Sam Easter looked funny shoveling snow in his shirt sleeves and green tie, but nevertheless this was the first job that the entire Associate had been hired to do. A little money had come in before that: a welding job for Keith, built-in bookcases and cabinets for Jim, an antique appraisal for C (not to establish worth, just age), and an income-tax-form check for Sam, hired by Marv Yoder, who had been notified that by random his 1950 forms had been pulled by the government and that he was to be prepared to substantiate all claimed exemptions. But the second snowstorm of any reasonable size had brought The Associate together digging out Mike's Standard. They charged what it would have cost him for a tractor with a blade to do it. The money was not coming in, and Rabbit paid his own bank the next installment on Sam's loan. C was not sleeping well. His son noticed that things were not as they had been. Cell grew larger.

Sam was drinking cheap wines and whiskeys, sitting around on the first floor of the house, avoiding at all cost being trapped in the same room with Cell, whose piercing looks had begun to fray even the few sharp, clean corners left of his nerves. Glove was also something to be avoided, not at all costs, but at least while he was drinking, when his bereavement over having come to Ontario and come up to the house was easy to forget, but easily brought back by Glove wanting to know about sheriff frogs, six-guns, and small radios that could be hidden in your pocket and talked into. Another way of forgetting, however, was buried in the midst of those times when he would be so engrossed in telling a story to someone who would listen that he would be lost from the sense of real things.

C had one pleasure: the experience of waiting with Cell and Glove for the coming of their new baby. The Yard business was good, tremendous; but his stock of pieces was diminishing. His neighbors traded food, more food than was fair, but C took it, ashamed, knowing that he had to, that The Associate had to eat.

When the time came C pushed aside all these things and went with his wife to the hospital, leaving Glove with Sam. Cell told him that Ester Wood had talked to her in Parson's and had said that if, just if, they needed money for the hospital, money for proper attention and to keep out of the disease-ridden indigent ward, money would be available. But even this C pushed aside as they entered the crowded room where women lay in metal beds mostly without visitors and waited for their turn. C waited, and two hours later Cell was taken into another room, and six hours later she came back, pale and thin, and slept for three. C smoked and no one told him to stop, despite the sign. He felt good and even thought of running home for another one of the pills that Sam had gotten somewhere that he said would keep him awake and did.

Cell woke up and looked at him and he remembered, like a bad dream, how he had been afraid that Glove would be a monster and how now, not even five years old, he took an interest in the Yard and C wondered what he and Cell had ever done without him there to watch and talk to.

A nurse came through the doors carrying what C assumed was his child and he looked at Cell.

"Isn't it wonderful?" she whispered. "Isn't it a blessing, even in the middle of these hard times?"

"Wonderful," whispered C and took hold of her hand.

"Put that cigarette out," said the nurse. "There's no smoking allowed here." C put the cigarette out on the floor and the nurse looked at it as if it were a place where he had spat. "It's a boy," she said, laid the baby down on the bed to the side of Cell, and left.

"Ain't he beautiful?" said Cell.

"Shhhh," whispered C, "he's asleep." And it did look like he was asleep, breathing so easily with his eyes closed.

"He's a lot like Glove," whispered Cell, "when he was a little baby."

"Glove was heavier."

"Not much."

"BOY, HE SURE CAN SLEEP."

"It's wonderful, C. What—" And then the baby opened his eyes and looked at Cell.

"Look, Cell, he's got his eyes open. He's awake."

"He's looking at me. It's just like he's really looking at me."

"Babies can't see anything, Cell. They can't focus their eyes. But it is kind of cute that . . ." and the eyes turned to C and rested there, the black-dot pupils in perfect focus.

"He's looking at me," said C. And the baby did not stop looking at C, or move or make any sounds or anything. It's staring, thought C; my God, it's staring.

"He seems so intelligent," he said. My God, stop that, he thought.

"He's beautiful," said Cell, thinking, Now it comes. I knew it. I knew that it would happen. First Sam to begin the curse, and now the terrible destruction, the retribution begins, and the crying. Oh, my God, help us.

Another nurse came through the swinging doors and came to them carrying a clipboard and a fountain pen that she jabbed at the paper to make the ink flow.

"And how is the little fellow?" she asked, troubling with the pen.

"Fine," said C. "Fine."

"And have we thought of a name for the small fry?" He was staring at her now, but she did not notice.

"Baron," said C.

"Perhaps," she said after a pause, "your wife had a choice she'd like—after all, Baron . . ."

"No," said Cell, "Baron. Just Baron. We've always liked that name."

The nurse went away to find another pen and did not return.

Baron's eyes watched her leave and then returned to C, who lit another cigarette before leaving.

"RABBIT," SAID ESTER, AFTER EIGHT HAD GONE AWAY FROM THE TABLE carrying her doll, "I've got to talk to you."

"Haven't got time," said Rabbit, finishing his last drink of milk half in a dribble and going off to watch that Eight did not hurt herself.

"Let her go," said Ester. "She can't get into anything. You've gone through that room every day for the past eight months to be sure that there's nothing dangerous within her reach."

"Well, still," said Rabbit, but knew she had him cornered and knew already (from one of the men that worked for him at the bank) what it was.

"Still nothing. Maybe I shouldn't have, but I did. I wanted to find out what it was—what it is about C Easter that upsets you so much. Ever since their baby, even before that—the mention of the Yard sets you off for a week, and you don't talk to anyone but Eight, and read."

"Still, to name a kid Baron. Why would anyone name a little kid Baron?"

"That's not it," she said, waiting.

"And do you know that Cell won't let anyone see that baby, and doesn't even talk about it? Just keeps it in the house all day. Glover even said at school that he hardly ever sees him."

"His name's Glove."

"The boys at Scouts call him Glover." (Actually, that had been Rabbit's own doing, because on his first day, when he stood shyly against the wall while the others romped around the room,

Scoutmaster Rabbit had taken him by the hand and introduced him in a full, strong voice as Glover Easter to all the boys, some of whom he already knew.)

"So what?" said Ester. "What does that have to do with you?"

"Nothing directly, but—"

"But nothing. So I went down to the bank while I knew you'd be in St. Clair and inquired. And I found out that every month you pay money to Sam Easter, who has been back for probably a year and a half now and whom everyone invites over for dinner because he can talk about such interesting things and has such an interest in finance, but whom you'll never go see or go to a sale of his or anything. Now if you're in some kind of trouble, let's hear about it, and if somebody's breaking the law—like blackmail maybe—then we can get the police down here. Now if Sam's got something on you, let's hear about it."

Rabbit had not known that the new television would have such an effect on Ester's imagination. Despite that his neighbors everywhere invited themselves over to get a look at it, he rarely watched it himself because of the unpredictability of the plots and the feeling he had when a program did not end in the way he had thought it must. "No," he said, "it's really nothing."

"It's something," she said. "It's something."

Rabbit felt desperate, stepping along a narrow walkway between two immense ravines, knowing that he must fall and that, though deep, the one trip down was like a finger's depth to the bottomless pit of the other, which not only went down but megaphoned out as well, the jagged rock outlined in purple and cold white. He could choose. "When I was young," he said, "in the fourth grade, to be exact. Because I was fat, and slow, I guess, people picked on me."

"Come on, Rabbit—"

"No; it's true. It's something. It's important. They picked on me too because of my clothes (I even got so I would take them off on the way to school and put on well-soiled working clothes which

I wore until returning home) and our money. They teased C too, but it wasn't so bad for him because they were afraid of his father. One day, during recess, while the teacher was out of the room, five or six of them were rubbing the chalk from the erasers on my face, saying that it would make my skin crack like old Mrs. Jackson's hands. I was hollering. Sam walked by the door on his way outside and came in. He was a sixth-grader and much bigger and stronger than any of my persecutors. 'Knock it off,' he said. 'It's just *Rabbit*,' said a sneering voice behind me, 'the stupid fat banker's kid.'

"'Knock it off,' he said again, as though he would wait for them after school with a razor and a clubbing stick, him and some of his buddies, because he always had friends, and everyone could remember his hands bloody in the schoolyard behind the backstop, fighting with boys bigger than himself, his violence frightening to watch. After that I was left alone and was not physically abused again, though this may well have had more to do with passing through one mind set particular to a certain age and into another one, rather than them remembering the experience with Sam."

"But the money! Every month."

"I just showed you how it is that I owe Sam something. Anyway, I won't be paying much longer. The Associate seems to be getting some work. Because I did pay for a while—that's just insurance. Cheap, easily obtained insurance for our family." And he went off into the living room, following the crashing of something to the floor. Ester stayed with the table of dishes and resolved, looking deep into her food-splattered plate, that the issue would not rest and she would find out about it.

"I thought that I hadn't been over for a while and decided to stop in."

"Come in," said Cell, "and get away from all that clamor." She referred to an argument between Sam and Lawrence Ranger, a small but very concentrated affair that spread out in noisy waves, filling the entire Yard. "It couldn't be fixed!" shouted Ranger. "That friggin' tractor had a crack in its block big enough to shove your head in."

"I never said it didn't."

"You implied it."

"This is a junk yard. If you wanted a used tractor, you came to the wrong place."

"You said—"

"I said it was a good tractor in its day."

"Which implied—"

"Nothing."

"You claimed—"

And they closed the front door and then another before settling down into one of the less sprawling rooms on the second floor. "That's better," said Cell. "Do you want some pop?"

"No," said Ester. "Where's C?"

"He took Glove over to fish in Millet's pond. He said he didn't expect to catch anything—that there were too many snapping turtles in there—but he always wants Glove to know about the old things."

"It's important," said Ester, picking up a small pillow and following the seam around and around with her fingers as though she were unraveling it and saving thread. "Where's Baron?"

"He's in another room," said Cell with a finality of tone that sped up the unraveling.

"I suppose you can hear him from here—if he cries, I mean. I agree with you, little children never really need the attention that people lavish on them."

"He never cries," said Cell, dealing the last blow to the topic. "He never cries."

"Such an ideal baby!" said Ester, watching her own feet.

"Ideal," said Cell, and got up and left the room. Ester sat with the pillow, cursing herself for her inability to talk to people—to come out and have intimate, free-and-easy talks with people. Why? she wondered. Why can't I just come out and say, 'That's ridiculous. Even I know that turtles have nothing to do with fish'? Why do I have to be so stupid all the time? She heaved the pillow across the room.

When Cell returned she had with her two soda pops without glasses and carried them both over to Ester. "Which kind do you want, red or yellow?" she asked, noticing the pillow lying in the corner. "Red," said Ester, thinking, As long as I have to have one. Cell gave the strawberry to her and carried her own back to the gray chair.

"I didn't know," Cell said. "Sometimes people don't always say what they mean—I mean, you ask them if they want a drink of water and they'll say 'No, thanks' even if they're dying of thirst, just because they think that's polite."

"It's funny," said Ester, "how things are like that," setting the bottle down beside her, determined that nothing, nothing could ever make her taste it. They talked of the rain and the weather and other women.

"You want a glass?" asked Cell, her lemon soda one third gone.

"No," said Ester.

"I'll get you one," said Cell, and got up to go trotting out to fetch it. "Sometimes I get used to just having the men around here, and they don't—"

Damn, thought Ester, and grabbed up her bottle of strawberry pop and swallowed four ounces before balancing it daintily on her knee while directing Cell back to her chair with her eyes.

"How's little Eight?"

"Fine. Just fine. I guess that Glove and Eight will get to know each other someday—I mean it's a small town and there's a relatively short time between them. Maybe they'll pass each other in the halls of the school. Wouldn't that be something? Isn't that odd to think about now when they seem so small?"

"Glove's getting pretty big. He'll be bigger than C."

"It's hard to tell—at this age."

"I can tell," said Cell.

"Eight will be two grades ahead of Baron."

"What!" said Cell as though she were broken by force out of a pleasant thought. "School . . . the same grade. I never thought about . . . When does it start?"

"School? It starts in the fall. It's going now."

"Now!" But then Cell regained her sense of time and adjusted herself to the room, keeping in mind that Glove was not yet old enough for school and that he was four years older than Baron; and in time something could happen. Something could change before men in hats came to take him off to school. He could be different by then. He could be normal. "Of course," she added, "how foolish of me. Sometimes everything seems so timeless here, with the Yard and the people—especially in the winter."

"It must be different with an association here."

"It's fine. Things are more lively—with all the arguing and bickering all the time."

"Arguing?"

"Not real arguing. Just deciding out loud, like if they should use parts from the Yard on jobs, or if they need a car to drive to Des Moines and look up laws."

"Look up laws?" Ester was not actually interested and had not come for this reason, but nevertheless she became sidetracked into caring about how The Associate was finding work and if it was crooked. What she learned was that this group of men were hired occasionally to act as arbitrators—arbitrators with no power—in disputes between neighbors. Since there was (and still exists) great anxiety concerning any dealings with the law, any direct dealings with it, Sam or Jimmy Cassum would drive to Des Moines and copy down the wordings pertaining to fence rights, landowners' responsibility, tenants' rights subject to law, penalty payments, trespassing rules, right-of-passage statements, inheritance regulations, or whatever the people wanted.

The Associate would then decipher the laws and write down easily understood sentences which one of the four would read to those involved. For example, Keith Kullisky, sitting between two squabbling relations, saying, "The law read . . . that if no will is left by the deceased, his wife will receive at least half of his money, land, and machinery. If she is dead too, then it will be divided equally among his children, and if there are none of these, the brothers and sisters of the dead man may divide up equally among themselves with no preference given to age or familiarity to the dead man, given that their parents are dead too. Along with this must also pass the dead man's debts—all amounts and things he legally owes to anyone else for services or items, also borrowed things. These are to be divided equally too, with no preference to age or familiarity to the dead man." After this, Keith would be paid in the name of The Associate and the dispute would be settled, because it was not the intention of any of the people of Ontario to break the law—only to come to know it. If the laws were broken, it was of no consequence to The Associate, who merely hired out to make the laws known. No one thought of hiring them to enforce, because simply if a man *knew* what was right, then he could do it, or go about stopping it done, by himself. No law enforcement is necessary when everyone knows the law, the laws are clearly stated, and the names of the involved are known by people who can find their way around in the night. Ester Wood learned that The Associate, under the especial management of Jimmy Cassum, worked on houses and did any job within the imagination of the owner. Keith Kullisky, with the parts of the Yard at his disposal—a concession he had won hard-fought from C—claimed to be able to fix anything that had worked within four months, at less the cost of new. Sam did sales and gave talks to organizations—talks that he did not know beforehand or remember after, but that had full-grown men falling out of their chairs from laughter. He bought an adding machine and started an

income-tax filing service and, with C as an assistant, acted as
a financial adviser. And even when the rest of them were too
lazy to take on any more work, Sam could usually be found
at some time during the day in the Prospect Tap, and he never
turned down a job. "Sure, haul it over there," he would say,
"Keith'll fix it." Or, "If you can find C, tell him to take a look
at it for you. There's almost nothing that he doesn't know
where it came from." But most of this he took on himself and
worked harder than some men thought anyone ought to work,
for health reasons, and told him so. Sam would laugh and tell
them a story about bicycle thieves in Illinois who thought that
same way.

The Associate was alive. It was an instrument for people to
use. Through it they could hire men, their activities, and even
their thoughts.

"I'm interested in Rabbit and C and Sam when they were
young," said Ester. "I believe they were about the same age and
knew each other."

"Yes," said Cell.

"What do you know about it?"

"About what?"

"About their friendship."

"Sam and C were brothers," said Cell. "You knew that, didn't
you?"

"Yes. I mean them and Rabbit."

"Oh, well, I don't think there was much."

"What do you mean?"

"I mean Rabbit used to follow them around, especially C. Sort
of idolized him. But then Rabbit was so . . . unworldly when he
was young. I guess C tolerated him, though, and Sam, which is
more than the others did."

"Is that right?" said Ester, trying to keep from spitting the
words across the room through her clenched teeth.

"Yes," said Cell. "Many of the other boys used to pick on

Rabbit because he was incapable of defending himself. I think maybe he was kind of a pansy."

Ester was quiet.

"Is that what you wanted to know?" asked Cell, satisfied to herself that she had revealed her friend's husband's childhood personality to her, possibly to the end of explaining some of his out-of-the-way actions at home.

Ester said calmly, carefully, and slowly, "I was wondering what it was about you, you Easters, that upsets Rabbit, why he is always so interested in what goes on over here, but won't come himself, and will pay . . ."

"Rabbit never had any friends when he was little. I think maybe he was spoiled by his rich father. Even—"

"I wondered why every month he paid money to Sam and why he referred to that money as insurance."

Cell was quiet, then said, "That money is payment on a loan that Sam borrowed. He and The Associate will pay it back. C said that Rabbit was the kind of person who would behold himself without telling. He must have been joking about insurance."

"But why would he do it?"

"I don't know. He's *your* husband."

C, MORE THAN ANYONE, NOTICED CHANGE. WHILE THE SIZE OF HIS YARD appeared to everyone else to stay the same, he could tell that it was shrinking—that the pieces that had been traded for food (and sometimes money, he suspected, when Sam had been there alone) before The Associate became the lucrative unit it was had not been replaced; some had been stolen; Keith, who took actually very little, nevertheless ruthlessly scavenged through it, picking a piece here and a part there, leaving indentations and holes that would never be filled. These losses brought C sadness, which he rarely portrayed openly—and then with reluctance—to Glove, who, though barely school age, could understand and with whom he enjoyed a relationship that even in its silence—long quiet times

spent together fishing, walking, and sitting on the porch—was
a communion.

Baron, or The Baron, as C and his wife sometimes jokingly
referred to him, did not improve, and did not change into being
anything short of terrifying to them. Seeming never to sleep, he
would, from wherever he was dropped, stare at objects in the
room, or at them. He didn't make those cute gibberishing noises
that other children make when they're using their tongues as
joy bars rather than instruments. Even pain—hot light bulbs,
dropped screwdrivers and pliers onto a bare leg—passed unex-
pressed, as though *everything* drained into him and whatever happened then, thought C, can't be good because it doesn't come out,
which is O.K. for the good things, but how about the bad? What
about absolution?

His concentration was demonic and a simple clothes pin given
to him to chew, fumble, and discard would occupy him for three
weeks, never leaving his clenched fingers except to be revealed before his eyes in the round. He did not move, but remained quietly
where he was set down, lying or sitting. When carried outside he
would scream, beginning as soon as the door was opened and con-
tinuing uninterruptedly until deposited back inside. They would
pick him up at bedtime and lay him in his small bed, but no one
ever saw him sleep . . . of course he had to, everyone does, but if
you were there, he wouldn't. At nearly one and one half years old,
closer to two, without ever having crawled or even attempting to,
he stood up in the middle of the living room and walked across
the floor to the window, professionally resting both hands on the
ledge between two of the potted plants. (They had been an idea
of Cell's, to fill the house with outside plants so that he would
someday be able to cross outside by himself without a blindfold
and Sam's curtained automobile to take him to the doctor, unobserved by the neighbors.)

"Look, he can walk!" said Cell, eyeing him from the kitchen.
"Wouldn't he be much happier in a room of his own? Wouldn't

he, C? He's so self-contented . . . wouldn't it be better to let him have his own room?"

He can follow me around now! He'll always be behind me, stalking about the house.

And so Baron was furnished with his own locked place on the third floor, where occasionally Glove could hear him walking from one end of the room to the other, there being no rug and little furniture to absorb the small tramping.

"OF COURSE HE'LL LEARN TO TALK," SAID C. "EVERYONE LEARNS TO talk, unless there's something wrong with their hearing. He hears fine. It's just that he doesn't need to practice. He didn't need the practice of crawling to walk. He'll be fine. The doctors say he's normal."

"I know," said Cell, "I already said that one of these days he'd start talking, and that as soon as he did, everything would be better."

C was quiet and picked up a novel to read. Glove sat in the corner behind a chair, listening with dread, as though he could hear through a concrete wall his own sentence being passed by a warlord. He remembered a week ago when his mother had come out to the frozen pond where he played with Sam's dogs and asked him if at school—if from his own experience—at school—with the kids and the teachers—if he thought that if someone came to school there—say just starting in kindergarten—and couldn't talk—if people would make fun of him—or if they—the students and the teachers—would understand that some people don't talk. This memory funneled into another memory of sitting straight-legged on the porch with his father while he had explained that some people, most people in the world, placed too much emphasis on talking—in fact, on words—and that there were many more ways of thinking and doing that were not verbal. He had said that a day might come, and TV and radio were help-ing to bring it about, when words would be no more important than any other sound, and when someone said something to you, you might not even hear it because the crickets and wind or the color of the sky would be more interesting and more meaningful. He had told Glove that the first men weren't able to talk at all, before the languages evolved, and that they got along by watching each other and listening for signs of danger and comfort. He had begun to say that animals don't talk, but had stopped. But Glove knew.

From behind his chair he decided, at six and a half years old, to teach his brother (secretly in the dead of night) talking. And that night he stole from his room and up to the third floor. He didn't know if Sam was home yet, supposed that he wasn't, and lit a candle in the hall to find his way. He walked close to the wall so the boards wouldn't creak, something he'd learned from Sam in a story about cat burglars and Chinese millionaires. He reasoned that if by chance Sam saw the faint light from outside while walking to the house he'd stop and wonder about it. By that time Glove would be inside the room and have the shades drawn to the bottom of the windows. Sam would think his eyes had played tricks on him and nothing more. At the end of the hall he blew out the flame and took a skeleton key from his pants pocket, reflecting then for a moment on its name, going over again how it had come to be called that. He placed it in the lock and—as carefully and slowly as he was able—twisted. A fast series of falling clicks sounded inside the lock near the end of the turn, and seemed comparable to a siren. He withdrew the key, knowing that he had done well enough. The house was quiet again. In the basement the furnace kicked on. Next time, he thought, I'll wait for that exact time. He pushed at the door easily. It didn't move. He let the knob uncoil back to its rest position and fell to his knees, feeling under the door with his fingers; there was clearance. He felt the crack running up the side, as far as he could reach. There was clearance. The squeeze was at the top. He wound the knob back tight with both hands, knelt on his haunches, pushing the front of his feet against the door and pulled down with the weight of his body hanging. The door popped open, clearing the top of the frame, into the room. Standing up now, he pushed forward again, and three minutes later inched through the narrow opening. Glove closed the door until it stuck at the top. The room was very dark. He took off his shirt and wedged it under the bottom of the door to keep the light from stretching out into the hall. The match flared and he lit the candle. Clean melted wax dripped down into a Ball jar lid taken from his back pocket. He settled the candle in, waited for the wax to harden, and placed it near the door so the light would be less perceptible through the crack at the doorjamb. He crossed the room and pulled together the heavy blue curtains hanging beside the windows.

Baron had sat up and was staring, his flannel pajamas buttoned clear to his neck. He climbed out of the cribbed bed and wormed his bare feet into a pair of furry slippers with thin leather bottoms. He went over to the middle of the room, outlining his body behind him against the wall, the twitching black image three times his own size, like a great guardian demon. He sat down in the middle of the room and looked at Glove.

"Shhh," said Glove, though six trained cats could not have heard his brother's passage from the bed. He was very quiet. Glove turned away from him and back to the door for a moment to listen. Then he turned back and said, "We have to be careful, Baron, so no one don't hear us. I came to teach you talking." And he sank to the floor across from him, leaning on his elbow, sideways to the light. "Get over there," said Glove, and pointed to a place where Baron would be able to see his face while he talked. Baron stared at him.

Glove got up and led Baron over to a place where the candle would not be directly between them. Glove sat beside him. "You have to use your mouth to talk," he said, and Baron looked back at his eyes. Down on the first floor the front door closed and Sam walked down the hall and into his room. His refrigerator shut and a bottle cap popped; water running, then nothing.

"If you don't open your mouth, can't nothin' come out. There ain't no place for it to escape. Go ahead and try to say somethin' without your mouth open."

Baron breathed and stared calmly at him.

"Well, anyway, watch." He pursed his lips together so tightly that they turned pale, puffed out his cheeks, and made some humming garbles. "See . . . nothin', really nothin'. No words. You got to have a mouth that's open for talking."

From two feet away his brother eyed him.

"You don't got to catch on right away. All learning takes time. Just watch me—see opening my mouth and using my tongue . . ."

Baron was watching him.

SAM, ONLY HALF DRUNK, HE TOLD HIMSELF, WAS WALKING THROUGH THE Yard feeling as though the drizzly December slush and cold had penetrated to the fibrous center of his mood. He carried over $100 in his shirt pocket, given to him by Isaac Hanson for the practical service done for him during the process of his divorce from what he claimed loudly in court to be an "immoral and awful woman." And another $250 he didn't want to think about. He'd stopped for a drink before driving back to his room and had stayed three hours, long enough for him to become troubled by the way he was living. He'd left the lights on in his car, and when he returned, the battery was dead and could not even budge the motor.

Walking through the snow toward the house, he stopped, noticing a faint light on the third floor moving from one window to another—down the hall, he suspected. Then nothing. Sam never doubted that his eyes had perhaps gamed with him (even in those times when most of us are willing to concede an aberration of perception in order to preserve a more sane world, Sam wouldn't), and now he had seen a faint light on the third floor being moved slowly from window to window, a light that he suspected might have come from a candle. Again he saw it. This time through the windows in Baron's room. Then the light was hidden from him by someone or something drawing together the curtains. He remembered a time when a square-dance caller had given him a nickel-plated pistol and, instead of putting it away in a drawer or an attic, he had carried it loaded with five shells, for two years, without ever once taking it out of its shoulder holster underneath his brown suit jacket. He had later given it away to a woman in a trailer court who was afraid of patients from the mental hospital escaping. It was for the kind of situation he now faced that he had carried the revolver, but, like those times before, this, he suspected, would also not lend itself to being drawn on . . . mediocrity, presented for a moment colorfully and mysteriously.

Knowing that it was possible for someone to have seen him walking toward the house, he decided that the best action would be to do nothing out of the ordinary, at first. He walked up the steps, kicked the snow from his shoes against the house, and walked inside to the water-stained hall, where drops and puddles of melted snow had left fog rings in the wood. He walked down this to his room, opened the door, closed it, crossed over to his refrigerator, took out a bottle of beer, opened it, sat down on a kitchen chair, took a drink from it, and listened intently for noises other than the somniferous hum of the furnace. He finished the beer and thought. Then, taking off his shoes and coat, he slipped silently through the room back into the hall and toward the staircase. Stepping quickly, two stairs at a time, he mounted to the second floor, where he stood and listened again. This time he could hear the low notes of talking. He climbed to the third floor and moved along down the dark hall, lingering by the doors. The murmur grew louder. Sam stopped beside the door to The Baron's room, listened, smiled, and sat down.

". . . and the only way you can tell if the frog is a sheriff or a crook is by listening, because the crooks work without noise and the sheriffs holler, 'CROOKS, CROOKS!'" Then Glove stopped for a moment and asked Baron if he had noticed how he had been talking. Baron looked back with his tireless eyes. Glove began again:

"There was one time in a small town in Illinois when this guy thought he would make a lot of money against the law. His plan was to cheat honest people—old ladies with dead husbands—out of their savings. His evil idea was—No, wait, something else; his whole family was evil. His father was shot by a neighbor for frying down full-size sponges in bacon fat and feeding them to his dogs. The sponges would get in the stomachs and swell up again, murdering the dogs and puppies."

That's nice, thought Sam, even embellishing. I never had that part in there. He leaned against the hall and continued to listen to Glove's version of one of his own tales. He felt a sense of place, a serenity that he wondered if he had ever felt before. His stories and his talking he had always thought of as being self-expression, a kind of nervous reaction to situations where there was not enough to occupy him. The idea that someone actually listened, *actually listened* and would remember and retell, made it something else. It was simply a shock, one he hoped would even last into sobriety.

Glove's voice was deadly earnest, almost sanctimonious, as he fought to remember the exact phrases Sam had used—to reproduce exactly that small, boiling world inside his mind for his brother, feeling that if everything was not just right, if the story was not told with just the feeling that Sam had given it, his brother would never learn to talk.

Sam's nerves changed for a moment and felt more like warm water than the spring steel he knew they were made of. Relief, he thought, comes from unexpected places; perhaps relief is always unexpected. But soon then he was reminded of his aloneness, reminded by nothing except the pauses in Glove's narrative, the sudden silence after the furnace clicked off. He thought of The Associate and his nerves drew up. Harold Burdock had asked him to "investigate" his wife's activities while he was gone driving his truck. This man—this Burdock—racked with hidden fears, had come to believe that his wife was seeing another man, a divorced man living alone in an apartment, and that their intention was finally to kill him. Sam had shunned the offer, saying that such a service was too time-consuming, too ridiculous, too degrading, and most of all too boring. Burdock had taken a wad of money from his pants pockets and thrown it on the bar counter. Most of the bills were twenties, several were tens, and in the turned corner of one was a fifty. "One week," Burdock had said. "One week."

Sam had taken the money and would tomorrow begin watching Becky Burdock. C must never know about this, he thought. He wouldn't approve—and neither do I, but anything to leave. Then he thought of his father and the spring steel wound up a full turn. He shivered. "You must learn to live with your feelings," his psychiatrist had told him. No, he had thought then and now, that's nonsense. I must learn to live away from them.

". . . and in court," Glove continued, "the judge admitted that no law had been broke—that is, no law *would* be broke if the caskets he had sold the old ladies were delivered before they could be needed. Not just any caskets either, caskets of 'best beauty, hand-carved, with real silver crosses on the lid.' So this guy is right now being watched by the police while he puts every dime he can earn into building these coffins and sending them to the old ladies— the oldest first—in time."

Baron looked at his brother, whose voice had grown tired, and who this time didn't ask him if he'd seen how the talking was done. Glove got up from the floor and took him back and nestled him into his bed. Sam quickly, silently descended to his room. Glove, with less elaborate, more tired precautions, stole down to the second floor and fell asleep.

"Look, Rabbit, are they paying you or not? It's just that simple. It's law. If they pay, then everything's fine. If they don't—if they aren't—then that's breaking the law. They can't do that."

"It's not that simple," said Rabbit, looking out of his steaming window. He'd been losing weight. Eight was in school. He'd managed to be elected to the head of the school board and had gone to Iowa City and hired two honor graduates from the University to teach. One to teach kindergarten.

"It is. You make everything too difficult. Are you still paying for Sam?"

"No. They're paying. They're ahead, in fact. But still it isn't right—hiring out to do anything . . . having a little kid that no one has ever seen."

"That's none of your business," said Ester.

"I don't believe that," said Rabbit and went into another room to call up the Millers and ask if everything was all right at the pajama party, the second time that night.

Watching Becky Burdock was more difficult than Sam had at first imagined it would be, but no less boring. The Burdocks' house was in the middle of a block of houses—no stores, building sites, parking lots, or other places to safely hide and look. There weren't even trees or bushes. Sam drove the Associate car up in front of the house, turned it off, and got down under it as if it were broken and he was working. Following Becky to the grocery store, he talked to the people he passed. He showed the money to Jimmy Cassum, who lay under the car when Sam was sleeping and followed Becky about town on foot or in his own car parked around the corner, spying on her. Each hour they wrote down something in a notebook, to be given later to Harold. Sam and Jimmy Cassum joked together about their ludicrous situation.

"What did she do?" Sam would ask, coming back to begin another ten hours of watching.

"I think we've got her now, Sam. She took some of Harold's shirts to the cleaner's, then stopped over at the Methodist Church pot luck."

"No!"

"I'm afraid so. There's no doubt about it. And what's more, she picked those same shirts up six hours later. Doesn't that seem strange to you? Almost as if she was trying to be caught."

"She's keeping pretty silent about her murderous designs, all right. In fact, both she and that Donnelly fellow are playing it so cool that they never see each other."

"So cool that they've probably *never* seen each other."

"What precautions!"

These dialogues would continue sometimes for an hour. They both agreed that it was easy money, and that Harold Burdock was the kind of man one didn't mind making easy money from, especially when the object was to prove to him the faithfulness of his wife (whose benevolence was known to be many times his own).

Sam, in the beginning, had wondered if maybe someone, even Becky, couldn't have managed to muscle some drama into their lives. He thought there might be a chance at least. Not everyone was stuck into a way of living that was neither exciting nor unhappy—at the best, *fun*, but mostly just bland. What could really be the crime in trying to beef it up a little? But within two days both he and Jimmy Cassum were without any reasonable doubt. They traded the post every four hours as the weekend neared, and it was difficult while following her, even walking, to keep from falling asleep—sewing circles, laundry, underwear departments, bakeries, friends. They comforted themselves with looking again at the money and imagining the way it must look wadded up in their pockets.

"HI, JIMMY," SAID BECKY, BUMPING HER SHOPPING CART INTO HIS LEG as he fumbled for another box of cereal. "I keep running into you."

"Very funny, Skidway," he returned (a grade-school pun on her last name, Sidway).

"Now that's not fair, Cassum. I'm married now, and old names don't count after that." And she even blushed just the slightest at the word "married."

"Oh, fuck," said Jimmy Cassum, and her face fully exploded, "I'll always remember you as Skidway, the great heroine of Greek drama whose father took her out of every single play there was a swear word in, and who couldn't say the pledge of allegiance because her mother figured the 'one nation under God' part wasn't right."

They laughed.

"Don't make fun of my parents," she said. "Time was different then, and maybe a little more of then now wouldn't hurt anything."

"Want some beer?" He picked up a six-pack and put it in her cart.

"Stop it!" she said, grabbed it up, and set it back on the shelf.

Jimmy Cassum remembered then how she had looked when she walked out of the church—the look on her face—Harold beside her, marrying her because of the threat on his life by her father (walking in front of her) and no one expecting him to stay even into the next week.

THEIR WEEK OF SPYING WAS UP AT NOON. SAM AND JIMMY CASSUM made a joyful dash to the bar and drank out of frosty mugs and played hand shuffleboard. They gambled for small change and were losing. Harold Burdock arrived there before dark, shutting the door and shaking his massive head several times slowly from side to side, adjusting to the different lighting. The bar's lights were run continuously from the time the owner opened in the morning until after cleaning up, and even then several of the electric signs went on through the early morning, guarding the beer and the undeposited money with blue and silver lights from pictures of running water in the wilderness. The change from outside was at once noticeable.

"I don't know if I can bear to tell him," said Jimmy to Sam, getting ready to whiz a chromed puck down the slideboard and dislodge some of their opponents' counters. "It may kill him." The disk left his hand and at incredible speed flew off into the sawdust gutter.

"You may be a great spy," said Sam, "and you may have been thinking that because of that you could be good at other things too . . . but that was our last chance."

Jimmy went through the motions of shoving another puck. Harold Burdock had bought a bottle of beer and was carrying it to a table in the back of the room, looking as though he were nervous or had the flu.

"Just like in the movies," said Jimmy. "Let's hit him with a mug of beer."

"I think we better go over," whispered Sam.

"Look, I'm really sorry about the game—I mean, that last shot. I don't know what"—he swallowed down the last half of his drink—"got into me."

"Forget it," said Sam. "I'd never forgive you anyway, so there's no use in talking about it."

Burdock was looking over at them anxiously.

"We got to go over," said Sam, whispering, but not being as silent as he intended.

"I hate that guy," said Jimmy; the tone of it had a bad note. Their opponents picked up their earned nickels and ushered them aside to make room for two other challengers.

"Gratitude," said Jimmy, and everyone laughed because they were friends.

"Come on," said Sam, "it'll be over soon."

"I really don't like that guy."

"We owe it to him—at least to let him know what a fool he is."

"But you won't let him know. You're always too nice."

The two bought more to drink, for strength, and went over to the table. Both sat across from him. He asked to see what they had. Jimmy Cassum told him that they didn't have anything, that there was no dirt on his wife, that any simple fool would know enough to know that much, and that probably the only seedy thing she ever did was to marry him, and that if he wasn't so uselessly stupid he would know right away how utterly stupid he was. Burdock waited determinedly through this and in a deadly manner said, "Let me see what you got."

"We got nothing," said Jimmy, his hand tightening around his glass. "I told you, we got nothin'. You spent all that money for nothing."

"Wait a minute," said Sam, sliding over to the end of the booth, in order to be able to give Jimmy more room and also, should something begin across the table, to get away clear. "He's got a right." And he took out the small ringed notebook from his jacket and passed it over to Burdock, who took it without taking his eyes from Jimmy, looked a minute longer as if to say time out, and opened to the first page.

"The days are marked," said Sam. "And the time is written in the margin."

This was obvious. In many places throughout the notebook, because of having nothing to do but sit in the car, several of the times were underlined with arrows pointing at them and doodles. Burdock, word by word, emphatically inspected each page, as though it were in secret code. "What does this mean?" he asked several times, pointing down into the tablet. "This '10:15; rooms, rooms, rooms.'"

"That's when she was cleaning the house and watering the plants," said Sam, "going from room to room. I guess it could have been clearer."

Harold went on. This is stupid, Sam thought. We should never have done this, whatever the money. It isn't worth it. Jimmy Cassum was looking up at the ceiling, holding his glass between both hands, thinking about breaking it. Burdock went on down the page, carefully noticing everything, thinking to himself: These men are idiots. They are incapable of knowing subtleties. But their time is worth it, because of what they may have noticed . . . what to them seems like one thing may down in the darkness of it be another, be evil. I can take their abuse. I know what they're thinking in their little minds: "He's crazy," they think, "he's a crazy truck driver who read a story about something and with no more information decided it was true about him too." Idiots. They don't know the dark emotions; but the witch knows. But they could never recognize that. Life is so simple for them, living on the surface. There's something. I'll find it.

And he did. Three quarters of the way down through "Friday" he saw a notation that had particular significance for him. "This"— and he pointed down into the page—"what does this mean?"

"You mean 'King Kong'?" asked Jimmy Cassum. "What does 'King Kong' mean? You think somehow it means something special . . . like maybe that's supposed to mean a giant fuck was laid on Becky? Is that what you think it means?"

Burdock's bulk began to rise, and with it the table, which he intended to use to pin Jimmy Cassum to the back of the booth and then with one lunge squash him like a bug. Jimmy was up to meet the thrust, but Sam pulled him out of the booth and told him to leave, and that he would join up with him after Burdock was satisfied—that Burdock had that much coming. Jimmy Cassum left.

"He's lucky," said Burdock. "I could've killed him."

Sam picked up the notebook from the floor and sat down. "Maybe," he said, "but either way you would never've walked out of here."

Burdock was back with the notebook and didn't listen. He recovered the Friday page and pushed it over to Sam. "That," he said, pointing down. "What's that?"

"That's a laundromat. It's called King Koin."

"I thought so," said Burdock, closing the book with a look of troubled satisfaction on his face, "I thought so."

This seemed odd to Sam. Burdock lit a cigar and ordered a drink for both of them.

"Aren't you going to look through the rest?" asked Sam.

"No need," said Burdock. "No need. I found what I wanted. Such things are sad."

"Listen," said Sam, "I don't know what you're talking about, and I'll pay for my own drink, thank you," and shoved some coins across the table at the bartender, who was irritated that they hadn't come over to the bar to buy.

"I wouldn't expect you to," said Burdock.

"Whatever King Koin means to you, it shouldn't. She took three shirts and picked them up a couple of hours later. Your shirts."

"Yep," said Burdock, sipping his drink, and yelled out for a sandwich. "How's The Associate, Sam? How's C and—what's that kid's name? . . . Yeah, Baron. How's Baron?"

Sam had reached his threshold. One more swallow would be too much, and he pushed aside his drink. The insinuation that he and Burdock were now to be friends was too much. He stood up from the table and left without so much as saying anything. Harold Burdock sat and sipped and chewed on his sandwich and turned things over in his head, about Becky and how King Koin was run by Donnelly's parents, an aging couple whose good judgment and even wills could probably be twisted by the darker emotions of their son and his slut. The confusion of beer and sandwich and saliva in his mouth tasted good.

Sam rejoined Jimmy Cassum, who had not yet given up on the prospects of the night and thought of two immediate, almost simultaneous possibilities. The first was to go outside and wait for Burdock to come out and take him by surprise. The second was to forget that and mosey on over to Lucy Lourn's place, a warm, colorfully lit house in town where Jimmy Cassum turned in secret desperation and joy and Sam could come too because she had a roommate. About the business of thresholds: Sam knew his was considerably lower than Jimmy's (who was steadily gaining on it), so after first dissuading him from murdering Burdock or breaking his legs with a two-by-four or even waiting around just to check if maybe he wouldn't stand out somewhere in the open, the two companions left for Lucy's place. They called for a taxi, but the only one in town wouldn't pick them up. They explained their concern for sober citizens on the highway, but the argument cut no ice with the Willard Jones Taxi Service. Sam helped Jimmy Cassum walk, knowing that because of his condition it would be he, and not Jimmy, who would interest Lucy when they got there.

"YES, YOU'LL BE GOING TO SCHOOL SOON, BARON. WON'T THAT BE NICE— all those little people to look at, and things to learn? . . . Won't it, C?" She put several more carrots on Baron's plate and he began eating them one at a time.

"I guess so," said C, stirring his coffee with the handle end of his knife, wondering if it was the iron or the rust in the water that made his coffee turn gray instead of golden brown when he put half-and-half in it. Sam drank his black, so he didn't notice. Glove was pushing his food around on his plate, eyeing Sam from across the table, asking quiet, shy questions of him that might lead Sam to tell a new story about the world or living in Illinois.

"Everybody goes to school. It's fun . . . right, Sam?"

"Right," said Sam, thinking he would rather be in town or down in his room or anywhere but here eating with his brother's family (C, he felt, was never really fully present around the rest of his family; at least, not the C Sam thought of as being C), which he did every other Thursday night without fail. And sometimes he even took them out with him to a restaurant. But such things were done with the full expectation of how boring they would be. Each knew what the other felt: one's family being intruded upon, the other feeling that it was being forced down his throat. Both of them looked forward to these times and were bored and irritated in the peaceful warmth of their feelings for each other.

"You'd better be careful," Sam said to Glove, as though Glove had been pulling out a knife under the table, or leaving a hint about the bank robbery behind at the scene of the crime. "Many good men have been lost by that."

"What?" said Glove.

"That, what you were doing," he said and went back to drinking his coffee and looking off into space.

"What?" asked Glove. "What?"

"Staring at someone's eyes that way. A smart man can tell when someone is staring at his eyes—even if they don't see the other person. Like maybe they're looking through a hole in a wall or something. It's real useful knowledge when you're tracking killers or headhunters, stuff like that. The trick is, when you're doing the looking, focus on the mouth and even then keep looking away. It's good to not look at eyes anyway because they can kind of hypnotize you and you'll find it difficult to tear away in case you need to make a fast fly for one of your guns."

"Headhunters!" said Glove.

"What!" said Sam, as though he were completely interrupted from another distant thought. "And, by the way, you were looking at my eyes, weren't you? . . . Weren't you?"

"Yes," said Glove.

"Well, there, you see?"

"How can you tell?" asked Glove.

"It's mostly feeling," he answered. "You have to feel the eyes on you." And if this game had been serious, Sam might well have had so much feeling about the eyes of Cell being on him that he would have been thrown back against the wall and cut up into little pieces.

"You try it," said Sam, not looking at Glove, then turning and saying, "You were doing it again . . ." and Glove, who seemed unable to look anywhere except at Sam's eyes, now that he was thinking so hard about them, had even drawn his hands up so that the top portion of Sam's head was severed from his vision.

"Go ahead, try," said Sam.

"Come on, Sam," said C, wanting to take his coffee away from the table, "don't tease."

"No, he can do it. Go ahead and try, Glove. Close your eyes."

Glove did and sat with his forehead wrinkled, waiting for the feeling. Baron watched.

"Now," Glove said, and opened his eyes. Sam's were straight ahead into his.

"Pretty good," Sam said. "Try again."

Success three times running, though Sam said each time that it was a little slow, that he, Glove, wasn't familiar enough with the feeling yet, and that he would have to work it out by himself, because game situations—testing the power—were unfair, and were almost immoral. Even talking about such things was risky, but then Glove could keep a secret and would probably someday be a great tracker or woods hero. Cell had left the table and was staring from the kitchen, getting more coffee for C, hating Sam.

"Did you hear about Burdock?" asked C.

"No," said Sam, offhand.

"I thought maybe Keith had told you when you came back from the lumber yard."

"He didn't. Haven't seen anybody all afternoon, except Old Man Sanchez, who finds out about everything a couple weeks late and then forgets it. I don't know how he makes any money out there. It's too disorganized . . . and I don't know if I'll be able to figure out a way for him to . . . What? He drive his truck over a cliff?"

"No, but he put Becky in the hospital."

Sam pushed his chair back from the table and fastened his eyes on C.

"It was pretty bad, I guess—that's what Ray Millet says and his boy's an orderly there at the emergency entrance. Welts and bruises and even burns all over her body."

Sam took his mug of coffee and placed it carefully on the table, a slight tremor beginning in his hand. Inside he felt his nerves expand and unravel. There was nothing he could do to stop them. His face was very hot.

"She didn't file a complaint, evidently, and said nothing about it."

"I hadn't heard," said Sam. "I guess what goes on in one family is none of my business—or yours, for that matter, C."

"Oh, the family part, sure, I agree," said C. "But she said something about her husband being tricked."

"Probably nothing besides the usual trickery that takes place in Burdock's mind every time he tries to use it." Sam got up from the table and went downstairs to the first floor, where he sat for a minute before leaving to find Jimmy Cassum. He found him halfway between their respective homes, Jimmy having actually traveled farther, actually running when Sam first saw him. They talked. Jimmy said it wasn't their fault, that what they did could in no way be seen as having anything to do with what happened to her. Sam felt differently, but was slowly convinced by Jimmy that they were not guilty. Then Jimmy started talking about how they never should have done it, and Sam convinced *him* that it made no difference. They set off then for the package store in Jimmy's car, and drank far into the night, far past Sam's threshold. They called Lucy, but she wasn't home. Jimmy's Chevrolet was driven very slowly into the ditch and stopped, with no physical injury to the road, the fence, the car, or the sleeping driver. People driving by saw the lights growing fainter and fainter, until the taillights looked like low-burning wood coals, and then finally nothing, after the battery was dead.

Sam stumbled home across his neighbors' back yards, holding on to substantial objects here and there.

He stumbled into the house and drank up the rest of the orange juice in his refrigerator. Sitting at his kitchen table, he heard the now familiar sound of Glove stealing down the hall from his room toward the staircase. He listened to the faint snap as

Baron's door came open. Then he started up for the third floor as quietly as his condition allowed and sat down outside Baron's door. Many times during the last year he'd done this, unknown to Glove, because of the calm, contented feeling that it gave him about himself and about the world, and he never had need of it more than now. He listened:

"So one of them comes in very handy when tracking head-hunters, who run wild in certain parts of the country and dogs can't trail because they have no smell . . ."

Nice touch, thought Sam.

"IT'S RABBIT," SAID CELL, FROM THE WINDOW.

"Coming over here?" asked C.

"Well, he's walking into the Yard, and headed this way."

"Funny. He hasn't been over here for . . ."

"Just a visit, I'll bet," said Cell, thinking, I'll bet Sam hasn't been paying on that loan and now we all have to leave . . . or, more likely, he's a school-board member coming to take The Baron. C went downstairs and Cell continued watching from the window, though standing partially behind the curtain so that Rabbit's roving eyes would not find her.

C met him at the door and they went into a downstairs room that Keith had taken over for a shop to fix small electrical appliances. They sat down on metal-rung kitchen chairs with holes burned through the red plastic by drops of liquid solder. He looks so old, thought C . . . even his hair is turning color. How old are we getting to be? he wondered.

"You know about Becky Burdock," said Rabbit.

This isn't a visit, thought C. "Yes."

"Well, I went over there to talk to her, and finally she said that someone had convinced her husband that she was cheating on him—someone for some reason had told him something. He's sick, everyone knows that—but I wondered who would do that. So I went to see him, and he was defensive at first, but I expected that, and I told him that I was going to do everything in my power to convince his wife to file a complaint and send him away for the rest of his life—"

"Maybe that's none of your business," said C.

"Maybe," said Rabbit, "but maybe not, too."

He's grown up, thought C, at least he's decided that being just like his father wouldn't be such a bad way to be.

"So," Rabbit continued, "I talked to him and he said he'd hired some men to watch her and that he'd learned from them of his wife's dirty actions. Then I left, and sitting at home I began to wonder who he could find to do that, who *would* do that. And I thought that the only place would be here—The Associate, a group of semi-professionals who hire out to do anything."

"Nope," said C.

"It's not right," said Rabbit. "It's not right. You and Sam can come to work for *me*. I can use you. It's not right, doing these kinds of things. It will lead to . . ."

"We had nothing to do with that," said C.

"Yes, you did. Sam and Jimmy Cassum did. I found out."

"Sam!" yelled C. "Sam!"

Sam came out of his room a little later and walked into the small shop.

"Rabbit says you and Cassum did some work for Harold Burdock, that true?"

Sam looked over at Rabbit and Rabbit's eyes fastened on him. *He knew*, there could be no doubt.

"That's right," said Sam.

"Well?" asked Rabbit—Rabbit, who was older now.

"Well, what?"

"That's the difference," said Rabbit, standing up, "between you and me. It's not right, living the way you do here. Good day, C." He put his hat on. "And I think it's wrong to keep little Baron away from people," he said and left.

Sam explained the job they'd taken, exactly what they'd done, and how much they were paid, and even how they felt about it.

"I probably would've done the same thing," said C, "but from now on why don't we—all four of us—get together and agree on the jobs before we accept them, unless it's the kind of thing we've done before?"

"Sure," said Sam. "Sure."

That night Sam left on the road. He drove to Quincy, Illinois. He went to see a friend, a woman who he had once thought could take him in and care for him and would keep him. Then he came back alone, and only C noticed that he'd gone.

ONE YEAR LATER

"You know, Glove's been teaching Baron how to talk. It's the damnedest thing. He goes up there when we're all asleep and sets his brother in front of him and tells him stories, letting Baron watch his mouth. It's how the boy has learned to understand talking." Sam told this to C.

C was pacing back and forth over the red-and-black flowered carpet in his living room, his sock feet hardly making any noise. He went over to the coffee table and began rolling a cigarette from a tin of Velvet. "What stories?" he asked, licking the paper.

"Just stories."

"Stories," said C. "Maybe a lot of those stories that he's heard from you. Nothing good can come of it . . . nothing good can come of it, I can tell you that. I should never have let Cell put him up there." He resumed pacing.

"Come on," said Sam, "cut it out. What's to worry about?"

"Don't let Cell know, O.K.? Don't tell her."

"Come on, C," said Sam. "Everything doesn't have to be something more to worry about. You know that kid ain't normal, but he's happy enough, and he's learned to understand—he's learned language. He just doesn't talk yet."

"He hasn't learned real language," said C. "He's learned about fantasies."

"Language is language," said Sam. "Mind if I turn on the TV? The news is coming on."

"Go downstairs and watch it. The news always depresses me."

"Everything depresses you," said Sam. They looked at each

other. "It's true; everything depresses you. There's something wrong with your head."

"Maybe," said C. "Maybe. But I wish you would've told me about those talking lessons before—before it was too late."

"Too late! Come on. Too late for what? What do you think's going to happen? Language is language. What's the difference if he learns it one way or the other?"

"Real language is learned by real associations, real things— reality. What he's learned is fiction. I don't know what'll happen, but it won't be good. Nothing good can come of it."

"You worry too much," said Sam and went downstairs to watch the news.

C put an end to the language lessons. Glove was eight years old then. It was, nationally speaking, the beginning of a very long troubled time when many people began to think, even though they weren't philosophers or particularly sensitive anyhow, that maybe things could be better for everyone; and many didn't see it that way at all. A few only wanted more money. It was the rhetoric of these last few, and their employees in Congress, that depressed C when he watched the news.

CELL SAW THREE MEN IN BLACK HATS WALK INTO THE YARD. ONE CARRIED a small briefcase. They did not dwell on pieces of old machinery here and there; they came straight toward the house without even talking or looking at each other. She didn't know who they were. Sam was downstairs; she could hear his radio. It's too early for trading or jobs, C's still asleep, and Sam usually isn't up yet, she thought. But these men are not from around here; they don't know. Pounding on the door—twice, hard and decisive. Sam answered it. Cell heard him shut the door, then murmured talking, then walking toward the staircase. "Hey, Missus C," called Sam. "Someone to see you." She heard footsteps on the stairs. Around the corner down the hall she met them, seeing Sam at the bottom of the stairs, looking up. She wished C were there, but wouldn't wake him. She was afraid.

"What do you want?" she asked, not pretending—in the manner familiar to the country around her—to be nice. They didn't care. She didn't either.

"Our records show that you have a boy, Baron Easter, born December third, 1955, who should be in school. He should have entered pre-school. He should have entered pre-school last year, and we're here to see that he is enrolled this year—in fact, this very day." An affidavit signed by two judges was lifted from the briefcase by a pair of white hands and thrust out for her to take. C, she thought . . . C!!!

Sam came upstairs. "There must be some mistake," he said. "Baron isn't a normal kid . . . he's, well, not so well in the brains department." Cell had stumbled backward down the hall and into the living room, collapsing into the chair next to Glove's card table, the piece of legal paper still in her hand. Far away, she heard Sam call for C.

When the men left she heard one of them say "noon." She got up, and at the window watched them walk disdainfully through the Yard. C came into the room and looked at the affidavit. "They say we got to take Baron to school by noon or they'll come after him. It's either that or take him to an institution. I guess Rabbit put them up to it—not that they wouldn't have done it anyway; but he brought it closer to their attention."

"I was thinking of bringing him, anyway," said Cell . . . "after he had enough time to get ready."

"Everything'll be fine," said C. "Everything'll be fine." Pause.

"I know," said Cell. "I never doubted that. It's just wonderful that Baron will be in school, like Glove. It just startled me—those men."

"Sure," said C. "It's just this thing," and he held up the paper by its top corners. "A thing like this would scare anyone." They both laughed. Then C read it out loud and they laughed together

about the legal language and the odd punctuation. Sam came upstairs to see if they wanted to hide Baron in his room for a couple
of weeks and found them sitting across Glove's card table, staring
at the affidavit, laughing quietly.

"Get the car started," said C. "We're taking The Baron to
school this morning."

What a couple of phonies, thought Sam, and went out to start
the car. He pulled it around in front of the Yard. He waited and
watched as C carried The Baron through the dead metal, a black
blindfold put over his eyes so that he would not scream, Cell
walking alongside and behind.

Baron sat between his parents in the back seat. Sam drove. At
the school he was taken out and his father said, "You can walk
now. Keep a hold of my hand." And he walked into the school-
house, into large, cinder-block gray halls with large clocks and
low drinking fountains. His blindfold was taken off, and Cell
slipped it into her pocket. They found the door marked KINDER-
GARTEN, and passed several tough-looking little kids in the hall,
scurrying back and forth from the bathroom. C opened the door
and stood inside. The teacher came out and Baron looked at her.

"This is Baron," said C. "He belongs here. You should have no
trouble with him, except that he doesn't talk, but he can understand and will do as he's told. Also, he won't go outside or stand
by open windows."

The teacher, who C thought was too young to have mastered
the profession, went down to the principal's office. Seconds later
Mortimer Value pushed his head out and waved at C. The teacher
came back, skin showing above the wrinkles in her knees.

"Fine," she said. "Come along, Baron, the other boys and girls
will be happy to meet you."

"Go ahead, Baron," said Cell, though he had already begun to
walk into the room and didn't even look back.

Cell and C went back to the car. C opened up the back door,
not thinking, shut it, and the three rode in front. "Look at that,"

said Sam, and pointed out a black car parked at the side of the school building, on the unsodded lot. C looked, and inside the car sat the hatted men, who pulled out and drove behind them for a ways, and then turned off.

Baron went into the room. The other children looked at him. He stared at them. He got a colored pencil, a lead one, an eraser, and a paper tablet from Mrs. Fitch. He put them underneath the seat of his chair on the little holding platform, where the others had theirs. Mrs. Fitch told him, and the rest of the class, that they had been hearing about raccoons, a fictional family of animals that wore ties and drove bulbous automobiles. She continued reading where she had left off. Baron leaned back in comfort.

At noon recess, after the lunch cart had gone, Mrs. Fitch asked Baron if he wouldn't rather go outside—rather than look at the others through the window. Baron looked back, and Mrs. Fitch hurried on down to the boiler room, where she and her fellow teachers not on playground duty relaxed with a savored cigarette and coffee. The child is harmless enough, she thought.

Baron stayed inside for afternoon recess too, and lay awake during naptime, though his head was down on his mat and he was quiet, as he was told. But every noise in the room would open his eyes as quickly as those of a bird. At three thirty his parents came and picked him up, smuggling him out to the car with a blindfold over his eyes. Strange, Mrs. Fitch thought . . . but nothing more.

Inside, at home, Cell asked Baron how his first day of school went. He did not answer. She knew he wouldn't, but he didn't look any worse for the experience. At the table Glove listened to his parents talking about what must have happened at Baron's first day of school.

Mrs. Fitch didn't have any trouble with Baron. The other children seemed to like him, and she thought to herself that communication—at that level—is more than words. Her job as a

pre-school educator was to make the children familiar with working in a learning environment, make them familiar with pencils,
books, large green cards with letters on them, sitting at a desk, and
following a schedule. There was no reason why Baron couldn't
learn these things. She began to love him.

Looking at him coloring in his book, for instance, she would
think of how frustrated he must be—but how well controlled
he was. All the torment kept inside. He would be an artist, she
thought. He will be a great artist. He will be able to see clear into
the core of the human experience.

Baron was unaware of any of these thoughts. The only thing
he knew was that sometimes when he looked up from his little
desk, Mrs. Fitch would quickly move her eyes away—that and
sometimes she asked him about things, about how he felt, when
he knew C had told her that he didn't talk.

He won't go outside, she thought, looking over at him standing next to the window. She had been forgoing her cigarette break
in order to stay in the room with him and try to get to know him.
Why won't he go outside? she wondered. Why must he always
have walls around him?

"Why won't you go outside?" she asked after a while. Baron
turned around and looked at her. Again she saw frustration in his
face. He's trying, she thought. He's trying to tell me. "Come on,
Baron," she coaxed. "Why won't you go outside?" He was trying! They were communicating with their faces. "Try, Baron. Try.
Please. Why won't you go outside?" She saw his mouth begin to
move. She thought she could hear murmuring sounds. She didn't
take her eyes away from him. "Come on," she whispered. "Why
won't you go outside? . . . Speak."

Baron opened his mouth:

"A frog can tell when he's being looked at, when something's
looking at his eyes. Sheriff frogs, tracking headhunters, using pall-
bearers to carry their packs through the jungles, where snakes grow
over thirty feet long and can encircle a man in less than a second,

and carry him seventeen miles through the mushroom trees to keep away from the walking canine cadavers living on the ground, up to a cave, a witch's cave with painted orange walls and signs of the devil, bones of bats hung from the ceiling to ward off . . ."

And out of his mouth began to flow a relaxed, easy story, a gargantuan, enormous story that was a part, and most all, of all the stories that he had heard from Glove during the midnight hours in his room.

"O.K., Baron," Mrs. Fitch said. "That's enough. You can stop now." But he didn't. When the outside bell was rung she was shouting at him and the first-grade teacher could hear her all the way down the hall. "Be quiet, Baron. Stop it!" When the other kindergartners came in, he was still standing next to the window telling his mammoth story, talking without emotion. In tears Mrs. Fitch ran to Mortimer Value's office and they ran down the hall together. Other teachers left their better students in "patrol" and hurried after them. Baron was still talking.

"You there, Baron!" shouted the principal from across the room. "You stop talking!"

Baron didn't even look at him and continued talking, looking absently down at the floor.

"What's he talking about?" asked Mortimer Value.

"I don't know," wailed Mrs. Fitch. "I don't know. I asked him why he wouldn't go outside and he looked at me and then began . . . this."

"I'll call his parents," he said and ran off down the hall, through the clump of teachers huddled in the doorway.

When Sam and Cell and C arrived at the school, there was mayhem and confusion. Children were running up and down the halls, yelling and accosting each other. In one room was a water-balloon battle. Mortimer grabbed C by the hand and hurried them to the kindergarten room. Cell collapsed when she emerged through the throng of teachers. Baron went on with his gigantic tale.

"Shut up!" yelled C.

But of course he didn't.

"Get him," said C, his arms gathering up Cell from the floor.

Sam rushed across the room and picked him up and carried him down the hall, still talking.

"The blindfold," said Sam.

"Forget it," said C, and they went outside. Still he didn't stop, but went on telling about the Amazon, zip guns, marked cards, Indian burial grounds, and woods animals that actually disappeared when looked at. Some of this Sam recognized, and in the car, with Baron and Cell and C in the back seat, he said to his brother over the talking:

"Honest, C, I had no idea this would happen."

"I told you nothing good could come of it. I told you nothing good would ever come of it."

Back in the mansion-like house, C coaxed Cell back into the conscious world. Sam phoned the doctor, then several more, and within one hour two arrived, looked at Baron, took his pulse and blood pressure, were afraid of taping his mouth shut, and decided together that he would have to be sedated with a local tranquilizer. They gave him a shot and waited. Two hours later they gave him another—enough to "put a full man asleep." Then they gave him another.

At about one in the morning a practicing psychologist was called in—the phenomenon believed to be a mental disorder, a kind of shock.

The psychologist arrived and quickly told everyone to leave the room. Then he came out and explained that it was an attention-getting trick and that if Baron were ignored he would quickly stop. Sam, with Glove, listened through the door, waiting, thinking to himself, He hasn't even repeated himself yet, just one long descriptive action.

"He's saying meaningless things because he thinks that it will upset you," said the psychologist.

"Those are stories his brother told him," said C, "in order to teach him how to talk. This is the first time he's ever said anything—only screaming when he's taken outside."

"What!" said the psychologist, and Cell and C told him what they knew of their son. Hours later Baron was still talking.

The psychologist had many explanations for what was happening, but none of them helped to stop it. Finally, he thought the Baron should have another shot—this time a more powerful one. They taped his mouth shut, but four hours later, without sleep, they took it off and he continued on.

"Sometime he'll stop," the doctors said and left.

The next day they came back, and the day after that. "He's repeating himself," Sam told them.

"Doesn't he eat?" they asked.

"Nope." I never thought *this* would happen, thought C.

"Sleep?"

"Nope."

"It'll kill him," they said. "If he keeps on, it'll kill him."

"No!" screamed Cell, who had had little sleep herself and was shaking and vomiting every few hours.

"With all that—tranquilizers in him—no sleep, no food. It would kill any of us. No water."

That day Baron fell into a comatose sleep for a long time on the floor. When he woke up in his bed, he didn't talk. C brought him some food and he ate it. Then he went back to sleep and within several days was like normal, silent.

"If he ever does that again," they said, "he'll die."

Baron didn't go to school any more. Rabbit absolved himself by believing that it would have happened sooner or later, and sent anonymous creative things for the child to play with. He looked into private institutions, but was disappointed.

When Baron was well enough to sit at the table again, the family had dinner together. Cell's hands shook. They'd never stopped. And now wherever she was she would play quickly with the fringes on her sleeves, a fold of cloth from her dress, the curtains. At dinner she ate little, said nothing, and shredded her napkin. C was having her take Valium, but it didn't seem to help except to make her eyes look more glassy and cause her to fall asleep in chairs. Still she maintained everything was fine—how lucky they were that all the bad times were past. Mr. Parson, who owned the drygoods store, asked her to take some time off, and when she wouldn't and said she was fine, fired her. Rabbit heard about this from a woman who had overheard. The next week a health inspector visited a restaurant that Parson also owned and condemned it as a health hazard. He applied for a beer permit and it was denied. He put the building up for sale and no one would touch it; the only man who had been interested complained that he couldn't swing a loan anywhere. Parson left for Illinois. Rabbit repossessed his house and put it up for sale.

"You know what I think?" said Glove, hollowing out his dinner roll with his finger.

"What?" asked C. "Don't pick."

"I think maybe Baron's a genius."

Baron looked over at him.

"Oh," said C.

Cell was looking first at Glove, then at Baron, back and forth, her fingernails bitten down to where they were bleeding.

"Yes," said Glove. "I read in the encyclopedia that a genius is supposed to be a person who can put things together in his head. Well, Baron put all those stories together."

"That's right," said C. "He did." Then he looked at Cell. "But it didn't make any sense."

"He just needs practice," said Glove.

C turned to him and said, "Don't you ever. Don't you ever."

Glove was quiet.

"We're going to have another baby," said Ester to Rabbit.

For just a moment he didn't know what he was thinking. For

just a moment he was immune to his thoughts, and such times (those few that he'd had) he'd decided privately were glimpses of heaven, tiny, tiny suspended winks of time when you were allowed to walk on God's garden path. Then his thoughts began to creep back in and he refamiliarized himself with what it was normally like to be himself, and began to worry, walking about the room as though looking for signs of trouble. Such preparation was needed.

Ester, on the other hand, saw very little of this. What she saw was Rabbit's eyes lighting up as though they were little blue suns, fired diamond hot, and pursing of the lips and wrinkling of the forehead accompanied by an almost inaudible humming noise. He stood up and let himself drift around the room, across the Persian rug, over to the bay window, feel a plant, hum louder, say, "That's good, Ester, that's good," over to the solid zebra-wood stereo, back to the chair, sit down, get up again, over to the window to check if Eight was coming home from school. What she saw was Rabbit being happy. She smiled to herself, a smile that kept a secret, because if anyone else knew—people at the bank, businessmen that came to see him, school-board members—what Rabbit Wood was really like, they'd . . . well, they just wouldn't believe it.

"Sit down," said Ester.

"No time," said Rabbit. "No time for sitting down. Must think. A lot of changes got to be made around here—a lot. This is no place for a little kid to grow up in. It may be fine for Eight, now that she's used to it, or you or me, but there's always changes. There's no doctors live close around here . . . the people at church, did you tell the people at church? Too big. We need some smaller rooms. Little kids are scared of big rooms . . ." Rabbit went upstairs.

Nothing could be done, thought Ester. He's off again. Perhaps it was better that this would be the last one (because of overpopulation). But nevertheless Ester was excited too and went upstairs (partially because Rabbit would later decide climbing stairs was out from now on, and fuss over her; and it had been a long time since she was fussed over in that way). Besides, this child would be their last, because of overpopulation.

Fall had always been that time of year, and every time it came— even before you would see it, but could walk out of the house and know it was coming because of the smell and the plants making a final rush, a glorious, powerful last stand—it was the same. This year Sam was ready, and by the time the walnut husks had begun to turn brown he had three dogs that were used enough to him that he could work with them. The corn was still green but beginning to droop and sag on the leaf ends. The sweet corn was picked, even the late-planted rows, and the raccoons had turned back to the field ears. A lush time of year. Flies were thick everywhere, and healthy, so that if you didn't smash them flat against the window with the swatter, they would fall to the floor, shake themselves off, and be back rummaging through the kitchen.

Cell, unlike her husband, remained throughout the night on the edges of sleep and woke up startled, as though Sam's alarm clock downstairs were a barred owl under the bed. She could hear his dogs clawing against his door. They did not bark. He'd trained them. He'd told them that talking to him in the morning would wake C's wife up, and that noises frightened her. She had heard him. She listened to Sam walking downstairs, opening the refrigerator, rattling glass bottles, closing the fat refrigerator door, letting his dogs into the room and them going insane running up and down, jumping on Sam, Sam telling them to be quiet, to get down, to calm down, to stop acting like children—"Sled, get out of there, you lame-brain. Get down, Hose. You can't have nothin' to eat if you don't get down . . . Settle down. Settle down . . . This is coffee, stupid . . . Coffee. If you're not careful, you'll be just—" Cell couldn't hear the last part, and got quietly up, out away

from the bed, her wire-like body disturbing neither the tilt of the
mattress nor C's sleep. "If you're not careful, you'll be just . . ."
she thought, like Baron, like his mother, like everyone upstairs—
because of his mother . . . them dogs . . . them dogs . . . them dogs.
She walked to the window and looked outside where the sun was,
where the world was. She looked at the flies trapped in between.
She looked at them. Her hands began unraveling the edges of the
sleeves of her sleeping gown and picking at themselves. Them
dogs, she thought, watching the flies, them dogs. C turned over on
his back. He don't miss me, she thought. He don't miss me now
. . . an' won't later. If I was gone, he wouldn't miss me . . . Them
dogs. They are good dogs. They are good. I hate them. Flies, not
awake, not asleep. Not awake, not asleep. Them dogs.

Sam opened the back door and turned them loose. They fought
to be first out, and ran among the pieces and piles of junk like
three very fast children in a toy department, looking for something that will run away from them, something they can chase.
The morning sun had turned everything in the Yard cold pink,
and vertical shafts of colored light were opening up through the
dark-pillowed sky. Sam's heart tightened. These times, he thought
at the door, looking out into it, are what make all the rest worth
it. He put those things he wanted in his pockets: a metal package
of tobacco, papers, wooden matches, a knife, a sandwich, three
apples, a flask of whiskey (which he felt silly carrying but took
nevertheless because of its flatness and light weight), a pistol
that shot .22-caliber shorts, and a paperback edition of a novel
he intended to read. He walked through the Yard, watching his
dogs, who came back together and separately to check on him and
would be off again jumping and careening past each other.

Just at the edge of the Yard he stopped to roll a cigarette and
turned to avoid the wind, though it was not very strong, and
noticeable only by its touch on his face, no movement of grass
or leaves, five to ten miles per hour, he thought. Several people
had awakened and an occasional door slam or car motor could

be heard, but they were only part of the morning, and seemed far away. Sam pinched the tobacco together and glanced at the house. In a window on the second floor he saw Cell's thin, dark shape. He looked at her, but she didn't turn away, as though she were looking at something on the window surface. He felt sad about what it might be like to be going crazy and looking out of that window from that room. He felt sad about what it might feel like to be C, waking up and seeing her there unraveling with her fingers. Directly above her, on the third floor, he saw the small head and shoulders of The Baron, staring out at him. He dumped the tobacco back out of the cigarette and into the pouch, let the paper fall, and walked down across the street and got in his car. The battery was not strong, but had surprising endurance. The motor churned over. He finally worked it enough so that it started working itself. Sam pushed the choke halfway in and drove off down the street, his dogs circling around him, across yards, behind houses, running alongside barking. Several of the men looked out of their houses and wished to God that they didn't have to work all the time and could be in that car with Sam, or in their own, heading out in the early morning for a day in the woods. Some of them even stepped out of their houses, half dressed, and waved as he motored by, watching his fine dogs running.

"You better be careful with those tires," one called to Sam.

"I know," called Sam, "don't run over any rocks." Sam's tires were something of an interest in Ontarion, after he had bought them at a fantastic saving in a big shopping-center store in Des Moines, bragging about what suckers people were to pay so much for tires, and had worn away the tread in about three weeks of hard driving and looked like inner tubes. They watched him drive on out of town.

On the blacktop he pushed his choke in all the way and kicked up his speedometer to a little over thirty, forcing his dogs to run pretty much directly behind him in order to keep up. This way, by the time he reached the woods they would be at least a little less apt to run away because that first, initial surge of excitement would be over. He turned from the blacktop onto a gravel road. From here he could see the forest on the horizon. He waved to the farmers when he saw them. They smiled and waved back from their tractors: good, genuine smiles. He stopped to talk with one and wait while his dogs caught up.

"How's doin'?" asked Sam.

"Fine. Couldn't be better."

"Good year?"

"Good enough," said Henry Sutton. "Must come over sometime."

Sam drove on a ways and looked out on the poor corn, damaged by hail, with whole parts of the fields nearly dead because of there being too much water in early summer. Fields dirty with weeds because of their having been too soft to get in when the corn was growing up. He knew that Henry Sutton had been forced to take a job in Middle River. Sam's dogs were running alongside the car now. At the creek he pulled off the road into an access lane to a field. In the ditch were burdocks and goldenrod. He left the keys in the ignition in case whoever owned the field wanted to move it.

The sky was completely blue now and the first layer of mist had lifted up from the ground, though the air was still heavy and cool. He walked down to the wooden bridge. C and he had called this creek Little Creek when they were young and had come to wade, make dams, and eat packed lunches with their mother on Sunday afternoons when Ansel was going about church business and counseling. He remembered those expeditions and his memory began to run on over more times, but he could still choke it, and again he gave up rolling a cigarette, let the paper fall into the clear water and float with the current, making a shadow on the pebbly bottom. He went down into the ditch, around a galvanized culvert, climbed over a loose barbed-wire fence and down along the creek bank. Two of his dogs were already in the stream, running and splashing. The other one, J. B. Hutto, did not like the water and was walking disdainfully along the sandbank.

Sled, the largest of the three, left tracks in the soft mud as big around as a hoof print. Sam walked under the bridge and out the other side. Piles of sticks and logs, all covered with a netting of mud and silt, layered the creek banks—remains of the flooding water. Turtle tracks with the characteristic tail drag. Raccoon. Creek willows grew out from the stream ledge, out as much as thirty feet from the water, with twisted, long trunks, as though something very wrong had happened to the organizing intelligence of their seed.

Sam went down the stream for a ways until he was forced to scramble up to the top of the bank or walk in the water. He ambled away from the creek and up the hill, noticing as he went that it had been a long time since he was in the area; the look and coloration of the terrain seemed unfamiliar. The dogs came up out of the creek after him. He began looking for dead elm trees, ones that had not been dead for too long and still retained most of their bark. Finally he found the kind he wanted and picked off some mushrooms and put them in his pocket. He did not take many because he did not particularly like the taste, but enjoyed looking for them and feeling their cold, fleshy bodies and always felt obliged to take some along, as though some wood spirit would come jumping down from the trees, telling him that he had committed a violation by finding them and then not wanting to take any.

The part of the forest he was in now was predominantly oak and Sam wandered around in it, hoping to find some bur oaks, which he had decided were his favorite trees after reading about them in *Homeland*, a book written by an Indian—an Indian who claimed to have known Chief Blackhawk. This book had said that on the great plains there were sometimes fires, prairie sagres, started by lightning or by natives in order to chase buffalo. (In fact, the book had said that prairie grass—real prairie grass—would grow only if it was burned down every year or so because it needed some of that burned-grass chemical of itself in the soil.) These fires had evidently wiped out millions of acres of green. They had burned for miles and miles, chasing animals, driving herds of buffalo to a place where the Sacs or Crows could get a shot at them, unchecked by rain, wind, small rivers, anything but bur oaks. These trees were so hard, so tough, with bark so thick, that a stand or break of them would be a natural barrier to the fire. And after several generations the forests of Iowa, as seen from far in the distance, would appear to be all bur oak, which in actuality grew predominantly in a border around the other trees, guarding them.

He found one, studied the shape and color for a while, then sat down under it with his back against the gnarled bark. He took out his tin of Velvet tobacco mixed with Bugler, whose strand cut helped keep the shorter, heavier cut of the Velvet together. There was a piece of banana peel in there for moisture. He rolled a cigarette. J. B. Hutto was sitting beside him. The pattern of the sun through the leaves onto the brown mat carpet of the woods floor was like a thousand small stars and crosses in gold. The air had warmed up, but here and there a couple of pellets of dew clung to the dark side away from the sun, and you could see them. A red-tailed hawk of the black phase stepped off a high snag near the Little Creek, opened its tremendous wings, and headed for a cornfield in the distance. Sled, who was also down there, barked at him. Sam looked behind the bur oak and saw the hawk sitting in the air, letting the wind carry him downstream. Foolish dog, thought Sam, and watched until the bird was out of sight. He wished a rabbit would run by in front of him, because he had a feeling that J. B. Hutto could outrun one—though he knew he could never catch one—and he wanted to watch. A ragged V of wood ducks went overhead, but they might have been teal. A warbler in the distance.

He was satisfied. But in the middle of all this he did something that had always been the never-ending, painful regret of his life. He thought about death. Always, when just about up to the gates, he would think about death. He remembered a friend of his who had told him that he was afraid of death; but then he had been afraid of so many things. Shortly after that he had killed himself.

Sam lay down, fell asleep, and slept for several hours until the hot sun overhead woke him, while J. B. Hutto sat keeping vigil in the way a good dog will love a man and watch over him and, should even the king of hell come walking up for him with death on his face and fire in his hands, protect him. Sled and Hose spot-checked the two every ten minutes or less, then were off again in their natural playground, looking for things to run away from them.

When he woke up he discovered himself to be hungry, and decided to shoot something. Although he was almost too sentimental about nature to kill anything, he was still old enough to have a good part of himself back in the earlier days, the days he had grown up in, when he'd loved to hunt and loved to call himself a hunter, and his idea of what a man was was tinted by the memory of the earlier feeling. He ate his sandwich first, which didn't go very far after he had given in to handing out bits and pieces of it to the dogs, and an apple, then set off in search of a squirrel (an animal which was of course in some way sacred but which Sam had little respect for—it having very little character, not like a fox or pheasant or raccoon or gopher or ground squirrel or a deer, badger, etc.). If he'd thought he could find a couple of chipmunks, he'd have gone after one of those.

Moving quietly among the trees was a problem for the dogs, who had no reverence for that kind of thing, and were confused by Sam, who kept shouting at them in a whisper and calling them idiots—knowing he was upset, but not knowing why. So Sam decided the only thing he could do was head for the nearest cornfield and walk around the trees next to it (where most of the squirrels lived) until they chased one up a tree, and then hope that it was a tree without holes in it and without leaves thick enough to hide him.

Almost the entire afternoon was spent doing this. The first three trees Sam had to give up on because one was so bushy with leaves that a man could hide up there until winter; the second had a hole, or at least what looked like one; and about the third he was sure his dogs were wrong. They found another and Sam circled the river birch again and again, knowing that if he could finally see it, the same thing that hid the squirrel from him would enable him to keep it in view while getting into a place where he'd have a shot—the squirrel, overconfident that he wasn't being seen (even when you were looking right at him). When he did see it he took out his pistol, but then decided (with deliberation) that it was a young squirrel, probably born in the summer; so he coaxed the dogs away and found another—shot this one and started a fire. He thought of roasting an apple, but ate it raw. He stripped the squirrel and cooked it on a stick. It was very tough and tasted wild. He nibbled at a couple of the flattened mushrooms and threw the rest to the dogs, who were expecting something better and waxed indignant. Even warmed up, they wouldn't eat them.

By now the sun was in a very calm position in the afternoon sky and being in its direct light was comfortable, the shade having a tiny edge of coolness. You could almost look at it. The noises in the woods were just that much more tranquil, nature being by then well fed and lazy, but not ready quite yet for forgetting the day. Sam sat by his fire until the sun came perching down orange on the horizon, admitted to himself that he was hungry and had not brought enough food with him from home, and began walking back to the car. Besides, he thought, he had a book to finish, and it would soon be too dark to read.

ARRIVING HOME AT 8:30, HE LET THE DOGS OUT OF THE CAR AND WALKED with them through the back yard. In the front were seven or eight

men talking and playing horseshoes. C was there among them.
This was unusual. Things were just not as they had been. Almost
no one came to trade any more—only to hire The Associate, and
then there was little work. People stayed home more. Sam took
a long drink of the whiskey and put the flask back in his coat
pocket. Then he rolled a cigarette. The house payments were being met, and sometimes double the amount was paid each month.
But still they owed, and Sam wondered if maybe he would never
be free from the burden of living in this kind of shoddy way.
Laughter from the front yard. C would be enjoying this, thought
Sam, knowing how the only time it seemed that his brother was
without worry and fear came when the Yard was full of people
who had come just to spend the time. He knew too that C was
thinking maybe of sending Cell somewhere for therapy, but that
he'd never say it out loud. He walked around into the Yard, and
was soon telling them all the only way to hunt squirrels.

When the last of these men had left, C remained in the Yard
with Sam, playing horseshoes. The metallic clinks and zings carried throughout town. They played under two yard lights put
up for the purpose many years ago by Rabbit, who was afraid
of someone being hit and paid for the electric current. At first
Sam had not wanted to play at night because it had seemed that
he was under examination, but later—two years after Baron's
unsuccessful attempt to enter school, when business had begun
to slide and there just wasn't that much doing—he'd learned that
no one paid any attention, and if they did, it was merely to look
out of their windows to see who was out there in the dark. One
could distinguish the four throws, allow a specific amount of time
for the walk to recover the shoes, a second or two for knocking
off the dirt (tiny, bell-like sounds), and then more sounds of the
shoes falling upon each other in the clay pit. Sam's dogs were under the porch. Upstairs, Cell had fallen asleep in the chair she had
pulled up to the window in order to watch. Glove had taken her
off to bed and gone up to the third floor with some cookies for his

brother. The brothers could hear only those throws that struck the stake or another shoe. Glove brought him something else too.

"WE NEED A COUPLE BIG JOBS," SAID C.

"Yep," said Sam.

"That are worth some money."

"Yep."

"You know, I'm beginning to think that money's more important than I thought before. A lot more."

"It can be useful." Sam missed his second chance for a ringer and went behind three more points. "What were you thinking of doing with it?"

"Sending The Baron away to a school where specialists could work with him. . . . Cell thinks we should."

"Oh," said Sam, moving forward one point.

"That, and I figured you were probably saving up for another dog, a special one that would be worth a king's ransom— one that would destroy everything, never sleep, and would bark continuously."

"Very funny," said Sam, handing him his second shoe. Both laughed. "Best out of five."

"Oh, by the way, Glove thinks Hutto doesn't have a dog's soul, but is inhabited by Bluebeard, and that's why he's so conscientious, because this is his last chance."

"Oh," said Sam.

"You know," said C, falling behind for the first time, seven to five, "sometimes when I talk to him—after a while, on the right kind of day—just listening to him, I even begin believing that, sure enough, old Bluebeard is walking around in the back yard."

"Maybe when you take The Baron they'll let you stay for a while with those specialists," said Sam, slightly elated despite himself at being ahead for two rounds. "Just to talk."

"No, seriously, that boy will be something someday."

"Maybe." Sam thought, I could have been something too, but

here I am, stuck with less and less hope of being able to leave . . .
of ever being more than I am now, which is nothing . . . but then
everyone could be something. It's just those that manage to keep
from getting stuck. But whose fault is that?

"Maybe we ought to look up James . . . no, Johnie Fotsom—
remember that guy who wrote all those cheap books about the old
man? Maybe there's some money—"

C stopped his pitch in mid-swing, and turned to his brother.
"No," he said. "We'll never do that. It might as well be blood
money. It's worse. Nothing that—"

"Go ahead and shoot. It was only a suggestion. Damn, but if it
isn't hard to tell what might make you upset . . . the oddest things,
just about everything is like that to you. Why can't you relax? You
remind me of Ernie."

"I wonder what ever happened to him," C said, completing a
double ringer—moving the talking away from himself.

"Probably left for the sunshine of California and all those
hard-nippled girls." Sam put one ringer on top of C's two. "Either that or he opened a beauty parlor, specializing in facials."
Sam's second ringer fell into place—nullifying C's. He was almost
laughing, he felt so happy, but C, who in a game with someone
better could and would do that maybe twenty times, thought
nothing of it and was already halfway down to the south pit.

"You know," he said, "I figured it all out—how it was."

"All what?"

"The old man, and how he was."

"You mean you don't believe he was a saint?"

C had sat down on the bench just out of the direct shine from
the yard lights. Sam kept throwing the shoes and walking back
and forth between the pits in the heavy yellow light, listening to
a voice that no one, unless they were right there, could see . . .
so that it looked as if there was no one there but Sam playing by
himself, and talking coming from out of the Yard itself, with him
answering it.

"The way it must have been was that somebody told Ansel when he was very little—and it was probably a woman, though not necessarily—that everything could be just the way he wanted it—that the world should run according to how he saw fit—"

"That doesn't explain—" began Sam, throwing the last of the four shoes and beginning to walk after them.

"Just wait. So anyway, he's very little, probably very lonely, his father and mother, from what he can tell (if indeed he knows them at all), are having a hard time of it, and he begins to believe that everything should be the way he wants it—that they should never fight. The misery and the smell of their crummy little house goes right on. His father beats his mother and he listens to the screams and the curses from the drinking . . ."

"Go on," said Sam, who, although very hungry, had had to pay a man money to be able to do what C was doing now—talk about their father—explain how so many people could love him and how especially his sons should because a son loves his father . . . but hates him. This is what I have come back for, thought Sam, to listen.

"So Ansel leaves school early, of course—what does anyone but the idle rich have to do with school?—and begins working in the mines. Imagine him thinking while he's down there that money—money can save him. He's young and looks things over very carefully and decides, as though in a great revelation, that his family has no money and is miserable, but that other families are not unhappy and have things to do—things that money can buy. So he mistakenly thinks that money, or rather the lack of it, is the root of misery, and that if he can just make enough, then it will go away. (And maybe from some position that looks at least partially true, except people who think like that can never make enough money.) So, imagine him down grubbing in the ground, pushing ore cars—believing he needs money—realizing that he is still dirt poor although he works hard six days a week and wakes up Monday morning in a secret terror. All of this and still clear back in his mind is the feeling that says things ought to be the way you want them."

Sam didn't play so well by himself, but C didn't notice; he cared very little about horseshoes (which he was good at, so good that occasionally people from other towns would come on Sunday afternoons in hopes that they could watch him play someone else very good) except for the company that went on during it, which many people felt he was not nearly so good at as Sam.

"So he thought to himself, Things shouldn't be like this— hell, he was probably only fifteen. Anyway, imagine him thinking this to himself, and working, with arms that could break a man's head open. And time . . . while he smolders in the ground. Then finally he comes up into the daylight and explodes, telling everyone what has been going on in his mind—that living is not so good, at least that much of it that he knows—that working in a mine is not so good—that watching friends killed by faulty supports and equipment is not so good. And of course his voice is like deep, controlled growling. And because the people he talks to work with him, eat the same food, live near him, they think, Yes, he's telling the truth. They want to listen to him."

"It shouldn't be like that," said Sam, paying less attention to the stake and more to his brother, who, he was beginning to realize, had thought everything out in much more detail than he had ever imagined—knowing C wasn't making it up as he went along.

"That it shouldn't be never matters. What does matter is that people wanted to hear him talk about how bad things were, enough to give him money for it. And so now he has money, more than before, and in order to keep up this way of life the only thing he must do is tell everyone how bad it is, even though from his point of view he is up walking around on the surface of the earth instead of down in it. And here you can begin hating him, and this is just the beginning."

Sam leaned against the light pole, and looked to anyone watching as though he were weary and resting, with his eyes studying the ground in the middle of the night, looking for something he had already given up on. Only that and the talking.

"And in the back of his head is this idea that things should be the way he wants them. He doesn't do that well as a speaker, mind you, but it's a far cry from grubbing in the ground. *Right away* he decides that he's of a much better class than the people who support him—because if they were smart, like him, they could've found a way out. Now this is an important part here, and it's easy for it to slip by unnoticed: see, first he was *told* everything should be the way he wanted it, and now, when he's better off than his parents were their whole lives and their parents before them, he thinks it's not good enough for him, and what he wants isn't respect, it's honor and an easier life."

Sam, who had been looking at the ground, lifted his head toward his brother, because for a moment he'd been startled, for a moment he'd not been listening to the words and had heard the voice, the intensity, the hatred, the pure religiousness—the voice of his father in the pulpit. He walked out of the light and sat down next to C and, without saying a word to him, helped him rescue his voice, and his hands no longer shook while he talked.

"He married a woman whom he had seen before wearing a red dress, and moved. He learned that much—most—of his parents' misery had been because of where they were living, and had they only known and moved a mere thirty miles, things could've been different. The homes were better. The streets were better, safe. The food was cheap, and better. Money was easy. Laws were not to hurt them. Loans were not from loan sharks. He took a job as a boiler man for a large corporation, smoked while working, and complained with his fellow workers about the short length of the afternoon coffee breaks. But he wanted more.

"Before, people had thought of him as special—as having had something, some spark of fire or genius. Now it wasn't like that.

Everyone liked him all right, but they didn't appreciate how intensely he could talk about life—how bad he could make it out to be. Even when they were striking for another five cents an hour, there was a humor behind it, because in a clutch everything was really good.

"Then of course Mom has you and later has me; so we begin walking around on the earth, looking a little like him, but mostly just a couple of kids.

"Naturally, the idea of the ministry occurs to him. What else could fulfill his life? What potential! He could be a prophet. Where else could he have so many people's undivided attention for so long? He went to churches everywhere. Every Sunday a different pastor would look out over his congregation, gathering them in, so to speak, to his spiritual aura before beginning to talk, and there, sitting close to the front row with eyes like polished metal disks, was a man whose intensity the people sitting beside him could tell was ready to erupt, small radiants of the energy creeping out of him and startling the comfort of their lives like a gush of cold air. The pastor would feel those eyes on him and would begin and then feel compelled because of this man and the demands he was making—Ansel studying him closely and taking out a small notebook and pen, pushing him on to excel—to try even those special orator tricks that pastors could do, that they had done maybe once or twice to move congregations and restore the community need for them. Calling forth these displays of emotion. Doing these and watching this man write down into a small pad with a pen, looking up as if to say, Fine, now what?

"After a half-hour into the hour sermon, many of these men would decide it was time to pull Ansel into their tow, and interrupt themselves, as though they were just aware that a newcomer was in their midst and wouldn't he introduce himself to the Sharon Center Baptist Church. This was a rash move, and many felt a little guilty about so embarrassing a man who'd done really nothing tangible against them or their groups. But these regrets were soon over when the steel-eyed man stood up, turned, and said, 'Ansel Easter,' clearly and powerfully, and sat back down with such perfect finality that there was nothing left to do but begin a hymn. . . . And he would wait afterwards too—to see how they talked standing on the steps of the church.

"This only took up his Sundays, mind you. He was still making money in the boiler room."

"But that doesn't explain—" began Sam.

"It will. Today they call that kind of person a socialpath."

"What does that mean?"

"Nothing. Really nothing. Just that's what they'd call him today—if they had him, but even—"

"Settle down," said Sam.

"So he began telling everyone that he had been a minister, and, as fate would have it, he was asked to be a guest minister in a sick preacher's church. Even people other than the regular congregation (and they were all there) came to listen. Ansel walked up to the pulpit from the back of the room, without smiling, stood up in front of them, and began: 'I am new to you, but I can tell you of the things I've seen . . . of all the things I know on God's earth. . . . I know that there is suffering . . . suffering beyond comprehension—terror beyond imagination . . . eternal suffering . . . crying that never ceases, and tears that run forever. There is death . . . death and dying . . . and more suffering for those poor abandoned left behind, abandoned on this earth . . . suffering beyond endurance. Unreasonable suffering . . . even in small babies . . . even they can be born into a house of misery. And I know of misery. . . . But I can tell you this misery, this suffering, this dying . . . and these deaths . . . are like joyous laughter compared to that eternal damnation of hell . . .'

"And his descriptions of the misery in hell, of the tortures and the fiends, made the small children cry. His stories of the tragic lives, the suffering of God-fearing families brought tears to the eyes of women. He cursed the men for living such soft lives when the service of God was the only real occupation on this earth worthy in His eyes. They listened and went home feeling as though they didn't want to talk with each other or go to a restaurant for Sunday dinner. Later, when the position became available, they hired him. They paid him. And he thought to himself, Things are the way I want them."

"Say," said Sam. "Don't mean to hurry you, but I'm awful hungry, and the only part I'm really interested in is how you explain that terrible stuff—how McQueen lost his hand in the fan—how Mrs. Bontrager happened to step in front of the car out by her mailbox—how George Frazer stumbled head first into the deep freeze where he worked, or the acid in Lester's eyes . . . how Terry came to be hung. How and why."

"You've got to wait," said C, and Sam knew he had to.

"He'd just begun to get used to respect, honor, money, and reverence. He began to feel safe, and WHAM the Depression came. Few people came to church. Those that came didn't even try to fill the collection plate. No one paid the electric bill in the parsonage. They expected him to be just like everyone else—suffering.

"He'd been cheated. He'd built his house and it had been smote down. Then the beatings began, when he would take us down into the basement and beat us senseless with black belts for petty things—sometimes imaginary—as though we'd been the instrument that had forced him to go scrabbling in the ground with the others for food. And so by working, stealing, begging, enduring like everyone else, we came through the Depression to here, and he was put back up into the pulpit.

"But he was different now. He wouldn't be cheated again. He would not fall again. He'd build himself such a high station that nothing could take him off. Things should be the way I want them, he thought.

"So he began preparing for that next inevitable Depression that never came, and he finally ceased to care even about that, and went on preparing himself not to meet God but to *be* Him. An entire day of self-righteousness wasn't enough. He began writing at night—volumes and volumes on the subject of himself and his blessedness. He fabricated stories that he thought should have happened—stories of his own grandeur. He found some disreputable, self-deprecated character who he claimed wrote down these accounts like a faithful biographer, and who even admitted to doing so, and had him publish them as books. Yet all in the supposed name of our Lord. A perfect choice, because Fotsom was a failure at everything he'd tried to do—but still vain, a perfect foil.

"Of course he never cared about us, or Mother. We were only extended parts of himself walking about in places where he couldn't be at once, continually bringing him in more reverence. When we finished mowing the grass in our yard we'd continue down the block, doing those of the old and infirm, without pay, and we were punished according to exactly how well he felt we carried this out, this reflection of him, and where we should have been better. The sanctimoniousness of those whippings in the basement. Remember, Sam? Remember how he used to say at the dinner table, 'Sam, I want to see you after dinner in the basement'? Then make everyone sit through dinner, eating, imagining in all clarity your screaming that would later come racing upstairs, and the sound of the leather striking skin again and again. Do you remember, Sam?"

"I remember," said Sam, "but it doesn't make any difference one way or another to remember it. Go on."

"So still this isn't enough—the grasp he has on his family—the almost incredible hold he has over the whole community—how everyone thinks of him as being just the closest thing to God—the slowly increasing literary place for him that causes an occasional reporter or feature writer to show up here. He wants something more, like an exaggerated, myth-like testimony to his benevolence. So he looks for something that will do this for him,

and finds Ernie. Do you remember Ernie, Sam? I know you remember Ernie. But do you remember what Ernie was like, Sam?
Do you remember what he was really like?"

"That's stupid," said Sam. "It's stupid to keep going all through
this stuff. Of course we remember Ernie. Of course we remember
what he was like."

"In a traveling carnival he found him, and like a slave bought
him from a man who had chased him with dogs down South and
had trapped him . . . three hundred dollars. And from the kitchen
window Mom saw him come walking back toward home with
this thing, with people from his community following him, thinking, What kind of man would befriend such a hideous creature
and live with it? How could anyone . . . ? The abuse, all the sub-
ordination, all the barriers to letting real, sweet life into her home
rose up at once and she left."

"If that's true, then why didn't she take us with her?"

"Maybe for fear that we would have denied her feelings and
abandoned her with nothing to help overshadow her memory of
all those years.

"And we were asked—told—to take little Ernie in. And he
lived with us, and we would find him torturing rats he'd caught,
with fire. Murdering our pets with jackknives. And when we'd try
to interfere or give the impression that all was not just as it should
be, we were taken down to the cellar for a cleansing experience
with the leather strap."

"But at the same time—"

"I know, the deaths and mutilations . . . I don't know if I can
explain those."

"What good is all this, any of it, if you can't explain those?"
The moon was becoming unveiled by the dissolving dark haze.

"I mean I can explain them, but I doubt if I could tell exactly
how it all worked.

". . . What I think is that there is more to heaven and earth
than anyone knows—that there are powers and possibilities that,

if understood, would seem so unnatural to the way we normally
think of living that their recognition would shatter even the basic
foundations we have. And somehow he got in the current of one
of these possibilities. In other words, he believed in his power
to have things the way he wanted them for so long and with
such intensity that the actual physical truth of it became real
as well."

"Give me an example of something else that works like that,"
said Sam.

"Hypnotism, I suppose, is one."

"Who believes in that?"

"Well, take Fotsom, for example. There's a guy nobody liked,
who had no feelings for decency, who had no talents and no prospects except to maybe go into politics. Still he has this ego that
kept telling him, in spite of the world or the way he was in it, that
he was special and should be respected. So along comes somebody
and makes him a writer without him ever pushing a pen."

"Well . . ." said Sam. "Not quite the same thing. What you're
saying is that voodoo, necromancy, and the black arts are moving forces."

"Not quite. I know it's awful close to it; but not quite. See,
the black arts require that certain rituals be met—for instance,
candles, words, lines, pieces of bone and snake teeth arranged in
a particular order, and then that order causes whatever happens
later to happen. That's what makes it superstition, because it's not
intelligible, exactly, how it works, even to the ones who believe
it. So at best it's a kind of controlled accident. What's different
about the old man, and what makes him worse, incidentally, is
that he wasn't acting through anything else, bones or teeth or
chants. He was in complete control. He knew, for instance, that
summer when he and Ernie were trying to collect money for the
church and McQueen, drunk, slapped his wife across the face (an
obvious affront to the goodly minister)—he knew that he could
make him reach his hand back behind him and into the fan. He

knew he could make him do it so quickly that more than just a finger would be lost. He knew he could do it, and that it would seem like an accident. And he did it.

"That was the first time he'd done something like that—the first time he'd realized that he could do it."

"You don't think he made a deal with the Devil, then?" asked Sam, growing very sleepy on top of his hunger, but nevertheless somewhat amazed at his being awake at all. All of the lights in the house were out now.

"No. I don't believe in the Devil. I don't believe in anything other than the terrible powers of men."

"It seems almost sick to think that way. I'd think that would be an indication something was wrong with you. Very wrong."

"Things have always been easier for you, Sam."

Sam knew he was right about that, and that was why he was sitting where he was, hungry and tired, able to listen, but not to empathize.

"You think too much," said Sam.

"Maybe. But that's not important. I'm almost finished anyway. Listen: Dad became more ruthless with his power. The horror of his crimes culminated with Ford and Bontrager, and after the body of Mrs. Peters was discovered lying half eaten by animals, a change took place in the minds of the people here. He'd overstepped himself. Instead of reverence, he elicited fear; instead of honor, hatred. No one came to his church. He was asked to leave. Rabbit's father had enough nerve to do that—to tell him that he had to leave. And then he realized that he'd been tricked again—that things were not as he wanted them, and that nothing could ever be done to return back to what it had been like before.

"Then he had this house built from the money he'd made from the books, as a triumphant rebuttal. But after going inside it, confronted with himself by himself, too weak to admit that he was lonely, that he was at last just a man and all the rest was just flourish, he did what there was left to do. He killed himself. Somehow he managed to talk Ernie—who would do anything for him—into chopping him up with the knife."

"What ever happened to Ernie?" asked Sam. "Did he ever come back here?"

"No. At least, not that I know of."

"I wonder."

"Probably dead by now. He probably got used to being around people and forgot that most everyone would shoot him the first chance they got, just because of the way he looked."

"I don't know," said Sam. "Somehow that doesn't sound quite right. But I'm hungry and tired and I've got to get something to eat." He got up and started to the house.

"Wait," said C. "Sam, what are we going to do?"

"About what?"

"Money. We need money."

"I don't know," said Sam, "but I don't think that's your problem—at least, not the important one."

"What?"

"Cell. What are you going to do about Cell?"

"Don't talk about that," said C. "Everything will be all right. Don't talk about that any more."

Sam went into the house, and from his room listened to his brother mounting the stairs. Outside the window, on the ground in back, he saw a square of faint light go out, the candle being blown out in The Baron's room. Upstairs, C's wife pretended that she was asleep, although she wasn't, only breathing as she thought she did when asleep. Those pills is wearing away, she thought after he had come in beside her, those pills he takes so that he won't have to come to bed with me . . . those pills Sam gives him from hate.

SHE HEARD SAM GET UP IN THE MORNING AND WENT OVER TO THE WINdow. Outside, the ground was not wet. There was no trace of nighttime ever having been there. Sam let his dogs out, then later walked himself down between the stands of junk. Them dogs . . . them dogs. Them dogs.

C woke up and looked to the window. He slipped from the bed and put his arm around her. He could see Sam walking toward his car.

"He's going to the woods," said Cell.

"I know," said C. "He shouldn't go. We need him here."

"No, we don't. We don't need him. We don't need him or his dogs—anything. We need peace. There is nothing peaceful in this house."

C tried to go back to sleep.

"I want to see Rabbit," said Sam. The clerk went far back into the bank and returned with Rabbit Wood, who studied his employees while he walked. It seemed to Sam that he would not be a bad man to work for, but maybe one that would make you nervous some of the time. They walked back into his office together.

Sam told him that every week he was going to send money— all of the money—to the bank from the plant. And this payroll check was to go toward the mortgage. Rabbit was surprised, but pleased, that Sam was beginning a real job. He asked him how he came by it, now when so many people were out of work— especially a good-paying job. Sam said that by chance someone had told him of a death, and because he'd gone right over they'd taken him rather than sift through the waiting file.

"There wasn't anything else to do," he said. "Keith and Jimmy Cassum started working two weeks ago. There just wasn't any work."

"It's better anyway," said Rabbit.

Sam asked how long it would take to pay off the loan. Rabbit added some figures with an adding machine on his desk, and told him three years, four months, one week, and three days— assuming his overtime would cancel being docked here and there. Sam looked outside, then back at Rabbit.

"How long if I worked five days a week?"

"Five!" said Rabbit. "That's full time. How much you going to keep yourself?"

"None."

"You'll need some," said Rabbit.

"I've got some. How much at full time?"

"From Harold Burdock?"

"How much at full time?"

Rabbit added and read the final figure from the tape. When he looked up, Sam was at the window, watching the leaves, the fall, blow along the ground.

"What are you going to do when it's over?" asked Rabbit.

"What's over?"

"Paying on the loan. You know, you should begin thinking about starting a life for yourself."

"I already have one, thank you."

"You know what I mean."

"There's no life here," said Sam. "All I want is to get away."

"Someone told me the other day—"

"Someone's always telling you something, Rabbit. I think maybe you're always asking someone."

Rabbit paid no attention. "—that Cell was getting worse."

"Could be."

"Well, if it's true, she needs help. Has C ever . . ."

"He won't talk about it."

"Then I think I better go see him."

"Do what you like." Sam began to leave, but had not escaped the office before Rabbit confessed that he was happy, very happy, that The Associate was disbanded. And now with Sam going to work tomorrow, a real job . . . well, he was sure that life would improve, and that even C might see, from him, that real work was the only way to make a living, and also recognize that Cell needed professional help—she and The Baron. Either that or they would both improve just because of the living situation being so

much better. They might even have all the junk taken away from
the Yard and the house painted. The telephone on his desk rang
and he answered it. The voice said that several dogs were outside
pestering the bank patrons. Rabbit said that Sam was coming and
hung up. By then Sam was almost through the front door and into
the street.

"SAM GOT A JOB," SAID GLOVE. "HE'S STARTING TO WORK TOMORROW
morning."

"Who told you that?" asked C.

"He did."

"Where did he say he was working?"

"At Ruttford."

"The plant?"

"Yep."

"Give Baron another piece of meat," said Cell. C put a round
hamburger on his plate, and he ate into it. He sat next to C. "I'll
bet he's lying," she added. "I'll bet he's lying."

"Maybe," said C, knowing that Sam would never have made
up something like that. "Well, I guess that's O.K." He'd considered working himself; but still, he wouldn't have imagined Sam
would ever think of it, let alone do it.

Baron finished his meat and put his fork down in the middle
of his empty plate, pointing directly out from him. Cell stared at
it, thinking, On purpose he's fixed it on me. "Make him move his
fork," she said. C reached over so that it pointed more toward
Glove. "Not that way," said Cell.

"Go on, you're excused," said C, taking the fork over onto
his own plate. Baron got down and went off into another room.
"Tomorrow morning?"

"Tomorrow morning," said Glove. "At least, that's what he
told me."

"Odd," said C.

"Very strange," said Glove.

"I'll bet he's lying," said Cell. "I'll bet he's lying."

"Those little books upstairs in the attic . . . in that trunk. What—"

"Those are your grandfather's."

"Ever read them?"

"Probably a good idea to leave them where they are. Why?"

"I just wondered."

"Baron will never know how to read," said Cell, thinking then that Baron's eyes were somewhere on her, slapping her face again and again with moth wings. He was back in the kitchen. "Make him stop," she said.

"Go on now, Baron," he said, and Baron left.

GLOVE

Sam had worked faithfully for three weeks and two days—
twenty-one days if he'd finish out the week. He reviewed this
fact to himself. The first week he'd worked a Saturday for the
overtime, but decided it wasn't a good practice. He needed the
whole weekend. The noise from the plant, even his own machine,
was almost inaudible, until it was shut off, and then the silence
was awesome and no one talked for at least five minutes as they
walked back to the lockers. His machine had a whine, punch, and
whir of its own that he often thought he heard when he woke up
in the morning, hidden within the clamor of the alarm. Indeed,
every machine, everything that made noises from metal, was a
related member of his own machine and carried its sound. He'd
not made quota. The plant foreman at first had said encouraging
words to him, and helped him get to know the other men. But he
obviously expected better and now had a way of making Sam feel
somewhere very out of place whenever they were together in a
group. And it wasn't just the work. "Don't let it get to you," he'd
been told. "Old Doberman just got his own way of feeling out the
new men. Morley started here last year—no, the year before. He
really got a hard time from him. But hell, now everything's good
between them. Even put him up for shop steward."

The five-minute bell rang through the plant. Sam slowed to
a near standstill, thinking only of the coming break and the time
when the machines would be shut off. Other workers, he'd noticed, who could make quota and more, who could earn nearly
thirty cents an hour more, depending on how fast they wanted to
push themselves, could keep working dead on through the bell,

clear up until twelve o'clock and still not be caught with a rivet or brake clamp in their machine when the plant shut down. Sam fingered in his pocket for a cigarette, found one, and fitted it into his mouth. He turned away from his machine and sat facing the EXIT door. Phil Doberman came up the aisle, laying the checks for last week beside the workers. Sam reached out for his, but Doberman put it beside the machine and looked at the cigarette.

"It isn't lit," shouted Sam over the noise, and smiled.

"No, it ain't," Doberman said, and walked down to the next worker.

Then the plant shut down. Even the high overhead lights wavered for a minute before coming back to full, silent illumination. Green light hovered close to the metal walls, let in by thick green plastic windows, two rows of eight-inch-square panes. Without talking, the workers filed out. The janitors came out from the shadows and began sweeping under the machines, working quickly because an unkempt area would be reported on the return of any worker and there were plenty of people who wanted work.

Most of the men went into the locker room, and the talking slowly started up, once the clamor of the louvered doors disturbed the silence. Sam and several others left the plant for the bar across the street. There was no regulation against it. The identifiable alkies were required to take a dose of Antabuse each morning before work. Sam ordered an infrared sandwich and a glass of beer. Snels Larson sat down beside him. Snels was, as Sam came to find out, twenty-eight, nine years younger than he, though Snels easily looked much older, so consistent were his mannerisms and speech.

"I'll tell you," he told Sam, "working in a place like that, I think a man dies a little every day. Every day he goes to work he dies just a little. It kills him . . ."

Sam turned to Snels, nearly astonished at the conversation, giving him his full attention.

"What I mean is that anyone, no matter how healthy they

are—no matter how high their goals are, how far up they can imagine themselves—no matter how tiny of a dream they have when they come here, each day they die a little. Each day is another that they put aside what they want to be for what they have to be." Then he stopped talking, as though there was no more to say.

"How long," asked Sam, "have you been here?"

"Seven years."

"I know this is going to sound funny, maybe, but why don't you get out—find a better way to live somewhere."

"Debts," said Snels. Their sandwiches came.

"What kind of debts? House debts?"

"Of course. Furniture, car, borrowed money here and there for vacations and whatnot. It adds up. I've had a couple OM-VI's."

"How much?"

"Maybe five thousand dollars."

"To whom?"

"The credit union."

"Well, in a couple years. You could save up, couldn't you?"

"You know, I could." Already half of his lunch gone without chewing. "I've got one of the best machines in the plant. Saturdays aren't that important to me any more since I lost my license. . . . I probably could."

"What would you like to do?"

"I don't know." Snels was no longer thinking about work. His mind was centered on his second sandwich, which had just arrived. The five-minute whistle blew from across the street. Long silence.

"You won't, will you?" said Sam.

"No. You know why? I'll tell you." Here he began talking very earnestly, looking insistently into Sam's eyes for any sign of his betraying their intimacy. He was telling one of his innermost secrets. "See, my old man worked here. He worked here for twenty-five years. And things are rotten now, but they were a lot worse for him. He had it rough. So, when I was young I used to give him a lot of shit—we all did, us kids—took advantage of him. Of course, he was kind of slow, stupid really, so it was partially his fault. But, God, I did some terrible things to that old man (was over forty when I was born) . . ." He paused and got off the stool, rinsing down the last bite. "And now . . . well, because he worked here . . . I don't know. It just seems like maybe if I keep working here where he did—that maybe it will pay him back for what I did."

Sam hadn't finished either part of his lunch. "You coming?" asked Snels.

"No," said Sam. "Tell old Dobe that I wasn't feeling good and so I went home."

"You going to tie one on?" asked Snels, and his eyes lit. "I'm game if . . ."

"No," said Sam. "Really. I don't feel so hot. I'm heading back up home. Must be a touch of flu. Go on now or you'll be late."

"Hope you get on better."

"I will. So long, Snels."

"Say," he said at the door. "Thanks for listenin', Sam."

"Sure."

The plant started up across the street and Larson shut the door. The bartender gave Sam another cold beer and took his warm one away.

"Say," said Sam, "you know anything about these payroll checks?"

"Some. I'll cash about half of 'em tonight."

"What's this for?" he asked, and pointed down at his check to a place that took ten dollars away from his total.

"Oh, that's for union dues."

"Oh," said Sam and put it back into his billfold. There was a table in back, and because they were alone now, Sam asked him if he played.

"Sure. But most games are kind of boring for me. Too much luck."

"What do you like to play?"

"Three-ball." The bartender filled up a glass for himself and they walked back to the table.

MERLE WOOD GUIDED HIS NEW LINCOLN CONTINENTAL SILENTLY into his son's driveway and turned it off. Rabbit saw him from the kitchen window, sitting and looking around before getting out, and was struck by how old he looked, as though gray death already had taken a swipe at him, leaving only the core. Rabbit saw him with a frightening objectivity: he was an old man, much thinner than he had been, with an almost comical—if you looked at him in just the right way—lean to the way he walked, the perfect confidence only the old can have, inching along in his judicial, appraising attitude. He rapped on the door briskly.

"Hi, Father. Come on in. Good to see you."

"Well, I happened to be in the neighborhood," he said slowly, looking up at the ceiling to see how well it blended with the pale yellow walls, inspecting the water fixtures and counter top, the refrigerator and the table in one great sweeping glance. "Place looks pretty good here."

"Well, thanks. Here, sit down. No, come on in the living room. It's more comfortable there. Eight's gone right now, but Fisher's around somewhere. Ester, why don't you see if you can find him and tell 'im his grandfather's here?"

"Hello, Ester."

"Hello, Merle. If you'll excuse me, I'll just rush off and see if I can't hunt up Fisher."

"Fine." He followed Rabbit into the living room. "Still got the old mirror, I see, and that ugly black chair."

"That was always your opinion. Let me show you the rest of the house. . . . Did you stop over and see Mother? She'd want to see you . . . if you were in town."

"I stopped over for a little while. I think I'll just sit here for a time. Driving that infernal car around tires me out. If you can lose some of that weight, you'd feel a lot better, and let me tell you, it's a danger when you get older . . . or so my doctor keeps telling me." He sat down in a chair where he could look outside. "Looks real nice here, Rabbit. What'd they hit you for it?"

"Well, I saved quite a few things from the old place."

"Lumber keeps getting more expensive."

"How about something to drink?"

"No, thanks. Say, what's going on over at the Easters' old house?"

"Sam and C and his wife and kids live there now."

"I heard that. Where's all the trash from?"

"It's a junk yard, I guess."

"You don't get over there too much, I don't suppose," Merle said, staring out the window abstractedly.

"Not too much."

"I imagine it was them, then, who went down to old Ansel's grave and pulled away some of those cement slabs."

"You go down there?"

"Earlier this morning I did."

". . . What for?"

"Oh, I just thought I'd like to look around. Thought I'd drive out and talk to Ray Millet, and then while I was there . . . I just sort of thought I'd walk down just for curiosity's sake. See, I don't know if I ever told you or not . . . Ah, nothing."

"What were you going to say?"

"Just that I always sort of liked that fellow Ansel Easter. He and I used to get together down there in the basement of his church and play shuffleboard and argue religion. I always figured he was as likable as they come. One of those few people who ever really listen to anything you said. Everyone felt that way about him . . . before. I was glad to see someone took some of that concrete away."

"Maybe it was one of them."

"Had to've been the both. A single man couldn't've lifted many of those pieces."

Fisher and Ester came in from the kitchen.

SAM'S ALARM WENT OFF AND HE HIT THE TOP OF IT TO MAKE IT STOP. He was very tired and lay in bed alternately opening one eye and then the other. Upstairs, the familiar noise of Cell secretly leaving the bed and walking over to the window came like whispering down through the ceiling. He shut both his eyes and then opened them, got out of bed, and dressed. Then he let the dogs in and gave them some grain and yelled at them softly, cursing them and pretending to kick J. B. Hutto, who in turn attacked his shoes. He had suggested to C that his wife spend some days with the dogs because they would help make for better chances to get out of the house and into the air. But C thought that was stupid and didn't really want her out of the house, or the dogs upstairs. Sam could hear her murmuring to herself and ushered the dogs out back into the Yard. There was a faint knock on his front door then, the one opening to the long hallway. It was so faint that he ignored it, but listened more closely nevertheless; Cell's voice rose nearly to a talking level when she saw the dogs, and the tapping returned.

Sam opened the door and found Glove standing on the other side of it.

"Come in," he said. "You want a cup of mocha java, chief? I was just about to make myself some. Instant, of course. You want some?" Glove looked troubled and came in. There was no place to sit because of clothes covering everything. "Just move whatever you need to on the floor and sit down. Now, you want some coffee or don't you?"

"Yes," said Glove, and smiled a little because his uncle made him feel like a man, but in a way he didn't have to be one or live up to anything. He found a small, long case next to his chair and picked it up. Inside were two pieces of a pool cue that would screw together in the middle with a yellow metal screw.

"Where'd you get this?" asked Glove.

"That! Oh, I won that from a bartender the other day. But it's a cheap one, and it cost me about twice what it's worth in drinks."

Glove put it together. Sam poured the hot water into the cups, on top of the crystals of coffee, then stirred them both and handed one to Glove. He took it and Sam noticed how large his hands were becoming.

"Now, what did you have on your mind?" asked Sam.

Glove took a drink of his coffee. "Is that talking upstairs—is that Mom?"

"Yep."

"She do that all the time?"

"Every morning. Other than that I don't know."

"Who's she whispering to?"

"Herself."

"Can she hear us down here?"

"I don't think so. Unless you were to start a fight or something. She hears the alarm go off in the morning."

Glove drank more coffee. "If I helped you move your stuff, would you change rooms—somewhere that's not right below her and Dad?"

"It doesn't bother me."

"But it wakes Mom up," said Glove.

"She wakes up anyway . . . during the night."

"Then this isn't the only time?"

"Well, no. Sometimes I wake up and hear her murmuring to herself upstairs, walking around in her bare feet. It's sad, Glove, I know. But there's nothing to be done. Is that what you wanted to talk about?"

"What I really wanted to know was if you couldn't get me a job where you work."

"You aren't old enough . . . even if there were jobs."

"I'm almost fourteen."

"That's what I mean. Anyway, what do you want a job for? You ought to appreciate not working. What a waste that being young is left to young people. They don't know what to do with it."

"Don't joke, Sam. We need money. We need money bad. You don't know how bad things are upstairs. Dad—I don't know what'll happen to him. And Mom's taken to going to the third floor and teasing The Baron sometimes when Dad and I are gone—sort of yelling at him and calling him names and threatening to do things to him. And pain."

"Come on," said Sam, "how do you know that if you aren't there? Cell wouldn't do that."

"I can tell," said Glove. "I can see it in Baron's eyes. I can tell by the way Mom looks at him at the table."

"It's not true," said Sam. "But if you wanted to make some money on your own, there's only two things I can think of. First, you could go look up that guy Johnie Fotsom, he used to write these . . ."

"No! The writer, you mean. That guy who Grandpa used for a name?"

"I know C thinks that's true, but—"

"No! I'd rather die before I'd have any of that money."

"You're awfully stuffy for your age, Glove, you know that? Maybe it's time you started seeing that some things of your father aren't so good, and maybe being just like him—in all ways, I mean—wouldn't be the best thing."

"Maybe," said Glove, and set down his coffee on the floor, half gone. "What was the other idea?"

"The other one is to comb through all the junk out in the Yard—sometime when C isn't there, of course—and pick out the old things—like that dresser in back with the marble stone on top, or the—"

"And sell it, is that what you mean?"

"Yes. Not around here. Gather it up and I'll drive you to Davenport or somewhere."

"No," said Glove.

"I suppose you feel the same way as your father does about that too."

"Listen," said Glove, but he would not look at Sam while he talked, because he was afraid he might cry. "Dad is kind of a symbol—I was telling The Baron about it the other day . . ."

"That's a big word, Glove. Do you know what that means? . . . Because I don't think people can be symbols."

"I looked it up. It means something that stands for or 'represents' something else. I know that Dad isn't as strong as you or Keith Kullisky; he's not strong at all, though he pretends to me he is. But he 'represents' to me everything that is good, everything that is kind. If I'm happy, I imagine I'm seeing things like Dad sees them. If I've done something good—something I think is good, like helping someone or aiming at a bird with my gun and then not shooting it—then I'm being like Dad. So if he doesn't make it"—and now Glove began to cry—"if things get so that he can't go on any more, and I know he's thought of killing himself because he talks to me about how that's the worst thing to ever think about . . . If that happens, if things are like that for him, then, then . . . then I guess it's my fault. And taking away pieces from his Yard—pieces that he would miss, because we know everything in it, even though not much trading goes on now—that's bad." Glove broke down into full tears and put his head in his hands.

"Shh, Glove, keep it down. Can you imagine what might go through your mother's head if she heard that? She might think it was me. She might think anything. Nothing's going to go wrong with C. Nothing that money would help—the kind of money you could make. If only he knew how you felt about him."

Glove mostly stopped crying. "Why won't anyone come to The Associate any more, Sam?"

"That's just the way things are now. There's a war going on in Asia, and because of that, people are out of work and money is hard to come by. Times are bad. Riots, tear gas, shootings, revolution. Not much of a time to go hire four people to do something for you."

"But it's not here in Ontarion. None of that stuff."

"No. Not most of it. But the feelings get here—the hating and suspicions. Fear can come in, and it's more dreadful sometimes because it stays longer and gets bottled up."

"Let's don't talk about the war, Sam."

"Why?"

"Because it's wrong. It's enough to hate it deep down inside of you, hate it and all those that make it and support it and let it go on."

"O.K."

Glove picked up his coffee again, and drank some more of it. Sam was beginning to glance back and forth at his clock. He would be late for work, surely. They sat in silence. Glove took apart the cue, put it back together, and looked down it to be sure it was straight, several times. Sam got up and put on his coat. "I'll tell you, chief," he said, "if you want to do something, you can take special care of your brother. I think that he might be able to pull something off, if it just got clear in his head what was wrong and what should be done. Some kind of magic."

"I wanted to talk about that too," said Glove.

"About magic? I don't know much. What I do know I learned from an old hag that lived in a rotten tree stump, so everything she said is—"

"The Baron. I was wondering if you might be able to keep him down here, sort of secret."

"Down here? In this room?"

"I think Mom is trying to get him put away somewhere—in a place."

"Down here?"

"O.K., forget it," said Glove.

Sam opened the door and stepped halfway through the opening into the hallway. Cell was talking louder to herself, but still whispering.

"You want that?" asked Sam.

"This cue?"

"Sure. It's yours. Keep it. I've got to run off now."

"O.K., Sam. Thanks." Glove's eyes were shining now as he screwed the cue back together and sighted it to make sure it was straight, now that it was his. Sam went down the hall and out the front door. The first snowfall. Slush and wind. I know what is wrong, decided Sam, kicking the mud from his shoes every half-dozen steps; things need to be worse. He remembered his father owning an automobile that was like a metallic plague. He'd filled the trunk with broken parts and began putting them in the back seat, the weight causing it to bottom out on railroad tracks. Yet still it remained a lemon and continued blowing gaskets and hoses, all the more because of the extra weight, until one morning it flew to pieces and the flywheel came wandering up through the flywheel casing, up through the floor, past Ansel's right elbow, and through the roof. The transmission fell out onto the street with a big clatter, followed shortly by the drive shaft. Only then could he be free of it—could he walk away from it and think for the last time, You will never do that to me again.

TWO YEARS PASSED.

EVEN IN THE SNOW, C EASTER, NOW WITH HIS OLDER BOY FIFTEEN YEARS old, with such an overwhelming sense of place that being in his Yard was like being also invisible, liked to sit on the porch. Today his son sat with him. The sun on their faces was warm. The snow was melting from the floorboards and dripping into puddles. Drops of water fell in dreamy runs from the overhead porch roof, down from the clogged eave drain, creating a magical curtain between their place and the outside.

"It's nice," said Glove. "Maybe we ought to try to bring The Baron out here."

"That's what you thought last time—last summer. Remember?"

"Maybe summer isn't his time of year."

"Maybe not. I doubt if winter is, though."

"He's older now."

"Your mother wouldn't be able to get over it if he started bellowing again."

"You're probably right," said Glove.

C reached back behind him to strike a match on the side of the house in order to relight his pipe. So turned, he could clearly see his second son standing directly behind them, separated by a window.

"That kid is sure quiet," said C. Glove turned around and waved to Baron, who waved back and smiled. Glove motioned with his hand for him to come outside. Baron looked confused and absently frightened. It was clear, however, that he loved his brother and would do everything in his power to do what he wanted; but perhaps this was too much. C watched him, puffing contentedly on his pipe. Today, he felt, despite whatever, would be a good day. "If he comes," he said quietly to Glove, "remember not to excite him. If he makes it out here, remember not to get him talking."

Baron had come around to the door and was looking out at Glove and then at the water falling from the roof.

"He won't come unless he knows he can handle it."

"He might," said C, "for you. He might try and then whatever it is'll catch up with him."

"No. It's the water falling that'll help him," said Glove. "He's watching now to see if it is enough."

"How do you know—" But C didn't finish. Baron had opened the front door and pushed the screen aside, but still stood inside.

"He's coming," said Glove. "He's going to come."

"Don't talk," said C. "He's got a right not to be pressured."

Baron stepped out onto the porch, very slowly, his wild eyes looking everywhere at once, flashing back and forth. Both ends of the porch, Glove could see, terrified him. "Just look ahead," said Glove. "Just look out through the water. Everything's cool." He smiled and The Baron smiled. The word "cool" used like that was a joke between them. Baron became more comfortable. He walked over between them. C got up from his rocking chair and offered it to him. Baron didn't move.

"He won't take your chair," said Glove. "Here, sit on this, Baron." And he pushed over an orange crate that up until several seconds before had been filled with galvanized pipe fittings and couplings and elbows. Baron set it under him as though it were a box of unexploded dynamite, interlocked his hands, and began to smile, looking out through the falling water.

"Why?" asked C to Glove.

"It's easy. He just doesn't like to be 'outside.' He's fine as long as there's something between him—like a window or, in this case, dripping water—and everything else. That's why he was afraid to look out to the sides. There's nothing there to protect him."

"Protect him from what?"

"I don't know. It's just too much, being there in the open."

C looked over at his younger son. Baron turned his head to him and he was still smiling, sitting there as a child might who had climbed to the highest place on the barn and, once there, sat absolutely still, being proud of himself but afraid to move even an inch. Then C began to relax. There was plenty of snow on top of the house and the water supply, at least for the day, might as well be considered inexhaustible. Baron looked over at Glove and watched him whittling on a stick.

"Here," said C. He took his own pocket knife out of his pocket and handed it to Baron, then handed him a large stick. Baron took it, looked carefully at C, made his own legs cross in the

way his father's did, and began to work on the stick, looking
over every once in a while to see if his project was looking like
his brother's.

"Here comes the banker," said Glove, and, like magic, Rabbit
appeared, picking his way through the muddy Yard distastefully.
C looked out and wondered for a moment if he shouldn't take
Baron back inside, but then thought, No, I will sit here with
my sons.

Rabbit came up the steps and rain ran off his hat down onto
his big corduroy overcoat. "Hello, C, Glover, Baron. What's up,
Baron?" he asked.

Baron looked as if he was beginning to open his mouth, but
Glove quickly shot his hand out in front of his brother's face and
he stayed quiet.

"You can talk to him," said C, "but don't ask him any direct
questions."

"O.K. Sorry, Baron. Sometimes a man this fat can be fat-head-
ed too." Baron smiled at him, and proudly went back to working
on his stick, sitting like his father. Rabbit went inside and brought
out a chair. "You still got a pop machine, C?" he asked. C nodded
his head. "Be right back," said Rabbit, and disappeared.

C saw a car pull up in front of the Yard and two men get out.
He put on his hat and left the porch. Rabbit came out with a soda
and made to sit in C's rocking chair, but was challenged by Baron
frowning at him, so he used the chair he'd brought from inside.

"C got a customer?"

"I don't know yet," said Glove. "Maybe he just wants to look
around. But he'll tell me."

"Do you have some signals worked out?"

"Yep. Dad wanted for me to be able to learn about trading,
especially about people's faces. So, for instance, if he lifts his hat
off his head and scratches his hair like he's befuddled, that means
that the person has something in mind that he wants. Then I'm
supposed to look in his face for what gave it away to Dad."

"But it's too far away to even tell who it is . . . except I haven't seen that car before, and I don't think I know those people."

"Dad says you've got the best eyes of anyone he ever knew."

"Maybe," said Rabbit, and finished the last corner of his soda. "Great day . . . Seems to me, though, that the best eyes would be—"

"There," interrupted Glove, "see?"

"Sure enough. He took his hat off and scratched his head. That means what?"

"It means they want something."

"Fascinating. But the best eyes should be useful for something. I don't do anything more with mine than you do, or Baron does. So what better are they? None. Why would he give the sign when you're too far away to see their faces and learn?"

"Probably because he knows we're watching, because Baron's out here, and he's showing off."

"C? Showing off?"

"Yep," said Glove, and looked proudly out through the water at his father, who moved closer into the Yard with the two men. "There isn't anyone better than Dad. When he comes across what they're really after, he'll light his pipe—whether it needs it or not."

"Hmmm. You or your brother want a bottle of pop?"

"Nope."

"I'll be right back."

"Hurry up, or you'll miss—"

"I'll be right back." And he was, with a different brand of pop, as though somewhat dissatisfied with the first one. He drank half of the new, it seemed to Glove, in less time than it would take to pour the same amount out on the ground, and only checked himself then because he wanted to save it.

"Your mother at home, Glover?"

"She's asleep. Look, they're going over to that brass bed. They can't want that."

"Eight—you know Eight?"

"Sure, I know Eight. She's got a birthday sometime this week, she told me."

"Hmmm. Well, we're going to have a surprise birthday party for her, and I wanted you to come if you could make it."

"When?"

"Next Saturday . . . in the afternoon, around two thirty. Her mother will take her shopping."

"O.K. If Dad doesn't have anything for me to do that day. Or Sam."

"How's Sam doing?"

"He's good, I guess. We never see him any more."

"That's because he's got a life of his own to put together, Glover. He's got responsibilities."

"Dad said that that's because he has a job, and not a very good one either. He says that that's what happens when you have a job, you can't even stand to be at home at night and the only thing you want to do is drink beer."

"But you don't feel that way, do you, Glover?"

"I don't—Look at those two guys."

They had picked up the bed and were carrying it over to their car.

"I guess you were wrong about them not wanting that bed."

"No. If they'd wanted it, Dad would have lit his pipe. They don't want that bed, but they're sure trying to use it to their advantage."

C was walking along behind them.

"Strange," said Rabbit. "You haven't seen Keith Kullisky, have you? Or that scoundrel Jimmy Cassum?"

"No. Why?"

"Because they both quit their jobs, and I was wondering if they'd been over here bothering your father and Sam about starting up that Associate again . . . just making trouble for you."

"There, see!" said Glove.

The men were carrying the bed back again to where it had

been. They set it down and walked away from it, over toward several sinks and bathtubs. Still C didn't light his pipe.

"Your mother's taking a nap, right after lunch. It's not good, you know, to sleep right after eating meat, unless you just had soup, or egg sandwiches, or something."

"We didn't eat any lunch today," said Glove, and handed a larger stick to the banker for him to hand to Baron, whose piece had almost disappeared except for a very small, pointed chunk. The rest had been transformed into little curls of wood. Rabbit gave it to him, and he smiled and took it, first putting the stub into his pocket. Rabbit could think of nothing to say to him that wasn't a direct question.

"Does Baron read?" he asked Glove.

"No. Not yet, at least."

"Do you think he could come to the party too?" The rest of his pop was gone in a sort of liquid bite.

"No. This is the first time he's ever been outside . . . without a blindfold."

"Why did you quit the Scouts?"

"Just decided I'd rather be here instead of doing those kinds of things."

"With your father."

"And Baron. We get on real well."

"It seems so odd, talking about him while he's right here. But then I guess he can't really hear, or understand."

"Sure he does. Look at him."

Rabbit did and then said, "Eegad, you're right. Probably makes you want to be mealy-mouthed."

Baron started laughing and almost dropped his new stick.

"What's he laughing about?"

"The phrase 'mealy-mouthed.' He thinks it's funny. There it is! See. They're after that old metal bed frame. Boy, are they taking their time. They must believe that old story too."

"What old story?"

"That bed used to belong to Hollie Purdue and, like everyone knows, she had a fortune stashed away in her house and took it out and looked at it every night before going to bed."

"How does everyone know that?"

"How? Because she never went anywhere, and even had Old Man Bean delivering the groceries. Of course she had a lot of money tucked away."

"You've been talking to Sam. Say, it isn't good, going all day without food. Do you do that often? Maybe your mother's not getting enough nutrients. They're walking away from the bed." It was true; they were. "I guess they don't want it after all, despite the treasure."

"They want it," said Glove. "They're just pretending."

"What's the signal?"

"If they want it a lot, some, or hardly at all."

"Then C might not make a trade."

"He'll make one. It's just a matter of what he can get for it."

"You mean they think there really is a treasure in that old bed?"

"I guess so. Sam thought that there was too . . . but it only turned out to be a little over five dollars in nickels and dimes."

"So it was true."

"Still is, sort of," said Glove. "Sam and C fixed it so that the only part of the posts that will come open will have a five-dollar bill, too far down to grab, though."

"You mean—"

"There, see." Glove pointed excitedly, quickly withdrawing his hand when all three in the Yard turned their heads. The two had split up, one staying with C, the other walking back in the general direction of the bed, poking along and stopping here and there, picking up this and that. The three on the porch said nothing and watched as he carefully pulled at the post of the bed, hidden from C's view because his friend had him conveniently turned around in the opposite direction looking over something else. The top of the post came off and he looked down into it, then put it back and walked away. Though the three on the porch knew he would make some sign to his friend, they didn't see it, even Rabbit, so they must have had some kind of word code.

"Your mother . . . is she still acting funny?"

"No. Not really." .

"How come Baron's outside—for the first time?"

"Because nobody asked him to try before . . . when it was raining or water was running down, that's all. Maybe too, he knows more what's possible for him, because of growing up."

"Don't you think he'd be better . . ."

"What?"

"Nothing. Look, they're coming back to the bed." They did and carried it to the car. Then they began bringing things out of the trunk and back seat . . . things to trade. But even from the porch they could see C didn't like the trades, and was ridiculing them by laughing and putting his hands to his head. Glove handed Rabbit another stick, and he said, "Here," as he handed the stuff to Baron, who had during this time changed his legs to look like his brother's . . . more spread out. The three men were walking toward the house. C eventually came to remain on the porch. The other two went inside.

"How's everything?" asked C.

"Good," said Rabbit, "despite the fact that the country seems to be going bankrupt over this war . . . financially and morally."

"And emotionally," said C.

"What are they doing in there?"

"Calling a friend. You got something on your mind, coming over here on a muddy day?"

"Well, yes and maybe. I've invited Glove to Eight's birthday party. That's something, isn't it?"

"That's something."

Then the two strangers (Rabbit had not seen them before, at least, but guessed they lived without peace or contentment in barely heated, dim, grim, tight little homes) came out, shook hands with C and his fat friend, and fled off into the Yard, wanting to get back to their prize. Soon, from far away down South Street came a pickup, a valiant soldier of a vehicle ready to begin for the third time around the odometer should it be demanded, without any more complaint than the clankings and clatterings. It stopped and a man came out of it to help the other two heave the bed and five-dollar bill into the back. Then, loaded with three temporarily wealthy citizens, prodded by a single long backfire, a kind of old engine-horse fart, they departed, heading back up South Street toward some unknown, sorrowful destination.

"Think it was worth it?" asked Rabbit.

"I don't know. I've got the keys. Let's have a look." Both adjusted their hats, braved the water, and were back down into the mud. Glove rose to follow them, but C asked him to stay with his brother. Rabbit walked behind C, who knew a less troublesome way to the road and his new automobile. The motor started. C was sure the compression was good and the oil consumption would be low. Rabbit was less sure, knew little about engines, but was sure that merely starting one didn't imply all kinds of other good things. Both soon became lost for a while in investigating the paper rubbish in the glove compartment, and, like children, they unfolded letters and tried to piece together connections and plot lines from calendars with dates circled, pictures, road maps with routes drawn in, and match-book covers with names of establishments.

"Where's the title?" Rabbit finally asked, after they'd both been led to the fanciful conclusion that the car had been owned by a man, or men, who went about their business in lurking darkness and mortgaged young bathing beauties into lives of sin and transit prostitution, blackmailed several jewel thieves in another country next to the border, and cut the throat of a friend of theirs who had betrayed them to an officer of the law whom they had to bribe for a sum of $53.19, for which they were given a receipt signed by the traffic court to cover up.

"I haven't got one," said C.

"Then when they find out that—"

"I know," said C. "They were in such a hurry they forgot about that."

"They'll be back."

"Probably."

"But this is still legally theirs. They haven't signed anything."

"I know. But I never intended on keeping it anyway. I don't need a car."

"I don't know, C. You're a good man and all . . . Of course it's a terrible thing to be, well, almost cheated out of your car, along with a carload of junk, and made a fool of too—and to have to come back again and admit it and demand to have your broken-down thing back again, now that the treasure didn't make better things possible—but still I think you're a little foolish too. It's all a game to you . . . but then Sam's here and—"

"Just once I wish you could stop trying to teach me how to live. O.K., you can't. I just wish to God that someday we could . . ." Here C stopped and looked very old. Rabbit, who was younger by one year, looked away.

"What was it you came over here for, Rabbit?"

They got out of the car. The time to be back in the world had come and it would be a sacrilege to stay sitting in that same place where they had, with maps and pictures and letters, eloped for a moment.

"There's a clinic," said Rabbit. "A free clinic that's been set up by the federal government. It has professionals—people who can help. Send Cell there. We can take her tomorrow . . . voluntary commitment. She can leave whenever she wants. No one will abuse her. Tomorrow. Let's take her, C."

"Maybe," said C, "we could take Baron there. She'd like us to take him away. But think, if he was cured, then he'd be a big, stupid kid, twelve years old, not knowing how to read, anything about dealing in the world, and most of all unprotected by the unawareness that shields him now. Why should we want to do that?"

"It's not for us to decide," said Rabbit, ". . . only our duty to make them normal—to make them right. Of course, we have no way of knowing if right is right, or if it isn't."

"Forget it."

"Anyway, Baron doesn't concern me. When I fall asleep at night, it isn't him that comes stalking out from the corners to chase me back into the bedroom. Your wife, C, is getting worse. She may become dangerous to herself, to you."

"I'd think with a family of your own you could keep mine out of your dreams."

"So what! Do I apologize for that? Your wife is mad, C."

"No. She's coming out of it, I think. I think she's merely worried about Baron."

"She's not 'merely worried,' C."

"You don't know," said C. Then a terrible scream cut the air again and again and again. C and Rabbit ran for the house. On the porch Baron stood huddled over, shaking, bewildered and frightened, next to the awesome open side of the porch, his knife lying on the floor in front of his box. Glove was taking his mother off the outside wall of the house, where she'd backed up, screaming, to protect herself. She must have been coming out toward the front door to check on C or to watch the melting snow, saw Glove sitting there, and wanted to ask him through the screen if it wasn't too chilly. Baron, Outside, Knife. Something in these three things frightened her. Perhaps one, or all three, or simply the rapid succession with which she'd been confronted with them. But something was wrong.

Glove had taken his mother back in the house and upstairs before they reached the porch. C mounted the steps and stopped. He took in everything and motioned with his hand for Rabbit to come slowly. The Baron was very frightened and tears were streaming down his face, but behind all that was a rock-bottom terror, an unknowing that was wildly searching about for a handle, a crowbar of some kind to pry into the face of the situation and wreck and destroy and finalize . . . something that might well be done for him by his other mind. He was about to do something, had not yet decided what it would be, but was having his unconscious mind made up for him quickly. And C sought in himself for a way of not showing any emotion other than normal-living serenity (that he believed he'd learned from Glove) and so mesmerizing Baron away from his fears. Don't jump, Baron, he could hear his mind screaming, but, "Why don't you go get the three of us some soda pop, Rabbit? That sun's got some heat behind it," he said.

"Three sodas . . . coming up . . . or out, that is," Rabbit responded and disappeared inside.

C sat down in his rocking chair and rocked several times, then leaned forward and picked up his knife from the wooden floor, and was immediately afraid that he should have let it lie, that it might be a symbol to Baron of the experience before (which was why he'd dropped it). But C's back was to him and Baron could not see the changing expression of his face as he regretted picking it up, accepted that it was done, considered, and resolved that his youngest son was not an idiot, that he would not be fooled. Baron knew that what had happened had happened and he knew C knew. Furthermore, he knew Rabbit knew and he knew C was going to try to help him. So with everything out in the open, what C had to do was help Baron ignore it.

Rabbit came back to the porch, carrying the sodas. He stopped the screen door from banging with his foot, then let it fall back. He handed one to C and then pushed one at The Baron, who was no doubt overwhelmed at the size of his hands (making the twelve-ounce bottle of carbonated orange look like a kind of reproduction in miniature, made for sitting next to two other miniatures with shining hard skin and unflagging gazes sitting at the table in the dollhouse). He accepted it and Rabbit went over and sat in his own chair.

C held up the knife between two fingers and, waving it at Rabbit as though to make a point, said, "Those winter spirits, Rabbit. They're epicene, aren't they?"

"The winter spirits," said Rabbit thoughtfully, fixing his voice and face into a half-hum, as though it were very enjoyable—such a question, just thinking about it. "You know, I'm not sure, not sure at all. If we had been smart, we would have looked very carefully today to see."

"You're right. There were a lot out today, I bet. A perfect day for them." They took long, pleasurable drinks of their pop, letting the liquid swish around in their satisfied mouths before swallowing.

"Plenty of them."

Baron came over to his crate and sat down, very timidly. But during that next half-hour, as he heard about the winter spirits and how they were different from spring spirits in both size and color, and how they not only couldn't swim but, according to Rabbit, were deathly afraid of the water and had phrases like "water over your head" to mean bad things and how the snow covered them up as they slept and were angry at that but glad when the sun melted it away—so long as they didn't get wet—and on warm days in winter would come from everywhere together to high ground and dance and rejoice long into the night, and were often seen staggering home through the woods, saying foolish things and falling down occasionally, or singing, and what an epicene was—he relaxed, drank his orange pop, and settled back for an afternoon on the porch, sitting on the porch with the men, his legs looking like his father's, the water falling in front. After a while Glove came back and listened too. As it was getting dark, C told the boys to go back inside where it was warm.

"I tell you, C, you've got to take her down there to that clinic. Dr. Stephenson is there, and I found out that he—"

Very long pause.

"You know why I won't, Rabbit? Because I need her. Even the way she is, I need her, and him—Baron—I need him too. And we'll either get through it together, here with the Yard, or go down together. I have no respect for professionals when it comes to my family."

"Baron could learn to read at least. You could teach him that and he could have an outlet for some of his time."

"He's all right the way he is. He doesn't need to read."

"He probably couldn't learn anyway, I don't suppose." He stood up. "I'll be going, C."

"Thanks, Rabbit, for coming over."

"O.K." And off he went.

The air was turning cold, and heavy blankets of temperature were being laid over again and again, each time sending a tiny shiver, steadily increasing in intensity, through him. The images in C's mind, as he tried to gather them together, became metallic. He got up and turned to go back inside, unaware of Glove moving quickly away from the door and down the hall from where he'd been listening.

SAM WOKE UP BEFORE HIS ALARM, AND SHUT IT OFF. IN DEATHLY SILENCE he dressed and put water on to boil. The flame came on automatically, burning with a faint hiss and a flicker of funereal light on the dark walls. Looking through the window, he could see nothing of the outside, only his tired reflection asking him how long this kind of thing was going to go on. The atrophy, the desperation, and the despair. He rescued the water, mixed coffee, and dry-swallowed half a tablet of mild speed. He took the coffee back to his bed and the window and waited for the light part of morning. But before it came he'd decided not to go to the factory this day or ever again. Things will get worse, he thought, but then something will happen. He put on several layers of clothes and slipped outside, stole with his dogs through the Yard, and drove out to Meyer's cabin (a little hunting hut near the river owned by a lawyer who almost never found time to be there, knew that an access was available through an unlatched window to the back, but didn't care as long as his friends, the trespassers, kept order and replenished his wood supply) with J. B. Hutto in the front seat and the other two in the back.

It was in this cabin, laying fire to the not altogether dry wood while the dogs familiarized themselves with square acres of ground, that he realized that he was, essentially and for all practical purposes of useful definition, a worthless vagabond—a bum continually believing that his prospects were better than his circumstances, ability, or even his ambition. Sounds of woodpecking began, and he looked out, hoping, though he knew it not likely, that he might see a pileated woodpecker. He began a fire in the stove, and loved the smell. The cabin warmed quickly. He fried several eggs, which he'd brought with him, and found a bottle of bourbon.

Sam made voyages out into the wilderness and down along the river, returning only as the cold air began to be an irritation.

There is much that is dead and sleeping in winter—like rows of bees filed away in reed weeds, back to back—but much that isn't. Those things which are not sleeping take little pleasure in living, and merely do it. Of course the sleeping ones take no pleasure either, but they are less aware. Those who love winter are naive. Terrible things happen in winter. Everything hurts more in the cold. Tears freeze. Sounds have no compassion. Winds bite. The rough edges of crusted snow cut deep into ankles. How, wondered Sam, in all of this, can anything good happen? But still, to be outside in it is better than being inside.

In the late afternoon, Sam was walking back with an armload of wood when J. B. Hutto began to bark more than usual, and, arriving back at the hut, he could see another car parked down the hill next to his own. Wood in hand, he passed into the warmth of the cabin and also the presence of Abbot Meyer, looking all and more of his sixty-one years.

"'lo, Abbot."

"Morning, Sam." Meyer was drinking from a small glass of whiskey and snow.

"Hope you don't mind—"

"Forget it. I came out here, in fact, to find you. C told me you might be out here. We called out to the plant and I guess—"

"I quit."

"—you quit. So C thought—since the dogs were gone—and that you didn't care too much for the cold air—that you'd be here." Meyer's hand trembled as he raised the glass to his lips.

"Good guess," said Sam and sat down across from him on one of the wicker-bottomed chairs, a crude, square oak table between them with the bottle, Sam's one-third-filled glass, and a hunting knife on its top. Meyer shivered a little, as though his last drink had been a little over-anticipated and a little too large, as if a momentary sickness had passed down his throat and into his stomach, where it lay and made one tearing belch and stopped. He poured from the bottle without bothering to go for more snow. Sadly, with resolve, he looked down into the grain of the wood.

"I'm going to kill someone," he said.

"Got anyone in mind?" asked Sam, and moved the hunting knife to the other end of the table.

"I'm not joking," said Meyer. "I want to kill someone, only I want you to kill him for me."

"Come on," said Sam, "if you don't want me out here, just say so. That's crazy, Abbot. That's stupid."

"I didn't think you'd do it."

"Do what? Listen, Meyer, are you serious?"

"It's this simple," he said, his voice shaking slightly and faltering on the words, the sounds a man makes when he has made up his mind only after his feelings have hammered away at it, until it was either be won over, give in, act them out, and release them, or let them rip him apart. An ancient remedy for headaches is to find a bald woman in the dark of the moon, place your head against hers while she kneels on a rock and prays to make you well . . . and let her have it. Meyer murmured something Sam couldn't make out, then went on: ". . . kill Harold Burdock."

"Wait a minute, Meyer."

"Sam, I'm going to kill him. I'll do it one way or another. If I hang for it—if I have to, I will. One way or the other . . ."

"I admit he's not the kind of guy you would want for a roommate or—"

"I'll kill him," he said, that cold, that still.

"What's he ever done to you?"

"He's been with my daughter. He has defiled Judith."

"I'm sorry about that. I mean, I'm sorry for anyone to have to be that close to Burdock—she being very young too—but, really, that kind of thing happens all the time."

But his talking might as well have been the whistling of the wind, a background melody for the taking place of Meyer's own thoughts. He didn't listen; and continued, with great deliberation and precision, nearly ritualistic hand gestures on the top of the table.

"I don't ask you to be like me in your feelings. I won't convince you that you should. I don't care that you even see mine for what they are, foul, ugly, without any chance of redemption. All I ask is that you believe that this man"—and here there was a pause, as though Meyer were trying to get his breathing straightened out—"this Harold Burdock has taken my Judith, a young girl just working for the first time on her own, living in her apartment, fixing her meals, doing her laundry—he has taken her with him in his truck cab for weekends, performed on her animal, brutal acts, pictures of her hung up above the windows. He has frightened her, and I say to him, 'Stop, you must stop . . . I beg you to stop, she is frightened of you. She is frightened that if she does not do what you ask—if you are angry—then you will haul her out into the country and torture her, beat her, and make her do it again and again, in tears and screaming to never give you up, never deny you.'

"And to this he laughs. He says, 'I know your kind, you fancy lawyers, you men with money and grand morals. I care this for you,' and spits on me. And I've thought, What shall I do and what shall I do and what shall I do? and the anger mounted and even when I saw that I could protect her from him, take her away where he can never find her, still there's the memory, there's the spitting and the look of my youngest daughter—her face—telling me what he had done . . . the picture of him doing it. And there I decide, Yes, there is something. I will kill him."

Sam thought back, remembering his investigation of Becky, the satisfied look on Burdock's face when in the notebook he—Sam—forced his mind away from the memory. "What do you want with *me*, Abbot? You want me to talk you out of it or what?"

"No. You—your Associate. I want you to kill him for me."

"Forget it."

"No. I have money. I care nothing about money. You can have it all—only what I need to live—for Judith and Benji. Seventy-five thousand dollars. I'll give it to you."

"God, no, Meyer. Besides, if C ever found out—"

"C agreed."

"What!"

"C agreed. Jimmy Cassum agreed. There's only you and Keith Kullisky."

"Let's go back into town," said Sam, and they left the cabin.

GLOVE HAD TAUGHT HIMSELF TO WAKE WITHIN A HALF-HOUR OF ANY decided time. Two A.M. he was up. The winter, he noticed, was drying the house, and even in the moonlight he could see dust motes slowly falling from the ceiling, but so many and so slow that they were more like the light itself. The floor was cold and he put on several coats of socks. Heavy, soft clothes—clothes that would not rustle or rasp. Clothes for moving unsuspected through unlikely places. He adjusted his flashlight switch a half-notch forward so that the beam could be cast silently from a push of the button, and cut off by merely releasing the pressure of his thumb.

He cracked his door open and stood behind it. From down the hall he heard his mother, walking, murmuring to herself in a kind of interrupted yet continuous suspiration. He remained where he was, waiting to know if she intended a direction or would merely wander like a wraith about a stillborn child's grave. He saw her come from her room and move toward him. But he was well hidden in the darkness of the wall shadow. She passed his door and began her descent down the stairs, murmuring, "The papers. Legal papers. Gone. C, he taken legal papers. He give them . . ."

Glove relaxed. He would not have to follow her and could continue on his own purpose. He knew where she was going. Many times he had followed her there. From this room he had picked so that she would have to pass by him in order to go down, he had followed her into the only remaining room retaining a memory of The Associate—records in desks, receipts, telephone numbers written on the blackboard, and a safe. Her thinking was always that the legal papers—the marriage, the birth of the children—were not real, or were destroyed. She would go and open the safe, take them out, and hold them, wondering what it meant that they were there. Then would put them back, shut the safe, and go back upstairs. Besides, Sam would wake up if she tried to go outside. Of the family only C slept without easily waking.

Glove crept close to the walls of the hallway, past his parents' open bedroom door—he could see the lump of his father under the covers—past the room his brother had lived in before he was moved upstairs.

The door to the stairway was locked! Glove felt as if a segment of rotten mud had entered his life. He tried to wash himself clean, but only managed to roil what was already there: his mother, after he and C were asleep, had locked the door to the third floor . . .

in order that his brother—his brother might what? Might come downstairs? He closed his eyes and tried to turn what he was feeling into sadness.

The sadness he could suffer and went quietly back to his room and fetched a key which he knew would fit the lock. Downstairs Cell had shut the door of the safe with a popping thump. He hurried back to the door, opened it and locked it behind him, then went up the stairs. The door at the top was locked too. He opened the door, but didn't bother to relock it, thinking that his mother by testing the first door would be satisfied of the rest—until some time later in the morning, when she would open them all so that none of the enemy—everyone besides her—would know.

Glove passed his brother's room and began the last flight of stairs up to the attic—using his flashlight now. Very cold in the attic. A frightening place, because whatever could live there would have to be so thick-blooded that other things might be different too, like teeth. Also would have to move like a cat in order to move quickly on top of the ceiling beams. These were childish thoughts and he concentrated entirely on opening the big leather-hinged trunk. He swung the lid back. One by one he removed them, all twenty-six of them, took off his outer shirt, tied the sleeves shut, and spread it as flat as he could on the floor, placing them one by one on it. Buttoning several of the front buttons and holding other places together, like the neck, he made a sack for carrying them, shut the trunk, and turned to retrace his steps downstairs, unaided by the flashlight, which was in his pocket because both hands were occupied. From the moonlight he could see the head of Baron, just above floor level, looking at him from the steps. Boy, that kid is quiet, thought Glove. I wonder how he opened his door. I wonder how he could have heard me.

"Come here," he whispered, "and give me a hand with this. And be quiet." Baron hurried up to the top of the stairs and onto the two-by-sixes, over to his brother, happy to be a part of the mystery. "Take the flashlight . . . no, in my back pocket, stupid."

Baron got hold of it and lit it, giving them plenty of light. They crossed over to the stairs, went down, and closed the door behind them, then down to Baron's room. "How did you open this?" asked Glove, and his brother took out a piece of bent wire (originally from a coat hanger, Glove suspected), deftly intruded it into the lock, made a clicking noise and thrust the bar lock out into the air, then clicked again and brought it back in. "Who taught you that?" Baron pointed downstairs and, as if that weren't clear enough, pretended to tie a necktie. "Sam did, huh?" He nodded. "Get in here, I've got some stuff for you." They went into Baron's room and lit their special meeting candle, sealing the door underneath with a blanket, pulling the shade on the windows.

"First," Glove said, "we won't talk about this," and he patted his lumpy bundle. "We'll talk about this." And from his inside shirt pocket he carefully extracted a meritoriously rolled joint, holding it as though it were a contact lense. Baron smiled and his eyes flashed, in anticipation of its story as much as of the lighting of it.

"See this?" asked Glove, which of course Baron had, but he intended taking every bit of time. Baron nodded.

"Do you know what it is?" Baron nodded again.

"Well, you may *think* you do. You may *think* that this is just ordinary, plain old grass, like the usual stuff." Here he took a long pause. "But it isn't. No, sir. This here is Gold. Expensive, I admit . . . but worth it."

Baron was trying to keep from laughing, sort of timing his laugh into long sneezes.

"Now, this is serious, pay attention. I was in the high school, next to my locker, sort of looking out for trouble, but minding my business just the same, because that's a bad area to be alone in, especially just when school is letting out. But nevertheless there I was, wary, but knowing that if I was goin' to get any stuff I was going to have to take chances. There was a chance that the joint was staked out 'cause a lot of heavy dealin' had been going on there—"

Here they both started to laugh. Glove bit on his finger to stifle himself. Baron had rolled onto the floor, lying on his side, forcing all the air out of his lungs so that there was nothing there to make noise except on intake.

"So up comes this joker," Glove went on, very cautiously, "and asks, 'Hey, man, you want to buy some mighty fine weed? You want to buy some grass, man?'" Glove could see now that he was going to have to cut this short because his brother was about to blow a lung or at least give away their position to the neighborhood.

"So I asked, 'Is the ganj any good?' and he answers, 'Is it good! This stuff is heavy gauge. This is Gold, man. This is one toke dynamite super groovy opium-treated stemless seedless cool-burning good-tasting psychedelic hallucinogenic Fox River mind-bending eye-flashing thinking warping hard-core down-and-out good dope. Hey, man, you want to slip in here to the john and grab a snort or two, for the effect—that is, if you don't got to be anywhere for a couple days or at least long enough for the janitors to finish scraping your mind off the walls? Maybe you better just smell it while I take a toke.'

"So in we go, and he takes out his pocket stash and lights up a reefer. I took a couple pulls and he tells me to let it settle, has a couple himself, pinches out the coal, and sticks the roach back into his stash—so sure was he that we had had enough. And before long this little midget sneaks up behind me from the aw-ful sinks and hits me with a hammer, and this goes on for several more times and I'm really wasted, see, and my mind is as loose as an old convertible, only I know he's the same way and probably worse because it's his stuff and the frequency of it has taught his head where to be as soon as he lights it up. So I'm cool, see. I can't really see too good and I'm hearing things, but I'm cool, and say, 'What a burn. This stuff is nothin', man. Somethin' from your organic garden in the fields, no doubt.' He asks me if I want to try some more, and I tell him it's a waste of time, that I don't really

need any in any case, and that with the few acid trips I got left
I probably wouldn't ever come down far enough to even be able
to notice the fizz of that 'Gold' of his. He seems a little interested
then, but we got to split because one of the male battle axes, a left-
over from some intellectual Depression, comes in to take a whiz,
so out in the hall again, wary of plain-clothesmen (not wanting to
get busted), I whip out three of those tabs we got from a friend of
Eight Wood's—that stuff we took last summer, which since had
turned from light green to orange—good, but nothing fantastic.
But I'd put some food coloring on them and they were the deep-
est purple you could imagine and I go into a description of the
visuals of this righteous purple. And then because he's a friend of
mine I let him have one for himself, which I say is enough for two
twelve-hour trips. So he feels pretty good about that, but wants
more, for a friend, of course. And I say I only got three out of the
hundred or so I had, 'cause everybody wanted 'em, 'specially the
cats from Iowa City, which was where I got them. So he really
wants 'em now and wants to know what they sell for. And I say,
'Sell! Nobody sells this stuff! It'd be immoral and might burn
your mind to settle the score.' So he offers me that Gold again,
and I'm interested, but . . . still, the quality being what it is and
all. So we end up trading (me finding another tab to throw in) my
four (counting the one I gave him to begin with) for two of his
lids, which came out to be a little under forty-five grams.

"But not yet," Glove said, and put the joint back in his pocket. "Here we have"—and he unbuttoned his shirt and pulled it
apart, divulging twenty-six hard-bound journals dated only in
years: 1923, 1924, 1925, 1926, etc. "These are your grandfather's
diaries—the material either this guy named Johnie Fotsom or he
wrote into books—and you're going to learn to read . . . but no one
must ever know. No one must ever know, because they're secret."

They looked at the books for a while together; then Glove
lit up the "Gold" and they smoked it before he left and slipped
downstairs, locking the doors behind him. He crept down the hall

and into his own room, shutting his door with infinite patience, unaware that down from his room his parents' door opened a crack, just enough to let Cell's wild eye see into the hall down to his room.

THERE WAS A MEETING ONE AFTERNOON IN EASTER'S YARD, IN THE ONLY room with a blackboard and a safe, musty from disuse. C Easter, his brother Sam, James Cassum, and Keith Kullisky were there, the original members of a disbanded Associate, a group of general specialists who hired out to do anything, that had run aground due essentially, they believed, to a war in Southeast Asia. Now they were out of work. They met only to talk, and to decide finally whether these four people, under the name of The Associate, would participate in some way in murder, for money, and again just what that participation would be. Although no one in the town would believe it later, or probably would ever believe, they quickly decided that they would have no part in the killing, the actual physical aspect of it. They deemed that that—the throat cutting, stabbing, blowing apart, poisoning side of the business—went along with the emotion, which Abbot Meyer admitted to having and without which the action could never come about, except in some drunken outrage in a tavern over a forgettable slander and in that case The Associate would never be asked. The reasoning was carried on mostly by C at this point. A murderer is a fool, he told them. Thinking that a death, any death, can solve a rotten situation is near lunacy; thinking that *causing* death can is then again one step farther out in left field; and then beyond that to think, as was the case with Meyer, that some personal, emotional release could be obtained from doing just that is blind, full-tilt madness. This was agreed, with only Jimmy Cassum putting in that Harold Burdock could easily be everything Abbot Meyer suspected he was, and no one would mourn his passing . . . but that didn't change the argument so much as indicate the reality of it.

The next order of reasoning went on that, *given* someone feels in such-and-such a way and decides in his blind, full-tilt madness that he will murder someone, in this case Harold Burdock, and he comes to The Associate and says, *I feel in such-and-such a way and have decided to kill Harold Burdock, help me, I will give you money*, it could then be decided that Harold Burdock is, for all practical, reasonable purposes, already marked, and his death at the hands of Meyer is assured . . . only an indefinite time between now and then. But what help?

Sam interjected, What if the effect was the same, only somehow Meyer's purpose—what he wanted—was to be talked out of it? That too could be possible; and if it was, then the assumption that Harold Burdock was marked for sure would be wrong. So then what? Would not the help be more in the way of counseling? They considered this as well. They tried to think in the abstract. But Harold Burdock, all of them knew, was surely marked.

Then there was the law, but all finally agreed on a saying which they did not create but which was available to them from youth, an acknowledgment not only of the greed of the country as a whole, but of themselves as part of it: *It is not against the law to break it, only to get caught.* And of course they did not seriously believe that was a factor.

Perhaps the mistake, the error, so to say, in figuring this all out was that they hadn't done it before—before Meyer had come to them—and so as they deliberated this way and that, abstractly and hypothetically, figuring how they might be rich as well as heaven-worthy, still they could come back to the fact that they were talking about Meyer and Harold Burdock, and he (Burdock) was indeed marked for dead, and nothing they could do one way or the other, short of turning Abbot Meyer over to the police for doing nothing, would save him or even help. And they must have clearly believed, personally, though never saying it out loud, that this would be the only time. And all would have gone along with that except for the money, and Keith Kullisky, who had grown up in a one-room house with seven brothers and no father and all the things base and profound that go along with true poverty . . . it was Keith who maintained that it was not fair that only the rich can buy help. And the others agreed, probably more because they knew it was not right even for the rich. So they drew up a paper, made four copies of it, and everyone signed them. C put one copy in his safe.

They decided that the way they would help Abbot Meyer and so obtain $75,000 was to devise a way that he might kill Harold Burdock, a way that would leave him completely free from fear of being blamed for the crime—something foolproof, so to say. But still only information. They would have no part in the murder itself. Their service was one which anyone could perform himself with a level head (which of course a murderer never has, at least Meyer), could even do in fun sitting on his back porch thinking up perfect ways to kill, a game played by children again and again, there being no law against it. . . . Are children ever told how they might spend years in prison for coming up with these? No; it is the act itself and the emotion behind it that's blameworthy, that's unlawful. . . . It's the specific desire to kill that's punishable . . . and the act. Not the thinking.

It was agreed that in order for someone to divulge his own intentions of murder to four other men, he would have to be beyond the turning-back stage. But just in case he *might* change his mind they would always (still thinking in the abstract) take at least one month before delivering the information—the plan that one *might* follow, given certain malicious feelings, if he did not wish to be caught. No payment in advance. In the case of Abbot Meyer, a simple matter of economy of lives . . . one dead, Burdock, given; but one reprieved, Abbot. And on the papers it was written that anyone, regardless of his financial stature, could obtain such information at a price set according to his means. In this way they imagined that they protected themselves from transgression by making their information a commodity (if, indeed, it was evil at all) available to everyone and anyone—in the same way that the inventor of firearms cannot be held responsible for their use, since he did not confine them to one person or people, but gave them up to everyone. Then, as an ace in the hole, a kind of morality nullifier, they knew that whatever happened in a small town in Iowa had little consequence, good or bad, in the total system of things.

They got in touch with Meyer and told it all to him, finding it easier to explain the more they went over it. Yes, and the money was to be paid in one month (the time during which it was hoped he'd change his mind), right after the plan was revealed; not after the act, because it was only worthless information that they sold. Worthless, because only a madman would use it with his emotions.

EIGHT'S BIRTHDAY PARTY WAS SMALL BUT TIGHTLY ORGANIZED, with lavish, nearly wholesome pastries and cakes, punch, presents that filled up a davenport and took nearly forty-five minutes to open and marvel at, and a real magician who played pick-a-card-any-card to the continual delight of Fisher and Rabbit (the rest of the twelve or so members being too old, or at least at the wrong time of their lives for such hokery). Hard rock blasted from Eight's component stereo. Rabbit had found an authentic roulette wheel, put it in the basement alongside a slot machine (for which he provided the dimes), and wore a gaming hat. Ester flourished behind the bar, doling out refreshments. Eight and five of her close friends, unknown to the rest, converged in her bedroom and quickly consumed half a gram of black hash from her miniature waterpipe.

"Some doin's here, Eight," said Rolland.

"Sure."

"Cost your old man plenty, I bet," said Gloria.

"The blimp," said Eight. "He embarrasses me."

"Hey," said Glove. "That ain't right. He's an O.K. guy."

"Get off it."

"Come on," he continued, "it's too easy to goof on a guy like that—when he puts everything out front and you hold back and come down on it."

"He's just such a pansy," said Eight. "I think he's even afraid of me."

"Look, you want to hear somethin' that shouldn't make any difference? You want to?"

"Go ahead, warp my mind," said Max.

"O.K., listen," and Glove talked to Max, but with the intention of talking to Eight. "About a year ago, I guess, Sam was gone somewhere or it wouldn't have come about, I don't suppose. Well, Beef was over to the Yard and is sitting like he usually does on the porch, drinking something. And, see, these three toughs come into the Yard and Dad's out there and evidently they think that they've been cheated, or maybe they had a friend who thought *he* was cheated . . . anyway, they're giving Dad a hard time, the two of them. The other one, mean and big, is hanging back watching them jive each other one way and the other. Then he comes up close to C and says, 'I think I'm going to mess your face up a little, junk man.' And Rabbit, as though from out of nowhere, pulls Dad back and stands there like a post set six feet in the ground and says, 'Make your play, chubby.' And this big, mean guy backs down and goes away, and his friends are saying, 'Why, Lem, why?' and I hear him tell 'em, 'Maybe, maybe I could beat him in a fight, but if it was down to it—him or me, if it got to that, he'd kill me.'"

"Did he say that?" asked Rolland.

"Yep."

"That Mr. Wood would kill 'im . . . if it was down to it?"

"Yep."

"I'll bet—" began Eight, but didn't finish; then they went back downstairs. The only mishap of the party was later on, after Rabbit had allowed each teenager two glasses of wine. Someone thought Eight should have a birthday spanking and tried to organize it. Outraged, Rabbit threw him out of the house.

IT TURNED OUT THAT AFTER A MONTH MEYER'S CRIMINAL DESIRE DID not go away; instead it festered into a fierce, demon-like conviction. His will for revenge would hear no arguments or generalities. Even to where he insisted that if it was in the plan to be the throat, then he would hold the knife—down to the neck bones— and watch. He wanted that kind of participation.

So they sold it to him. They told him what he could do, if he would want to (and by then there was no doubt of that, and being near him was even frightening for them because by themselves it had been like a game, talking together, listening to Jimmy Cassum, who knew how his house was laid out, and Keith, who knew how those things in it worked, C and Sam offering ideas as to how someone might go about changing this or that just a fatal little . . . drinking coffee). They shuddered to themselves as they explained it to Meyer—seeing in his eyes and the way he held his hands when he listened that what had been a game before, cunning and deceitful but still a game, was a game no longer.

He refused the plan. It wasn't direct enough, he complained. Again and again they explained about the telephone and how he would know, only he would have to wait, because, no, he would wish no harm to her . . . but of course he was on his own now. He left.

Waiting was hard for Meyer. But finally, after talking to shop-owners, combing the town for information, even stopping her on the street, Meyer learned that on January 27 Becky Burdock intended to leave for her mother's and stay until January 28— that being Mrs. Sidway's birthday, and one of the few remaining which she would likely see before snuffing out in the middle there somewhere.

With binoculars Meyer watched Becky leave the two-story house, get into her car, and drive away. Through the glasses he continued to watch the house, Harold's goings and comings every so often taking him past the two converging circles of amplified vision and causing Meyer, three blocks away, huddling in the silent, cold car, to curse him, freezing the words into puffs of white frost in the near-zero temperature.

Two hours later Burdock extinguished the lights and went off upstairs, closing the stairway door behind him so that the niggardly heat which he allowed to worm out of the space heater would not escape upstairs, where it was not needed to keep the pipes from freezing and where one could sleep perfectly well in the cold. Meyer sat in someone's parked car, warmed internally by anticipation, hatred, and resolve, frantically scratching little holes on the fogged windows to see through.

Meyer had waited a long time for these coming moments, thinking them through with every detail his imagination could call up. Now he was going through them again, step by step, his passion boiling. He looked at his watch. Forty-five minutes since all the lights went out. The time had come when he would finally participate in his own fantasy. Immediately, all of his passion abrogated. In unholy silence, those appointed tools stuck separately in pockets so as not to rattle against each other, with no feeling other than decidedness, Meyer left the car and walked down the street, walking next to the fences in the lurking darkness. At the first intersection he went diagonally across so he would not have to cross the partially lit street twice. At the next intersection he stopped and looked for a long final time and then crossed into the block. And as though that passage were a kind of terrible initiation, he threw all timidity, whatever little of it still remained, out of his mind. The rest would be quick.

He passed through the front yard between the garage and the house, back to the five-hundred-gallon LP tank sitting like a huge bomb in the starlight. With fast, sure movements, actions he had performed again and again in his sleep, his hands even moving underneath the covers, he shut off the main valve, waited for that little dribbling of propane to run from the line until the pilot lights of the space heater and stove went out, disconnected the regulator, and with the proper fittings realigned the house line directly to the tank, then turned the valve back on, letting the unleashed pressurized gas pass through the tiny holes of the pilots like small holes in a dam. Leaving the tank, he moved to the covered outside electrical outlet on the back of the house, wired in series to the upstairs lights, and inserted an all-metal plug which he held at the end of a pair of rubber-handled pliers. There was a short snapping noise, one feeble burst of spark, then nothing. He stood by the house in the complete darkness of the roof shadow for what he knew must be more than forty-five minutes—what they had told him must be that long and for which he had paid almost $75,000, except that when it came down to actually getting the money he had been a little short of that. The time (and he was surprised by this) passed almost without his noticing it. Not believing his watch, he went to the window and put his nose to the crack. Yes, even through this he could smell the gas. Then he went back to the tank and rehooked the line in sequence with the regulator, letting only that little bit of gas through the holes that would normally pass through if the pilot lights had gone out by themselves, that little bit which would make up for whatever would escape from the windows or venture up around the closed door to the upstairs. Then he walked, nearly ran, over eight blocks to his own house.

Dialing the numbers, he felt his hands tremble as the passion returned. He heard the click of the connection and listened to the ring . . . Once . . . Twice . . . Three . . . Four . . . Five . . . Six . . . Harold Burdock, shaking his head like an animal, rose from sleep and walked into the hallway. The light was out. He tried his bedroom light and that failed as well . . . Ten . . . Eleven. He went back into his bedroom, took his Zippo lighter from his pants on the floor, struck it . . . Fifteen . . . came downstairs, and opened the door. The initial suction pulled his huge bulk like a piece of wood ash into the living room. Then Meyer, hearing seventeen, listened to the sound of the line going dead, not caring at all about the other noise, the one with sound, the explosion he could have heard if he would care to listen from eight blocks away, outside the city limits. He listened to the sound of his connection going dead. Listened until an operator cut in to tell him that there was no—

"COME ON, NOW," SAID GLOVE. "NOBODY SAID IT WAS GOING TO BE easy. It just takes a lot of time. Think the sounds in your head . . . w-w-w-w-w-w-r-r-r-r-r-r-r-o-o-o-o-o-o-o-h-h-hnnggggggggg. Wrong. Wrong. So what that says so far is T-h-e-r-e i-s s-o-m-e-t-h-i-n-g w-r-o-n-g . . . Now, do you know the next word?" Baron nodded his head. "Good, w-i-t-h." He pointed to the next word and Baron nodded. "T-h-e." He pointed to the next and Baron shook his head. Glove wrote it out on the tablet. "It's just his handwriting there. He liked to make flourishes. This is the word:" Baron nodded. "W-a-y . . . There's something wrong with the way . . ." But it was getting light outside. "I've got to go," said Glove. "Now make sure and hide this book and take it out only when it's safe. Circle the words you don't know and I'll be back, not tomorrow night, but the night after. You have to try."

Glove went down without having to unlock any doors, because since that night four months ago, when he had first noticed his mother locking them, she had only sporadically continued it and then sometimes only the bottom door. But now he heard her walking downstairs in her furry slippers and he quickly slipped out of the way of the open staircase and into his room, then into bed, not because he thought she would look in but because standing behind closed or partially closed doors made him feel decadent. "Money," his mother was murmuring to herself. "That money. That come from somewhere. That money."

Money? wondered Glove, but soon dashed off into a deliberately sound sleep that in two and a half hours would have to add up to a whole night of rest.

"I'M TELLING YOU TO FORGET IT," SAID ESTER. "JUST FORGET IT."

Rabbit followed her into the living room. "No, listen. Something's not right. There's something wrong. It's too . . . too accidental."

"People die all the time from accidents, and the good thing in this case was that—*I'm going to say it, Rabbit*—nobody really even cared. Besides, it was four months ago."

"But I was talking to Becky's insurance adjuster today, and those guys are thorough, and he said the fuse was blown—the upstairs current."

"So an accid—"

"No! Not like falling from a ladder, or being electrocuted with some power tools, or even falling down a flight of stairs, even that."

"Stop it, Rabbit."

"No! Listen. Here's someone who has many enemies; maybe even I don't like him, and don't think that doesn't work at me too. Everybody should care. It's not right to not care, no matter who it was."

"It doesn't matter," said Ester.

"It does. It does. Listen. Here's someone nobody likes."

"You've already said that."

"—and in the middle of the night he becomes unrecognizably blown to pieces and the second floor of his house falls down on top of him even before the fire truck arrives. Now, how did it happen? And isn't it funny, *isn't it good,* that Becky wasn't in the house? Isn't it a blessing that on this one particular day a person who never goes anywhere—"

"Rabbit! You think that Becky—"

"No, of course not, but just listen to all the ifs. If he had had a safety switch, that couldn't have happened. But the insurance man said there was one there. Peters, who works for the gas company, said so too, that it was put in less than a year ago; the whole stove was practically brand new. And what they say is the only

way for that much gas to get in there in that short a time (Becky
left at around nine o'clock) is if it came in through the burners.
Of course there's no way to check such a thing, to know for sure.
But then when they dug up the space heater and cut it off the line,
which had become welded to it because of the heat, they find the
burners shut off. Of course it could have done that later, and besides, if they weren't on, then it couldn't have happened—so they
say. So it's odd that not only did the pilot go out but the burners
stayed on and then *later* shut off." .

"That's the way with accidents."

"Not yet. There's more. Upstairs the electrical current is broken. The fuse blown down in the basement. O.K., we think that
happened in the explosion, when the house collapsed. But none
of the others are blown, and the power line broke when the house
fell. It's odd too because Harold must have been upstairs as his
house was filling with gas and waiting down there like a ton of
dynamite to be exploded . . . as soon as what? As soon as it's lit,
and the pilot lights are out. So how does it get lit? Now, if nobody
killed Harold, then he must have lit it himself, and because he
had a different opinion of himself than the rest of us did, then he
wouldn't do it on purpose—so another accident. He didn't mean
to light a house full of gas, but did it anyway—and the only way
he couldn't have known it was there was if he couldn't smell it or
see it, a man who is not only forty-some years old but also hauls
propane about the country with his truck and of course knows
the smell of it. So he must have been upstairs where the closed
door (another thing which had to be in order for an accident of
this kind) protected him from the smell, and he must have had the
match, or whatever, struck before he opened the door because he
wouldn't have done that afterward because he would have known.
So the only reason for coming down with a lit match (given that
a cigarette or a cigar wouldn't ignite it, and Dale Peters says no)
is if the lights upstairs are out—which they weren't when Becky
left at nine. But of course maybe he just walked downstairs (the

lights not being off then) and lit a cigarette *just* as he opened the
door—just as he opened the door. Or maybe he wasn't upstairs at
all and just sat watching the television as his house not only got
cold but filled with gas too, and then lit a match,"

"Accidents are strange," said Ester.

"Very strange," said Rabbit. "And strange that after going to
bed, turning the lights out, he would come downstairs just at the
right exact time—as soon as the room was lethally full, yet before he could smell it upstairs, before enough of it would weasel
its way up there to warn him. So why would he go downstairs,
maybe in the dark?"

"I don't know why," said Ester. "*I don't know why!* Go ask some
of the boys at the junk yard. I'm sure they've got ideas about why.
Isn't that about all that goes on over there anyway? C and his
brother sitting around with the rest of the town gossiping, while
the rest of his family goes mad? I just won't hear any more about
it. Never. Better to forget it if it bothers you so much."

"It's just funny," said Rabbit in a contemplative, yet hurt,
voice, "how things had to be just right before an accident could
happen. Funny too about C and Sam. Everybody went over there
right the next day, and the next week too, for that matter, and
he did a lot of trading and sold a lot of pop (it being spring, and
some tried to play horseshoes, but it was too muddy still), in order to find out and talk about Harold Burdock's accident. Gossip.
I guess that's right too. But even Sam, even Sam, had no ideas and
didn't venture to explain it, like how the CIA might have come
down from Chicago . . . and maybe they feel the way I do about it,
or at least the way you do . . . and they should be able to tell when
something's unnatural. They should know that."

"Then go talk to them," said Ester.

"Maybe I will," said Rabbit.

So it may be imagined that after the accident of Harold Burdock
more people failed to forget it than Rabbit. Not to say that they

held a suspicion and took it out in idle moments for re-examination, or that they (except for Rabbit) felt even particularly uncomfortable about the recollection of the details—only that they remembered it. And of course the four people who felt most about it fought never to remember. They told themselves again and again—six months—that it was the passion, the emotion, that took Harold to the block, not the plan. They comforted themselves because of the pact—a signed document proving they had no passion, and no emotion. They would do it—the information—for anyone, even without money, in no longer and no shorter than a month.

The money they divided into equal quarters, but most of it remained in C's safe at Easter's Yard. C and Sam paid each month on the mortgage, paid the utilities, bought food, and even reported some of it and so taxed themselves, sending a hundred or two off to the government. Other than that, they spent nothing, and believed the best policy would be to show very little indication that unexplained money had ended up in their hands. They furthermore found no enjoyment in talking to people about the accident, or how it might have been done. Nor were they compelled to belittle those who tried to piece it together. But many people forgot, and after several months even *they* were becoming adjusted to the memory; and, when they opened the safe to extract several bills to cover the necessities, were less reluctant to reach over and pluck an extra twenty or forty from another pile of smaller bills to fit into their wallets, for the unexpected and even unnecessary. Abbot Meyer had moved with his daughter to Minnesota, and so carried with him what Sam, C, Keith, and Jimmy Cassum hoped was the only knowledge of the agreement. They more than hoped this; they believed it. They believed it as anyone would who had done something that froze the fluid in his spinal column whenever he thought of it . . . and believed he would never have to do it again.

But Abbot Meyer hadn't carried the burden with him. He'd

confessed, half in remorse and half in triumph, to an old friend of his, a slightly younger man who was a barber and who had once loaned him money to finish law school and who'd cut his hair while he told, in detail, how he'd vindicated himself and who had helped him and how much it cost, thinking that the eyes into which he was talking were expressing interest and astonishment, not knowing that it was passion that fired them, the same passion and desire as Meyer's had been before it had been tempered through the action and the remorse.

". . . It is finished," the old man said to Henry Travis, as though telling it out in the right order, in the right way, was a kind of self-imposed penance. "Judith and I are going to Minnesota to live. We will fish on the weekends. It is finished. I feel, as I tell you about it, the last of it, the end of it. The remorse covers the hate. The freedom conceals the memory. It is finished."

"Finished," said Henry. "You've been lucky." He shook the chin apron, letting the small trimmings of hair spin and flutter to the ground, where, in the way of hairs, they lay quivering slightly to the eye, as though still alive. He brought out a broom and swept them up.

"I'll miss you, Henry," said Meyer. "You must come for visits with your family. We'll put knapsacks on our backs and walk for days in the forest, unknown to anyone but the animals."

And Henry, "That Associate. They did that for you . . . the information?"

GLOVE LOOKED OVER THE WORDS BARON HAD CIRCLED. SOME HE COULD not decipher because of the handwriting. Others he had to look up: "attenuation," "exculpation," "picayune." At times Glove himself was struck with something in the record . . . some explanation that Ansel would offer which he would neither accept nor reject, knowing as he did how much of it had turned out. His brother was soon reading several pages a day; then a dozen. The purpose was, of course, to discover how much could be believed that Ansel said, that C said (and, though he did not know it now, that his mother would later tell him). The purpose was to understand his grandfather, understand him in such a way as to explain what happened and how everyone else turned out; maybe even what happened to Cell was hidden somewhere, predicted between the leather covers. And that thing, that Ernie. But it was not up to him, Glove, to do this. It was not his responsibility or his calling; and whenever he felt as though he were seeing something new, some forgotten ingredient of his grandfather, he would remember that it was his brother, The Baron, who would finally bring it all together. And for him, Baron, it was not a responsibility or a burden, because that putting together, Glove thought, was what he would do almost without volition, merely what he was. So Glove neither prodded his brother with the problems nor presented them in such an order that they conflicted with each other. No, he must only think that he is learning to read, thought Glove; the rest he'll do himself. If only there is time.

All of this Glove kept inside. One semester he nearly failed because of skipping so many days—days he spent walking and sitting under bridges watching moving water.

"No," said C. "He was serious."

"Joyce Campton! What did she ever do to him? What did she ever do to anyone?"

"He wouldn't say . . . told me that was his own business and that all he wanted was the information, which he could pay for, in time (he thought it was an even rate of seventy-five thousand). 'I have been hurt, beyond enduring,' he said."

"Did you tell him to reconsider?"

"Sure. But it didn't do any good. He said that was something he had done too many times already."

"Did you tell him about the month?"

"Yep. He said that was fine."

"Think he'll change his mind? God, I never thought Meyer would tell anyone. Even if he had, I wouldn't have thought it would hurt to tell Henry Travis. Who would have—"

"He didn't look like it. Not intense like Meyer was, but not undecided."

"How much money did he have? Did you ask him that?" asked Sam. "You should have told him the rate was fixed . . . course we'd do it for less," he added, looking at Keith Kullisky, "but we'd easily see how close he could come to that."

"He said he could bring in thirty-six thousand when he gets the information."

"Thirty-six thousand! Where would he get that kind of money?"

"That's not our concern," said Jimmy Cassum. "All we do is sell information."

"I never thought there'd be two people," said Keith. "I never thought anyone else would come. How can it be, in a place this size? Joyce Campton? Meyer happened to tell just the person . . ."

"But that pact was your idea," said C.

"I know. But we agreed on it. Besides, it was important in something like that to protect ourselves and to think abstractly, to make sure we didn't make a mistake."

"And we haven't," said Jimmy Cassum, firmly. "We haven't, and we won't. All we sell is information. Information that suckers pay us a lot for. Who blamed Einstein for the bomb, anyway?"

"That's stupid," said Sam. "Einstein's got nothing to do with this. Telling someone what he might do, if he were crazy, isn't a crime. Who'd believe it anyway? It's too farfetched. We could just deny it."

"He wants insurance," said C.

"What!"

"He wants us to sign that if the plan doesn't work, and the police get him, then the money will go back to his family."

"No, by God!" said Keith. "We only sell information—worthless information. No insurance. He'd have to pay even if he decided against it. We got nothing to do with the action. We ought to have him arrested on suspicion."

"Right," said Sam. "No insurance."

"No insurance," said Jimmy Cassum.

"I told him," said C, "no insurance."

"I don't like it," said Keith. "I never thought that—"

"None of us did . . . in a town this size. . . . He'll never do it."

"Thirty-six thousand is a lot of money to be considering giving up. Besides, the pact."

"And anyway, all we have to do is come up with something that's so far out in space that nobody would try it. Then we get the money, we can get out of here, go to Chicago—"

"Nobody's leaving," said Sam. "Not right now."

"O.K. O.K. We'll just come up with this plan that he would have to admit would work, but that he wouldn't dare try."

"Let's sleep on it," said Keith.

"Who would have ever thought . . . ?"

"SHE'LL BE O.K. THERE. WHY WOULDN'T SHE BE? DID YOU SEE THAT REC-reation area, and the clean look of those big rooms, and the nurses? It's a good place. One of the best."

"I didn't like it," said C. "I didn't like the way that Mr. Venison—"

"Mr. Vernon."

"—said, 'Sometimes you just can't take care of them yourself.'"

"It's true," said Sam. "Sometimes. Severe depressions. Poor Cell hardly knows us from strangers, hardly knows herself even. Did you see the way she looked at us as we left home?"

"He said *them, it's hard to take care of them,* and smiled as though that old bitch standing behind him was quietly goosing him."

"He was just trying to be nice," said Sam, who hadn't liked the director of the home himself, but knew that he would be tucked away in an office somewhere and would have little to do with the patients. "Make up your mind," he said, and threw the paper debris from their awful lunch out the window of his car and into one of the trash barrels spaced at intervals along the park space in front of the hamburger stand. He waited for C to finish his orange drink, then threw the container out too. "If you want to bring her . . . for a visit."

"No," said C. "I've decided against it. Besides, she's been getting a little better lately. She might come out of it on her own."

"O.K.," said Sam. "Want to stop and get a beer?"

"No. Let's get on back."

IT WAS THE SPREAD OF THE STORY—THE DEATH OF JOYCE CAMPTON— that was fast, and soon everyone knew those scanty details: how she had been found crushed underneath the stone wall of her bedroom, the roof hanging unsupported over the gruesome scene like a Chinese canopy creaking in the wind. The other half of the room, opened to the outside and the acre of wood in back by the collapse of the two sections of wall and corner, remained exactly as it had been (or as everyone imagined it had been because it was not believed anyone was ever in it except Joyce, and she would no longer know, lying under the sum ton weight, if the perfume bottle or hand mirror were as she had left them on the dresser). They learned how one of the neighbors, Charlie Sanchez, who had looked after her—started her car in the winter, helped her rake leaves—had walked on the undisturbed carpet, past the clothes hamper with a round, smiling face Scotch-taped to it, drawn by one of her first-grade students, over to the securely closed door, the one the woman closed as a last, almost superstitious thought to keep out unknowns from the other parts of the house. He opened it, looked down into the intimate inside of her home—nothing moving, no sign of anything being wrong, the portrait of her sister grinning from the living-room wall—then back behind him, at the fallen corner and the outside, shaking his head in disbelief, then slammed the door as though to punish the jamb and the rest of the house for not giving at least the appearance of being hurt. Then he wrenched a fire ax from one of the rescue teams and set at the wide-grain pine. MacDonald, from the creamery, ran over and led him out into the yard in order to stop the hollow laughter that seemed to follow each blow of the pick end of the ax, telling him, "These are sad times, Sanchez. These are sad times." And Sanchez turned to the rest of them there and said, "These are evil times. These are evil times. Mark me, this was no natural thing happened here." The crowd stood back and let him pass through, knowing themselves that it was not natural, that there was no *natural* way for a person's house to fall apart in the walls and crush them. They knew it wasn't natural. But it wasn't supernatural either. It was an accident, a mistake of nature. A fluke. It would have an explanation (as earthquakes do) but it would not have a reason . . . or purpose. Nothing natural or supernatural *wanted* it to happen. It was an accident. But how? How would such a thing? No evidence like . . . like . . . like what? What could make that happen? No traces of tire tracks in the lawn where a truck might have careened off the road and smashed into her stone house. The neighbors had not even been awakened during the night by an explosion, scream, or anything; even Sanchez, who watched her like a brother and even woke up if high-school kids over-accelerated their cars, said he hadn't heard anything. In fact, there was no reason to go over there at all until she didn't show up at school and didn't answer the phone. So by ten o'clock someone went over. No evidence, except water lying around as though a fire hose had been turned on and left to spray over the lawn and the buried body of Joyce Campton for a minute.

That spread fast. What was not so fast was the almost textural effluvium of dread, depression, fear, and wariness in Ontarion, that seeped out of the breach in the stone house and, when that was fixed, seemed to be coming from where it had been . . . seeping out into the air. Even the breeze was a kind of moth wind that gave no joy as it exhaled sick, lush spring breath across your face. It was deadly to be there then, to breathe that.

The facts were all too simple and few. For the first several weeks the neighbors asked each other, "Do you have any ideas how Joyce Campton's wall could fall in on her, and the water?" hoping to be told, "Oh, didn't you hear, they figured it out yesterday, it was . . ." But there was never an answer, so they gave up the hope that it could *ever* be explained. And after they'd admitted that, then they didn't want to hear anyone talk about it. Anything further would be superstition. And no one came to Easter's Yard for fear that there might be some people there who had been on vacation or visiting in the East maybe, who would be unaware that no explanation could be found and would be sitting around smoking cigarettes with their heads in their hands, trying to imagine how such a thing could be . . . how a grade-school teacher could be dead—dead!—and there be no reason. No explosion. Even though the pits had begun to dry and they could hear C out there from time to time throwing the horseshoes back and forth, no one came.

This was that spring. This was the one that Glove waited for so that he could open the windows and doors and let the air and warmth in, the sounds of birds and crickets. He knew there was something wrong in there—some spiritual decay. He waited until what he judged was the correct time and then at just the special moment opened it all up. And in came the moth wind and the effluvium from the stone house. Only he thought it was heat. Baron watched him come in and open his window, and looked up at him from his reading, in disbelief. "Sort of spring cleaning," he said, and left to open up other rooms. Baron shut his door and quickly pulled his window back down.

Later, that night, he came back and told the story of the origin of owls.

Very far back—just this side of the beginning of time, there were many birds but few men. And the greatest and largest and most fierce of them all was the Owl, even greater and more fierce than the Eagle, who was king of all birds. Of course most birds (and the Owl was one of them) were not then as they are now and had yet to develop their individual characteristics. The only real developing that had gone on was that men were not birds, and they were not animals, and they were not fish, and they were not insects, and they were not spirits. But within these groups there was not much difference. Wren, for example, was as much a last name as an indication of unique characteristics, and all birds had eyes located on the sides of their heads, as we commonly think of them being on a snipe—one of the ancients.

Naturally, men were cunning, more so than birds or even fish, and before long they developed hobbies among themselves. In some cases these became sports and were enjoyments. Also, among the creatures of the wood there were tales of animals being held captive in men's caves, for amusement. In a state of trouble, the animals went to the spirits and asked them if these tales were true. Come back in five days, they were told; and in five days they returned to the crevice in the rock and learned that the tales were indeed true—that the men were holding animals captive in their caves. Why do they do that? What is the purpose? they asked the spirits, and were told to return in five days, upon which time they came back to the crevice in the rock and learned from the spirits that it was pleasure for which the animals were held in caves. Pleasure. This the animals could not understand. What kind of pleasure can that be? They were told again to return in five days, and then five days, and five days again, until one month had passed and even the spirits despaired of being able to discover what kind of pleasure there was in keeping animals captive in caves.

The animals sent a messenger, a smallish Rodent, to the birds. What shall we do? he asked the king. Do about what? came the reply. About animals captive in caves, came the answer. Why? And for what reason? Who? asked the king Eagle. Men, was the answer. Men, for pleasure. Ridiculous, said the king. Ridiculous. I

don't believe it. Go away. You are trying to fool us into some kind
of den of foxes and weasels. And the Rodent went away.

Some time later, as the cunning of men grew, so did their
sport. It was rumored among the birds that a great battle had been
fought near the caves and that men had badly beaten back the
animals by rolling large stones onto them, unloosed from the cliffs
by levers. But more terrible than all this was the firsthand report
from a Bluebird to the king that he had seen a trap set and sprung
and that men had carried off a Kestrel and put it in a cave.

Call the birds together, decreed the king to all of his subjects
who could hear his voice in that part of the forest. For we will not
tolerate this. We will have at them, and rolling stones cannot hurt
us. We will attack their eyes. Make especially known that the Owl
should come, for his fierceness is not surpassed among us.

A Pigeon took the Owl the message, and he replied in his huge
voice, Have no fear, for I will be there. Let the battle not be delayed. Let us leave tonight for the caves. And so the birds set off.
Only on the way (for the distance was overland as far as a Hawk
could see by eight times) the Owl began to think to himself: What
if I were captured and put in a cave? It would not be so hard on
the smaller birds, as they only live but a short time. But the length
of my years . . . in a cave. Becoming so frightened, he flew until
dark and then fell to the back of the army, and finally hid in the
top of a leafed tree and was not missed.

The battle was long and hideous. Screams tore through the air.
Blood ran and bones cracked. The men were nearly overcome, but
prevailed in the end by using a giant net to surround the remaining birds and club them to death with rocks—a net which none
of them could break. And they called out for the Owl to tear the
net, but he was not there, and did not hear them.

So the message went out through the land of birds (young
birds now, too young to have fought in the liberation war) to
bring the Owl into the courts. He was found and brought in,
and he stated, It would not be so bad for you to be caught, but

my lifetime is long and I could not suffer it to be put away. Who could blame me?

But they did—those who had lost their parents and remembered when the survivors had come home battered and beaten, with the story of the terrible net and how the Owl was not there to break it free. They blamed him and set his head in a wedge of trees so that his face would look like men, with the eyes smashed in front, and made him an outcast from the rest of the birds, forced to hunt at night, away from the sight of others, who would harry him in groups whenever he was found. His mournful cries continue in the winter, throughout his long years—wishing only he would have another chance to get at the men's eyes and redeem himself.

IT WAS EARLY IN THE MORNING IN THE BANK WHEN LARRY TIMBERMAIN, putting together the end-of-the-month statements, came upon, by chance, a check that had passed through the clearinghouse on the 3rd. It was not a check to The Associate, but it was a check that Henry Travis had made out to himself for the amount of $36,000 and cashed, having scribbled in black ink near the bottom, possibly out of force of habit because all the other checks were the same way: "for shoes," "gas," "new razor," "heat," and "The Associate." He put it back in the envelope and went on, but came back and took it out again. $36,000 . . . The Associate. $36,000. He tried to put it back, then took it out for the last time and, shaking in his voice, carried it in to Rabbit, who looked as though he had had no sleep, no good night's sleep, for several years.

"Look at this!" he blurted out, then pushed the door shut behind him as the other employees turned to look, and his face flushed because of his shyness. Rabbit took it between his fingers and placed it down on the desk with a look in his face of complete surety, complete and thorough belief that nothing written on any piece of paper—especially a check—could be ever of such concern, that the world of paper and writing and money was so peaceful, so pristine—compared to other things—that coming to work was a kind of escape into a comfortable, ordered fantasy, away from the deadly gray effluvium outside. And now one of his clerks, within this fantasy, had a problem that was merely a matter of a decimal perhaps, or a forgotten number, maybe even a wrong signature—such trivial things. He turned the check over, upward on top of his desk, and focused on it and read *$36,000* . . . *The Associate.*

For quite a time Rabbit did not see anything but the number and the words—that is, he looked at them without seeing, as though their meaning had come through before the figures, so that by the time they arrived (the *$36,000* and *The Associate*), Rabbit had already convinced himself that it must be a mistake, an accident of some kind—that is, the meaning must be an accident, and he had only to look at the figure *$36,000* and the amount written out in longhand and the scribbled words *The Associate* long enough and some true significance would come through and explain it all . . . a decimal point, something. "Did he get all this money?" asked Rabbit.

"Miss Jordan put it into his hand, counting it first. Then he counted it by himself and left."

"Thirty-six thousand dollars?"

"Yes. Thirty-six thousand dollars. Do you think that it means . . . What could The Associate sell that would be worth thirty-six thousand dollars . . . or what could they do?"

"He picked up the money when?"

"The first of the month. One week before—"

"Henry Travis."

"Henry Travis."

"Be quiet. Go back to your work. Keep whatever you think might be true to yourself. It's not the way it appears. There's some mistake. I'll inform you when I discover what it is. In the meantime, keep quiet."

"Yes, sir," said Timbermain and went back to his desk, shutting his boss's door a little more loudly than was his wont, startling himself a little.

Rabbit immediately called Henry Travis and received an electronically operated voice telling him that such access to that person was closed—disconnected. He called the business office of the telephone company and got hold of Marvin Walsh, the line foreman, and was told that Henry Travis had had his phone disconnected, the one at the barber shop too, and that he had moved.

"Where?"

"Somewhere in Moline, I think. Why, owe some money somewhere?"

"Maybe. Thanks, Marv."

"O.K., Beef, any time."

Rabbit called the police and one of the new members of the force answered the phone. Rabbit told him to go get Henry Travis, and quickly. Oppenheimer, on the other end, asked, Why? And who are you, anyway? Rabbit told him that Henry Travis had written a check that bounced, that it was for a large amount, and that he wanted him brought to the bank. The procedure, however, it was explained, was to make a formal charge and let the jail serve as the meeting place between the two parties. Forget that, said Rabbit. Get him and bring him over here or I'll have you fired. You can't. I can. The police end of the telephone connection went dead, but not before a pause, long enough in its silence to let Rabbit know that what he wanted done would happen. And because Henry Travis was not actually yet in Moline but was carefully rolling his garden hose up and putting it into the rented moving van with an elephant drawn on the side, it was less than an hour before they arrived at the bank, together with a lesser official of the police force, a time during which Rabbit had not yet committed himself enough to the terrible meaning to call the Yard and ask for C or Sam.

Larry Timbermain watched from his slot in the counter as the two policemen brought Henry Travis, the man who had written the fatal words on the check—the man who Timbermain had decided was in some way a murderer—yes, murderer—into the bank and quickly through to the back and into Mr. Wood's office, closing the door securely behind them. He crossed to a part of the room where he could see through the partially glassed wall, and saw Mr. Wood hold up the check and then hand it to Henry Travis. Henry Travis looked at it and handed it back. He was facing the wrong direction for Timbermain to see his face, but he made an offhand motion to the side as though tossing something lightly into the air from between his two fingers. Mr. Wood turned the check over and pointed at it, looking like he was still managing to talk without raising his voice, though not without some emphasis. Again the gesture. The two policemen alternately looked down at the piece of paper and stepped a little farther away from Travis. The younger of the two took off his hat and looked at it again. Mr. Wood picked it up, then made the same motion with his hand that Travis had made twice earlier, his face looking like he was humming, very ironically. With this same look, he flamboyantly took a pen from his pocket, looked as though he were thinking deeply like a famous actor in movies who is just about to have profound ideas, appeared to have one, and pretended to be writing on the check which he held in the other hand, near the date. Then he put the pen back in his pocket, became very angry, looked as if he was shouting, and thrust the check back at Travis. The older policeman took off his hard-brimmed hat too and looked again at the check. Then Henry Travis ripped it in half and with the same gesture, for the third time, cast the two pieces into the air, where they fell to the feet of the younger policeman, who looked at them as though he had never seen them before.

RABBIT SAT DOWN, SHOUTED ONCE MORE, "YOU EXPECT ME TO BELIEVE that!"

Henry, who was becoming very angry now, shouted back, "I don't give a good god-damn if you believe it or not."

"Listen," said Rabbit, changing very quickly to being earnest but calm. "There's something happening here that's not good." Then Oppenheimer spoke for the first time and asked him if it was indeed true that Mr. Henry Travis had not written a bad check after all, that the money was his own, in his own checking account, and that the only reason he (Rabbit) had wanted him brought in was because he had scribbled the words *The Associate* on his own check. Rabbit began to explain, or at least show how something might be made of it, how some people knew that he had once tried to start something up with—But Travis interrupted him,

"There's two reliable witnesses here, Wood. If you want to say something untrue, I'll sue you for every cent you own."

"Look," said Rabbit to the older policeman, Oppenheimer, "isn't there a law against using all that money and having nothing to show for it, like blackmail, or larceny, or obtaining money for no tangible product or service?"

"Did you obtain that money from an illegal source or obtain it in an illegal way?"

"No. I've saved over the last twenty years and I inherited over twenty-nine thousand of it last year . . . from my grandfather."

"He says he inherited—"

"I can hear," said Rabbit, remembering that that was true. "It's that Associate part I don't like."

"Oh," said Oppenheimer. "Let me see that."

His companion picked it up and handed it to him.

"Why did you write that?" he asked and shoved it over to Travis.

He took it and threw it away again. "Because I was thinking what I was going to do with the money. And one of the things was to go see if I could hire The Associate to help me move. So I wrote *The Associate*."

"And what did you say was wrong with that?" Oppenheimer asked Rabbit.

"If that was true, then he should be able to go get the rest of it, or show how he spent it. Make him go get it. If he can't or can't explain where—"

"Wait a minute, Wood. Making out a warrant for someone's own legal money. We can't do that." Then he put his hat on, apologized to Henry Travis for the inconvenience and told him he could go, then called him back from the door as he turned to leave and asked him to wait and they would give him a ride home.

Larry Timbermain saw the murderer make it almost to the door, stop at the silent voice of the police officer, and then, accompanied by the other police officer, walk out of the bank and into the squad car across the street. The other policeman reclosed the door and remained talking to Mr. Wood. Both looked very angry at first and then became more amiable, the way two people might calm down after discussing a fiendish crime, a brutal, near perfect butchery, and then feel better for the fact that the guilty were apprehended. Then the policeman left, got into the squad car with the murderer and the other police officer, and drove away.

Rabbit put on his coat, closed the office door, and walked through the bank, thinking, I told him to keep his suspicions to himself until I told him the truth of it. He is still bound by that agreement. However, Larry Timbermain thought, *What else was there to say? We all have eyes.*

"Hello, Glover. Is C here, or Sam?"

"Nope. They're both gone—over to Kullisky's, I think. You want to come in, Rabbit? Don't stand around on the porch."

Rabbit came inside. "You know when they'll be back?"

"No, not really. If it was just Dad, I might venture a guess; but with Sam nobody knows. Could be they never even got there. Or it could also be that they plan to hole up there till Indian Summer."

"You think quite a lot of your uncle, don't you, Glover?" he said, though not with very much tenderness, more as though just for something to say while he looked around the house, to be sure they weren't there by mistake.

"Sure, I suppose. But look, I've got to split. Why don't you grab a bottle of pop or something, and if they show up, then good, but if not, then leave a note if you want and have 'em call you. I've got to get back before study hall lets out."

"That's right, aren't you supposed to be in school?"

"Not really. I mean, it's O.K. as long as I get back for classes. I think they know I skip the study halls, but then what the hell, there's only another month before the whole thing's over." And he was gone, running out through the front door and down the steps, very gracefully, the way one moves when he knows every step, every dip in the ground by heart and can pace himself just right even when running fast over it.

Rabbit watched him leave the Yard and cross the street. He thought for a moment of his own son, Fisher, and wondered if things would ever clear up in time so that he, so that they, Fisher and Glove, could grow up without learning that things happen, terrible things, without anyone wanting them to happen. Of course Glove was nearly grown now and only needed the rough edges smoothed off, just those few things that he did which set him aside from being grown-up, like running instead of walking, being unsure and self-conscious about how his face looked, thinking that a good night's sleep or lying against the ground on a clear day could solve real problems—these things would have to go.

"Well, hello, R-a-b-b-i-t," Cell said from the end of the hall in front of Sam's room, her raucous voice speaking his name with bitter irony. He started, then recovered, measuring his speech very carefully, the way a person does who talks to someone he is afraid of, not thinking exactly that it will help, nor that he would be able to know before blurting out just those words that would make her flare up, but just not knowing what else to do.

"Hello, Cell. Long time."

"Too long. Isn't that the phrase, Rabbit? Too long?"

"I guess it is."

"What do you want?"

"I was hoping to find C or Sam here."

"C!" she yelled.

"Glover said they had gone to Keith Kullisky's house."

"Who's this Glover?" she asked, having ended her slow progression down the hall, standing ten feet away.

"I mean Glove. Do you know what C and Sam have been—"

"How would you like someone to call you Rabbiter, or Beefer . . . B-E-E-F-E-R?"

"I guess that wouldn't be so good."

"So what do you want?"

Rabbit gave up talking carefully. He felt exhausted. "I guess I wish someone would come along and tell me something, something that will make all the things I'm afraid are true, untrue. I guess all I really want is to be able to sleep well."

"Everyone wants that," said Cell. "What are you doing here?"

"Oh, just being myself, I guess. It's just the idea of all that money—" and in the time that word took to travel ten feet Cell's face looked like it had just seen some graves opening up. "What is it?" he asked.

Cell shook her head to indicate that it was nothing, but the look remained.

"What is it about the money?" asked Rabbit.

Cell shook her head again and began twisting her fingers.

"What about the money?"

"What about the money . . . what about the money . . . what about the money," said Cell.

"Did you—did C or Sam get a lot of money, thirty-six thousand dollars, from Henry Travis? Did C get a lot of money somewhere?" In sadness he looked at her.

"What about the money . . . what about the money . . . what about the money." Twisting.

Then Rabbit said something that caused him deep regret for many days. Before leaving the house he said out loud what he was thinking, something he had no right to say before he was sure, a fear that should never have been spoken until the facts proved it, something that, if it were true, no one should ever tell her: "That's not much money for a human life," he mumbled sadly to himself, as though a tiny rill of voice had carried his thought outside of him, then picked his way deftly down the steps and through the Yard.

That's not much money for a human life. Cell looked at the place beside the door as though the words, dead, had not left the air, but hung, now clarion, next to the woodwork in woodshadows. She was trying to think.

"RABBIT, COME TO BED."

"No, go on to sleep, hon. I've got something to think about."

"You'll catch cold out there. These nights are chilly."

"No, I won't. Go on to sleep. I'll be in soon's I get something thought out. I can feel events coming."

"It's something about the Easters, isn't it? I know it is, the way you sit next to that cold window looking out over there, thinking maybe you'll catch a look at The Baron in an upstairs window, hoping that that would finish it once and for all and you could know whether it was true that that crazy woman chains her son up in the room at night. I know it's something about those damn Easters."

"Don't say that, Ester. They may be cursed."

"They may be curs-*ed*."

"No, I mean through their father."

Long silence. Ester sat up. "There's something about the father, isn't there?" Then she talked louder. "There's something about the father. It's not them, is it, Rabbit? It's the father. Tell me about him. It's the father." Pause. Voice now more contemplative. ". . . All these years when I've thought it was something about them, some hold they had on your worry that sometimes drove you out of bed in the middle of the night . . . I thought it was them. But it wasn't. It was the father." Now just merely thinking out loud. "After all these years, it was the father."

"No. It's feeling. I love those people over there living in that junk yard. You have to love them too, those men who look like they're strong, and they are because they can look that way. But I can look at them and still see them standing there on the porch of that house, C not even twenty years old, their mother gone from them for three years . . . Ansel Easter having taken them in there and never come out again himself, ever . . . with this demon, this Ernie, sending them out for food, out into a town that was so afraid of their father and that demon that they could scream . . . I can see them standing there as Doc Mason and Henry Olmstead carried out their father, his head nearly cut from his body . . . I can see them there, standing . . . a crowd of people who'd hated their father, policemen who blamed him for the death of one of their officers, the women whispering still, 'Is he dead? Are you sure he's dead?' I can see them standing there," said Rabbit, "trying to be strong."

The Yard light that he had put up to play horseshoes by came on five blocks away, and under this white, cold light he could see C picking up the horseshoes . . . knowing that behind one of those darkened windows was his wife. *That's not much money for a human life.* The sound of the cold steel ringing reached his ears. "You must love them. You must see them standing there, the neck bones of their father white. You must see them and hear Sam, not much older than C, say, 'No, he ain't dead, lady, he's just resting. Can't you tell by the way he hangs his head?'"

"My God, I didn't know."

"Knowing isn't enough. You have to have seen them there. You have to remember what it felt like then to see C drive up in front of that house years later in a secondhand automobile, the only thing he owned, with a small-framed, dark little girl with a look in her eyes of living in orphanages, of beatings, of cold and hunger—carrying a pillowcase with bologna sandwiches. You have to remember how it felt to see them walk up the porch and go in, you have to remember how it felt to know that C had come home, back home to live, thinking that he could be strong enough." Tears came into Rabbit's eyes.

"You have to have seen C with his son Glover, walking with him, talking to him, wanting to believe that it was all over, but knowing he could never forget. Or what it felt like to learn that Sam had come back and was staying there, who had been living by playing mostly three-ball in the barrooms, honky-tonks, and all-night bus terminals with tables. Road dust on his clothes. And though he didn't plan to, because he hadn't known C was going to be here, he thought he would have to stay, because he thought that he was stronger than C, and that together they could be strong enough." C was still throwing ringing noises into the lurking darkness. "But now he knows he can't. He's thinking he will have to die too, like his father, without ever getting away from it. Maybe all of them. But what is misery to them? They have known so much, how can they be blamed for doing anything?"

"Some of this I don't understand, Rabbit."

"It's no matter. Go on to sleep."

"Come to bed. It's freezing out there."

"Go to sleep, Ester." Rabbit stared out at the faraway figure of C, knowing it was cold out there, but not cold enough to freeze. It was too warm in the daytime for it to grow that cold at night. Not enough temperature to freeze water. Frozen water, thought Rabbit. Frozen water. Cold freezes, expands, and frozen water . . . expands . . . cold expands and bursts a stone wall. If there was water between the two walls, and it froze . . . somebody could put water in between the walls of a house if they knew what they were doing and knew the mason work was poor and that no supporting rods connected the outside wall—which would break apart in pieces because of the mortar, soaking through to the inside wall. It could be done if someone wanted . . . to do it. Then the next day, if it was in the spring, the sun would melt it down to water.

That's not much money for a human life. Rabbit regretted saying that. But maybe it was true. Maybe they would kill for money. Maybe they were no longer going to stay in that house. Maybe they merely wanted revenge before they left it. And maybe even now, as C threw the horseshoes, he might know that he was not strong enough and that they (Cell, Baron, and Glover) would have to pay, either in blood or in memory, for the failure. And maybe he didn't care.

Rabbit reasoned how he could know for sure, a plan whereby he could find out, then either take C's family away so that they would not have to watch them die, or send all of them away from Ontario and their father's house, where they should have known they could never live. He could call the balance of Sam's loan due, foreclose the mortgage. If they paid it, that would mean, yes, they took money for killing; if not, then they would have to leave. One way or the other, Rabbit thought to have them out of his life within four months, or even less. He struggled with this plan inside his mind, backing down, then reaffirming its necessity, back and forth—then he told himself that just because it could have happened that way (the stone wall), it didn't mean it did. He didn't want to do it. But he felt he was forced to. And finally he did it. So it always is. Decisions have importance. Actions are clean. Considerations are dead. Feelings do not move the world, or even nudge it.

"LISTEN CAREFULLY. DON'T LOOK AWAY FROM ME. LISTEN."

"It can't be true, Mom."

"Listen. C is—maybe he has—selling Baron to the University of Iowa to experiment on. I'm sure that's the place. Some of the money's already been paid. More than Rabbit thinks. They will be here to get him any day."

"It can't be," said Glove.

"Don't look away! Rabbit Wood told me so. He didn't mean to, but he did. What I want you to do is go ask him where there is a place where he can be safe—an institution that can keep him. A free clinic, because none of the money will matter later."

The arguing of The Associate down on the first floor grew louder. Each voice, Sam's, Keith's, Jim's, and C's, in turn was louder than the din of the others. A concert of bitter discontent and worry. These arguments were not new, but had begun less than one month ago and seemed to go on continuously, as though they only allowed one member at a time to sleep, carrying the argument back and forth between the Yard, Keith's, and Jimmy Cassum's. Sometimes Cell did not even think the harried voices came from people, but instead came from four stereophonic speakers, woofers, and tweeters and mid-ranges, held in suspension, one channel louder at times than the others, but all projecting simultaneously. Shouting. Myra Kullisky had gone to live with her father in Indiana. Sometimes when she (Cell) walked into the room where the speakers were, they shut off, as though her body were a volume switch; the closer she came, the less sound, until finally nothing except the tortured faces, the hum of the needle in a silent groove.

"Find out where. Get him to make arrangements for tomorrow. Don't look away! Borrow Sam's car. Late tonight I will give you some money for the trip. For gas and so that he can buy clothes when he is there, or tobacco if he ever gets old enough to want to smoke. Now go."

Glove went, but he did not go to talk to Rabbit Wood. He went down the stairs and past the room full of shouting voices— ("Who would have thought he would have ever tried that? I never thought it would work. I thought the wall would probably just crack." "But it did," said Keith. "She taught my kid in school, that woman did." "Shut up," shouted Sam. "It's not our fault. Better that than a knife blade." "Is it? Is it?")—so out the door and down the steps. Sam's dogs scrambled from under the porch to see who it was, though they probably knew from the sound of the footsteps. Glove set off through the Yard in the direction of downtown, but as soon as he was out of sight of the house he veered toward the country, toward the river. He walked past the outer environs, the shanties, wood-burners, and trailers, onto the gravel road and into the country, Sam's dogs still following him. The spring, he noticed, had become summer. The road had that unmistakable dust lifting up into the air—like heat itself.

Once in the forest, Glove headed for a place he had always thought of as a sanctuary, a little island of ground formed in the meeting place of two creeks merging into a stream questionably large enough to be called a river—thus creating a situation on the island of water running in at you from the northwest and north-east and away from you to the south, the ring of water surround-ing the island a myriad of eddies, ripples, currents, subcurrents, undercurrents, and tiny waves. When he was younger, Glove had felt this ring of water, the only ring of water he had ever seen, was magic, and that by crossing it and then pulling the log over so that nothing broke the circle, many mysterious things would happen to his soul. The island itself was only about twenty feet in diameter usually, but as he looked at it now, the water was down from when he was last there and heaps of watertrash had washed up on it, here and there bottles and cans, stagnant pools tucked away from the current with pink-and-green film lying on the top (fertilizer and bug spray from fields); it seemed smaller. Dad would be sad, Glove thought, if he knew how long it has been since I was here last, and how I haven't taken care of this place. He would think that once a person thinks sacredly about a place, no matter how far back in the past, he ought to take care of it and keep it like it was.

He set about cleaning up the island and the magic ring, throw-ing the cans across, but carrying the bottles off into a stand of horseweed where he could later come back with a sack and carry

them into town. About the petroleum-like film he could do nothing—throwing clods of dirt and clay, battering the surface, but the
pink and green rising again. He choked his anger. It had no place
here. After setting right all he could, he crossed again over to the
island. Then he drew the log over and lay flat down on the ground,
his two legs following the course of the two merging rills and his
upper body and head straight in line with the outgoing river. It
was here he thought to find help, to get it from the water and suck
it up from the earth with the fiber roots of his body spirit.

Then J. B. Hutto, sitting between the two merging streams,
gave a low, deadly growl, as though to say to Glove, *There is trouble,
but do not concern yourself with it,* and at the same time saying to the
trouble, *I will wait, then kill you.* And then Glove felt someone,
somewhere, staring at him. J. B. Hutto growled again. If this is
true, Glove thought, still not moving, then they cannot be far
away, and if they are close enough to stare at me—close enough
to give themselves away by that—then J. B. Hutto, being a dog
and much more generally alert, must even know pretty well where
they are, and would naturally be looking that way. He raised his
head just a little to see where his uncle's dog was looking. He put
his head back down and tried to remember what was over there.
He wondered what a woodsman would do. He tried to imagine
what his father would do. His father would calmly tell himself,
*The way to know for sure is to imagine that if that same situation had come
along before in your life and you were remembering it, what did you do?
This,* he would say, *will tell you what's the honorable choice, and that is
the only choice to ever make.* Glove thought, If it's a man with a high-
powered rifle and a scope, he'll shoot me. It would be disgraceful
to be showing fear to anything else. He lay on the ground and did
not move.

By then J. B. Hutto was advancing, walking deftly with stiff,
tight legs, leaning forward, his head held low, menacing, stalking,
as though to say, *At the slightest movement I will come, full tilt, at
your jugular.* After he had gone fifteen yards Glove sat up.

"Glove!" yelled the voice. "Glove! . . . Will he bite?"

"Eight, what are you doing over there?"

But she did not answer and came walking out from behind a weed thicket, pushing J. B. Hutto away from her, saying, "Get down. Get down," as he jumped up trying to lick her face and bite at her shoe laces. She was dressed in very tight jeans and a shirt, the tails tied up in a knot around her waist, showing just a line of soft skin, carrying a book bag.

"What are you doing out here?"

"I saw you start walking out of town—get down—so I wondered where you were going and what was out here."

"So you followed me."

"Well, I had something I wanted to show you."

"So you followed me."

"What were you doing? Putting those bottles over there."

"Just cleaning up the place a little."

"That place?" and she pointed to the island.

"Yeah. When I was a little kid I thought this was a magic island."

"Out of sight. Can I come over?"

"Sure." Glove upended the log and let it fall across the circle. "Why were you hiding?" he said.

"I don't know. I can't walk over that."

"Sure you can. Just walk fast."

She did. "What's magic about this island?"

"There's nothing magic *about* it. It's just magic."

She laughed. "I mean what kind of magic is it? How is it magic?"

"Secret ways. Magic ways. Did you follow me out here?"

"Yes. I guess I did. But that's nothing. I've got something to show you." She opened her book bag. "Aren't you going to pull the log over? So not to break the circle?"

"How did you know about that?"

"I saw you pull it over, and I wondered why. So no one could come over and get you? . . . With Hutter sitting there . . ."

"Hutto. J. B. Hutto."

"Hutto."

They both sat down.

"Sam named him from a record."

"Is your uncle a pillhead?"

"No. Where did you get that idea?"

"I just wondered. Oh! You want to come over sometime and listen to some records? Mother and I went to Des Moines the other day and I got some out-of-sight stuff: Led Zeppelin, Grateful Dead, Ten Years After, Eric Clapton, Delaney and Bonnie, Russian Roulette, Snowman, Boston Blackie, Milk Carton, Business Makers, Purple Reason, The Double Bed . . . that's all I can think of. And I finally talked Father into getting me a pair of Bozak speakers instead of those ones I had, and they're fine. Heavy-gauge bass."

"Sometime, maybe. Now what did you bring?"

"Oh! And the St. Louis Freight Co. Did you know that Ken told Dolores that he'd like to be your best friend but that even though everybody likes you, you never let anyone very close? I mean you never get tight with anyone, even guys."

"Is that what he said?"

"Yes. That's sort of true, isn't it? If everybody thinks it."

"Probably not. Everybody thinking something doesn't make it true. What did you bring?"

"Oh, right. This," she said and pulled it out and handed it to him. "I bought it in Des Moines. After I read it I asked Father about it and he said that the Ansel Easter in it was your grandfather, and that those things in the book were real." *The Broken Lantern*, by Johnie Fotsom. "Is that true?"

"I don't know," said Glove, "I haven't read it. And it seems like things that happened in the past get lost—I mean, there's something about the past, the truth of it, that gets lost and no one can ever be sure of it, of whether it really happened or was just imagined."

"Foolishness. Things either happened or they didn't. You're

kind of weird sometimes. Anyway, there's a part in here about Ansel Easter walking into town for food with thirteen cents in his pocket and a rabbit falls out of the sky at his feet. Did that happen?"

"I don't know."

"Or the time when Sam was shaking a catsup bottle because it was stuck and a big blob of catsup flew into the air and landed on his father's head. Or when he spent all his money on a motorcycle, drove it out into the country, wrecked it, and walked home. Is it true that every part that broke on his car would end up in the trunk so that the car would have to carry around the extra weight?"

"Is that in there . . . that last one? Because I think that might be true."

"You keep it. I knew some of it was true. I just knew it."

"No, take it back. I don't want it."

"Why?"

"I don't like to read."

"That's not true, Glove. I know—"

"O.K. I'll keep it." And he shoved it into his back pocket.

"What should we do here on this magic island? Shouldn't we be doing something?"

"We could be making love," said Glove.

J. B. Hutto lay down, chewing on a stick.

"Would you want to do that, with me?"

"I guess." Neither of them was looking at the other.

"Out here in the daytime in the open with Hutter over there?"

"He won't come over."

"Those other dogs, where are they?"

"They've gone home by now."

"He could come over on the log."

"Are you serious, Eight . . . that you would?"

"I guess . . . if you really wanted to, with me. It's no big deal."

Pause.

"No big deal . . . because why? Have you done it before?"

". . . No. But it can't be a big deal. Not that big."

"But babies and."

"Father's made me take birth-control pills ever since I was fifteen, since he saw Ronnie Milling looking at my bod when he came over to pick me up. . . . Mother told me that."

"Wait a minute," said Glove, and pulled the log across. "How should we begin? Should it be—"

"Kiss me."

"IS IT GOING TO HURT?"

"We'll see," said Glove.

"IS YOUR MOTHER CRAZY?"

"No . . . well, sort of, but she's getting better. Now she has thoughts and makes plans from them. It's where those thoughts come from that worries me."

"DO YOU FEEL PEACEFUL NOW?"

"About you, and everything about you. Not about something else."

"I wonder if I'll ever be the same—as I used to . . . now?"

"Probably not."

"I COULD LAY HERE ALL NIGHT."

"I could too, but I got a lot of stuff to do."

I can hide him in the Yard, thought Glove. In one of the old cars. Have him shut his eyes and take him out there. At night.

HE WOKE UP. IT WAS TWO O'CLOCK IN THE MORNING, ONE HALF-HOUR before the time he had wanted to get up. He listened, but could hear nothing. Dressed.

He heard her downstairs and waited. When he heard her down the hall, he stepped out of his room. He met her at the top of the stairs.

"Take this," she said. "It will be enough. It will be the last of it."

"The last of what?" he whispered.

"None of your concern. Your concern is your little brother, getting him out of here. Mustn't blame C."

"It can't be—"

"Don't look away!" and her thin, ravaged fingers dug into his arm. "Did you get Sam's car?"

"Yes."

"And you know where to go?"

"Yes."

"Then go get him. Put whatever he wants to take with him into a pillowcase, and be gone by three, and back—How far is it?"

"About a hundred miles."

"Be back as soon as you can. Give the money to the people there."

"Almost eight hundred. Where did you get this money, Mom?"

"Never mind. Git."

Glove went upstairs and into Baron's room. He was already awake because of the talking downstairs. Perhaps he even knew what had been said. He smiled when his brother came in.

"This isn't a visit, this is more like the beginning of an adventure for you—for us. It'll be very difficult. It'll be hard. Do you love Mom?" Baron didn't move; the smile was gone from his face. Anger came into Glove's eyes. He said it again: "Do you love Mom?" Baron nodded his head and then Glove's face relaxed. "Then what we must do is go outside. Get the things together that you want and we'll take them. Remember, you may never be back here again." He was glad when Baron brought the diaries, all twenty-six of them, and put them on the bed for him to put into the pillowcase—even those that they had already read. At the front door Glove asked him if he wanted a blindfold or if he could trust himself to keep his eyes shut. Baron motioned that he could trust himself, but Glove saw the apprehension and thought that this was no time for it and tied a blue bandana around his head, and led him out of the house, through the Yard, and into Sam's car. He started it and drove away. Baron took off the blindfold after he knew all the windows were rolled up.

"Mom said for me to take you to a nuthouse. She gave me this money." But he only put half of it on the car seat. The other half he had his own use for.

"Of course that's out of the question. So I decided you could live in the Yard, way out back there, in an old bus. I've already taken most of the seats out, put in a bed and a heater—though you won't need that for a long time. I set up sort of rooms in there, some of them with windows blocked off so you can sit up in the daytime or read at night. The others—the ones where you can see out—you'll have to be careful with because even though you'll be hidden partially by some of those weed trees, a sharp eye might spot you moving around in the daytime. Of course I'll bring food out to you, and I'll even fix up a 'frigerator later—there are three or four around here (and I always wondered why so many)."

Baron looked frightened, and stared out the front window at the road whipping by in the night, animal eyes in the ditch.

"It's O.K. to be a little scared. That's because this is an adventure, and all adventures are scary a little—half. That's what makes them adventures and not just events. And I'll stay with you all night tonight and sort of get you familiarized with the place. And do you know what I brought with me for just such a night?"

And he took out a small lump rolled in foil from his shirt pocket. Baron unwrapped it and pointed at it, indicating he did not know what it was.

"Opium," said Glove, and the word hung in the air like a mystical chime and all the connotations of the Orient—opium dens, Fu Manchu, Opium War, dark Hong Kong streets, hatchet men—filled the car, and Baron smiled; the other half of adventure.

AT FIRST LARRY TIMBERMAIN ONLY TOLD HIS WIFE. FROM THEN ON
in he was careful, only opening up to his closest friends and their
wives. Then only those people, those good friends, who could
trick him into giving away the secret, sort of getting him talking
about Joyce Campton and murder, maybe even Harold Burdock,
so that without thinking he would blurt it all out, even down to
the fact that no one had seen Henry Travis again, not since he was
taken into permanent custody by the police and his family moved
away from town. Those few who knew that Henry was not in jail
at all ignored that part of the story and entertained at least the
other part, about The Associate killing people for money. And if a
person filled up a wall with water, in late winter. The mere explanation that someone could have done it, that it could be explained
that way, was frightening enough. The question of why someone
would want to do it never came up. It was too early for that.

Rabbit went back four months in one of his many ledgers.
Nothing, nothing, nothing. Several of the people who had left
had merely—Abbot Meyer's account closed out: $74,873. And
everyone knew about Harold and Judith—at least he did. And
now Meyer was gone too. Rabbit decided again what he must do,
to be sure.

Many did not believe it at all. Not yet, at least. July
Montgomery, Steve Linquist, Paul Kraus, Arthur Friday, Lyle
Cote, M. Mossman, Jay Greenhaw, Jim Frye, Ken Burr, Charlie
Sanchez, Phil Odell, Leonard Barrett, Jacob Forbes, Morris
Holsten, Burton Chase—these men didn't believe it. There
was even some fighting, but mostly threats and pushing and
others holding back. Many of these men went to the Yard in
order to make sure it was not true. Not testing, just reaffirming.
They went in groups, and sometimes alone, picking through
the Yard, trading for this or that, giving Sam and C (and Keith
and Jimmy Cassum, if they were there) friendly greetings, hoping that in the conversation that followed—without having to
come right out and ask, *Did you take money to kill Joyce Campton*

or Harold Burdock?—it would come out whether it was true or not.

But they received no word or indication. Someone (Charlie Sanchez) had even said right out to Sam in front of four men, "Some say . . . some say that wall could have been filled with water . . . if someone wanted to, maybe if they were paid money for it." And Sam had said, "How much money, Sanchez, would that have been worth to you?" No one spoke for a time after that, but July Montgomery and others wondered why Sam hadn't come right out and denied the implication. Why did he pretend he didn't know what was being asked of him? When he knew that everyone there was waiting for him to say, *There wouldn't be enough money for something like that,* or even pick up a piece of angle iron and threaten to clean Sanchez's wagon if he didn't revamp his thinking or keep it to himself. When he knew that little was asked of him, of them, so that everyone could go home again and forget it. July Montgomery looked at Sam and thought, Perhaps because he knows what is being said of him and his brother, who never did anything in their lives to harm anyone except the memory of their father . . . perhaps he will not stoop to even recognize it, thinking that merely denying such an accusation is not enough, thinking that only by ignoring it—by abrogating it in that way— would it be pushed out of existence. Only if it had never been could it go away.

But they had come, some in groups and some individually, to be told that it was a lie, and none of the four told them that. And so what could be done then but wait? Because if it was what Larry Timbermain had said it was—if it was that—it would rise to the surface. They would wait, and when the covering was pulled back and the events were clear, they would know what to do. But of course it couldn't be true. Accidents. Gossip. Fear. Men with minds of old ladies. Nothing more. Yet still, July had been there when they had carried Ansel Easter out, when Sam had said, "He ain't dead, lady . . . resting." Looking at them all. What could death mean to them? Wouldn't that have done something to them, something to their insides, so that if someone came and said, *Will you kill for money?* they would not turn away like normal people, horrified, but would remember and their faces turn to stone. *How much?* And of course if that was true, then how could you blame them (when Harold Burdock had been there and so had Joyce Campton, younger then, and their father dead, dead for what reason)? Nothing they could ever understand. No, not that young. They could never have understood when it was their father who was killed by someone in town, though no one ever knew who, but everyone had known for a long time that it had to be done, that someone would do it, whether it was true about him or not, just so that the thought could die too. Everyone knew but them. They could never know. And if that was true, though you couldn't blame them, they would have to be stopped, like animals.

Yet they were not really frightened then. Not until later. They were mostly waiting, thinking that the police would be turning over some stone any day, every day for a week, then two, then a month. Waiting. Rabbit had decided what he must do, but waited, hoping something would happen so that he would not have to do it at all; aware that Timbermain had not kept their secret. Knowing that the harm had been done, but secretly hoping that the harm would help bring about something that would ferret out the truth, so that he would not have to do what he knew he would do. Watching his daughter leave the house with Glove and get into Sam's car and drive off into the night, letting her go, making her promise that they would go where they said they were going and come back without unexplainable forty-five minutes or hours between when the movie house let out or the pizza parlor closed.

They were not really frightened until later. Until Steven Sterns, a bachelor by divorce (having settled out of court three years ago for what everyone believed ended up being more for her than any judge would allow), living in a low-budget apartment complex, owner of a small thirty-five-cent laundromat where he spent his weeks making change and doing dry-cleaning and paying close attention to the use of his top-loading machines, was irritable one morning, and snapped at Mrs. Gregerson for leaving her clothes in a dryer while going about her business in town, though there were not enough people there to demand the concern. Later he screamed at Susie Peterson for letting in fish bugs through the screen door, holding his head every minute or so as though he had a severe headache. Nothing more until the following day, when he did not open until afternoon and chased several young people away, saying they could not buy soda pop unless they were doing laundry. By then the slightest noise, the starting of a machine or the infinitesimal click before shutting off, seemed to frighten him nearly to tears. He drove everyone but Mr. and Mrs. Morris out and then began flinging laundry from his dry-cleaning machine around the room, spitting up saliva which he seemed unable to swallow but which also flowed unchecked from underneath his tongue. Gagging. Then his body began to jerk and he began screaming and did not stop for over two hours, not even later at the hospital. He lay on the floor and was spasmodically rippled with muscle convulsions prompted by the sounds of running water in the unseen lines in the walls and under the floor or by someone touching him to carry him away, until he was dead. A quiet, noble man, dying like that.

Rabies. And his cat, the only thing he had seemed to get away with after his out-of-court settlement three years ago, was taken in for observation and died six days later of the same symptoms.

Then came the fear. Quickly. As though it did not even need to be thought out, as though it no longer needed to be true, as though the fear only needed that word "rabies" to feed on, for all the rest, the supposed, the fact that because of Steven Sterns' cracked lips and bad gums someone could have found a rabid animal, taken some serum from under its tongue, enough to infect a city, followed him into the grocery store and when he wasn't looking, perhaps while he talked pleasantly to the store owner or a neighbor, injected an apple. Then after waiting a week snatched his cat as she snooped around the apartment lawn looking for bugs or a private place to defecate, and infected her too, knowing that there would be no symptoms of the animal to give the disease away to Sterns until it was too late and he was mad. Then the doctors would have to admit, No, it is not absolutely necessary that the animal be mad itself before passing the disease, it could be done before, and of course with the condition of his body after writhing for several hours, some of that time on rough cement, it would be a joke to look for the tiny scratch mark that might have begun the virus. Someone could have. No, merely the word "rabies" did that. And as if that weren't enough, what it also meant was that if a man living like that, surrounded by people, with no chance of anyone working over the apparatus of his living situation without being seen, could be made to die like that, then no one could be safe. So it was fear.

Ed Simpson came to the Yard at night. The Associate was in the room downstairs. The rest of the house was dark. Arguing. He slipped into the house and knocked on the partially closed door. They called him in. He demanded to know if Don Lable had paid them to kill him. No, he was told, he hadn't. They did not take money to kill, what they did was supply information, worthless information. Then Don Lable had done that, hadn't he? Ed was sure. No, he hadn't. But Ed was sure he would, if he had the chance. (If he did, then Ed would have to move on him first.) "So how about this worthless information? How much is it for you to tell me how to kill Lable?"

"You have to wait a month. Then we know what you can afford."

"One month!"

"Yes."

"But I think he's leaving in one month."

"Too bad."

"But maybe he isn't."

"Why don't you forget it anyway?" asked Keith. "If he's leaving anyway."

"After what he done to me!"

"Wait a month," said Sam, "and maybe we'll do it and maybe we won't."

Then he left.

FROM THE THIRD FLOOR GLOVE WATCHED HIM STUMBLE AGAINST A LAWN-mower handle before crossing the street. He finished rolling a cigarette, lit it, blew out the flame when the paper had flared up, and turned on the radio. The green, fierce button tinted his hand. He put on the headphones and waited for the low hum of electricity glowing red and yellow in the tubes.

"Hey, Baron, you there?"

He heard some rustling around inside the bus, then the three pops of his brother's fingers on the microphone, signaling that he was there listening.

"I've been thinking about that part you showed me, *There's something good about Ernie*. I can't understand it either. It seems to me, from the rest of it, that he couldn't think that. From everything that I know, it couldn't be thought. I think he says that several other times, later in the diaries."

He took a couple of puffs on his cigarette and blew the smoke, unseen, out into the darkness. It was a black night outside.

"Have you found another mention of that phrase?"

Two pops.

"In the 1946?"

One pop.

"1945?"

One pop, loud.

"1947?"

One pop.

"1948! The last one!"

Two pops.

"1948!"

Two pops.

"Very curious. I don't know how he could say that. Especially then." Pause. "Anyway, I haven't got much to say tonight. I just got back from seeing Eight. You know, for a girl she's got a lot of feelings. They're still arguing downstairs. I guess Keith is moving into one of the rooms next to Sam. All of them are acting funny and never talk when you come in the room. I overheard a little, but couldn't make much out of it. Something about some agreement, on paper, that's all. I'm nervous about staying down too long 'cause Dad gets so mad if he catches you down there. But they sometimes use the word 'murder,' or 'killing.' Whatever it is, it's got me worried, and them too. Jimmy Cassum's wife took her kids and went out of state. Dad sits up with Mom sometimes now at night. Last night, again, Dad asked her about you, but she won't tell where you are (or where she thinks you are) and just says, 'He's safe. He's safe.' Usually they don't talk at all, but sit up in the living room, Dad looking out the window and Mom looking at him. Once he said, 'The Yard. If I would have stayed with the Yard, the way I was doing when we first came here, when things were good. Now we'll all pay for it.' He talks odd like that, like he's afraid of something—well, maybe before he was, now he's just waiting. What black thoughts. Hardly worth going to sleep on. I got to go, O.K.? Everything all right?"

Two pops.

"O.K. Be cool. I'll try to get out tomorrow night. Want anything?"

Two pops.

"Food type?"

Two pops.

"Solid?"

One pop.

"Liquid?"

Two pops.

"Sweet?"

Two pops.

"Orange soda?"

One pop.

"Root beer?"

Two pops.

"O.K. Anything else?"

One pop.

"Want to try anything else to read?"

One pop.

"O.K. 'Bye."

Three pops.

Then Glove flipped off the amplifier and took off his head-phone. He relit his cigarette and smoked it down to a respectable short length and snuffed it out. Then from a desk drawer under the short-wave radio he took what had cost him the other part of the money Cell had given him, and carried it, held closely to him, back into the end of the room on the other side of the corner, where he could look out into the back yard, from where he could see the bus in the daytime. Tonight was so dark that he could not even see to the ground. This may be too dark, he thought, and took it out and put it to his eye. Through it he could see the cross-hairs against the side of the bus, not clearly, but well enough. There was a faint light inside the bus . . . Baron reading by candlelight inside one of the partitions with painted windows, the brighter light coming from lines near the edges where the paintbrush had not reached, thin pencil lines of light hidden be-hind leaves and woodshadows.

He waited and rolled another cigarette, keeping the burning end cupped with his hand so that Baron could not know that there was anyone in the window. Just as he was ready to give up and go to bed, he saw the light inside the bus go out and, later, his brother emerge from it, his eyes pressed closed but without the blindfold. Without the blindfold! Yes, he had known it would happen. He would trust himself to keep his eyes shut. After that, in the blackest of nights . . . Yes, thought Glove, he will open them. No, he will never be able to walk around in twilight . . . still, in the dead of the night, in the lurking darkness he will move around some. The thought filled him strangely with a kind of pride—pride in being Baron's brother—in having a brother who he knew would be able to move about in the blackness as silently as an eyelid opening, more wary than any animal, quicker than a bird, smarter than anything. He watched Baron return from the hidden outhouse and approach the bus, like a ghost, no sound at all, as though the dark figure was only appearance, no substance. Glove reached a finger to the screen and made an inch scratch of noise. Baron stopped and stood absolutely still, so still and for so long that Glove thought several times that what he had thought was Baron before was really some shadow or piece of something vaguely that shape—that his brother was in the bus. So he looked away and back again. And then without his ever having seen it move, the shadow was gone. Then he saw the back door of the bus closing but heard no click of fastening.

MORE

"I see it," said Glove, as his brother pointed again at the line *There's something good about Ernie.* "And this is the third time?" Baron nodded. They were sitting in the room with the refrigerator. It was late at night and they were reading with a candle. The salamander heater was turned on and sent a blast of warm air into the bus. Glove was pleased at how well the bus could hold heat, being as old as it was, but was nervous about reading in one of the rooms with unpainted windows. They had both become too confident, he feared, and he thought of how he might find a way to warn his brother to be careful about leaving footprints in the snow without letting him know that he knew he was coming out of the bus when it was very dark and roaming like an animal about the Yard. He decided to say nothing—Baron would know himself not to do that.

Glove went over to the window and looked out. It was snowing in fine, misty flakes, sounding like straight pins falling on the roof of the bus. He stared out into the snow toward the house, then saw someone—a figure (it was too far away to tell more)— slip off the side of the front porch and into the Yard, carrying something. Coming toward them. He turned absently to tell his brother to douse the light, hoping to be able to keep what he had seen to himself, but Baron read his eyes as soon as he turned, pinched out the candle, turned down the thermostat so that the blower would not come on, and was at the window beside him.

"Over there," whispered Glove, "just coming around the tractor, next to—" Baron touched him, indicating that he saw. The figure came forward, deliberately, step by step, straight toward the bus. After half the distance Baron touched his brother again. "I know," Glove whispered. "It's Mom." Closer. Glove could feel that The Baron was afraid.

She came up to the bus and then walked around behind it. Baron closed his eyes. Both waited for the door to open, waited to see it open outward and her stand there, and for this reason did not hear until later that the footsteps carried her on past the door farther down into the tangled growth of trees. "She's going away," whispered Glove. But Baron was already on the other side looking out the opposite window. He motioned for Glove to hurry, and pointed.

Cell had stopped with her breadbox-sized bundle, which looked to her sons like one big ball of wadded-up newspaper, and put it down. She knelt beside it and little bursts of light jumped from her hands and went out. Finally a corner of the paper caught on fire, and spread. Soon it was all burning and Cell stood back from it, looking in the snow and darkness as though she had walked into a wall of light, and the light, like paint, had rubbed off and was now glowing red and yellow from her forehead, cheekbones, shoulder tips, underneath her small breasts, and most brightly from a huge swath across her dark skirt.

"I don't know," whispered Glove.

Cell broke off a length of stick and prodded the fire, plunging its sharp end into the bits of unburned substance that fell away, bringing them back to be burned. And as she knelt next to the fire, making sure no phoenix would come from the ashes, her face betrayed no emotion, no madness, and otherwise no indication of what purpose she could have set for herself. After the glow was gone she covered the ashes with snow carried by hand and scraped with the side of her slippers. They could tell she was shivering. Glove started for the door as the pile of snow continued to grow and she began talking to herself a little, the shivering making the words stagger and falter. But Baron touched him to say, *Wait.* Then she began walking, past the bus and back to the house, even running after she had reached near enough to the front steps so that she could run without falling.

Glove turned up the thermostat again and let another blast of warming air into the bus. He felt very tired. He felt very sad.

"There's events coming. I can feel them."

Baron nodded. Glove did not talk about the burning. He had suddenly known what it was that she was burning, though he did not know where she had gotten it to burn. And he knew that later, after he had gone back to the house, Baron would go and uncover some ashes and know too. Then they would both know without one having to show or tell the other. And they would both know as much about it.

"Did you hear what she said today . . . about Grandfather, about an hour after I brought you the sandwich and that Wood kid went back home with his birdcage?" Baron nodded. "Good. I hoped you wouldn't be asleep." Pause. "The way she explained it, he—Ansel—thought there was something good about Ernie . . . because he thought Ernie was human. At least, that's what *she* thought. But I don't know how she would have heard about all that . . . Who would have told her? Not Dad. Not Sam. I don't know how it could have been human.

"I've got to get back. She might start looking for me if she checks my room before she goes to bed. You know, she's got a picture of that Ernie inside a little trinket on her arm?" Baron nodded. "Oh, I guess you could tell that from listening.

"Anyway, I got to go. Be cool." He slipped out of the bus and back toward the house. Baron watched him go, knowing that now, this minute, it was he, Glove, who was afraid, not of Cell, but of those events which he felt were coming. Baron wanted to run to him, to touch him in the snow and let him know that everything would be all right. But of course he couldn't let his brother know that he knew Glove knew that he could move around at night outside the bus. He could never let him know the full extent to which he knew anything. But now, just now, he wanted only to let him know that if need be he would not have to stand on the front porch by himself as they carried out . . . Baron left the bus and went quickly to the pile of snow his mother had left. When his brother had heard her murmuring, he had not known that she was praying. Baron knew. He had heard her before. Sifting through the wet ashes, Baron thought of her words: *Know the power of my Lord, know the power of my Lord, know the power of my Lord.* He knew this was no ordinary prayer, but that because of the undirected *know* and the *my* instead of *the* before *Lord*, it was a kind of prayer prayed by someone of little faith who sought merely to familiarize herself with the feeble power inside herself in order to do what she felt she must, and to make it through another day, asking for no more, daring no more. Such a prayer Baron prayed. Then he set out across the Yard, though he feared the moon might rise from behind any house, through many things, down into the woods, moving like a wraith past rabbits and deer who noticed him but did not move, just watched more carefully.

Just before daylight, like a vampire, he stole swiftly back to his bus, not having found what he was looking for. He slept until almost six in the afternoon, and set out again that night, this time with no fear of the moon rising because his brother had brought him a *Farmer's Almanac.* He hoped he would be brave enough later to go to Joyce Campton's house.

"BE CAREFUL THERE, FISHER," SAID RABBIT. "DON'T MOVE AROUND IN THE boat or you'll tip it over."

"Ah, Dad."

"And be careful with that fishing pole or you might get a hook stuck in your finger." Rabbit worked the oars deeply through the water, sending their little boat gliding over the top of the pond.

"This is a good place here, Dad."

"I'm afraid it's too shallow here. Fish like to be in deep water near weeds."

"If I was a fish, I'd sit just there and BANG I'd swish up out of there, and ZOOOM back down under!" Fisher made violent gestures with his hands, rocking the boat. Rabbit couldn't help but smile.

"Careful there, Fisher. Don't tip the boat."

"Look, look, there's a turtle! Look, Dad, look!"

"Sit down, Fisher." Rabbit had let go of the oars and was holding on to the sides to steady the rocking.

"There he goes, PLUNK down under. Dad, can I take this ole jacket off?"

"No."

"It's too hot."

"It isn't hot at all. Mine feels just right. See there, that's a great blue heron. Watch him when he flies. He'll keep his neck folded back."

"Wow! He's big. Why's he that big?"

"He just is. Now, right over there looks like a good place to me. How about you?"

"Where?"

"Over there."

"It's O.K."

"All right, we'll go over real slow, being careful not to make much noise—just drift in, set the anchor—"

"I'll do that!"

"Right. But carefully and slowly. We don't want to scare the fish."

"Why are fish scared?"

"Because they don't want to be caught."

"We'll get 'em, though," said Fisher. "Won't we, Dad?"

"Yes. Now we have to start being quiet."

"Why couldn't Glove come with us?"

"He probably wouldn't've wanted to."

"Did you *ask* him?"

"Well, no. He's got other things to do."

"You promised!"

"I know I did." Rabbit felt terrible. "I know I did. Next time we'll both ask him to come. But you have to remember, he's a lot older than you and he's got other things to do."

"I know," mumbled Fisher dejectedly. "But if he was here, he'd know how to get 'em. He knows everything."

"Nobody can know everything."

"He knows all the important things. Do you know how strong he is, Dad?"

"Well, I guess I don't."

"He's *real* strong. He's stronger than a bear, I bet."

"We have to start being quiet now."

"O.K. . . . . There! Hey, I just saw one, right down in the water!"

"Quiet, Fisher. We'll just let 'er drift on over now. Hand me your pole and we'll put a piece of cheese on the hook."

"Can we buy this boat?"

"Why?"

"Don't you think we should?"

"Not as long as Mr. Millet will let us come use it whenever we want to."

"But it isn't ours."

"It's just as good as ours, though. Now don't move around, just hand me your pole."

"I want one of those long bobbers like yours."

"O.K. Here, we'll just slip it on. There. Now for a little piece of cheese, just fish-bite size."

"Are the Millets poor, Dad?"

"No. They have a comfortable income from their farming."

"Could we have a farm?"

"What would we do with a farm?"

"Start a junk yard!"

BARON COMMUNICATED TO HIS BROTHER THOUGHTS THAT HE HAD DURING the day by circling words in the diaries as he learned to write.

Once Glove came to visit him after several days of being too busy, and in one of the diaries Baron had circled one word in a green pencil . . . "lonely." Glove felt as though a knife had entered his heart.

"I'm going to get a job," he explained, "working at the foundry. At least, I hope so. I'll try to get out every day, but I can't promise when we'll be able to get you back in the house. Do you miss the folks much?"

Baron nodded.

Glove felt his nerves begin to quiver. I've got to get some sleep, he told himself. His brother, as though looking into his soul, motioned to his own little pallet along the side of the bus. "No, thanks . . . heck, I don't want to go to sleep now that we got a chance to be together. Here, bring those cards over here. I've a feeling you won't stand a chance against me tonight."

Baron brought over the cards and they settled down to play crazy eights. Outside, big ragged snowflakes fell silently out of the sky.

JULY MONTGOMERY, PAUL KRAUS, JIM FRYE, LYLE COTE, KEN BURR, Billy Jackson, and Mal Rourke were drinking in the Farmer's Tavern under the dim overhead lights. They talked in slow, purposeful voices.

"Did they find anything else?" they asked Lyle Cote, who had a brother-in-law in the police force.

"Only that his cat died of rabies too. Only Bud called it something else. Some long word."

"Hydrophobia," said Paul Kraus.

"Nothing else?"

"Not that he said."

At that time the front door burst open and Don Lable came in, out of the snow. He got himself a double whiskey, no ice, and brought it over to their table. His face was flushed from the cold. He took a long drink and told them he was "marked" by The Associate . . . that someone, and he wouldn't say who, had paid them to kill him before he left for Denver.

"Ah, go on," said July.

"I tell you, I've been marked. They're going to try to kill me."

"Who hired them?"

"Somebody."

"Ah, go on," said Mal Rourke.

"WHAT IS THAT!" CHALLENGED C, POINTING TO A BULGE UNDER HIS brother's shirt.

Sam said calmly, "It's a gun."

"Get rid of it. We're not going to start carrying guns. My God, get rid of it."

"Don't be a fool. Jimmy Cassum almost got beat to death last week by a shady bunch with two-by-fours. And it wasn't the goodness of their hearts that stopped 'em either. It was because they couldn't run that fast. Do you think something's not going to happen?"

"Get rid of the gun. I mean it, Sam. Get rid of it."

Sam threw the sleek little automatic from inside his shirt back through the open door to his room, onto the bed. Then the two of them continued down the hall and into one of the front rooms, where they could watch the Yard.

"Keith's going to leave," said Sam. "Maybe tonight and maybe tomorrow."

"Won't that sort of mean something?"

"You know, C. Nothing's any good now. Even if we took that agreement and nailed it up on the front door to read. It wouldn't do any good. You know that, don't you, C?"

"Maybe. They won't come here. They're not that sure."

"Do you believe that?"

"No. Who's that?" and C pointed out through the window. Someone was running toward the house. C's eyes were not as good as they had been, but, refusing to admit it to himself, he lived in a cloudy world rather than have glasses.

"It's Ed Simpson," said Sam.

"I suppose he'll want his money," said C. "Keith will."

"I suppose."

Ed Simpson burst in the door.

"In here, Simpson," said Sam.

He came in.

"Quick," he said. "You got to tell me. Lable's leaving! I just found out. He's been keeping it a secret, but now the bastard has got his kids and wife already gone, the big furniture moved out during the night, and is just now picking up his tools and such and putting them into his car. I tell you, he's leaving!"

"Is that a fact?" said C. "Did you hear that, Sam?"

"Who's that?"

"Lable, Don Lable, he's leaving."

"No! Leaving! Where's he going?"

"I don't know. Where's he going, Simpson?"

"Damn it. Give me the information."

"Well, listen, Simpson. What we decided is no more information. In fact, we have become citizens again . . . and anything you say now might be held in evidence against you."

"We had a deal!"

"No," said Sam. "You made a mistake in your thinking. There was never a deal. Now get out."

"You'll be sorry," Simpson said. "Lable won't get away, and neither will you. Bastards."

"Get out," said Sam.

"You'll be sorry." Then he left and ran back through the Yard, jumped madly into his car, yelling still, but now inaudibly over the screech of his tires as he fled on downtown, toward Don Lable's house.

"There's one we can't be blamed for," said Sam.

"True. This one should be sloppy and out in the open. Maybe that'll help."

"Maybe," said Sam. "But I doubt it. Merely a matter of time, getting up enough nerve."

"Why did we do it, Sam?"

"Which one?"

"Any one. Why did we ever do it?"

"For money."

"How can that be? It sounds so simple. So stupid. There must have been more to it than that. We must have hated—"

"Joyce Campton?"

"No. We didn't think he'd do that one. Even Cassum didn't think it would really work, and it was mostly his idea because of knowing about the walls being set up that way. Who would have thought—"

"Snap out of it, C. We've been over this how many times? The only thing to do now is keep from going . . . get out of here."

"Mad. Like Steven Sterns. Can you imagine what it would be like to feel—God, Sam!"

Sam hit him, not easily, but with a full half-swing, and knocked him out of his chair. Blood ran from his mouth onto the floor. He shook his head, got to his knees, then stood up. "That'll cost you," he said, and tried to kick Sam in the face, but he moved to the side and the blow caught his shoulder and spun him out of the chair. Then C hit him and he went back against the window. C picked up a chair and came at him again. The window splintered. A bleeding crack opened up above Sam's eye. C spat out two of his own teeth and his mouth flooded with blood. Then he felt a rib snap.

Keith and Jimmy Cassum burst into the house from outside and grabbed them, and were able to keep them apart because of the weakness that had set in from the exertion and pain. "Listen, you idiots—God, look at that, Cassum, two teeth! Don Lable is dead."

"What?" said Sam.

"Him and Ed Simpson; both of 'em killed in a wreck. Cassum and I was on our way here from my house and we heard a noise that sounded like an accident, so we went over there, and by that time a whole crowd of people were there—a kind of funny crowd, too, because they weren't acting like people usually do at an accident . . . were too excited—and what it looked like was that Simpson had come barreling down Lincoln, and Lable, who had just thrown those few things in his car that the movers had left behind, was pulling onto Lincoln from Clinton, that street running in front—"

"I know where it is," said C.

"He either decided to or couldn't help it. In any case, he ran smack into him, drove him clear across two yards and into a swing set, and killed them both. God, you should have seen them. Awful. And old Beef from the bank almost threw up looking in at Lable and told us we better get out of there.

"Then he sent somebody for July Montgomery. Did Simpson come back here again?"

"He came. But we told him what we decided, to get out."

"Anyway," said Keith, "there's one they can't blame on us."

The telephone rang and Cell answered it upstairs.

THAT "FUNNY" CROWD WAS WAITING FOR JULY TOO. IT WAS SATURDAY, so most of the men were home, and had been absently watching the movers carry the furniture from Don Lable's house. The man who had said he was marked by The Associate . . . thinking that he was going to get away, and that there was nothing to the story that . . . watching him carry out his box of tools, overshoes, a radio, stand for the TV, cardboard boxes, and two lampshades, put them in his car, back out of the driveway and down Clinton. Many quit watching him then, and only heard the crash and came out of their houses, some holding cups of coffee. Rabbit too, who, after he had looked inside the wreckage and almost thrown up, saw Keith and Jimmy Cassum there and told them to leave, to get back and tell C. He walked them over to their car, keeping himself between them and the "funny" crowd. Then he sent for July Montgomery and when he came they (Rabbit and July) and five or six of the men went across town to Rabbit's house and he told them that he would see every last one of them hang if they did anything before they knew for sure, and that they could know for sure in less than two weeks. That he would tell them. But before then—he would see them all hang.

"O.K.," said July. "But they won't get away."

"No, they can't blame us for that one," said C.

Upstairs, Cell hung up the phone and came walking down into the front room, from where she heard the voices.

"Keith's decided to leave. And I guess I'm going with him," said Jimmy Cassum. "We'll leave tonight."

"O.K.," said C, and turned to sit down in the chair. Cell saw him then, staring at the blood on his hands and shirt.

"Rabbit called," she said. "And he says we got two weeks to pay for the mortgage. He says it's legal. It's legal and if we don't pay in two weeks the cops come and throw us out . . ." Her speech had gotten slower and she stopped talking when she took her eyes away from her husband and saw Sam.

"Go upstairs," said C. And she went.

"He's trying to get us out of here," said Sam. "He's telling us in as kindly a way as he can to get out of here."

"No," said C. "He's trying to make it easier for them. He wants to see it happen, but he wants it done out in the open so there's no question. He's afraid somebody might think he did it."

"Bankers don't think like that," said Sam. "All he cares about is money. They never do anything except for money. He probably just learned that it was legal to foreclose if so-and-so many payments are late. He just wants—"

"Don't mean to interrupt," said Keith. "But Jim and I don't really care. And besides, you can just pay it anyway. It's not as though you don't have the money, and it's also not as though we haven't waited long enough to start spending some of it. And it's about time we divided it up, being's as Jim and I are leaving tonight anyway."

"Don't you see that you can't leave now?" asked C.

"Of course we can."

"Look." And he pointed outside, where in front of the Yard sat two automobiles with three men in one and two in the other. "He's trying to force us out of here. Those men are from July's bar. That's why he sent for July, 'cause he doesn't want Glove or Cell to get hurt. He wants us out there in the open."

Keith and Jimmy looked out. And stared.

"We can get by at night," said Jimmy, the first of the four finally to believe that what they had feared even to imagine had happened. He was the first to see that what was outside was not a nightmarish illusion. "Let's divide up the money. You can do whatever you like. I'm getting out of here."

So they went into the room with THE ASSOCIATE above the door. "I won't leave this house," said C. "No one's going to take me out of here."

"Then pay him," said Keith.

C opened the safe and swung the heavy, fat door aside. Then he sat back on the floor and gazed, put his hand in and stared. "It's gone," he said. "The money's all gone." Jimmy Cassum and Keith rushed to look in, and even put their hands in too, grabbing through the few scattered papers and letters as though all the neatly packed money, in mostly tens and twenties, that had taken up half of the space in the safe was hiding somewhere. "It's gone," said C again.

But Sam had known from the finality of his voice that it was no mistake, and did not have to look.

"You're right," he said. "He's trying to force us out in the open. He knew about the money, and now he knows we don't have it—that we can't pay."

"The pact," said Keith slowly. "The pact."

"C, the pact."

C shuffled through the papers; then again. "It's gone," he said. "They've taken that too."

"They know everything."

"Then they know we didn't do it," said Jimmy Cassum. "They know it was only information—that we had no passion, no desire to kill anyone, only worthless information. They can't want to hurt us now." And he ran out and opened the front door. The others ran behind him and stopped there, looking outside. The two cars in the distance across the Yard opened up and men came out of them. They looked at each other. "They're going to kill us," said Jimmy Cassum. "They're going to kill us." They shut the door and went back inside. The telephone line was dead. The men from July's bar climbed back inside their cars, out of the cold. C went upstairs.

He went into his living room and sat in the chair next to the window. The room was unnaturally clean. He heard her coming, but did not look up. His whole face hurt.

"Cell," he said. He looked at her and looked away. "You've got to get away from here. Take Glove and go away. You've got to be strong now, and never come back."

"C!" she said and ran to him, throwing her thin arms around his legs. "C . . . it wasn't Sam that took the money. It was me, C. I took it and I burned it. Beat me, C. Beat me with your fists, please." Crying.

"You took that money?"

"Yes. The other night, I took it and burned it."

"You took the money and the pact?"

"And that paper about needless information for free, that too. I burned them. I burned them in the Yard."

"Why did you do that?"

"Oh, C"—she was crying very loudly now—"I want you to beat me. I thought you were selling Baron. I thought that money was for—"

"That's why you sent—You thought I was selling—What made you—"

"But I know now that it wasn't true. I knew when I saw you

downstairs, with your teeth on the floor and blood on the window and on your shirt, and Sam too . . . I knew because you're good, C. You're good. It's me what's brought all this on us. I burned the money. Even with blood on your face, there was no hate, and C, there's always hate in me—" C put his head into his hands. "No, don't look away, listen, C. It's been me. I burned the money. I hated The Baron. I did things to him when nobody was here, trying to make him jump out his window. I burned the money, and the paper. C, it was me. Beat me, C."

"Why did you think that I had sold—"

"Jellybelly Rabbit. He said, *That's not much money for a human life.* He said that to trick me, to make me burn the money, 'cause he knew inside of me is hating, hating, and that when we couldn't pay he could throw us out. In the winter. We've got no money, C. I burned it. Nobody ever comes here any more. They will never bring us food, now that *they* know, too, about the hating."

"So Rabbit knew about the money?"

"He kept saying, What about the money, what about the money, what about the money, do you have money?"

"Then he didn't see it?"

"No."

"Is it all burned . . . all of it?"

"Yes. I burned it all, even the corners with the numbers. It's all gone. I'm sorry, C. I'm sorry I ever came here with you."

Then tears came down C's own face, and ran over the dried blood, freeing some of it, and down onto his shirt and onto Cell's hand. And she said, "Don't cry, C. Don't cry. Sam will get us some money. Everything will be all right." And he took her up in his arms and carried her over to the other window and told her to look out at those cars and those men who were going to kill him, not because of her, but because of him. He told her he loved her beyond anything else in his life, even the Yard, but he would not try to run away, like Keith and Jimmy Cassum would, tonight probably . . . and maybe Sam. But he wouldn't leave. But

she must, and take Glove with her. He told her she would have
to be strong, and she stopped crying and said that if he wouldn't
beat her, would he undress her and live inside her for so long that
they might remember for a minute what it was like when they had
been young and had no refrigerator.

He carried her down the hall and into the bedroom, shutting
the door behind him. Glove stepped from behind his door, from
where he had heard that the money was burned and that Rabbit
had called in the loan, but the rest, when they were next to the
window, he had not been able to hear. He did not hear Cell,
from inside the bedroom, say, "I won't go away, C. Neither will
Glove." And because of this much that he knew, he also knew
what he would have to do. He remembered the day before, when
his father had talked to him in his room, talking in an abstract
way, as though he (C) would be gone or leaving, telling him that
the Yard, that he would have to save the Yard, stay here, so that
sometime again people would come to trade, for comparable size
and weight, play horseshoes, drink soda, and watch the cartoon
colored time pass through Iowa. He knew what he would have
to do. He went into the living room and picked up the phone.
It was dead, yet almost a sound in itself. He went upstairs to his
room and put his whole stash of euphorics into his pocket, then
downstairs and outside. As he stepped onto the porch, several
cars opened up and men began to come out of them, but then they
closed up again. Glove thought nothing.

"They won't hurt him," said Sam from a front room, and
watched him walk out through the Yard, start up his (Sam's) car,
and drive away. It was getting dark.

TURNING INTO THE DRIVEWAY, HE HIT A PATCH OF ICE AND SWERVED
from side to side in the snow, oversteering and overaccelerat-
ing, up to the house. He walked to the house and knocked on
the door. Arness, Ester Wood's maid, let him into the enormous
kitchen. Fisher was there.

"Hi, Fish."

"Hi," said Fisher. "You want to see that secret now?"

"Well . . . I sort of got business. But O.K. Arness, you tell Eight I'm here?"

"O.K.," she said and went out to find her.

Fisher and Glove climbed the back staircase up to the attic.

"Spooky up here, Fish."

"Don't be scared," said Fisher. "Ain't anything up here hurt you. Just animals and wind and wolves."

"Wolves!"

"Sometimes. Anyway, look." He pointed down at the aviary. It took Glove some time, because of the darkness, to see anything in it.

"It's a sparrow," said Glove.

"I know it," said Fisher.

"Keeping him for the winter, huh?"

"For the winter?"

"Sure. Through that time when it's rough for birds." ·

"Why not longer?"

"Longer! You weren't thinking of keeping him longer, were you, Fish? No. That was just a joke—pretending you didn't know about the Tabulation."

"The Tabulation?"

"Sure. When all the animals and birds—wolves too, there's millions of them there—get together after the winter and tabulate just who's who in the other world. And so having this little guy here there, you've got someone to put in a good word for you. And sometimes that helps—with the wolves, I mean."

"What with the wolves?"

"Oh, well, you know, don't you . . . about how wolves get at people sometimes, tear out their throats and such?"

". . . Sure."

"That couldn't happen if there had been someone—some animal—at the Tabulation to put in a good word for them."

"No, I don't suppose it could."

"Of course, if you're worried . . . there's a way to know for sure."

"How's that?"

Downstairs, Eight called, "Glove."

"We better go," he said, and started downstairs. Fisher, coming down the stairs behind him, asked, "How can you know? How can you be sure?" Glove stopped and told him that the only way to know for sure if the information was needed right away was to let the bird go—give it a chance to fly away, and if it took it without a moment's hesitation, then it would mean he couldn't wait until spring, that the good word was needed now, before the wolves began their midwinter feasts.

Fisher stayed on the second floor and Glove continued on down to the kitchen. Only Eight was no longer there calling for him. She was in another room with her mother, yelling at her, and crying. But Rabbit was there.

"Hello, Mr. Wood."

"Hello, Glover. Did you bring something for me, from your father?"

"No," he said, and saw in Rabbit's tired, worn face a kind of never-ending suspiration. Then it changed.

"I've got something to say to you. I'm going to say it quick and . . . I guess what I mean is that I'm going to say it and whatever responsibility—concerning your thoughts of me, how much you may not understand, and hate—I take it all. I expect Eight home tonight before eleven. And after that don't ever come here again. I won't have you near here or near Eight. Do you understand that, Glover?"

"My name is Glove."

"Do you understand?"

"I understand."

"Do you agree?"

"I agree that after eleven o'clock tonight, when I bring Eight back, I will never come again. Unless you change your mind."

"I won't."

There's something else here, thought Glove, looking at Rabbit's face, something more than the money . . . something more in his mind. He looks at the floor, not at me. He looks like he might cry, but there is no water. A desert in his face. Not just the money. Yet he barks out the words. Not just the house. Not just the money. But I must pretend that is all, because I don't have enough time. Perhaps there'll never be enough time to know all that must be known in order to act. *The Yard—you must save the Yard.* Knowing cannot act; it is dead. Honor is action. Feeling is honor.

"You will," he said. "Remember that you take—"

"The responsibility."

"Where's Eight?"

Rabbit Wood called his daughter, who came into the kitchen bundled in her tremendous white furry winter coat, her eyes red, looking hatefully at her father. She began to speak, but Glove took her mittened hand and turned her. They went out together and shut the door. They clasped at their clothing as a bitter wind tried to rip them naked and fled, running sideways down the driveway and into the old automobile. Rabbit watched them.

"You shouldn't have let her go, Rabbit," said Ester. "You shouldn't—"

"They deserve it," he said.

"They deserve!" she yelled. "Do you know what could happen tonight, because of letting them be together, them feeling the way they do, knowing they will never be allowed to see each other again? And young? You're as much as telling them go ahead, go ahead, this is the last time, go ahead and . . ." Between rage and hopelessness she could not find more words, and when she did they went on as though what was left out in between was not missing at all. "It means nothing to men, just an adventure, just fun. But she'll never forget. All her life."

"It's for her," said Rabbit. "Tonight's for her. It's Eight that deserves it. What can possibly mean anything to him? It will be nothing to him. It's she that deserves to have a sordid little fumbling experience in the back seat of a freezing car out in the country to hang on to—something she can use to hate us with—some dirty little deed she can think was worth it all. So that after he's gone, forever, she won't have to torture herself with why all the fear, why all the killing, why all the blood, and only a simple, naughty little night. Something she can keep and confess to her husband years later and maybe even tease him with—perhaps herself too, telling herself, If it was only Glove who was here now. It's for her. It's Glove who you should feel sorry for. Nothing can help him, not a lifetime of petty sins."

"I will not," Ester said slowly, "argue with you. I can see that you feel what you're doing is right. But I wonder and I want *you* to wonder if there isn't something with that boy—if there wasn't always something with that boy ever since he came here for Eight, maybe even before. I wonder if maybe you didn't all along want this to happen, want him to be the one."

"Maybe—"

"Wait. I want you to ask yourself about that. I want you to wonder if maybe you didn't think you could be him and she could be me . . . the way you wish I was."

"I did what I had to."

"I know," she said, in that slow, precise language, and went upstairs. Rabbit went into the living room and turned on the television, to Channel Two, and watched everything that came in front of his eyes and spat through the cathode-ray tube, scanning back and forth quicker than anyone could see. Watched until five minutes of eleven, when he heard Sam's car. He listened to two car doors slamming, then the opening of the kitchen door, then the closing. He listened. He listened to one car door slam; and then the other; the car pulling out of the driveway and away. He sat and stared at the televison, but did not hear it. I would never have wanted this, he thought. I would never have in one thousand years wanted this. And he went into the kitchen. Without turning on the overhead light, he picked the paper from the floor, written by her:

DEAR M & F,
Back at 11:00. Glove and I are married. Will never be home again.

Eight

Rabbit folded it neatly and put it in the pocket of his Van Heusen shirt. He went up the back staircase to the second floor. There he met his son.

"What are you doing up, Fisher?"

"Nothing."

Rabbit sat down in the carpeted hallway. "Your mother's not going to be happy about something I did."

Fisher looked at him. "You want to see a secret?"

"A secret?"

"Yep. Come on." He led his father up into the attic. "There it is, see?"

Rabbit pulled over an old chair and looked down into the cage. "It's a sparrow," he said.

"Yep."

"How long have you had it? In the cage?"

"Not long."

"You been feeding it?"

"Sure."

"No salt."

"No salt."

"Where did you catch him?"

"Up here."

"Must be some holes in the roof. Cold up here."

"Do you want to be sure if the word is needed?"

"What?"

"Before the Tabulation."

"Tabulation?" He could see, even in the gloom, that his son was happy about his not knowing what he was talking about.

Fisher opened up the cage, and the sparrow was instantly gone, through the hole in the roof and out.

"Wow! It must have really been needed."

"What's this about tabulation?"

"Not tabulation, *the* Tabulation, where millions of wolves are gathered. But that's in the spring. Archie had to get—"

"That was Archie?"

"Yep. He had to get back to the wolves before their midwinter feast, to give them the good word about me, and you too, 'cause you were here too, and Glove."

"Was Glove up here?"

"Yep."

"Did he know about the Tabulation?"

"He knew a little about it."

"Do you know what he's done, Fisher?"

"No."

"He's taken Eight away. He married her. See this note?" He handed it to him.

Fisher read it with a secret penlight.

"What do you think?"

"I thought he was smarter than that."

"What do you mean?"

"I never did know why he wanted to be with her. She's really stupid, Dad. She doesn't care about anything like wolves or mysteries and such."

"When you get older"—he paused—"neither will you."

"Glove does. I'll never be older than him, and he'll always care about those things. And so will I."

"And so will I," said Rabbit.

"Don't worry," said Fisher. "He'll care about them again. He's like Samson."

"In the Bible?"

"Yep. He's like him; he's just lost his hair now. But no one will ever blind him, and one of these days he'll find some rusty thing out in the Yard that only you and I will know is in the shape of a jawbone."

"Even Samson couldn't do anything for him now, Fisher. He's really in trouble. More than you know."

"I know," said Fisher. "I know how Eight can drag you down. I've probably spent more time with her than you have. I know how she can drag a man down. But Samson could do anything. Even when he was blinded and weak from starving and hunger, he asked that guy, 'Hey, could you please put my hands on the pillars?'"

"He might do that," said Rabbit. "Bring it down on top of him."

"But Glove ain't blind—except about Eight. He's just got his hair cut off now. And Samson had to do that 'cause he knew he couldn't see. If he could have seen, he could have broken his chains and found some jack handle to clean their wagons."

"DAD, MOM, YOU KNOW EIGHT."

"Sure. Hi, Eight."

"Hello, Mr. Easter."

"Kind of late, isn't it, Glove, for you two to be still running about the countryside? Better be thinking of getting her on home soon."

"She *is* home. We're married." And he held out the paper, and displayed his half of the rings. She took off her mitten for the other half.

"You're married," said Cell. "You two?"

"Yes," said Glove, "us two."

"Are they, C?"

"I guess so."

"Good," she said, and smiled. C smiled too, but he did not say anything then, only later, when he said, "Your uncle will want to

know. You should tell him. Even if he's asleep, he'd want to . . .
No, forget it. Tell him in the morning. Hurry up now. You're still
too young to be staying up into the middle of the night, even if
you *are* married."

They left the living room. Cell watched them clear to the
stairway from the door. Glove showed Eight the bathroom, then
scampered down to his radio, flipped on the switch and, as soon
as he caught the hum, began saying, "Baron, you there, Baron?"
No answer. Then he turned it off. It was cold in his room. Eight
came and they closed the door and for a little while absolved
themselves of everything not of fingers and flesh and warm frol-
icking . . . Too early yet for Glove to begin wondering how much
longer now until he comes and says to C, Your son is mine, my
daughter is yours. Oh, yes, and take the Yard.

"Remember, they've got spotlights," said Keith, "those kind that
plug into the cigarette lighter. And they may have a couple of
watchers in the Yard." All of the lights in the house were out.
"Come on, Sam."

"No. I'm not in shape for the kind of activity you're talking
about, running and all. And I'm afraid you're underestimating
how many men and how much they want to get us."

"But it can only get worse. It ain't going to get any better.
Besides, this kind of thing drives me buggy. You ready, Keith?"
They stood in Sam's room next to his outside-opening door, wearing dark winter clothing. Keith drummed his fingertips against
his arms.

"Take this," said Sam, and held out his pistol to them.

"Keep it," said Keith. "If we'd need that, then it would probably be all over anyway. That, or I'd blow my own foot off just
before I got into the clear, during the last mad scramble."

"O.K.," said Sam. Then they looked at each other long before
opening the door, in a way to say, You and me, maybe someday in
Chelsea. Then they opened the door and slipped out, up against

the side of the house, their eyes like minks. Sam did not look out for them after that, but sat smoking, wondering when the noise would begin . . . a scream, two shotgun blasts maybe. He knew July Montgomery well enough to know he would never let them go, not after he had made up his mind. No, they would be out there waiting for them.

Jimmy and Keith stayed by the house until they were sure they could never see anything except dark shapes everywhere, some of which they could recognize as being wrecked cars, or oil-burning space heaters, knowing they would have to get away from the house, which acted like a light backdrop behind them. They hurried over to the automobile and stopped; they moved forward again twenty feet to an immense pile of metal roofing. They stopped. Murmured talking behind them. Snow crunching. Jimmy Cassum pointed back toward the house. Two figures divided by a dozen steps came forward. Flashlights. They started off again, but in front of them, forty yards ahead, two more lights came on and began searching with their luminous tunnels into the roofing. Keith looked at Jimmy. They were trapped, and could go neither forward nor back. Sam waited inside for the noise. And then at the same time they felt someone touch them. They turned and, as though out of nowhere, a young boy, maybe as old as fourteen but no older, had materialized from the dark air, and motioned them with a nudge of his head to follow him. He fell down on his hands and knees, crawled forward several yards, and completely disappeared. They fell down and followed, into an unknown length of corrugated culvert, large enough to crawl in but not much more, that had been hidden by the covering of snow. Keith judged they had traveled a little less than three rods before the culvert ended and he could see the boy crouching in the opening waiting for them. Another four-rod progression under the protection of a giant grain elevator, up to another automobile, under it, moving on their stomachs, west. Behind them voices.

Finally the protection of the weed trees. Then crawling in a ditch to the road and another culvert in order to avoid the headlights on the road where three or four cars moved in slow, hunting repetition. Coming out on the other side of the road, the boy motioned for them to continue moving west, and then was gone. "Jesus," said Jimmy, "that kid."

"Let's think about it later," said Keith, and they moved off west. "I don't think they ever saw us."

As Eight slept, Glove lay awake. Carefully he got out of bed and went over to the window. Flashlights in the Yard. He remembered the cars with men in them that were out front when he had left and were still there when he came back. He did not worry about them finding The Baron, if that's what they were after, only that he might get stranded in an unprotected place until morning. Glove got his scope and looked through it. He could see figures in the Yard. Now, he thought, the events are coming. For the second time today he understood that he did not know enough, but, unlike the first time, now he did not believe that knowing would make any difference, because he knew now that his father knew something more about the flashlights and the men, and he could hear him downstairs walking around. He wasn't doing anything about it. No, there was nothing for Glove to do until just before morning, when he must find out where his brother was, so that he would not be left out in the open. And he knew that his uncle had a gun and that he could get it. He was too tired to think. Here, on his wedding night, with Eight, whom he loved very much but who looked nevertheless like some tramontane visitor sleeping under his covers. But perhaps it was the sleeping itself, his reasoning offered, the way sleeping will do. There is nothing so private as a dream, and no way to open it up even if you want to—that is, let someone else in. And because he couldn't be there, it was as if she were a stranger. Glove was very tired.

He tried to relax. But the confusion and sense of foreboding wouldn't settle. He tried to overcome them by thinking of cold, running water. Then he heard a faint noise outside in the Yard and he slipped quietly out of bed, dressed, and left. Finding The Baron safe in his bus, he returned and for over an hour sat and watched prowling figures moving in the Yard through his infra-red scope, wondering, Where are the dogs? *Where are the dogs!*

The next day he was to go see about working at the foundry.

SOME OF THE SNOW HAD MELTED DURING THE DAY AND WHAT REMAINED had a thin, hard crust. Baron was dismayed. Moving around quietly would be much more difficult. And now he would have to take the biggest chance in his life—something that would kill him if he failed. Last night had been clear, and even after the moon had hurled across the sky and disappeared, the starlight had been too bright and his terror wouldn't let his legs work. He'd waited until morning on the chance of an overcast, then had crawled off to his pallet on the floor. But tonight was dark. The moon would be late. He put the note in his crude handwriting next to the radio, *G—back soon,* and slipped out of his bus, hearing in his stomach the snow crunch. He passed unseen by the men around the house and moved slowly away from the town. He could not move as quietly as he wished, and staggered the pace of his walking so that someone hearing him in the snow might have an idea of his weight (as he couldn't hide that) but not of the number of his feet or the nature of his body, or its distance from the ground. Several times he thought he saw things fall out of the trees along the creek and light without a sound on the ground. And it was in his mind that these things did not go away, but followed him with extreme caution from distances to the side and behind him. Old stalks of corn stood up like the broken swords littering a battlefield. He went up a slightly rising hill and over the crest, traveling the fence line, then along to a small gorge, an untillable chunk of alluvial land where the runoff began, a moderate stack of cans and bottles and bedsprings, creek willows, one thorn tree, and several scattered graves: Emmett Miller, Silas Miller, Lorri Treadway, the markers looking like soft stones split once and engraved with a nail with the terrible efficiency that possesses the remaining relatives of someone unloved, whose death is an inconvenience, nothing more, and as he was treated in his life, so in death would be set in a clean, decent grave dutifully marked with a split rock and engraved with a nail and forgotten. Not in vengeance or hatred, merely without love. Baron knew this was not a good place, but he didn't believe that the dead could hurt him. Again he went over what he was going to say. Walking was more difficult in the deeper snow.

He stopped by these graves and listened, and did not move until he was sure that if someone had heard him before, they would now be unsure if it had been real at all. Then across the creek, where he picked and stumbled over the jagged ice-covered pieces of concrete, back toward a bank of earth where a pile of broken concrete rose up in a mound the size of a small igloo. Baron was frightened. Facing the bank of earth, not more than a foot and a half across, was a hole opening into the mound. Baron got down on his hands and knees and crawled in, knowing that going inside was the last thing he would have to do if he was wrong. If he was wrong, he would never come out.

The air was foul and heavy with the smell of animal. Very dark. But not so cold as outside. He stopped and waited. The drone of silence surrounded him. He crouched for what seemed a long time, his senses so keen that a heartbeat from anywhere inside would have been registered. He was alone.

He crawled on the dirt floor until he located where the heat had come from, the coals not dead, but covered with dark ashes or dirt, put on to insulate and keep them. Finding a thin, long bone, he stirred them, and with their red glow they dimly lit the cave, the walls composed of huge pieces of concrete, pieces so large that it would have taken two normal-sized men to put them there. The floor was littered with bones of small animals and one skeleton of a larger animal, the head missing. Perhaps a steer. White, completely bare bones. Eaten clean, he thought, and shuddered.

Then he saw it: the dim red light illuminated the bone head of what had been a giant bull, the horns still fastened midway down the skull and pointing outward, the eyes empty. It had been mounted on the top of a pole and stuck in the ground at a level not far from where it would have rested on its body in life. It stood in the back of the cave like a guardian, its nostrils and eyes terrible, as though even in death it could sweep forward with its horns and kill whoever would enter the small hole next to the earth bank—whoever would trespass inside. Baron went back to it and found what he knew would be there, directly underneath, so that if the protecting bull had been alive, saliva from its mouth would have dripped down on it. The square stone had been pieced back together again from its fragments, and though it was sunk into the ground to hold it together, some of the cracks were over a quarter-inch wide. Still it retained the name. *Ansel Easter.* That was all except for two coarse blankets beside the grave that were laid out for a pallet. And to assume from convention that Ansel lay with his head below the stone marker and his body stretched out in the direction where the bull's hollow eyes were directed, then the space of the grave and pallet was no more than a trundle bed, opened out. Baron looked at the bull again, and its monstrous horns. Superstition, he thought, idolatry. Then he was not so sure of it, because there was something else, there was also something peaceful and kind about it (and about it having been set there). Then he saw that the way the horns came out from the head, the outline of the whole affair was like a . . . no, he thought, it couldn't be. And if it was, it was an afterthought. Then he heard the noise of the snow, as clearly as thunder. There was nowhere to hide, and the noise of walking came nearer. It took a long time to get close, and by then the noise was deafening. Now, Baron told himself, now I have to talk. Then a figure entered the dwelling, dragging something not yet entirely dead.

"Hello, Ernie." His rough, unused voice was broken and faltering.

Ernie sprang forward to the center of the cave, his eyes flashing red from the coals. The animal he had brought in struggled back on outside into the snow, dragging its own bleeding back legs.

"I know you can understand me. Ansel was my grandfather. My name is Baron. I know all about you."

Ernie circled him, like a dog around a spitting cat up against the side of a house.

"I came here to talk to you, not to hurt you. Do something about that animal out there."

Ernie circled, jumping forward once as if to grab him with his wire-like fingers, then back. So fast that Baron had no time even to flinch or draw back, completely at his mercy. Then Ernie stopped and went out, caught the raccoon, broke its neck, and brought it back in. He threw it over by The Baron, as though maybe he had wanted it. Then crouched back on his haunches, waiting.

"You're old. How old are you, Ernie?"

Ernie looked down at the dirt floor, making noises like light snarling, only two of his pointed teeth remaining in his mouth.

"You're sixty-eight years old, Ernie. I know that you killed my grandfather. I knew it was you who had taken the rocks off his grave when I heard that it'd been done. I knew that you would have wanted to do that. I know all of it, Ernie."

Ernie went over to the coals and put on several pieces of wood. This will be the test, thought Baron. He'll see how well I know. He'll look for me to show a horror of him. I must not.

"Sixty years ago—sixty-eight . . ." began Baron.

Ernie came up and took the raccoon and brought it to the fire. With his teeth he ripped it open in the belly, and with his slender hands he tore apart the skin. Blood ran down his arms. He reached inside and jerked free the liver and popped it into his mouth. Then the heart. Blood dripped down his mouth, onto the floor.

I must not show it, thought Baron. ". . . conceived and born of a normal father and mother who were maybe a little closer to each other's blood lines than they should've been, but mostly it was because of a trick of nature. You're an abnormality, Ernie. You're an accident. Even your mother wanted to have you killed. Your father, when he found out that they, the men in the hospital, wouldn't destroy you, demanded that any record of you belonging to him be burned."

Ernie ripped away the head and ate at the neck.

"Some rudimentary tests were performed, but pretty much no one really cared about something so far from normal as you were and they farmed you out to what was known then as the state institution. You stayed there until you were twelve years old, then climbed down the side of the building from the roof, over the fence, and into the trees, where you began living in the ways and attitude of an animal, because that animal nature was all that up until that time you had had to rely on. No one had ever talked to you, nor looked at you with anything but disgust. Then hunting parties went out with guns and clubs and dogs, because after you were out of the state institution it was forgotten that you were of human born—and there was little of you, as seen out of a window as you grubbed in some garbage pail for meat or marshmallows, to suggest it."

Ernie began poking at the eyes.

"Look, cut that out. I know Ansel knew you were mostly like an animal. But put that thing down or I'm going to walk out of here and never come back."

Ernie threw the head away and tossed a handful of ashes onto his fire in a disgusted manner. The wood burned with yellow flames.

"See, I know that you were kept moving, mostly in hill country, from community to community, living as much as you could from dead animals and ones you could catch, but relying still on garbage cans because of the ease. Sometimes you'd live around the outskirts of larger cities, but were afraid of penetrating deeply into them for fear of being trapped. Thirty-three years you lived like this. I know you can't understand all of this, but that's O.K. I also know you've heard it before—that you heard Ansel tell you.

"Then a man began to trap you and stayed after you for a long time. Then you began your carnival career. Except what Ansel didn't know was that you enjoyed that. You enjoyed the chains and cages, the food, sleeping without fear of dogs, and, most of all, the recognition. You desired the scorn. Each person who came in to look at you was acknowledging your horribleness. Sure, you hated them all, but in being a spectacle you felt in some way they were being mocked. It also confirmed everything you thought of yourself. After all, you had no reason to believe you were anything more than a geek. Maybe if you were born today there would be some interest taken in teaching you the language and to think linear thoughts in your head, but not then. It was the acknowledgment."

Baron felt his words getting away from him, as though his mind were going to sleep, and a slight dizziness. He could not even conceptualize through a simple sentence before the associative thoughts caught hold. Losing his balance, he stumbled and bumped against the head of the bull.

"Stop it! Stop it!"

Ernie changed positions, muttering, and threw another handful of ashes into his fire.

"I know about that too. I know you can concentrate on hate so hard that I'll be aware of it, some foreign, disconcerting element in my mind. But that's not so remarkable. I could do it too, if I wanted to.

"But Ansel loved you, didn't he? I know he did. In fact, he wanted you to have this." He threw Ernie a leather coin purse hung on the end of a small gold chain. "Put it around your neck," said Baron, watching as his spider-like, bloodstained fingers put it over his head and fondled it as though it were a baby rabbit. He looks so old, thought Baron.

"See, I know that Ansel was the first one to ever love you.

Forty-five years old and no one had ever loved you. You had no morality. How could you have? Isn't morality always concerned with love in some remote way? The idea of something being wrong or something being right had to have been foreign to you, until then. But when Ansel took you, and fed you, and protected you, and loved you, in your animal way you thought something was being asked in return. And as Ansel later found out, you felt it was demanded. Even when he told you, No, Ernie, don't do it, don't do anything to fix things up. Leave them alone. But you thought it was demanded, because when he thought, 'This is good,' then there was nothing for you to do. You were out of the picture then. But when he thought, 'This is not good,' you could fix it up. You could do something for him. And because what you did horrified him, you thought all the more that you must do it because he was incapable of it; being an animal, it was your duty. I know you felt you had to kill him, that he wanted you to."

Ernie began to murmur unintelligibly and stir the fire with a bone. Baron had no way of knowing for sure if he understood anything other than the senses of what he was saying—the moods his speaking voice created, like a dog.

"Your hands are cut. Rub this into them," and Baron tossed over a small, tightly sealed bottle of liquid. Baron took out another and as an example poured out the liquid and rubbed his hands in it. Ernie's fingers broke the top off the glass, and poured the mostly clear, thick liquid into his palms and rubbed them together. Baron's eyes filled with tears, but he choked them back.

Then, disregarding the question of whether Ernie could understand at all, Baron sat down and began his own story of Ansel Easter that he had formed from all that he knew. His language was stilted and harsh, and he'd memorized all the words over and over again, so that at the last word he could end. The experience at the school, he believed, was because he was afraid and because he hadn't known what was expected of him—that and those drugs. But now he knew exactly what he intended, how he would say it and where he would end. And there was no fear of how he would say it and where he would end. And there was no fear of Ernie asking him a question or interrupting. He was sure he could do it.

"OVER HERE!" CALLED OUT ONE OF JULY'S MEN.

July left his car and hurriedly picked his way across the side of the Yard.

"Back in here," the voice directed him.

Then he saw the powerful flashlight and went back into the stand of naked trees.

"Look. Someone's been living in this bus. There's a heater in here and food and books and everything."

He stepped inside and looked around.

"Lights too," said Ken Burr, flipping on a light switch beside the door.

"Somebody sure fixed this thing up to live in unobserved. Look at the paint on the windows."

"Looks like kids," said July. "Come on."

"No, wait. It might not be. It might be Cassum or Kullisky out here. Whoever it is, I wonder where they are now."

"Plenty of footprints around here," said Jim Frye, coming in from outside.

"Look." They found the piece of paper next to the radio: *G— back soon.*

"Well, whoever it is is coming back. Then we'll see." All of them could hear Ken Burr's gun cocking outside.

"Put your guns away," said July. "It might be just the kids. We'll find out soon enough. You two, take your lights and hide out back. Ken and I'll get around the side by the elevator. When someone comes, let 'em get up real close, then as I turn on mine, get your lights on 'em."

"ANSEL EASTER WAS A GOOD MAN, AND CARED DEEPLY ABOUT HOW things were in the world, and how they should be, and how they appeared to be through his own eyes. All his life it was these three, *the real, the ideal, and the appearance.* In their assimilation was his joy; in their autonomy, his despair. He never once claimed to be saintly or even pious, and indeed looked as though any minute his hands would go back to grubbing in the black ground, tearing out pieces of coal, or ripping away at wood with large-toothed saws. An intensely secretive man with his family.

"Yes, he was a miner, and was raised by woodsmen, protestant Protestants who had an ax-handle way of dealing with problems, to whom morality was not much more than fierce, communal bigotry, and who taught him to respect pain and avoid pun-ishment and seek solace through physical exhaustion, and that any solace he might find even in that way was to be ashamed of because it indicated weakness—people who would never real-ize that difficulties were anything more than hunger, cold, and sprained muscles.

"So the amazing thing is that he was ever any different than that at all. He was short, and so one would think he'd be more susceptible to that way of thinking than someone else. And a part of him was. So is it any wonder that when he was he couldn't be all that way—that there was a conflict in him that had to be voiced or it would tear him to pieces? Is it any wonder that he wouldn't be able to express it quietly, but would holler it out so that he could be heard above ground? He had to raise his com-plaint to the issue level of hunger or sprained muscles in order to be recognized.

"And when he began to holler about what it was like down there and how maybe the way it was and the way it appeared to be were very different from the way it should be, miners listened. He told them they had a right to a better life—to have comforts and respectability—and the *way* he said it—because it was rough and strong—made it something not to be ashamed of. They had a right to be disgusted. Of course the old ones shouted it down, saying again that it was the broken bones and the sweat and the iron-hard muscles and veins in the neck as big around as your finger, and only these, that offered solace (because all feeling, to them, was solace). And then it was the power—the same broken-bone sweat, iron-hard muscle hollering that said, No, bastards, it ain't just that at all. There's more. There's got to be more. It was the power that made it all right for the others to listen, and made it all right for them to agree, and later made it all right for them to hire him out of the ground at night to talk to them in their pasteboard shanties about not what should be, but what had to be.

"Later, he married and moved, and worked as a boiler man, and this was conflicting too because he had changed his lot and, though he was still below ground, at least his station had improved so much that when he remembered, he felt guilty. Sam was born. He remained silent. His wife grew round again, and still he was silent. But he could no longer deny that the battleground had returned—in fact, had never been gone—and demanded expression.

"Where else to turn then but to religion? What else offered the expression? He must have realized by then that the conflict was larger than the trivial inconveniences of his daily routine. Perhaps he had even overheard the professors talking while he was checking valves and blowers in the buildings, complaining of their rough lot, and realized that that kind of thing could go on forever. The issue must be spiritual. And once he admitted that, he was hooked, and his old hollering startled his new neighbors because many of them had never heard anything like it, and thought it was good and that the power of the Lord was in him, where it was really his old fear of weakness.

"All of the training came from the churches he'd visited, the Bible, and what he remembered from the bigotry. The Depression came, and no one escaped that without some inconvenience to their souls, but by then he knew that his problem was spiritual and was as much in his mind as outside of it. His worries had a larger dimension than the physical things he could attach them to. He tried his whole life to be happy.

"He ended up here in 1939 as a community minister, living in the parsonage on Everett Street. And this was his right place. After several years people began to hear the feeling through the power, and listen for it, and began to love him. And this was the first time for that. Even as he knew it was happening he was astonished. Even Grandmother had married him for the power. Because the conflict within him was so great, he could give spiritual aid to others as freely as casting pollen in the wind. There were stories of the help he gave to July Montgomery's father as they played shuffleboard in the basement of the church, at a time in Montgomery's life when every morning his neighbors expected to see him through the window hanging from a coat hanger. Supposedly Elmer Carlson, a confirmed alcoholic, was visited one night by Ansel in the depths of his misery and after that never touched another drink, and went on to do many worthwhile and creative things. Ansel, a man of such gargantuan stature and good will that the whispered gossip that he shot dogs with a BB gun from the church basement to keep them away from the flower beds amounted to a full-scale scandal and sustained talk and suspicions and wonder and went on for years. More: he sees a rabbit fall at his feet from out of the sky (this was back in the Depression, but wasn't brought out into the open until later, by Grandmother); puts broken and cracked automobile parts in the trunk of his car for retribution; finds spiritual release in everything, even sawing wood. Working is prayer.

"Now, the thing with Johnie Fotsom, who was not, I agree, a very likable character, was neither one way nor the other; he didn't write the books alone, and Ansel didn't write them. Fotsom did most of the work, but Ansel made the information available to him, though what he did with it was very different from what Ansel had expected. Ansel wanted further expression. He had wanted Fotsom to say, 'If this kind of man can achieve any contact at all with heaven, then anyone can.' But of course what Fotsom did was show how difficult a struggle it was for *even this kind of man* to come near to heaven, so everyone else might as well give up. And after the distortion had already happened, he was caught double and couldn't out-and-out deny it without also denying the very point he had wanted to make in the first place.

"But none of this explains the unbelievable stupidity. In fact, there's no way to explain the stupidity. It wasn't even predictable from the fact that his wife got to know him more by the brute force of the years than by his ever letting her into his life. No, it can't be explained either symbolically or by religious inference. Just that he went one day to a carnival and mistook you for a complete human being." Here either the words or their directness seemed to cause Ernie to flinch. "Anybody could see you weren't. Even small children. But he thought that if a part of you was good, then it was wrong to keep you the way you were, not knowing, of course, that you had *wanted* it that way. You'd never *asked* to be treated well, or equally. In some way, your dignity was *involved* with the never ending mockery of your own appearance. It sustained you, because it made it possible for you to separate yourself in some way . . . No, it didn't take much to understand that this person was different and couldn't be set right by snapping up flies or showing your pointed teeth (which were sharpened for you, but if you'd been unwilling it could never have happened).

"You were paid for and brought back—to the house on Everett Street. Naturally, you didn't know what to think, and hated him along with everyone else.

"The people in town were a little set back. They didn't know what to think either. They were like you, just as sure that you belonged locked up to look at and toss pieces of popcorn to. They never changed their opinion, and neither did you, really. They hated you, you hated yourself *and* them, which I guess would've been an O.K. set-up but for Ansel. He loved you for what you were originally supposed to've been. And after about a year you couldn't help loving him in return. But *not* in the same way. You loved him with the devotion of an animal. Everyone else still hated you, but did so quietly, thinking after all that you were harmless."

Here Baron felt the foreign element enter into his thoughts again and he became confused. The power of the force was twice what it had been and it frightened him. Even to try to walk out of the covering of concrete would be nearly impossible with the condition his mind was in. "Stop it," he pleaded. Immediately his thinking cleared and Ernie stirred the fire with the bone. "I know you can do that. I could too, if I wanted to. Ansel finally knew too, but it took him a long time to recognize it, longer than you'd think a quick-thinking person would take.

"It was only natural for you, of course—once you started loving him devotionally—to want to fix things up a little. The first time was in the tavern when Ansel looked over at McQueen, who was belittling his wife and finally slapping her next to the pool table and you *knew* that Ansel felt badly about that. So with all your concentration you hated him from where you were, producing the confusion and dizziness in his already intoxicated mind, and in an act of reaching back for the chalk he put his hand into the turning fan. The same thing with Paul Green and John Bean, both situations where not being in full control of their faculties caused them to make costly mistakes. When that wouldn't work—at least, in some cases—you'd go out at night and hang people or cut their wrists and put them in a bathtub. With your strength this was easy. Like I said before, you had no morality. You were just an animal. It'd never occurred to you before to kill somebody, or even hurt them—sure, you liked to torture animals sometimes, but that was more out of boredom than anything else. The idea only occurred to you because of Ansel: he would see things he didn't approve of—that caused the same old conflict to come up between the ideal, the real, and the appearance. It was only because he wished things different from what they were that gave you the idea of bringing about a change. When he would think, *It's too bad there are such people*, you took it to be your duty to *do* something to them—because you realized that he was incapable of it. But, being the animal you were, it was nothing to you. You imagined that you were doing it all for him. You were *proud* that you were able to do it. As time went on, you had things happen less and less in front of him because you could sense he didn't want to see it."

Ernie paced restlessly back and forth before the fire.

"Three years passed between when he'd first taken you with him and when he realized what had been happening. I suppose for a long time he was haunted by the coincidence of it all—how his private thoughts had seemed so curiously connected with terrifying happenings. Perhaps for a while he was even duped into thinking he *did* have something instrumentally to do with them. Let's hope not. Anyway, after he saw what was happening—what power you had—the only thing that occurred to him that he could do was kill himself or kill you, and because he couldn't do either one he had that big house built for him, big enough to contain him inside for the rest of his life, and as soon as it was completed he moved into it, resolved never to go outside of it again, for fear he would see something that might upset him.

"Then once he got into the house his sanity began to fade, and he'd wander from window to window looking out, and would never talk to you and always turned his head away in disgust when you'd walk into the room. He blamed himself. He imagined that it all began clear back when he was young. It was his weakness to ever have let anything short of hunger, cold, and broken bones disturb him. The setting apart of the ideal from the real from the appearance was the beginning of all the evil, as he saw it—the avoidance of personal physical pain the only virtue. He

tried to teach this to Sam and Dad—the last thing he hoped to
leave them with—and beat them severely for things like leaving a
hammer out on the porch.

"You probably understood none of this, having only knowledge of the most physical of emotions. All you knew was that his
attitude toward you had changed, and that he was tormented, but
by what you didn't know.

"He couldn't just turn you out, set you free on the world. At
least, he felt he couldn't.

"A man for whom people and nature and fresh air, work, running water and laughter and trees had always meant so much, re-
duced now to peering out of an upstairs window so that he could
see farther, in a room with what he'd decided was a demon . . .
the rest didn't take long. He tried to get up enough courage to kill
you, but by this time he was alternately sure and unsure if you
were real or just a phantom of his own evil nature. And finally
when he thought you were asleep on the floor and he came with
the cleaver and you easily took it away from him, he asked you to
kill him and you understood because you could sense the hatred
he had for himself—stronger than even the hatred you could
generate. And because you'd never stopped loving him in your
animal way, and there was no choice." Baron could feel that he
was going to be able to stop talking. He could picture the last of
the words he had to speak come floating up toward him, hanging
there in the darkness of his mind, and falling away as they were
spoken. He was almost at the end of them and he had only to finish. By now he knew that Ernie understood more than just senses
or moods.

"Listen," he said. "I'll be back to visit you when I can." He
took out a photograph of the big house on South Street from the
back, carried it over to the fire, and laid it down in front of Ernie,
whose eyes watched him with needlepoint black pupils. "You
remember," Baron continued. "Here, this room," and he pointed
to the window, then the door of Sam's room. "If you want to see

me again, come to this door." The last of his words went away.
He stopped talking. Taking a pen out of his pocket, he put an x
on the door. Then he turned and left.

The night was still overcast. He set off toward home. At the
cornfield he stopped and listened to be sure Ernie wasn't following him, though he feared he might not be able to tell even if he
was. Tears came as he began walking again. A spot in the clouds
dissolved, letting Sirius, the Dog Star, shine through, filling him
with terror. He closed his eyes and tried to feel his way along the
barbed-wire fence, stumbled, and fell. He began crying out loud.
Keep moving, he thought. Get up. I can't. Though two miles from
home, he nearly called out for his brother, squeezing his eyes as
tight as he could hold them. Keep moving. Snow had gotten up
next to his wrists and hurt like tightening metal bands. Then the
space in the clouds filled again. He could sense it even with his
eyes closed. He needed sleep badly. Usually he wasn't so fragile.
It was the idea of being in an open field. He got up and went on,
knowing that he wasn't being as careful as he should be.

He crawled under the road by way of the culvert to avoid
the notice of the prowling cars and even then knew something
wasn't right. But in his desperation to be safely back in the bus,
he pressed on. Again a sense of foreboding came to him, but again
he neglected it and came closer, his footsteps breaking the top of
the snow.

CELL HAD NEVER BEEN ASLEEP. SHE'D WAITED UNTIL C'S FAMILIAR, UNBRO-
ken breathing had started, waited for him to roll over onto his
right side and the furnace come on, then resumed her thinking.

It's Glove that needs me. C don't miss me now, an' wouldn't
miss me if I was gone. He knows what I done. It's Glove, he
needs me. And she got silently out of the bed, pulling her faded
terry-cloth robe around her. Stepping only on one board all the
way to the door, she turned the handle and let herself into the
dark hall. Glove needs me, she whispered. He don't know what

I done. She pulled a strand of her unkempt hair away from her head and twisted it until it hurt, watching her thin feet as they went two steps toward Glove's room. Like cheese, she thought. Sliding her hand along the wall, she went several more steps, stopped, and tried to remember something. There was something she was supposed to remember. She hovered for a minute next to the plaster, wondering if her feet would carry her downstairs or into the room. No, this is where I was going, and she grasped the round, cold knob and twisted. It was locked. She turned it again and pushed harder. Glove, let me in.

"Who's there?" came a voice from inside.

Then she remembered. Glove was married. He worked at the foundry. A stranger was in there. Feet and legs like cheese. A dark hole opened in the door. "Oh, hello, Mrs. Easter," it laughed softly. "That's so funny. I mean, that's *my* name too. Hadn't you better be going back to bed? It's cold out here. . . . Is something the matter?"

"No," said Cell. "I just thought I'd stop and make sure. Glove's not in there, is he?"

"No. Remember, he's working tonight. It's his first night."

"Oh. I thought maybe he hadn't gone. You're not scared, are you?"

"No. Scared of what?"

"I mean just scared. Don't be scared."

"Well, I'll try not to be. Now why don't you go on back to bed? We can see Glove in the morning. Do you want me to walk you down the hall?"

"No. I'm going back now. Do you want some cookies or milk?"

"No. I've got to be getting back to bed now, Mrs. Easter. Let me walk you down to your room."

"I'll go myself. Goodbye."

"Good night." The long black hole closed.

She turned to go back to her room, but continued past and into one of the spare rooms filled with cardboard boxes and toys

Glove and Baron had grown out of. From the back of the door she took a piece of nylon clothesline and carried it upstairs to the room directly above, Baron's old room, got down on her knees, and carefully opened the floor register. She tied one end of the rope to the metal grill and let the length of it fall through. Then coming back to the second floor, she re-entered the room and looked at it hanging like a snake in the jungle. Then a scream tore through the night outside, into the cold layers of her body, the dark lining of her womb, and lay quivering in her soul like a silver needle. That was her son screaming. She ran down the hall and downstairs toward the front door.

Sam stood in her way, a blue pistol stuck under his shirt. "Don't go out there," he commanded. "Go back upstairs."

"Nooooo!" she cried, and with a powerful burst she charged forward, knocking him back against the hall wall. He sprang forward to grab hold of her before she could get to the door, but too late, and she was on the porch and off into the snow, her unbuttoned robe streaming behind her like great hooped wings.

Baron was crouched in the snow crying, holding his hands over his eyes, four separate flashlights trained down onto him. July Montgomery was walking slowly forward from the bus. "Come on, kid, go on out of here. Get your brother and go. There ain't no place for you out here," walking closer to him. Baron was shaking, and crying uncontrollably, and just as July reached out to touch his shoulder, Cell, with the metal fencepost she'd picked up while she ran, swinging it like Odysseus himself, cried, "Let him go!" July jumped backward, barely missing having his extended arm smashed as the post came down, and in one tremendous leap Cell planted her bare feet in the snow between him and the young boy, shielding Baron from the yellow light with her thin body, her eyes glaring wild, bent forward with her legs spread apart like an ancient warrior. "Turn off those lights!" she yelled, and one by one they snapped off and the cold darkness returned.

"Now, Mrs. Easter," began July, advancing a little.

"Get back!" She held the post as though to jab it in his eyes.

"Take your boy and go back in the house, get dressed, and get out of here."

The screen door closed and Sam came out onto the porch. Ken Burr's gun cocked.

"Go on now," July insisted.

Cell took her son by the hand and led him to the house, still crying but not as loudly. Sam opened the door for them. C was running down the stairs with Eight behind him. He held her and greeted The Baron, put a blanket around her shoulders, and went off with Sam into Sam's room. Eight went back to her room, wishing desperately for Glove to come back. Cell and Baron went to his old room on the third floor.

Baron looked down at the grate with the end of rope tied to it. "Oh, that," said Cell, quickly dropping down and untying it and letting it fall to the floor below. "Eight put that there; I don't know what for, but she never used it, so we don't need it now." Baron was concentrating very hard, his brows knit together into a frown. Very deliberately and slowly he said, "Mom, I can talk."

Cell looked at him and carefully let herself sit back on the bed. There were so many things she had to sort out and remember. Important things.

At the foundry Glove thought, *He's got to acknowledge me. Any day now he's got to come over to acknowledge me.* "Oh, yes, and the Yard. It's yours."

During the next week Sam and C waited, C refusing to be made to run from his own house like some rabbit out of its nest into a ring of men with clubs and heavy boots, and Sam deciding that after all this time, all these dry, wasted years, he couldn't leave his brother now. C hadn't the courage to tell his family why the men were outside, especially Glove. He urged them to leave the house, but they always refused. Baron seldom came out of his room and seemed to be nearly ill with anguish. The men in the cars with nothing to do but think of Joyce Campton and rabies became less patient, and began to be less afraid of hanging. They still thought all four of The Associate were in the house. Glove and his wife were sent out to buy food and bring it back. Charlie Sanchez got out of the car to ask him something. Tempers flared. Several blows were exchanged. Then the other men stopped them. C had Sam's gun and was halfway through the Yard by then, but Sam reached him and brought him back. Baron watched from the window.

"That's Wood's daughter," July growled to the men in Sanchez's car. "God help you if anything happens to her."

Sam was lonelier than he had ever been. That was before Sled came limping back home and died terribly, Sam finally killing him himself, because of some tearing pain inside, put there by someone in the cars. He put his other two dogs in the basement and after that didn't want to see anyone. He resolved to get some of them for what they'd done to his dog—get one or two of them in the throat when they finally came in.

Cell was in that ground in between sleeping and waking, where she could hear Baron pacing in the darkness upstairs, and see his footsteps becoming little brown plants, one at each sound, and it all making perfect sense. This middleground between the conscious and subconscious was the seat of madness itself, terrifying, yet drawing her into it, threatening to turn her life into one waking dream. In her weaker moments the lure of this place of symbolic imagery could attract her from any thought, away from any reality. Now she saw the brown plants writhing and twisting and they became more like flesh, dark brown and cheese, and in their changing and motion there was a little drama taking place that one side of her could understand clearly, reasonably, and the other side (the waking one) thought strange and grotesque, waiting to see if it would be bad enough to have to wake up. Then mouths opened up in them and they seemed to be dancing in green water. The water began to change and frightened her and she sat up, holding her hands to her head. She began to get up out of the bed, wanting to get away from the regular, slow breathing, but there was a face in the window. A hideous face, pale olive in the moonlight, the size of a shrunken head, with tendons and veins pushing out against the tightly stretched skin. The terror and loathing she felt drove her right to the threshold of shock. Then the face disappeared, with almost inaudible scratching noises down the sheer side of the house. She went to the window and looked out. Nothing. Only the cars and the snow. There was never even the possibility that it could be real. The face was her own madness, finally having reached through from the middleground to penetrate the membrane of reality. She realized it wouldn't be long. One or two more times like that and it would be the end of it. The thought was almost a comfort. Things could continue to get worse only so far, then peace. She lay back down and tried to picture how brave she had been, the exact words that C had said to her when she'd come in, and Sam had said, "She's as brave as a whole army." Then she tried to pray.

Two days passed and she hadn't seen it again.

LET IT BE ASSUMED, FOR THE SAKE OF THE BARON'S CONSCIENCE, THAT the demon did not wait very long to come after him. Sitting in his dwelling, at the first tiny hint that his animal senses were becoming confused—at the first sign of headache, as soon as he tried to swallow but couldn't—he was out into the darkness and after him, his long fingers straining in expectation of tearing Baron's face open. He moved fast, using less caution because of his anger at having been betrayed, no regard for his own life because he could feel the grip of the virus.

"DID YOU SEE SOMETHING?"

"No."

"Over there, just at the edge of the Yard."

"Nope. Who'd it look like?"

"Not who—what. I must not have seen it very good. But I'm sure there was something."

"Better go see if anyone in July's car saw anything." He went over into the clear night and tapped on the window of July's car. It came rolling down.

"What?"

"Did you see something just a minute ago?"

"Nothing . . . why?"

"Never mind, I just—"

"Wait. Look!" said July, and pointed. A small figure darted around the side of Easter's house and disappeared. "That's crazy. Nobody can move that fast. Give me that flashlight." It was handed up to him from the back seat. July got out of the car. "Where did you first think you saw it?"

"Over here."

They took the light and panned it out on the ground. "Footprints. But what would be barefoot, asymmetrical . . ." and then they heard the report of a hand gun from the house. "It's . . . It's . . ." July was trying to say, but was too excited. "Get the doctor." And Dr. Lawrence was called out of one of the cars, a professional man who had been with them only because of a sense of duty. No passion. "Come on," said July, and they started for the house. Charlie Sanchez too. This is it, the other men thought, and came along behind them.

C was down in his brother's room. Sam was explaining how he had been nearly asleep, then heard the snow crunching outside the door, and scrabbling noises, how he had taken out his revolver and thought to himself, I'll take some of them with me. Then the door had opened. "It's him, isn't it?" said C. "It's really him. He came back." Running footsteps on the front porch, the locked door burst open in a tremendous charge of weight . . . and down the hall and into the room, July Montgomery's big frame leading them. They stopped.

"That's Ernie, the demon," July said, looking at the body on the floor, naming it the way one names geological specimens. He went over to it and turned it over with his foot. "That's the demon," he said again, and looked at Sam. Charlie Sanchez began hollering and pushing and clawing his way forward, throwing even July out of his way. "This," Charlie said, tearing the chain from Ernie's neck, "belonged to Joyce Campton. Everywhere she went she carried it. This was hers. Her coin purse." He kicked Ernie in the face, before July got to him and the doctor had knelt down next to the demon.

"Wrap it in a sheet and bring it," Lawrence said. "Whatever you do, don't touch it."

Cell stopped them in the hall. Sanchez pulled back the sheet, allowing her to see the face. She stared and said nothing, then walked into one of the off rooms. Glove and Eight watched from the staircase.

On the porch July stopped the doctor, but he only said, "I don't know yet. Rabies, maybe. July, we may owe these people, for what—"

July motioned Charlie past him and stood for a moment without speaking. Then, "As soon as you know, tell me. I'll be here."

All of his men left the house and went back to the cars, where it was warmer, except for those who went with the doctor.

"I don't get it," said Sam. "I don't know why he would ever come back. What could have ever possessed him to come back here, sneaking around in the middle of the night? What could ever have prompted that?"

"Who knows? Probably looking for Dad."

"Right."

". . . Actually, I wish I hadn't shot him, and if I'd waited, and seen who it was, I probably wouldn't have. There was just no reason for him to ever come back here. How was I to know it wasn't one of those men . . . and the way he came in!"

"Why do you think the doctor had him wrapped up and didn't want anyone to touch him?"

"I don't know. But I was glad when July stopped Sanchez from kicking him again. This is all very odd. Sitting out there for over a week and a half now, waiting to kill us—they get the entering of the house done and then leave. I don't get it. Do you suppose they sent Ernie and hoped he would . . ."

"It's Rabbit. It would be like him to threaten them with something like hanging if they don't wait till we're out in the open, maybe even when we're away from town. After all, he's worried about his daughter."

"What do you think about that coin purse?"

"Who knows?"

"But I wonder," said Sam and hurried off to the front room.

C followed, but saw Cell in the shop room and went in to her. She had her bracelet off and was shredding up a small piece of paper from inside one of the ormolu trinkets. "What're you doing, hon?"

She let the paper fall into a pile as big as a fingernail on the workbench. "I want to use that," she said, and pointed to the propane torch. "To burn this."

"Here, let me help you," and he opened the gas valve, lit it at the tip, and, holding the metal tank together, they burned the pieces until not even an ash remained. "O.K.?" he asked, and she nodded. They went down the hall to the front room.

"No," Sam said. "They're still there, waiting."

"I don't know why you'd think they wouldn't be."

They sat down in the dark and stared outside. The sun was just beginning to come up, with its cold white light. Nothing quite so exhausting as that kind of morning in Iowa, seen from the night before—the haze, the astringent color beginning in the east and maybe a little north, frozen crows flying and making that hungry, enduring noise of utter surrender and abandonment, cold machines, ice and frozen mud slick as a cat's ass, all this together in one breath, when you can't believe it's real. They watched it, and just as the sun came to perch perfectly round and red-orange above a faraway house like a great balloon, another car came up in front; someone got out and went to July's Oldsmobile. They talked. July got out and they walked together over to the other two cars. These drove away toward the cars in back. July got into his own car, then the other man went back to his. Then everyone left.

"I don't understand it."

"They must have realized that Kullisky and Cassum got away, and are going after them."

Cell sat quietly. Glove and Eight were upstairs with Baron, whose sickness seemed to have exploded with the shot. He'd become feverish and sweat ran from his face.

C, Cell, and Sam looked outside. An hour passed. The morning reached full maturity. Then a fearful grayness came over their faces.

"Look! What's that?" asked C.

Some of Cell's color came back then.

"I don't know," said Sam, and his voice was grave. In the distance something loomed toward them, something as big as a small house, and black. It was taking up almost both lanes of the street. Several men, the size of plastic soldiers, were walking along beside it. Great rumbling noises. Then they could make out that it was a truck tractor, pulling something very awesome and round. It progressed to the T intersection at South Street and made the corner in one tremendous, full, wide sweep. Huge valves came out of it as big around in the pipe as a man's head. Black as coal. The men had disappeared, and the gigantic object, tied to the trailer with great log chains, came to rest directly in front of the Yard, blocking the view into town completely. Then July Montgomery himself stepped out of the cab and came meandering through the Yard up to the house. They watched him come, but just before he made the porch, C reached out for his brother's arm. "It's a molasses barrel!" he said. "It's a molasses barrel from some granary. Somebody finally showed them we were innocent!" He ran out into the hall, threw on his coat and ran to the door, stopped, opened it slowly, casually, and went out onto the porch.

"'Lo, July," he said.

"'Lo, C," the big man answered, and sat down on one of the snow-filled chairs.

C joined him.

"Wouldn't be thinking of getting rid of that?"

"What?"

"That barrel."

"Barrel?"

"Yep. That one out front here."

"Oh. No, wouldn't consider it. Too useful."

"Well, I can see that," said C. "You could keep a lot of stuff in there."

"I was thinking of making a garage out of it."

"Hmmmm," said C. July's men, and others too, were coming into the Yard from cars parked everywhere along the street and in the snow.

"But I was kind of interested in getting a school bus. I don't really need one, of course, but just for weekend trips in the summer."

"I don't know," said C. "I just happen to have one myself. But school buses are mighty fine things. A guy could live in them if he had a mind to. There're almost as valuable as a house."

"I thought you had one," said July. "I'm not really interested, of course, but why don't we take a look at it?"

"I don't really see the point," said C. "It being so useful to me and all."

The men, and some women too, were reaching the porch. "You got change for a quarter?" asked Charlie Sanchez. "Hi, C," said David Wornbroaker. "Cell around?" asked Mrs. Timbermain. "I hope you got that coffee pot on," said someone else. "Just your kind of weather, ain't it, Easter?"

"Go on in," said C. "Sam's there. Get him to open up the machine and get the pot plugged in."

All of them went inside.

"I'd sure like to have a look at that molasses barrel."

"There's no reason to it," said July. "You'd just be wanting it then, anyone would. And I'd never give it up, it being so useful to me."

"Maybe I could offer you a cup of coffee first," said C, hardly able to take his eyes off the barrel, the finest piece of junk he had ever seen in his entire life, an excitement that he had not felt since just after he had come with Cell . . . greater now.

"I guess you could at that," said July.

"It's a beautiful day," said C.

"Below zero, getting ready to snow again. Just your kind of day, Easter. And by the way, do you have any three-quarter-inch faucets?"

"Probably. But I was just getting ready to use them this afternoon."

"Hmmm." And they went inside.

LARRY TIMBERMAIN CAME TO WORK EARLY, AND WAITED IN HIS CAR FOR Rabbit. When he came walking in from the back of the parking lot, Larry got out.

"Mr. Wood, did you hear?" he shouted.

"Hear what?" Tired. Old. Still walking.

"The demon. They got the demon. It was it."

"It was it. I don't suppose you could be any clearer than that." Unlocking the front doors.

"The Easters. They shot this demon, and he was wearing Joyce Campton's coin purse around his neck from a gold chain . . . and he had *rabies!*" He said it again, "*rabies!* It was it, the demon, who killed them. It wasn't the Easters. They never took money to kill. It was the demon. And they killed it. Sam shot it last night!"

"Sam shot it!" Locking the front doors back up. "Sam shot Ernie! He came back. Why did—"

"Ernie? Why are you locking up again?"

"Bank's closed today. Take me home in your car."

"O.K., Mr. Wood. Let's go."

TRACKING SNOW INTO THE HOUSE, NOT BOTHERING TO REMOVE HIS rubbers, Rabbit slammed the door and hollered out his wife's name and bolted upstairs shouting out that they had killed Ernie—that the demon was dead. He pounced on the bed; one of the posts broke completely in two, and they were rolled together in the corner, Ester screaming, "Rabbit! Rabbit!" over and over again. "Rabbit! What's this about?" and "What's this about killing for money?"

"They killed the demon," he said. Fisher came into the room in his pajamas, and listened. "Sam killed Ernie, the demon, as he was coming into his room in the middle of the night. Sam killed him! He had the coin purse. He had rabies, and might have been a natural carrier of it. The Easters never had the money."

"What did he kill him with?" asked Fisher. "Was it something that looked like a—Are you sure it wasn't Glove? Glove would have been the one—"

"No," said Rabbit and turned to his son. "It was Sam, Fisher. It was Sam all along. Samson was him. It was always him. You can't ever know, because you didn't see him when he was your age, you didn't grow up with him. It was always Sam."

"It could've been Glove," said Fisher and went back into the hall.

Rabbit began then the long story of what he had known that he had not told her, and what he had thought he had known that wasn't true. She listened to everything, then asked, "Can we get the police *now*, to go get her?"

"I don't understand," said Rabbit. "Why do we have to do that now?"

"She's only sixteen."

"So was your mother."

"Times are different. She should go to college."

"They're married," said Rabbit.

"Foolishness. She'll get over it. When she's twenty-five it'll be like it never happened." The telephone rang. It was Whitney Nickols at the police department. Mrs. Simpson said her husband had gone out that morning to kill Don Lable. Rabbit came back to the bedroom.

"Glove can go to college too."

"He couldn't."

"He could. He's a lot smarter than Eight. All of the teachers have said so."

"How do you know?"

"I asked them. He's got drive. He's only seventeen and already he's working at the foundry. That's hard work."

"They live in poverty over at that house. Filth."

"Maybe," said Rabbit, "it's just different."

"It's poverty. What you mean is that you'll take care of them."

"No, I won't."

"They can't even pay back the mortgage."

But Rabbit was thinking and said, "We'll see," and began smiling and pacing back and forth.

"BARON," SAID GLOVE, QUIETLY COMING INTO HIS ROOM IN THE MIDDLE of the afternoon, and finding him sitting, gazing out of the window. He shut the door. "The trouble's over," he said. "And the story is incredible. Everyone suspected The Associate of murder for money—you know, Joyce Campton, Harold Burdock, Don Lable, and even Sterns. But it was Ernie. He did it—at least the two of them for sure. Simpson did one. The other might've been an accident. Ansel was wrong. There was nothing good about him. But I'm going too fast. Listen to the story from the beginning."

"No," said Baron. "Tell me only if he died quickly and without pain."

"Which one? Sterns?"

"No, Ernie."

"Dead immediately. Sam shot him in the heart. Extraordinary, he is. Sleeps with his spirit awake."

"You have to leave me alone now," said Baron, as his eyes began to cloud.

"No time for that, Baron. Everything will be fine now. Any day Rabbit is going to come over and tell—Are you feeling all right? Boy, I always knew you'd learn how to talk. Mom's so proud of you."

"Go away."

SAM ATE DINNER UPSTAIRS WITH HIS BROTHER'S FAMILY, THOUGH BARON didn't come down and Eight sat in his chair. There was no shredding of napkins. C ate with the honest resolve of trying to keep a straight face, but kept smiling. Eight poked at Glove, and every once in a while they threw pieces of corn at each other. Sam picked at his food and answered Glove's continuous queries about how he had heard. If it was a sixth sense, where his gun was when he first thought he might need it? If it was loaded? How dark had it been? Wasn't it too dark to see well at all? Wasn't it more a shot aimed by listening, rather than pointing down the barrel? Could you tell by the sound it wasn't human? Listen for the breathing. Rabies! If the first shot would've missed, what chance did you have?

SAM WENT OUT THAT NIGHT OVER TO RABBIT'S HOUSE. HE RANG THE doorbell. Arness answered. Mrs. Wood came quickly up behind her. "What do you want?" she demanded.

"I was wondering if Rabbit was here."

"Oh, come in," called Rabbit from the living room, rushing out. "Come on in, Sam."

"Hope I wasn't interrupting anything."

"Oh, no. We were just playing a little cribbage. You should've seen the hand I had last game! Three fives and a jack."

Arness took Sam's coat.

"Mind if I play?"

Fisher was staring at him from the stairwell.

"Sure, come on in. But that wasn't why you came, was it?"

"No. But we'll get to that." And they went into the living room, where they played cribbage ruthlessly, and if one of them missed counting some of his points, the other pegged greedily ahead.

BARON SAT WITH HIS LIGHT OFF, LOOKING OUTSIDE. HE WATCHED THE car pull up and Sam get out and come into the house from the back door. The dogs were running in the Yard. He heard Glove's footsteps mounting the steps and turned from the window as the door opened, the hinges well oiled from before when he used to steal up at night to teach him to read.

"Hi, Baron. How's come you got the light off? I thought I'd stop in for a while before I left for the foundry. Golly, there's some tough-looking guys who work there—one who's got this chain *tattooed* around his neck, ex-cons and old marines . . ."

There was a faint pop as the back door closed. Baron motioned Glove over to the window. Outside, Sam was walking back toward the road, a large suitcase hanging from his arm. His dogs, J. B. Hutto and Hose, were running around him. He put the suitcase down on the concrete and stood for a moment. The tiny light of a match flared up. He tossed it and the red end of his cigarette winked up at them from between his fingers. Then he went to the car, opened the door, pulled the front seat forward, and tossed the suitcase onto the floor in back. Glove's face turned ashen. "No," he said almost inaudibly and turned to run downstairs. Baron stopped him with his hand and shook his head; and he came back to the window.

Sam snapped his fingers and the dogs jumped into the back. He climbed in and closed the door. The motor murmured softly, the lights came on, and he drove away down South Street toward the highway. At the stop sign they watched him turn left and watched him until the taillights disappeared behind the side of the house. Tears ran down Glove's face and fell onto his work shirt. He tried to speak but couldn't, then managed to say bravely before he left, "I guess I'll have to walk tonight. I better be going. Keep cool."

As he left the foundry in the morning, Rabbit was waiting for him, standing on the sidewalk. When he recognized him among the group of men, he hurried over. They walked together toward the Yard.

"Well, I guess you were right. I changed my mind."

"I was hoping you would," said Glove.

"So was I. Any time you want to come over to my house is fine with me."

Because it was still all he could think of, and all he feared he would ever think of, Glove couldn't help but say, "Sam's gone. He left last night."

"I know. I imagine that upsets you quite a lot." They stopped and waited for the traffic to clear on Billings Road. Rabbit waved to most of the people as they passed.

"I guess it does. . . . I saw him leave. I could've stopped him."

"Maybe," said Rabbit. "I think he had it pretty much in his mind, though. But now about you being married. I was wondering if maybe you'd consider having that annulled, in exchange for, say, the clear title to your father's house."

"Nope."

"I was thinking that was probably what you had in mind, going off like that, I mean. So . . . you win. You've got me up against the wall. What more do you want?"

"Nothing. The foreman says I can get a loan from the credit union and pay it back a little each week. So I guess we don't need your help at all."

"I guess you don't understand. No, I'm sure you don't. I want

Eight to live back home where she belongs. I'll give you anything within reason for the privilege . . . and to have the marriage annulled. It's illegal, for one thing, and I don't think you'd want to stand in the way of her future. She was planning to go to college. Did you know that?"

Glove's face looked as if he'd been slapped. He hadn't even thought about it. He'd selfishly been too busy with his own problems to think of her. He swallowed hard.

"Nope. If she wants to go to college, we'll find a way to do it ourselves."

"Are you sure?"

"Yes."

Rabbit seemed to leap straight up in the air in a gesture of perfect joy. He grabbed hold of Glove's arm with both hands and nearly crushed it. "I knew it! I just knew she'd never end up with a trifler, or that you would be one either. Wonderful spirit! Sorry for the deceit, but actually if you *would've* annulled your marriage, then that would've been the best thing. And I had to know. But now this is something different, hmmmm.

"Now don't get me wrong—just because I'm enthusiastic. I don't intend to take care of you. You're on your own as far as that goes . . . but as to college. I've been looking into a few places, and with your grades it looks like . . ." They walked on to the house, where Rabbit got a bottle of pop. C was already up and they went into the shop where they could be in private.

"Now see here, Easter," he began, "there're a couple of matters we have to discuss. As you probably know, Sam's gone now—"

"I know."

"And there's not so much as a sliver of a chance he'll be back. The way I see it, we've been at each other's throats for too long. At least, you've been after mine. But that's going to all change now. I guess you know your boy went off and married."

"That's what he said, at least."

"Look at it this way, C." And he slammed the half-finished

bottle down excitedly on the workbench. "Think of it! Glove
and Eight, Fisher and Baron growing up. They'll rock the world,
I tell you. There's no tellin' what things they'll be able to do.
Why, goin' out into the world'll be as easy for them as crossing
the street."

"Maybe," said C.

"Anyway, you'll have to admit we should have a big wedding.
I'll be happy to have it at my house—the reception, that is. We
can probably fit almost a hundred down there. We can get enough
chairs for the old folks from the church. July says he'll bring his
truck, and we'll bring 'em over right as soon as they come out of
the church. . . . You'll admit we should have one."

"Well, it would be nice."

"Oh, yes, I meant to tell you, Sam stopped over before he left
and we got to talking and playing cribbage—you should've seen
him the second game when I pegged out. And both of us seemed
to have this idea right off the bat—that the University of Iowa
might be interested in buying up that demon, Ernie, to sort of
examine. Anyway, we weren't sure exactly what they might want
him for, but I gave the Medical Building up there a call and they
sent someone over—I don't suppose you really care about all the
details, just what they wanted him for, study of genes and so on.
Well, I happened to be over there, and having Sam's power of
attorney, I struck up a bargain, and what it came down to was a
little cash—just enough to cover the balance Sam owed on the
house, plus a very meager sum left over. Now, Sam had said just
before he left—"

C knew he was lying. It was pretty obvious, and he even could
see that Rabbit knew he would know. He recognized that it would
be just the kind of idea Sam would have come up with—as an excuse. Whether he had promised to send back money every month
or whether Rabbit had taken it all upon himself, C didn't know.
But he settled back in the steel-runged chair and kept nodding
his head. It was no longer possible for him to live without help.

In fact, in order to live the way he wanted to, he had to be taken care of, and he found the idea wasn't so hard to live with at all. If it was freedom that was at stake, then the loss of it wasn't so great as the destruction it could cause. It was, after all, his family that was more important than himself. He and Rabbit fundamentally believed in that.

ENOUGH

Baron had heard most of what Rabbit said to his father, enough to know that he would have to go out once more. His last experience with the outside had left him so shaken that he looked upon the approaching night with dread; and when it came it justified all of his fears in being only thinly overcast. He'd had plenty of sleep and was as emotionally geared for it as could be expected under the circumstances, and could probably wait out the light spots well enough; but he'd have to be pretty fast. The moon, according to his almanac, was to come up at 4:30 A.M. The radio said there was an excellent chance of more heavy clouding and even snow as a northern front moved over, and he waited as long as he could reasonably delay, took the gunny sack from the basement, and left through Sam's back door, heading for the river, a small folding camp shovel and flashlight in his back pockets.

He moved fast, keeping away from the open fields, nearly running over the snow along the ditches and fence rows. He cut through a stand of timber, through a large patch of horseweed, the gray stalks breaking noisily, over to a place not thirty feet from his brother's magic island. Here, he kicked about in the hard blue snow until he uncovered the bones of the dead animal, and stuffed them into his bag. Then he quickly retraced his steps toward town. He was happy with his speed so far.

He moved through yards and along the streets. He wasn't comfortable with being in town, but it was darker now and he pressed himself to move faster. Once someone called, "Hey, Mike! Mike, is that you?" but he kept on without answering or looking. It began to snow.

The mortuary was completely dark. With his shovel he pried open one of the basement windows, tearing the fastener out of the wood, and let himself fall down to the floor, pulling the sack of bones after him. He listened carefully for the presence of someone else in the building, lit the flashlight, and, as noiselessly as he could, replaced the fastener of the window and closed it up as it had been before; then he began searching through the dark cinderblock rooms. His lucky star must have been on the rise, and after only a short time he found Ernie, shrunken from loss of water, lying in the makeshift coffin of a fruit crate, on the track where the bodies were let in to be cremated. A note card was stuck to the box: *For incineration, D.M.* Baron set the crate onto the floor and pulled Ernie's almost completely stiff body from it, put in the bones, and lifted it back onto the track. He cut two holes in the corners of his burlap bag for the pale olive legs to fit through and read the instruction plate on the face of the crematory, opened the door, pushed the little crate ahead to where the runners met with the conveyor which would carry it down to the burning gas where the ashes were collected and put in big jars. Then he pushed the red button, watched until the box began to move forward, shut the door, took up his bundle, and went to the side entrance door, where he let himself out, the lock fastening behind him. Among the morticians there might be some speculation and consternation, but basically they wouldn't concern themselves with something to which they attached so little importance.

His burden, he judged, weighed between forty and fifty pounds and, carrying it hung from his shoulder, he left town for Millet's pasture, the new snow falling wet and heavily—leaving him in supreme darkness, the darkest night that he'd ever seen. Everything was in his favor; he did not even seem to tire appreciably.

Only one mile out of town there was already at least one inch of snow above the road. He heard a car in the distance, threw his sack up over a fence, ran with it beyond a little knoll, and waited. The noise grew louder. Then the headlights came over the hill, moving no faster than a person could walk, illuminating the big flakes as they fell lazily onto the gravel, shining no more than twenty feet ahead. It passed the place where Baron had left the road and continued on out of sight.

He regained the road and went on, felt safe enough so that, despite the bad memory of when he'd been trapped before, he started across the barren cornfield. There was no other path but follow the creek, another quarter of a mile out of his way.

Walking over the twisted cornstalks was difficult; twice he fell to his knees. But he continued on and finally arrived at the concrete room. Dropping to his hands, he crawled in, pulling his burden after him. The room seemed quite different now it was cold. He could just barely make out the white head of the bull.

He lit the flashlight, found a small armful of sticks, started a fire on top of the layer of dead ashes, and illuminated the inside of the cave. Outside the low door, the snow was still falling. Over it, leaned against a slab of concrete, was the little black-and-white photograph of the house.

Baron warmed himself as the flames grew up from the wood. It seemed that the snow had let up. He took his shovel and began to dig directly underneath the pallet of blankets. It was very difficult work. Rocks lay hidden everywhere, many of them taking every ounce of his strength to pry out and roll away. He worked on and on, growing more tired and weak. Finally finished, he put Ernie down, the blankets over him, and covered him first with the looser dirt, then the stones, and sat for a moment to rest. As a last thought, he pulled the wooden post and steer head from where it was and moved it over to where it could stand looking out over them both, set it deep in the ground, and went to the nearly extinguished fire to dry the perspiration from his skin before starting back.

He went to the entrance and looked out. Far to the east over the blue snow rose the moon, cold and bright against the dark sky. He quickly retreated into the covering of the concrete, put a small stick on the fire, drew slowly into himself, and began to wait.

ABOUT THE AUTHOR

As a young man, David Rhodes worked in fields, hospitals, and factories across Iowa, nurturing his love of reading along the way. After receiving an MFA from the Iowa Writers' Workshop in 1971, he published three novels in rapid succession: *The Last Fair Deal Going Down* (Atlantic/Little, Brown, 1972), *The Easter House* (Harper & Row, 1974), and *Rock Island Line* (Harper & Row, 1975). A motorcycle accident in 1976 left him paralyzed from the chest down, which brought a temporary halt to his publishing career. In 2008, he returned to publication with *Driftless*, which has been heralded as a critical success and the "best work of fiction to come out of the Midwest in many years" (*Chicago Tribune*). He lives with his wife, Edna, in rural Wisconsin.

MORE FICTION FROM
MILKWEED EDITIONS

These novels by David Rhodes are also available in paperback from your local bookseller or www.milkweed.org.

"The best work of fiction to come out of the Midwest in many years."

—*Chicago Tribune*

"Each of these stories glimmers."

—*New Yorker*

"A profound and enduring paean to rural America. Radiant in its prose and deep in its quiet understanding of human needs."

—*Milwaukee Journal Sentinel*

"A fast-moving story about small town life."

—*Wall Street Journal*

"A wry, generous book."

—*Christian Science Monitor*

When David Rhodes' first three novels were published in the mid-seventies, he was acclaimed as "one of the best eyes in recent fiction" (John Gardner), and compared favorably to Sherwood Anderson. In 1976, a motorcycle accident left him paralyzed from the chest down, and unpublished for the subsequent three decades.

Driftless heralds a triumphant return to the Midwestern landscape Rhodes knows so well, offering a fascinating and entirely unsentimental portrait of a town apparently left behind by the march of time. At once intimate and funny, wise and generous, *Driftless* is an unforgettable story of contemporary life in rural America.

"A kind of dark but luminous *Candide, Rock Island Line* is beautiful and haunting in a way you have not encountered before. I read the book when it first came out over thirty years ago and it has lived in both my heart and head ever since."

—Jonathan Carroll,
author of *The Ghost in Love*

"Rhodes writes with both symphonic grandeur and down-to-earth humility in this galvanizing novel of 'the quick, naked bones of survival.' This is a descent into grief as resonant as James Agee's, an embrace of the heartland spirit as profound as Cather's and Marilynne Robinson's, a story that echoes Dreiser, Steinbeck, Gardner, and Bellow—and an authentically great American novel in its own right."

—*Booklist* (starred)

Born and raised in a small town not far from Iowa City, July Montgomery's early years are filled with four-leaf-clovers, dogs, and fishing. But this idyllic world comes to an end with the tragic death of his parents, after which July flees via the Rock Island Line, eventually landing in Philadelphia and fashioning a ghostly home beneath an underground train station.

When a young woman frees July from his malaise, they return together to the heartland. Restored to his ancestral home and yet perched on the precipice of a disaster that could herald his end, July must decide whether to continue running, or stand still and hope for the promised dawn of Paradise Regained.

MILKWEED EDITIONS

Founded in 1979, Milkweed Editions is one of the largest independent, nonprofit literary publishers in the United States. Milkweed publishes with the intention of making a humane impact on society, in the belief that good writing can transform the human heart and spirit.

JOIN US

Milkweed depends on the generosity of foundations and individuals like you, in addition to the sales of its books. In an increasingly consolidated and bottom-line-driven publishing world, your support allows us to select and publish books on the basis of their literary quality and the depth of their message. Please visit our Web site (www.milkweed.org) or contact us at (800) 520-6455 to learn more about our donor program.

Milkweed Editions, a nonprofit publisher, gratefully acknowledges sustaining support from Anonymous; Emilie and Henry Buchwald; the Patrick and Aimee Butler Family Foundation; the Dougherty Family Foundation; the Ecolab Foundation; the General Mills Foundation; the Claire Giannini Fund; John and Joanne Gordon; William and Jeanne Grandy; the Jerome Foundation; Constance and Daniel Kunin; the Lerner Foundation; Sanders and Tasha Marvin; the McKnight Foundation; Mid-Continent Engineering; the Minnesota State Arts Board, through an appropriation by the Minnesota State Legislature, a grant from the Wells Fargo Foundation Minnesota, and a grant from the National Endowment for the Arts; Kelly Morrison and John Willoughby; the National Endowment for the Arts; the Navarre Corporation; Ann and Doug Ness; Ellen Sturgis; the Target Foundation; the James R. Thorpe Foundation; the Travelers Foundation; Moira and John Turner; Joanne and Phil Von Blon; Kathleen and Bill Wanner; and the W. M. Foundation.

MINNESOTA
STATE ARTS BOARD

NATIONAL
ENDOWMENT
FOR THE ARTS
A great nation
deserves great art.

TARGET.

THE McKNIGHT FOUNDATION

Interior design by Steve Foley
Typeset in Griffo Classico
by Steve Foley
Printed on acid-free Rolland Enviro (100 percent postconsumer
    waste) paper
by Friesens Corporation